C000149598

A Yogurt Pot of Retribution

– BRUCE LAWSON –

An environmentally friendly book printed and bound in England by
www.printondemand-worldwide.com

Mixed Sources
Product group from well-managed
forests, and other controlled sources
FSC www.fsc.org Cert no. TT-COC-002641
© 1996 Forest Stewardship Council

PEFC
PEFC/16-33-415

PEFC Certified
This product is
from sustainably
managed forests
and controlled
sources
www.pefc.org

This book is made entirely of chain-of-custody materials

www.fast-print.net/store.php

A Yogurt Pot of Retribution

ISBN 978-178035-419-4

First published 2012 by
FASTPRINT PUBLISHING
Peterborough, England.

Bruce Lawson - Profile

After leaving work, Colin Bruce and David Lawson were faced with a true challenge as to what to do next. Being in their late fifties, it was evident that no company would want to employ them; neither, to paraphrase Groucho Marx, would they want to be employed by any that did. Therefore, they had little alternative but to do something for themselves .....and this is it!

"Remember! Retirement is not just about being put out to grass."

Anon 2012

Chapter One

The Last Hurrah

As Farewell Lunches went, this one had gone rather better than expected. A hubbub of forced informality pervaded the white-washed walls of the factory canteen. Cheery conversation of thirty plus people brought together by the common bond of Smith Screws was being fuelled by the heady mix of beer and a wide selection of fatty foods. Silver-foil platters of freshly cooked samosas and marsala dosas competed for popularity with sausage rolls and cheese and pickle sandwiches, without crusts. Neither the scent of greasy hot pastry nor the pungent aromas of cinnamon and curry could, however, completely eradicate the waft of herring and prawn that drifted up from the Open Sandwiches on rye bread set out on rival plates.

John Smith could not remember when the room had last hosted such a display of benevolence, culinary excess or multi-cultural cohesion. Triangular shaped Union Jack flags criss-crossed with similar shapes of Swedish white, yellow and blue to cover the bare walls of the room. Tables, normally littered with lunchboxes, much-thumbed copies of the morning tabloids and the winning hand from the lunchtime round of Poker, were now covered with white paper table-cloths. Cardboard packaging, that had once wrapped bottles of Sweden's most popular lager, sat torn and depleted; testimony to the notion that the country could at least provide a brew that was nearly as good as the local Meon's Export, even if their Open Sandwiches looked disgusting.

Farewell Do's for departing employees had usually been celebrated with a pint in the local pub a few minutes walk away from the foundry. A short speech of thanks for the employee's services to the company and a firm handshake were followed by a swift exit after an hour. However, the white banner hanging from the canteen's ceiling suggested a different routine. Black lettering was succinct and to the point – *"Good luck Gaffer! We love you!"* This time, John Smith, Chief Executive of Smiths Screws, was the one who was leaving.

'It will not be the same, once you have gone, Mr John, Sir!'

The black eye-patch over Ishy Hassan's left eye clashed with the chic Clark Kent-shaped glass frames. The look of menace of the long-serving Hopper Supervisor was at odds with a voice where neither hurry nor urgency much featured. John was impressed by his dark blazer, emboldened with the badge of Bisbury Cricket Club on the breast pocket.

'My wife, Ashi, will miss you also' Ishy continued. 'As will all my daughters. They say that they have really got to know you, even though they have never met you. They just listen to what I tell them about you and your Mrs Smith.' He reached for another sandwich and then continued. 'Also, we are all very grateful for our divvi. It was a very generous gesture of yours. It makes you a good boss. Ashi has great plans for our front room. Obviously, I have not told her the full amount I have received, but she seemed happy with what I gave her. I then have a bit for myself to buy more for my bees. Honey is very good for you.'

With that, the Hopper Supervisor put down his paper plate on the table by his side and started to rummage in the side-pocket of his jacket. Finally, he fished out a glass jar and handed it to John. 'This is last year's harvest.' A smile of pride showed beneath his greying moustache. 'You like the label design, yes? My son, Tariq, he did it with the computer. He is a very clever boy! He will go far, I am most certain.'

John took the jar, shook Ishy's hand firmly and thanked him for his generosity. He took a moment to acknowledge the lettering that heralded *"Ishy's Googly Honey"*.

'It's very ......different, but I don't see what googly has to do with bees or with the honey itself.'

Ishy was ready with the obvious answer. 'You bowl a googly on a sticky wicket, don't you know! So if you drop your honey sandwich on the floor, you get a sticky mess. It becomes a sticky wicket, don't you see? I thought it up myself.' His face was creased with an open smile as he looked to John for some sort of patriarchal approval. Before John could respond, Clive Hunt, the fatter of the Hunt Twins, but better known to his work-mates as Whattock, had come over to point his bony finger at the jar.

'So he's giving you some of his aphrodisial treatment, is he? It makes you very portent he told me.'

'Potent, I said.' Ishy interrupted.

'Rub it on my goolies, he said. My Daphne will love it, he said. Well, it did nothing for either of us. Nothing at all. We ladled on spoonfuls of the stuff and waited for the passion. Not even an erection, even with my Daphne dressed up in corset and suspenders.' Clive's disappointment was still evident. 'We ended up having a cup of tea and feeding the rest of the honey to the cat.'

'She wasn't meant to rub it in. She was meant to lick it and eat it. Very erotic, very satisfactory. Very good for love life.'

3

John wondered how the company had survived for as long as it had with these Absurdists in charge. Clive put his concerns aside and continued.

'That apart, Mister John, I just wanted to say that, in spite of everything.... including the times when I thought that you were a right pillock, it has been an experiment working for Smiths Screws.'

'Experience, don't you mean!' Ishy could not stop himself.

'Good luck to yer and we've also liked the money.' Clive continued unabashed.

At times, John had found Clive's combative demeanour as Works Convenor extremely trying. The lack of willingness to compromise during negotiations over working practices or on pay scales had been wearing and such a waste of both men's time. So John had felt genuinely touched by Clive's gesture of reconciliation, albeit addressed with a formality which he thought had stopped with the demise of the Trades Union leaders of the Seventies.

'Mind you..' Clive continued. '.... we will see how Smart Arse Andersson works out. I myself, personally, will be watching him like a hawk. In my capacity as Union representative, I will make sure that there are no contraceptions of the new agreement.'

Ishy giggled again. 'I think you mean contraventions, Whattock!'

'Ay, that's what I said. We're not going to be no shoveover.'

John had been pleased that the Staff Share Distribution had been so well received. He had deliberately kept the staff numbers at a manageable level. He had never understood the ethos of some fellow members of the local Chamber of Commerce who relished the notion of Bigger equating to Better.

In his mind, Bigger equated to Bother. Bigger was also expensive and more risky. He had never wanted to lose sight of the people who had worked for him. So a share of the Swedish purchaser's money to each employee, based on their length of service, had seemed a proper thing to do.

As John worked his way around the room, he was accosted by other members of the workforce, who shyly or proudly introduced their husband, wife or girlfriend to him. Many had wanted to meet the Gaffer at closer quarters to have their opinions confirmed or rebutted on the limited information that they had received about him. Ishy had already apologised that his wife had not been able to make it due to it being her turn to work at the fabric shop which she owned jointly with her sister, Ushi. However, John did notice that Ishy's plump nineteen year-old niece, Rashi, who worked two days a week in the accounts department, was enjoying her very own feast of carrot and celery sticks contained in her own plastic lunchbox. Seated next to a shape covered with a large white sheet, she smiled sheepishly at him.

'I wish you good luck in your future, Mister John.' Rashi's left hand clutched the ends of the sheet tightly in order to prevent any breeze from swirling through the half-open canteen window to expose what lay hidden.

Amid the babble of conversation in the small room, John did his best to listen to others whilst making sure that any utterances from him were not accompanied by minute particles of sausage roll or cucumber sandwich flying into the face of the attendant listener. John had not seen the Smiths workforce so smart and scrubbed up. Jackets and blazers were much in evidence.

'Alright, gaffer?' The tall figure of Chaffy Finch, the Senior Foundryman, had broken off his conversation with John's dark

5

haired personal assistant, Bridget Murphy, to acknowledge John's presence.

John was impressed by yet another blazer, whose breast pocket this time boasted the simple badge of Bisbury Bowls Club. The lapel of the dark green jacket was peppered with pin badges, further testimony to Chaffy's involvement with a host of other local clubs, including the Nurdley Pigeon Club. John wondered whether the dusting of white specks along the back collar was indeed extreme dandruff or just the legacy of a morning inspection of the pigeon loft before leaving home. A banging on the table silenced the room.

All Farewell Ceremonies needed speeches. Rumour had it that Clive Hunt had been disappointed not to have been selected in the ballot to be the speaker from the Shop Floor. Instead, the role had fallen to Ishy Hassan, who pulled a single sheet of paper from his pocket and started to address the assembled company.

'Mr John...... Mr Andersson, our new gaffer, and the rest of you tossers - sorry to the ladies. It's a cricketing term, don't you know!' There was mild giggling throughout the room as Ishy looked down to the large hand-written notes in his hand and started to read. 'I would like to extend a big thank you on this special occasion to the ladies for providing the teas, and to the umpires, to the scorers........"

Ishy stopped suddenly. He stared at his audience, a beaming smile stretched over his face. As Captain and principal off-spinner of Bisbury Cricket Club, he had had to speak at the Annual Dinner the night before, notes for which had remained in the pockets of his blazer. The blank sides of the monthly Newsletter from the West Midlands Beekeeping Association had been the only available sheets on which to write his notes for each speech. It had been understandable to forget which pocket had contained which speech. He quickly produced another sheaf of paper from the other pocket.

'That had you going. I bet that you thought that I'd really lost it! Don't answer that!' Ishy regained his audience. 'But seriously, Gaffer, on behalf of everybody here and for those who have worked for you previously, I would like to wish you a good and happy retirement with lots of fulfilment and lots of happy times with Mrs Smith.......know what I mean, like?'

At this remark, the snigger level increased. The men in the group identified with the expressed sentiment as they lusted mentally after Mrs Candida Smith, aka Smiths Screws Calendar Girl 1983 – 1988. John watched the puzzled expression appear on Sven Andersson's face. It had been too much to expect that sixty colour pages featuring the future Mrs Smith in various states of undress, displaying full tease and pout, draped amongst the works machinery for the annual calendar would have remained unmentioned, hidden away for posterity. John whispered into Sven's ear a few words of explanation before Ishy brought matters to a close.

'Seriously, Gaffer, Mr John. We have enjoyed our time with you. We may have moaned. We may have taken more sickies than we should have. We may have embroidered our timesheets a bit.' Guilty sniggers came from the listening group. 'But on the whole, you've been fair, you've been considerate, you've cared when it mattered and we really wish you all the best for the future. So I propose a toast.....to the Gaffer!'

This was greeted with a rumble of agreement around the room as everybody mumbled the toast before gulping down a fresh swig from their glasses. There followed a ripple of polite applause, followed by raucous encouragement for a reply.

Of course, John had been prepared. He had carefully rehearsed what he was going to say. He had however not been prepared for the finality of actually having to deliver it. This was the very last Hurrah, the Final Curtain Call.

'Colleagues, friends, Sven.' John drew in a full breath and then continued his last speech as Chief Executive of Smiths Screws Ltd. He felt a sudden shiver run through him. He wished that Candida had been by his side. 'It's been a long journey over these past thirty odd years. The track has been bumpy at times. There have been slides down. There have been climbs up. We have all had to endure considerable changes in order to reach this point. The fact remains that Smiths Screws has survived, still able to provide bread to put on the table. It is you who have made the business what it is and I can only say how grateful I am to each and every one of you for your efforts in making this happen. Throughout the company's existence, the Smith family has always prided itself on doing their best for its workforce as well as for its customers. As the last remaining Smith, I am enormously proud of what we have all have achieved together...........' He had not imagined that it was going to be this tough. His eyes glistened for a few seconds before he continued. '.....proud that you have been part of my journey over the past years.'

The group sensed his discomfort and started to shuffle. Bouts of muffled coughing and clearing of throats were starting to interrupt the initial rapt attention of hardened men and women from South Warwickshire.

'......... I'm sure that you're in for exciting times on the new journey with Sven and his team from Langstrom. You could say that he will be your new Screwdriver.......' John waited for a response. Both Sven and Charlie Weatherhead, the sales director, did not let him down, issuing booming laughs from the front. ' So, let me just conclude by saying how grateful, how very grateful, I am to you for your loyalty, for your efforts and for your good humour. I will certainly miss you.

However, that's probably quite enough from me. So I offer you one last toast ...to us, to Smiths Screws and to its future with Langstrom Dynamic Fasteners!"

The gentle rumble of assent and a ripple of applause were followed by a fusillade of nose blowing as the group adjusted its emotional state before approaching the remaining fatty food. The open sandwiches still remained untouched. More beers were consumed with gusto. Sven congratulated John on his speech.

'It is a pity that your wife was not here to listen to you today. I had not understood that it was her in those pictures.'

'She's a very busy woman.' John changed the subject quickly. 'It was Charlie's idea to introduce the calendar. It was a great success; very popular with many of our customers; it boosted sales considerably.'

'One of the benefits of being the boss, I suppose, is that you get to marry the pin-up model!' Sven's face was creased in a smile. 'She was a very attractive woman.'

'She still is.' John had been surprised that the topic had not come up before, during the sale negotiations. He might as well carry on, he thought. 'It was all rather a slow burn. I was much more concerned with the cost of the whole calendar project and with trying to keep the company afloat. So, we hardly met for the first two years.'

Sven seemed engrossed by John's sloppy outpourings. 'I suppose that it really started when Candida came to shoot the calendar for nineteen eighty seven. I had been staggered by how popular the calendar had been. So I wanted to thank her more...'John hesitated as he searched for the right word, without any sort of innuendo. '....genuinely. I invited her to have lunch with the photographer after the shoot was completed. Charlie was there also, I remember. She did look beautiful, but I remember that there was sadness in her eyes. She looked ......jaded. We then discovered that we shared an interest in horses. She came up to the house a few weeks later and I showed her the two horses that I owned at the time. She then told me all about her cheating husband and her miscarriage. Poor old thing! It all just tumbled out as we stood by the paddock fence. I remember it all so vividly.' John saw Sven's expression change as the soap opera continued. 'Anyway, she says that meeting my horses prompted her to take up riding again. I was able to help her out and our relationship developed from there.'

'My goodness! There was I thinking that it must have been her fine breasts that had attracted you!' Sven smiled. 'She was lucky to have found you at a time when she needed somebody.'

The hubbub had started to build up again. Clive Hunt tapped the table with an empty beer bottle. Silence took over as the diminutive Bridget Murphy stepped forward.

'I am probably one of the few women to have known Mr John the longest, although maybe not as well as Missus Smith. Nevertheless, as others have already said....'

John had considered himself fortunate that Bridget had been so loyal. He would miss the pink adhesive notes that had always littered his desk. He had come to rely on the terse instructions on what to do with the letters, the travel itineraries or the occasional birthday card to which they were attached.

'.....and so Mister John....' Bridget battled on. '......those who have worked for the company, past and present, as well as suppliers, agents and anyone who has known you, have all clubbed together to provide you with a little something for you to enjoy in your new life of retirement.'

John's mind was whirring. Oh God, please not a gold clock! That's what his father had received. It gave up the ghost many years ago long before he did.

Bridget strode to the side of the room to where the plump accounts girl, Rashi, had been sitting gently chewing on her umpteenth piece of carrot. Bridget pulled the drape to reveal an easel on which rested a large white board. *"Happy Retirement, Mr John!"* was written in large red lettering across the top, under which was pinned a large photograph of an enormous wooden structure on wheels. John was stunned for a moment, uncertain as to what it was. Whilst his concerns about a clock had been thankfully unfounded, doubts took over on what his response should be to what he had been given. The unveiling ceremony continued.

'Mrs Smith suggested that you would need something that would get you out of the house, something to which you could devote many hours in your new life. You might also be glad of the company, she said, since she does have a life of her own.'

John stooped forward to take in the text under the picture - *"Benson's Coop 'n Wheels. Give your chickens the penthouse feeling!"* Surprise at receiving such an extravagant present was competing with the expectations of Candida and her vision of their future days together. He just hoped that his look of grateful surprise had been sufficient to appease the smiles of Bridget and the others who looked towards him.

'I am very touched and very flattered by your generosity!' had been his immediate response. 'I will look forward to dealing with my new flock in much the same way as I have with all of you.' John could not be restrained. 'At least, they won't always be asking me for more money!'

'But they might down tools and not lay!' Clive Hunt shouted from the back of the room.

'A bit like you and your Missus, eh Whattock!' Ishy Hassan had obviously been wounded by Clive's earlier comments about the failings of his honey.

'I'll make sure that my chickens are productive at all times, Clive. I'm sure that they'll respond very positively to the work practices that I will introduce from the very outset!'

'You had once said that there was nothing to beat the taste of a freshly laid egg.' Bridget looked pleased that the present had found favour with her boss.

'When did I say that, Bridge? Not that I would dispute your memory for one moment.' John replied.

"Four years ago! I remember it distinctly. I made a note of it at the time.'

'You really are a treasure, Bridge. I don't know what I'm going to do without you.'

'I'm sure that Mrs Smith will think of something.'

++++

Chapter Two

Rattled intoTogetherland

"What breed of chickens do you think you'll employ?"

"Ones that will produce an egg on time, Chaffy!"

"What are going to do, gaffer, now that you won't have work to think about? "

"I'll just be glad that I won't have to worry about getting your face away from the racing pages, Suchak!"

It took John an hour to prise himself away from the flash of digital cameras having posed with each member of staff individually, collectively and then, one, for luck, just on his own. As he climbed the stairs, John passed the piercing eyes of the three previous Smiths that stared at him from their portraits on the wall outside his Chief Executive office. As he entered the dismantled muddle of the room, he realised that he had had enough. There was no need to linger any longer. He had done as much as he could. He gathered up the remnants of his work life that he wanted to take home with him.

'Ah! That's where you are!'

The chief executive of Langstrom Dynamic Fasteners, now new owner of Smiths Screws, poked his pale, pasty face around the open door. Sven Andersson marched into the room. His usual appearance of puffed-up peacock was looking a little dishevelled; the sleeves of his light blue shirt were turned up at the cuffs, the top button undone and his dotted yellow tie loosened and askew. Half glasses dangled on a gold chain over his paunchy stomach.

Throughout the months of protracted meetings and keen pursuit by the Swedish competitor, John had always been haunted by dilemma and uncertainty. Should he continue to pursue further riches independently? Would sales of the acknowledged superior *Gambit* range of screws hold up against unfairly cheaper foreign competitors? At his age of sixty one, would a comfortable sum of money in his back pocket *really* be enough to allow him to face up to the forthcoming twenty years of inactivity and physical decline? Could he just go off and leave the toil of his forefathers in the hands of other unrelated strangers?

John's hesitancy in making up his mind had resulted in Sven returning with bigger sacks of cash until John had determined that it would seem unreasonable, if not totally barking mad, not to accept the offer and run for the hills.

'This must be hard for you.' Sven had reached John's desk. 'The final day of the family business, the last day of your working career, the end of an era. It is a triple whammy, is that not what you call it?'

'You could call it that, I suppose.' John replied. Sven's monotone was becoming annoying. John had never really got used to Sven's friendly gesture of arm around the shoulder. He had never liked Sven's attitude that he was doing John a favour by taking the company off his hands. Smiths Screws had been John's life and it was now being taken from him.

'But now, there is so much for you to look forward to.' Sven's little smirk did nothing to calm John's agitation as he listened on. 'You now have no responsibilities, John. No phone calls. No e-mails. No worries about the next sale. All is swept away at a stroke.'

'You're right, Sven. But, what's going to replace them? I need some sort of brain food.' John hadn't meant the alarm in his voice to show so evidently.

'Your wife, Candida, will be there for you. She must be looking forward to spending more time with you. Is that not what retirement means? Settling into a less hurried way of life? Together? You have been such a busy man, working so hard for this business. It will be a pleasure to slow down, surely? You must have many plans.'

'Well, I'm not so certain. My wife is also a busy woman. She has her own interests. She really loves her horses. She has her own plans.'

John needed a distraction. 'I presume that you won't be needing this, Sven.' He had made his way over to the glass cabinet in the far corner of his office. He opened the door and took out *"Gambit Man"*, an eighteen inch statue made entirely from Smiths' Screws. Presented at a dinner held in his honour by the distribution company in Sydney, John had been deafened by the male guffawing as they watched him receive the assemblage of brass screws of varying sizes. The *"Gambit AWF 20 mm"* protruding proudly from the hero's groin, a manifestation of the "long and proud " association between the two companies, had caused considerable merriment. John thought that it would serve as a reminder of the fun times that he had had at the helm of the company.

Sven waved his arm dismissively as John carefully stood the statue in the cardboard box on his desk. 'Memories are important, John. You take what you want. Will you be joining Candida with her horses?'

'Alas, my own horse-riding days are long over.' John continued. 'They are a big commitment. I gave my horses to Candida after we were married. I didn't have the time to look after them. They were expensive to run.'

'Like my three ex-wives. That is why I have to keep working ...to pay for them.'

Sven looked out of the window towards the traffic snarling its way along the motorway towards the industrial heartland of Birmingham some forty minutes away.

'But it's not just the money that keeps you going, Sven, is it? You're a fundamental hunter-gatherer. You'll never stop work.'

'Most of the time, maybe, you are right, John. There are some times when I would very much like to be paid to leave. To go off with a large sum of money and never have to work again has its obvious benefits. To go up to the lakes in the north of Sweden or to the Goula river in Norway and fish all day, what could be nicer? There is much salmon and sea trout. The scenery is marvellous.' He sounded wistful. 'Do you do fishing? If you do, you must let me know. Maybe, you should take Candida with you. I will recommend to you great places for fish.'

'You don't know my wife. Watching ripples of water all day long would drive her nuts. If there's any watching to be done, it has to be of the four legged variety.'

'My daughter wants me to buy her a pony. I have said that I have to buy another company first before I can do that. She is not very pleased.'

'Consider yourself lucky, Sven, that it's only one horse that you are being asked to pay for. Now that I have some spare cash, Candida wants me to take over a set of livery stables in Bisbury. Somehow, Candida sees this as a great investment opportunity. It will give *me* something to do, so she says.'

16

'As well as looking after your chickens? You're going to be a busy man, John. It sounds like work. At least you don't have children to worry about.'

John sighed. He cast his mind briefly to the portraits of his father and the other John Smiths who had ruled the company since its humble beginnings. There would be no portrait of the latest John Smith. He had cared little for continuing the family line, deciding that the onus of being Son and Heir had carried too much expectation.

'Children can be so demanding and yet so delightful.' Sven was now facing John across the desk. 'It is a matter of regret that I don't see my three children as much as I would like. They live with their mothers and I get to see them at weekends when my work allows. It is not the best, but they are good kids. They love their Papa or so they say, as long as I give them money.'

As another grateful recipient of this Papa's money, John was not about to give Sven any more of his attention or undying love for that matter. He looked around the remaining chaos that had once been his office, scanning the walls on which an array of sepia photographs still hung. Expressionless faces and bushy moustaches of men in white cricket flannels, lined up for the first Smiths Screws cricket match, looked towards him. He wondered whether the occasion first introduced by John's great grandfather, John Bernard Smith, would continue under the new regime. Surely, the intricacies of leather and willow would be lost on somebody to whom a leg break was merely the result of a skiing accident.

The growl of a motorbike from outside caused John to look out of the window once more. He remembered something that had been on his mind for some considerable time.

'Look over there, Sven!' John pointed to the sign *"Smiths Screws for the world"* beaming in the darkening dusk above the adjacent factory building. Red and yellow neon shone either side of the middle word which remained unlit. John had been amused by the belligerence of the revised message. He felt obliged to point out the shortcomings of the sign as his last duty.

'I know that.' Sven replied authoritatively. 'I have ordered the name *Langstrom* to be put up next week. I thought that we should wait until you and Charlie were off the premises. You know...' Sven smiled as he suddenly thought of the joke. '...like ....Elvis Presley has finally left the building!'

John responded with a rueful smile before looking around the room one last time to see if there was anything else that he wanted. He placed his suit jacket on top of the box and made to move to the door. 'Well, Sven. I take your point. I'm going now. I need to be on my way.'

Sven stepped aside smartly. 'You are right, John. You should have gone ages ago.'

John could not decide what lay behind Sven's fixed smile. He hurried past the beady eyes and fixed expressions of previous Smiths on the corridor wall on his way towards the exit. John had determined that the only art that would accompany him in his retirement would be the distinctive, stippled Aboriginal paintings by Guffy Two-Fingers that had hung prominently in his office and was now in his study at home. Nevertheless, he wondered whether he had really seen the last of the portraits. He doubted whether stark paintings of self-satisfied Brass Triangle business folk would feature very long in the collection of the Scandinavian proprietor.

John entered the foundry, where only the gentle roar of the furnace fire could be heard. He walked past the line of pre-straighteners, die-cutters and headers, whose combined efforts had spewed countless billions of screws into the now empty hoppers. John noted the detritus of off-cuts twinkling on the floor like gold dust under the bright overhead light. Finally, he stepped outside into the small yard where coils of rusting wire stood awaiting their fate; some to be summoned inside for shaping and processing, others to be rejected as sub-standard and returned from whence they came.

John drew up suddenly as he took in the sight of the fifteen men and five women of the work force and straggling partners who had formed themselves into one long line. Duty and tradition had resulted in a full turnout as embarrassment mixed with smiling affection or resigned sullenness in the early evening chill. John lowered his box of possessions to the ground as a lump formed in his throat.

'Good Heavens, Charlie! What on earth are you all doing? I thought that we'd said our goodbyes in the canteen.'

The grey-haired ex-sales director and joint beneficiary in the sale of the company stood in his shirtsleeves at the beginning of the line and started to applaud. Handclaps echoing off the surrounding walls like rounds of machine gun fire gave way to a harsh sound of screws encased within tin cans being shaken vigorously by all those in the line.

John acknowledged the traditional ritual of being rattled off the premises. He went down the line extending one final handshake to each employee like Royalty being introduced to the teams at a Wembley Cup Final.

Chaffy Finch, factory foreman and one of the few pipe smokers in the team..... Bridget Murphy, five foot three in her stockinged feet, shivered next to Ishy Hassan, chief hopper supervisor and honey producer. As Clive Hunt stood next to his identical twin George, it was clearly evident why it had not been easy to differentiate between Whattock and Suchak. John shrugged his shoulders resignedly as he continued along the line. Shades of lipstick left by friendly pecks from each of the giggling women gathered on both cheeks. After a chaste kiss from Rashi Hassan, inevitably the last in line, John turned to face the group that had now broken rank to form into a semi-circle.

'Well, now that I have been well and truly rattled off, there's no going back. I said all I wanted to say at lunch. So, I just hope that you give Sven the same level of loyalty, hard work and commitment that you have given to Charlie and me. I hope...' John quickly corrected himself. '.... I *know* that he will look after you. So that's it, finally. Good luck to you all. I will be back to see how you're getting on. In the meantime, I must be on my way.'

He fumbled in his pockets for the car keys. Where the hell were they? The answer presented itself as Sven came towards him bearing his box of memorabilia as if offering it for sacrifice. Taking the box and his jacket, John quickly located the keys, unlocked the car and placed his property inside. He came back towards Sven.

'I love your quaint English customs.' Sven mumbled quietly.

'Rattling off long-serving staff members has been a well established Smith tradition.' John replied. '...started by my great grandfather and continued by all subsequent generations. I'm sure that they're no quainter than many of your Swedish traditions. Only we do them with our clothes on!' John saw Sven's face break into a smile at this unreasonable view of his fellow countrymen. 'I hope that you will continue the tradition. Globalisation must not quell individuality. The workforce is the lifeblood of any business. I hope that you will remember that.'

'Well of course, John.' Sven's face remained impassive. 'Langstrom is an honourable company. We always respect the workforce. Why would we do otherwise?'

Raising an eyebrow, John extended his hand for a final handshake. 'Good bye Sven. Thanks for everything.' He waved to the others before driving off on his last journey back home.

++++

Defined by a loose border of railway line, motorway and the A38, the Brass Triangle had been described in travel guides as *"the Welcome Mat to the Black Country"*. Others had referred to it as the *"Back Passage to Birmingham"*. It had however prospered as the centre for Brass alloy. Screws, door hinges, window fittings and drawer-handles were produced by the box load. The success of some family companies had led to their being acquired by more ambitious competitors. Others, more stubborn or more deluded, retained their independence, either to perish in the bankruptcy court or to undergo metamorphic change into Garden Centres.

By dogged hard work, good fortune and, more latterly, very favourable terms from Moncrieffs Bank, Smiths Screws had carved out a niche in a crowded market through the attributes and indigenous qualities of an alloy developed by John's grandfather, John Charles Smith. Still only in his early teens, JC had happened on a formula which provided added strength and durability to the fasteners produced by his father, John Bernard Smith. This discovery had coincided with the desperate demand for screws and rivets from builders as they rushed to construct factories for the burgeoning motor car industry on land thirty miles up the road. Unmatched by most competitors, the demand for *"Smiths All-Weather Fasteners"* ensured that the fires in the foundry would rage continuously whatever the effects of World War, recession, depression or boom.

All thoughts of what John was leaving behind were quickly replaced by what he was about to face as he steered his BMW onto the busy M42 motorway. The spark of John's own fire had been forced to ignite as he considered the options available on how to occupy the oceans of time opening out before him now. Having been frequently caught behind slow-moving tractors travelling at a snail's pace along the narrow winding roads away from the motorway, he had dismissed the idea of becoming a gentleman farmer; far too uncomfortable and much too unreliable. He would certainly have the time to tackle the cryptic crossword and complete it in full. He questioned the point of learning another language such as Chinese or Spanish. Who would listen to his bumbling, incorrect syntax in Shanghai or in Alicante, when their own grasp of the English language would be infinitely better? The possibility of referring to the old copy of *"Bert Weedon's Play in a Day Guitar guide"* which he had recently found in his garage had crossed his mind. Surely relearning chords on his old guitar that had stood dusty and unused for over thirty years would not be that difficult? John had certainly missed his music. Transferring the old vinyls of *Fairport Convention*, *Pentangle* and other members of the electro-folk age onto the i-Pod which he had bought in a duty-free shop in Sydney would certainly fill some of the days.

John steered the car onto the narrow lanes, where first signs of Spring leaf on the trees could just be seen in the fading light. Headlights from the occasional car passing in the opposite direction lit up the darkness. He pressed his foot down on the accelerator as if to hurry on his schedule of self-fulfilment, whatever it was going to be. He reassured himself that new interests would be embraced with his normal focussed efficiency. As he faced the dazzle of the setting sun, he slowed. Why the hurry? He had Sven's cheque! Life could be a lot worse. He was going home to *"Togetherland"* , to a closer co-existence with Candida, where, so far, negotiations on the Terms of Engagement had been disappointingly unilateral.

"Now that you really will have the time, Johnnie, the fences will need to be re-painted. The shed needs repairing. There are many small things with the house that require attention."

Candida's detailed list held deadlines that were, at best, unreasonable and, at worst, impracticable. It was clear that she had been saving them up in retribution for John's absences away on business over the years.

The presence of chickens in their Penthouse Coop would certainly provide a welcome addition to the Mulberry Farm regime. John's executive mind was already engaging the tricky question of recruitment. Whether to take on a team of prosaic egg layers noted for their regular productivity or instead to sign up a strut of ego-centric rare breeds whose colourings would provide beauty and elegance in their tasteful surroundings?

John hoped *"Togetherland"* would yield a rich seam where husband and wife could enjoy their co-existence cosseted within an absence of responsibility, other than to each other. He had been impressed by the ambitions of some portrayed in one of the Sunday supplements. *"Richard and Elpie's Jammed-in Preserves"* seemed an unlikely success for an ex-banker and his wife, where incongruous jam combinations of strawberry and nettle had proven to be very popular amongst the Foodies in Kent. Whilst John had doubted the merits of the other recipes being considered by the couple, he nevertheless hoped that his own wife's creative instincts could link with his business expertise in the formulation of a worthwhile project. He suspected that the spectre of Candida's expensive ambition for Mick Flanders' stables was going to fit this bill.

The slightly scratched royal blue BMW, acquired as part of Sven's package, turned the corner into Mulberry Lane. Long strands of green fern poked their presence through the thick hedgerows lining the lane and waved their welcome to the passing car. Others such as dandelion and bramble awaited their fate for possible inclusion in Eccentric Jam production at a later date.

John pressed the remote to instruct the electric gates to open before the car passed through and scrunched to a halt on the gravel outside the dark oak front door of Mulberry Farm. He had passed through the gates of his New Tomorrow. He lugged the box of relics from his previous life into the front hall of the house. 'Candida, darling, I'm home! This time it's for good!'

John's mobile phone bleeped. He read the e-mail on the small screen.

"Have just got confirmation of first order from new agent in Turkey. It's a big one. Many thanks and good luck. Sven"

"Bugger Turkey?" John thought. "From now on, it's chickens all the way."

John heard the padding of busy footsteps on the landing above as he watched Candida rush down the stairs towards him.

++++

Chapter Three

Re-entry of John Smith

Candida knew that it had been her husband's last day at Smiths Screws. They had both decided that it would not be necessary for her to go as well. They had agreed that it was to John that everybody was saying their farewells – or maybe good riddance.

"Be like the Queen Mother, God rest her soul, give the workers a taste of extravagance to brighten up their dull day."

Candida had scoffed at the suggestion offered by her friend, Mary Mortlock, on how she might greet the cessation of nearly a century of family history and the passing on of another chunk of local heritage to foreign owners. To have wafted in with a patronising farewell wave dressed in a wide-brimmed hat with flamboyant peacock feather and matching handbag and white cotton gloves was never going to be Candida's way. She had exposed more than enough of herself to the workforce to last a lifetime. The five years of Smith Screws calendars had just been one of many well paid chapters in her previous life. The title of being the Boss' wife had held little interest to her.

"You remember what we agreed when we got married." Candida had told John before he had left in the morning. "You deal with your swarms of tiny screws. I will look after my horses."

Candida had seized the opportunity, all those years ago, of John's offer to use his chestnut mare. The relief from the claustrophobia of London and the sadness of a failed marriage had combined with the gathering excitement of riding out with John and with other members of the Bisbury riding community. As the years had gone by, she had chipped away at the concrete wall put up by the bloody-mindedness of horse owners as she sought to encourage them, through bluff and flattery, to use her services to find the right horse to suit their equestrian skill or to sell on their current one because of their lack of it. *Candida Smith General Equine Sales* was proving to be a worthy and useful service to the local community, despite the cynics in the Brass Triangle who had referred to it as "CS GAS run by the topless tart using poor John's money".

As she towelled herself after the shower, Candida knew that she was courting danger by accepting the usual Thursday night game of cards with the girls. Her husband's plan for *"Togetherland"*, with implications of shared closeness and joint intent, was a territory of which she was not too certain. She was certainly not going to drop everything to be at his beck and call.

Candida studied the reflection of her figure in the mirror. "No bingo wings! Lucky you!" Many of her girlfriends had moaned enviously as they prepared themselves for the weekly Pilates class. She had always kept herself in trim after finishing her modelling career and had been determined to keep her wings well furled for as long as possible. Skin treatments, minimal exposure to the sun and a restrictive diet had kept her feeling good about herself. Even the boobs were holding up pretty well. She snapped on her bra before pulling on the white Tee-shirt. The size ten black trousers felt a little tighter than usual, but Candida knew that her bum would be hidden under the long floaty orange shirt.   Her hostess, Anthea MacMasters, always made the best of her rather plain self. Candida was less worried about the new recruit, Helen with the Cold, whose dress sense the previous week had been hidden behind a barrage of continuous tissues. Mary Mortlock would no doubt carry her usual look of ship in full sail with bright billowing cardigan.

After applying the last flicks of mascara to her eyelashes, Candida heard the sound of John's car come to a halt on the gravel drive outside. Christ! He's home already!   A bit too bloody early! Surely, he would have had one last drink with Swedish Sven? She heard the front door downstairs slam shut. She looked at her watch. Ten minutes and she was out of here, she determined.   She had been uncertain as to how to treat this change in their lives. Why was she in such a rush? What was she going to tell him? She took in a big breath before reassuring herself that she was taking the right course of action. Sod it! He had left her alone often enough in the past! Her life has to carry on, even if her husband's current one had come to a standstill. She opened the bedroom door and watched her husband coming up the stairs towards her.

'Darling how lovely!' she exclaimed sympathetically. 'You're home early. How did it go? Are you very sad......?' She saw a hint of confusion on John's face. She had hoped that the sincerity of her concern would be sufficient to allow her to brazenly carry on. '....having to say goodbye to everybody? I trust that they said lots of nice things about you?' She threw her arms around her husband's neck as they both stopped on the staircase landing. She had not been prepared for his response.

'Darling, you look gorgeous!' John realised that he had taken her high cheeked features for granted for far too long. Her magnificent sexy nose, her large doe-eyes still looked just as kindly on him as when they had kissed for the first time in the autumn sun after putting the two horses out in the paddock. He watched her orange and white draped figure continue down the stairs; he relished the fact that he was about to be with her for longer. He couldn't wait. He gabbled excitedly to her.

'I hadn't planned anything tonight, but let's go out and I can tell you all about it. Where shall we go? I'm ravenous.' His mind was now racing as he thought where he could treat his wonderful wife. 'I'll be very pleased if I don't see another samosa for as long as I live. It was a lovely spread, but there was never time to eat any of it ....' He paused to draw breath as he warmed to the anticipation of a cosy evening with his wife. '......where shall we go? *Mamma Pasta* in the village? Now that I am no longer working, we've got to watch the pennies.'

'I am so sorry, Johnnie darling. Not tonight!'

He had never been comfortable with being called Johnnie, not that he liked the name John much more. His name had always been a disappointment to him. Now he was being faced with the initial flurry of his impulsive excitement being blown away by the heavier wind of disappointment with his wife's plans. He watched Candida stop by the mirror of the hall to see if both earrings were attached properly.

'Maybe we can do it tomorrow night or even Saturday. I must look in my diary. But I did tell you. I'm off to Anthea's. It's Thursday night. You obviously don't remember. Why should you? You've usually had some business dinner to attend.'

John sat down on the stair and looked on bewildered.

'Have you seen my bloody keys anywhere?' Candida continued her frantic search in all the usual locations, the smell of expensive sandalwood perfume wafting about her. She stopped briefly, her mind clearly distracted, before she scooped up the errant keys on the hall table. 'Anyway, don't worry darling, we've got lots of time to catch up. We've got the rest of our lives together! I've got to be up rather early tomorrow morning. So I won't be late back. Mary's trying out her new mare. Terribly expensive. A bit frightening, if you ask me.'

There was increasing panic in her voice as she looked at her watch.

'Right, I'm off, darling! It's great to have you back. Try and relax, you deserve it. Love you!'

Candida bent down to kiss John on the lips before her heels click-clacked over the wooden floor towards the back door. Moments later, the muted crunch of her Volvo's wheels receded, thus welcoming John to the first hours of *"Togetherland"*

Like an urchin on the street corner, John sat on the stairs as he listened to the car accelerate away into the lane to be replaced by the sound of ....Nothing. No comforting noises from the creaking pipes in the radiator; even the clock in the hall could not be bothered to either tick or to tock. The early evening shrouded the farmhouse in a silence that he had not experienced since he shared the Room of Remembrance with his dead father. This time, there was not even a lifeless body to have a last chat to. He stood up and wandered aimlessly from room to room in search of a mystery guest who might suddenly spring an appearance.

Usually, John would have welcomed the still calm that pervaded the house. It had allowed him quiet time to immerse himself in the affairs of Smiths Screws. He would have opened his battered black flight bag which had accompanied him through much of his working life. A sheaf of letters, sales figures, balance sheets and other papers would have needed his attention. Other than last month's copy of *"Fasteners & Screws*

Monthly" and the two sheets of John's P45 tax form, the bag was now empty. Even the small screen of his mobile phone, normally alive with e-mails and important messages, could only fuel his previous addiction with limp, well-meaning endearments of farewell from previous business contacts. Like the junkie in the backstreet, he needed a new supplier of excitement.

John wandered out into the garden for inspiration. Suddenly, the light bulb in his brain lit up! He had a decision to make! In the gloom, he strode along the garden path that lined the far field. Finally, he stopped at an overgrown patch of grass which had been left untended, due to being out of sight from the house. The area caught little sunlight and was too small to do much with. An ideal position, therefore, for his new *Benson's Coop 'n Wheels!* John sighed with satisfaction at a job well done. The wind had died to complete the aura of silent calm. John looked out towards a few cows silhouetted against the dim light. He listened to the systematic tearing of grass as the cows continued to do what they did best. John adjusted his eyes to reaffirm his decision on the plot being far enough away from the crowing cock, but yet secure enough to beat off any interested fox. Assent to his decision was provided by the unedifying sounds of effluent being released onto the ground amid a series of spluttering farts and a violent gush of liquid. John determined that life was not going to be that bad. He determined that the occasion called for the opening of the very expensive bottle of Scotch which he had bought at the Duty-Free in Sydney airport.

The gentle peaty kick of the twenty year old Islay malt hung in the back of John's throat as he swallowed the first swig of the evening. He had settled into the soft comfort of his telly armchair in the drawing- room as he contemplated a future not offered to many of the Baby Boomer generation. The luxury of a sizeable sum of money and the lifting of the burden of running a business started by Great Grandfather Smith ninety six years ago had to be weighed up against his new role. No longer John Smith, CEO of Smiths Screws, but plain John Smith, relic from the past; the gravitas of a top executive position now replaced by the meanness of two measly syllables.

He had taxed his mother on the subject on several occasions. "Why just John, Mama? Why not even a second name like my forefathers? Why couldn't I have been called, for example, Peregrine Robespierre Albemarle Thundersley...... Smith ? That would be a really super name to have."

"Prat Smith? I think not, John !" His mother had replied dismissively. "Don't be so argumentative! All men in the Smith family have been John. Besides..." She was darning the hole in one of John's school socks and had paused to bite on the yarn to sever it from the reel.

"..... John Smith is simple, easy to remember. Your father says that simple unmemorable names are very good for tax reasons. It will confuse the buggers, he says. Befuddlement is more lawful than embezzlement. Mister J. Smith provides many options to confuse and to reduce our contributions." His mother put the finished socks to one side. "I can't see it myself, but then I've never been very good when it comes to money matters. That's your father's business." And so John Smith he had remained - an obfuscation for purposes of tax evasion.

John swirled the thawing ice cubes in his glass and gulped down the remaining whisky before reaching for the bottle on the coffee table in front of him. He poured out another generous measure before lying back in his chair. He reviewed not just the neatly puffed-up cushions of the unoccupied sofa, but also the comprehensive state of neat that was manifest throughout the wood-panelled room. He extracted his handkerchief to wipe the tell-tale ring left by his careless placement of his chilled glass on the top copy of the pile of *Bisbury Life* that was stacked on the low table. His retreat from the un-neat fiery furnace of the factory had clearly coincided with a visit from Mrs Wyatt the cleaning lady. It was as if Candida was laying down her own marker on how life was going to be in *Togetherland*.

John needed to stir himself from the onset of whisky-laced melancholia. It was time for some decisive action. He would call Brian McMasters, whose wife was hosting the Bridge Evening. Brian surely must be at a loose end as well. John felt like a small child asking a friend around for tea. He felt the need to talk to somebody who could relate to his newly acquired status. Brian had retired a couple of years previously after the law firm for whom he was Senior Partner decreed that, having reached sixty, he was surplus to their needs. Armed with a very sizeable pension and a gold fountain pen, Brian had previously explained to John in meticulous detail how he had worked out his own Retirement Plan. Life Drawing classes and a course on Egyptology at the local adult college had featured prominently. John knew that his own ambitions paled by comparison.

'Sorry old boy, no can do. I've got a GCC meeting.' Brian's Irish brogue sounded genuinely disappointed. 'It's really essential that I'm there. Otherwise, I would have loved to. Where have you come back from this time? You always seem to be away.'

'Just Bisbury. Alas, my travelling days are over, for good. I've sold the business. Today was my last day. End of an era. Anyway, what is a GCC meeting?'

John winced at his lack of knowledge of the parochial world that he had now entered with its own set of acronyms. He was like the new boy arriving at his new school, where verses of the School Song and the nicknames of all the school staff had to be learned in double-quick time. The owner of the village newspaper shop and the names of Mrs Wyatt's children had to be assimilated just as quickly. The urbane and all-knowing Brian seemed to have passed the test with flying colours.

'Golf Club Committee.' explained the Irishman. 'It's full-on at the moment. We're putting in for planning on an extension to accommodate the Lady members. Not a very popular idea in some quarters. Surely, you've read about it on the Club website.'

'Oh that! Is that still going on? I thought the matter had been sorted a long time ago.'

'If only! Feelings and opinions need to be overcome. Planners are in no rush. It has been very tedious at time, I can tell you.'

John had already recognised that increased visits to the shrine of the white dimpled ball that was Powder Hill Golf Club would have to become part of his new programme. He was reconciled to having to listen to the evangelism of fellow players as they expounded on the mysteries of the seventh hole and their continued belief that the bunker on the left side was too close to the green "unless you used a lob wedge to lift the ball onto the back". He would have to adjust his own agnostic belief that there was more to life than hitting a small ball in divergent directions away from your playing partners.

'Well, good luck with it tonight, Brian. Let's meet up next week sometime.' John had volunteered weakly. 'My diary looks pretty clear. How's yours?"

Brian then proceeded to outline in detail his calendar of activities and appointments which seemed to allow him little time to either eat or sleep. John was not certain whether he wanted his retirement schedule to be as hectic. They agreed to meet in a week's time, subject to Brian being able to get out of the monthly meeting of the Village Laundry Society or so it had sounded to John.

John punched the "off" switch on the phone. He was determined that his inactivity needed to be lanced quickly. His business life had been run by plans, objectives and strategies. His new life in retirement was going to be no different. He refilled his glass yet again and moved to his small study. He sat at the antique leather-topped desk that had once belonged to his grandfather. He pulled a pad of paper from the drawer and laid out pencils and a pen on the desk-top in readiness for action. John mulled over where to start. For a few moments, he looked at the books that lined the polished oak shelves as he sought inspiration for setting out his plans for the future. *"MAKE LIST"* followed by *"Friday, Tomorrow, Action Plan, To Do List..."* The vacuous was soon replaced by the abstract as his pencil meandered over the pad with meaningless shapes and scribbles. John's attempts at lucidity or worthy intention were getting nowhere. In a final burst of activity, he sharpened the lead of his pencil and then the other three that lay in a pencil box on his desk, before determining that there was little further need for objectives and strategies. He had the rest of his life to work them out.

'Oh bugger it! What's on telly?'

++++

Chapter Four

Candida and the Space Invaders

Candida had always driven fast. The journey to Anthea McMaster's small pile, Hatcher's, would take her no more than a quarter of an hour; time enough to rid herself of any last doubts about leaving her husband behind in his solitary state. She braked sharply, allowing a startled rabbit, rooted to the middle of the road by the glare of her car's headlights, to dive into the nearby ditch. A heavy blast of horn from a van did not deter her from crossing out into the main road as she contemplated *Togetherland*, now with its increased population of two. The rear lights of a horse box and the dark curvature of a horse's rear fuelled her impatience. Much as she loved them, now was not the time to be stuck behind any horses' arse. Much as she loved her husband, she was not ready to become stuck in the slow lane with him either. He says that he's got lots of plans. Well, so had she!

The horsebox had slowed to a snail's pace just as Candida prepared to overtake. She jammed hard on the brakes. The arse got closer, before the trailer turned off the road. Candida accelerated the car again, her mind racing with other potential scenarios. She can't have him just sitting around, leaving numerous cups of cold coffee planted around the house! There will be newspapers left all over the place! He'll want to *discuss* the news in the paper! Oh God! He had mentioned that they would have more time for sex! Appetites for such things have to be whetted. Lust cannot be turned on at will! As the car continued along the main road, Candida reassured herself that all will be fine, given a bit of space and time to readjust. She was most excited about the deal on Mick Flanders' stables.

Candida cast her mind back to Carlo's Coffee shop in Bisbury when Mary Mortlock had discussed her own husband's predicament.

"Roger and I had had no warning about his retirement. Just a phone call and the early train from London and, wham, my Space Invader had landed. We were both devastated at first."

Candida had always considered that Mary would meet any change of circumstance with robust equanimity. Mary's subsequent description of her husband's rehabilitation came as no surprise.

"But I soon got him into shape. He looks so much better, now that he's lost a little weight." Mary had reported. "He keeps himself very busy, spending a lot of time at the Bisbury Reservoir learning how to sail. He now wants to buy a boat! I suppose that I should be grateful that he still has some purpose to his life." Mary had paused briefly to finish her large Espresso coffee before continuing. "Look around the supermarket. You'll see some men brandishing the shopping list entrusted to them by their wives. I watch them hopelessly shuffling from aisle to aisle in search of yogurt or a loaf of bread! It's really quite pitiful. Men need to be kept busy and focussed. Mind you, when Roger first started to do the shopping, he would return with all the wrong things, many absolutely useless, but selected because they'd been on special offer or because they were cheap. I think that I've drummed that out of him now."

Candida had no fears about the capabilities of her own husband. He knew where to find stuff. What concerned her more was what lay beyond the Welcome sign of *Togetherland*. She thought of her dear dad. He had retired after forty years in the Army and seemed unable to grasp the outside world. She suspected that it was lack of opportunity, rather than any absence of will, that had resulted in his decline. He had been too young to die at the youngish age of sixty six.

'Oh crap!'

Candida's melancholy was rudely interrupted by her realisation that she had driven past the turning to Anthea's house. The lack of any turning point forced her to drive on for what seemed ages before she was able to turn round. Having taken the correct narrow lane, she braked the car hard on the gravel drive in front of the seventeenth century sandstone building. Candida breathed in deeply as she prepared herself for an evening of girly chat, sensible salads and indulgent chocolate puddings. She was dying for her first glass of chilled Pinot Grigio.

The outside chill of the Spring evening followed Candida into the hallway of the house, where she was met by Mary Mortlock, fully rigged in bright red cardigan, who took her to one side.

'Hello darling! You look lovely, but I think that we're all going to freeze. Anthea has only just discovered that Brian has turned off the heating. He says that there's no need now that Spring is here. So, you've been warned!'

Anthea McMasters greeted Candida and handed her a glass of chilled wine. The discomfort of her fellow guests seemed to matter little as the deep tan of her neckline was accentuated by the pure white of her linen shirt and the dusty blue cashmere sweater. Her wrists jingled with bracelets no doubt bought off the beach during her recent holiday on Mustique. Candida considered that her long blonde hair still looked in need of a proper shape and cut.

The fourth member of the group, Helen with the Cold, had been the newcomer at the previous session when she had distributed her germs with uncaring generosity. However, she knew that Helen lived in a small cottage on the far side of Wedlicote, where she had cared for her mother during the final years of her life. So she was not all bad.

'How are your horses?' Helen asked nervously.

Before having time to answer, Candida stood back as Helen's face reddened, her nose more puce as sneeze followed sneeze with some frequency. Germs were in free-fall. Candida determined that she would need to increase her dose of wheatgerm and vitamins from now on to counter the influx of alien bacteria.

As Helen recovered from her small fit of nasal activity, Candida moved towards Mary.

'Well, Mary. This is it! My own Space Invader has just landed.' Candida was suddenly embarrassed by her announcement. It wasn't as if she didn't want him at home - Johnnie was no ogre. She carried on. 'He seemed to be really delighted. He wanted to take me out for a slap-up dinner to celebrate. I had to dissuade him quite forcibly. He did look terribly disappointed.'

The other two had sat down at the card table. As the first hand was being dealt, Mary looked at her cards before turning to Candida.

'Don't be too soft on him, darling!' She continued. 'Tell him to go and get a job. He's still young enough. My dad worked until he was well over seventy. Three spades!"

The game was underway. Grumbles and grumps were now replaced by rubbers and trumps. After several hands, the women broke for supper. Soon they were enjoying Anthea's extravagant recipes with alfalfa and chickpea. In between mouthfuls, Anthea joined the review of the Space Invasion.

'Brian has hardly stopped since he finished with the firm. It's a bit sad. I wish that he would slow down and take life a little easier. He's never bloody here. He didn't even come with me for the few days in Mustique. Too much to do, he said. He didn't have the time to waste sitting on a beach.'

Candida listened sympathetically. Inevitably, Helen sneezed again as Anthea continued.

'I wondered whether he's having an affair. I've looked on his Blackberry for furtive messages. I've asked the kids. They don't know anything.'

Candida looked at Mary. If there were any liaisons or couplings amongst the good folk of Wedlicote and Bisbury, Mary would know. Her face remained expressionless. Maybe Brian *was* playing around. Candida had always thought his sweep of grey hair and his direct blue-eyed interest in what she had had to say were among his many attractive features.

'He sends e-mails and texts to the kids.' Anthea continued. 'We haven't had lunch together as a family for ages!' Anthea smoothed down her sweater in a gesture of self-reassurance. As they moved back to the card table, Candida placed a comforting hand on the arm of her hostess.

'I know how you feel. In my naivety, I just thought that my ex- husband was a very busy photographer. If I'd been as attentive as you, Anth, maybe I would have found him out sooner. I might not have been so shocked or disappointed! It never occurred to me. I had other things on my mind, like being pregnant!'

The evening continued, suits and points exchanged, the Pinot flowed as advice on future lifestyle changes was exchanged until Candida stood up and announced that she needed to go home.

'I've got one retired, unemployed Chief Executive to sweep up!'

Candida shuddered at what her husband might have done during these first few hours of their new arrangement. She turned the car into the drive of Mulberry Farm and into the wash of blinding white coming from the security light. As she entered the front hall, she could hear the tinny soundtrack of strident violins and muffled voices coming from a television within. The distinctive smells of whisky and curry had combined with a deeply unpleasant pungency. Yet, there was no audible sound of human movement, no response to her arrival. The noise drew her to the drawing room, where her worst fears were confirmed. Her husband lay in his armchair, snoring deeply, his glasses askew across his shirt, pages of the day's newspaper strewn about him. Candida bent down to pick up the plate of the remains of coagulated curry sauce and congealed vegetables that sat on the floor by the chair. She looked at the note pad that was nearby. She was about to be impressed by the intent of the scribble at the top of the page until the illegible scrawl told its own story. She was reminded of Mary's description of one of the by-products of the Invasion. "They have no concept of Order or Tidy. They think that both are self-correcting freaks of nature that can be activated by a click of a finger. To my mind, mess is an existential province of the male of the species that can only to be remedied by the female of the species in the form of my cleaning lady!"

Since Candida had abandoned her husband so summarily on the first night of his new life, there would be little point in a full-on rant so soon. She worked on a more restrained response to the scene of carnage by placing a kiss on his nose.

John stirred. 'Oh Candy darling.' His eyes slowly focussed on the apparition in orange standing over him. 'How lovely, you're back!'

The crescendo of violin over the end credits of the film on the television screeched in his ear as John struggled to his feet. 'Good night, was it? Did you win lots of money from the girls? God, I feel rough.' John scratched his head as he looked at the detritus around him. 'I'll clear it up in the morning. That's a promise. Let's go to bed.'

Candida sighed 'Welcome to *Togetherland*! '

++++

Chapter Five
Plans, Objectives and Strategies

The throbbing in John Smith's head did nothing to prevent him from moving robot-like to the shower at six thirty on the following morning. The normal morning routine was so embedded in him that he had neither bothered to look at his watch nor to question his actions. The dry mouth and blurred vision only intensified his efforts to hurry in order not get delayed by the motorway traffic. Suited and refreshed, he trod delicately down the stairs, so as not to wake Candida. The sight of the box of office memorabilia on the downstairs table stopped him. For the first time in thirty years, he had nowhere to go except to return upstairs!

'I was wondering how long it would take you to realise that you are no longer a captain of industry, and now purely a man of leisure.'

Candida lay in their bed, her head propped on one arm, strands of her auburn hair falling over one eye. John stood before her like a naughty schoolboy waiting to be told off. The clock under Candida's bedside light showed that it was far too early to be up on the first day of retirement. A hint of white-skinned breast protruded from under Candida's silk nightgown. John suggested that there was another agenda that could be addressed. Work clothes were discarded with careless abandon, John's chill nakedness slid into the warmth of the bed towards his semi-comatose wife. Candida edged towards him. She wrapped him in her arms as she kissed him lightly on the cheek. Her hands played over his back as she sought to bring her husband back to a temperature that was suitable for any further togetherness. She looked towards him through half opened eyes. Her hands stroked his newly shaved face.

John felt sensations that he had not enjoyed for weeks. He kissed her gently on the forehead as he looked into her sleepy face, her eyes now closed as John's hands worked their way under the flimsy silk and on to the firm flesh of her body. Candida's breath felt warm on his cheek before he let her turn away from him. John pulled her close so that she could feel all of him against her. He kissed the back of her neck. He could smell the perfume from the previous evening as he clutched Candida in a tight embrace, their bodies separated by the thin film of silk nightgown. He lay still whilst Candida twisted and turned in response to his touch. He felt that retirement was not going to be too bad after all until Candida suddenly lifted her head and pulled herself away.

'Christ, Johnnie, is that the time? I hadn't realised! I've forgotten that I'm due to meet Mary in half an hour. You'll have to do without me!'

The spirit of Carnal Lust wafted away like smoke from a doused candle. John watched Candida throw the silk to the floor as her tightly shaped bare buttocks retreated into the bathroom. A few moments later, she reappeared, showered, towelled and issuing orders.

'Now Johnnie, you may not have work to go to, but you have much work to do here. There'll be plenty of time for all that.' Candida looked at John's nakedness lying useless on the bed. She gave his bare stomach an affectionate pat before placing a kiss on his forehead and walking out of the bedroom.

John lay contemplating his own doused candle as he lay on the bed listening to Candida slam the front door behind her. He gazed outside through one of the bay windows. The wisps of white cloud looked equally frisky as they streaked over the morning blue sky. He could hear birds in the distance chirping their encouragement for him to join them outside. Yet John let out a wide yawn of indifference. For the first time in ages, he was accountable to nobody and nobody was accountable to him. No longer would he have to act as father figure to the likes of Chaffy Finch, the factory foreman and one of the chiefs of the Foundry, who had once accosted John outside the canteen, his small football face showing a large scratch on one cheek and a crimson blotch over his left eye.

"Had a bust-up with my Sheila last night." John had always wondered how the rotund Chaffy had ended up with the taller witch-like Mrs Finch. John had never been good with tears. His responsibilities as employer had been put under severe strain as he listened sympathetically to Chaffy's sniffing description of discovering " the male model from the Arts Centre at my home showing off his own Statue of David." John had considered it his duty to listen to Chaffy's announcement of Sheila's decision to leave him. "She said that I'd never satisfied the creative urges that had spilled out of her since she had joined the life-drawing class at the Bisbury Arts Centre." John had caved in to the subsequent displays of Chaffy's emotional state by offering him the services of the company's lawyers to represent him in the divorce proceedings. Fortunately, the fees had not been too high as Sheila caved in to Chaffy's demands. It soon became obvious that the law was not going to be siding with her own artistic representations of the male model.

With a cup of hot tea in hand, John took his lack of

accountability out into the garden, delighted that his involvement in their lives of others was at an end. Like the Lion King, he was free to roam his own kingdom with impunity. A slight breeze wafted early scent from the nearby lilac tree. He flicked at a magpie that had swooped towards a couple of blackbirds who were picking at some early Spring berries that had fallen onto the lawn. Responsibility for others' misfortune was hard to give up. On returning to the kitchen, John turned on the small television and listened to the blonde newscaster deliver the morning's news. Concerns about the plight of a tanker hijacked by pirates in the Arabian Sea or an alarming decline in the American housing market were all somebody else's problem. John's isolation in the kitchen was interrupted by the shrill of the house phone.

'John, it's Roger Mortlock here. I gather that you might be needing help.' John sensed that here was another carrying out instructions from his wife. 'Mary tells me that you've finished work. She tells me that Candida is worried that she'll come back to find an empty shell. She wants you to keep busy. You must come and join us at Katie Stumples' Fitness sessions. Strenuous exercise for forty minutes with the very fit Katie and a pint in the pub afterwards. Very enervating.'

John thought that he'd got enough to do on his first day of retirement. 'I'll certainly think about it, Roger. At the moment, I've got quite a busy agenda.'

'Ah, you've been given the Civil List by the wife, haven't you? Mary gave me pages of requests when I finished with Crosthwaites. I finished them all very quickly. Now I'm onto my own stuff, making a life for myself. Anyway, think about it.'

John looked forward to doing his own stuff.

++++

Chapter Six

Chickens, Mortlock and the Badgers

'You've spent the last thirty years going backwards and forwards between Bisbury and here, Johnnie. Now over this past week, you've hardly moved anywhere. Don't you think that you should embrace the world a bit more before you die?'

'I've kept myself very busy. There's been much to do around the house, as you have regularly pointed out to me.'

John lay in his bed with a feeling of satisfaction. *"Togetherland"* had just enjoyed a significant first. The absence of any responsibilities, the need to deal with only the most inconsequential items of life and Candida lying naked next to him reminded him of the heady times that they had shared in their first years together. It had been good to rediscover that playfulness, although he was less certain about his wife's post-coital inquisition.

'You spend more time feeding the chickens. You have longer chats with them than you do with me. I might cite them in our divorce as co-respondents. I've had more than my share of sharing with duplicitous chicks!' Candida had found it difficult to adjust to the idea that her husband really did have nowhere else to go. As she lay with her head resting on one arm looking towards him, she was not yet convinced that the Male of the

Species, when left to his own devices, was not fundamentally an idle tosser. 'You have at least spoken with Mick Flanders. It's going to be so exciting, Johnnie!'

John turned away to take a sip from his third coffee of the morning. The thought of entering into an arrangement with somebody who was certainly loveable, if not a bit dodgy, as a business partner had troubled him. However, John dismissed these fears about the future and turned back to the much more pleasurable present. He looked down to Candida and gently kissed each eyebrow. She looked back at him from the dishevelled pillow with a smile which acknowledged that making love at eleven o'clock in the morning had been naughty and nice. The memory of her earlier excitement that morning was still as fresh as her husband's dishevelled look of satisfaction. When he had replaced the handset in the kitchen socket and turned to announce Mick's acceptance of his offer, Candida let out a shrill cry of jubilation. Turning the stables into a fabulous Equestrian Centre was the fulfilment of a dream that had been a long time coming.

"You'll not regret this, Johnnie!" Candida had grabbed him and flung her arms around him as if she had corralled a small foal. She pushed him up against the kitchen cabinet doors and looked into his eyes. "It's going to be one of the best decisions you've......we've made." She reached her hand down to confirm that he was genuinely pleased to have her close to him as she began to kiss him with more urgency. Her hands had started to unbuckle his belt before she stopped herself. "Maybe there's a proper place for this sort of thing, Johnnie!" Candida had whispered as her husband lifted her pink singlet over her head. Lying half-naked amid the residual smells of garlic and onion on the kitchen table could turn a girl right off her food as she took her husband's hand and led him upstairs.

Candida's riding breeches and discarded riding boots,

together with John's creosote-stained trousers,   lay strewn abandoned on the floor of the bedroom.   The sun had streamed in through the open window as the new partners in the soon-to-be prestigious riding stables had responded to tender touch and newly found desire. Longing and exhilaration had combined in carefree passion on the bed.

Candida's review was on the move again. 'However, I am really glad to have you here. It's been nice to have you around more. We've both been buried in our own little cocoons.' She was lean over her husband's chest and started to toy with the grey hairs on his chest whilst she continued. 'I suppose that I'm just getting to know you better. Strange isn't it?   After fifteen years. I never sensed your reclusive tendency. Some people would question your affiliation with the chicken as not terribly natural. However, I suppose...'

'You know chickens are really quite a friendly bunch, if only you'd bother to get to know them.   They're just very shy and nervous when they meet people for the first time.'

'People I meet for the first time don't usually squawk and bite me!   When are you going to talk to other, real people, Johnnie? They're starting to think that you have a problem.'

'When they're not going to talk about golf all the time!   It's all they talk about!   They're the ones with a problem.'

'There are lots of people who don't talk about golf.'

'But they're all still working. Those who have stopped work gather at the golf club as if it were Mecca.   Whenever I do go out, all I hear is chat about the bloody game.   There's famine and a gathering financial crisis throughout the world and all I hear is the lament about the new bunkers in front of the fifth green!'

'Social intercourse is what you need, Johnnie. Not just this!'

The arrival of *"Mister Benson's Coop 'n Wheels"* had been a welcome distraction in John's monastic routine. The photograph displayed at the farewell lunch in the factory canteen had not adequately portrayed the size of the cylindrical roosting quarters as it had rolled slowly off the trailer amid the huff and puff of Saul Benson and his son.

"This is a great spot. The chicks will love this!" Saul had remarked as he stood back to admire his handywork in its new habitat. "There's lots of room for them to roost and to perch. You can sit and watch'em move about in the annexe without any worries from foxes. The spiked run will keep them out. Guaranteed!"

John watched both men, with stomachs that seemed to have consumed several too many chickens in the past, struggle to place the coop in its final position. He had been pleased that the flock of eight Rhode Island Red hens and one fully fluffed-up Cockerel had settled quickly into their Romany-style residence with en-suite wire-mesh exercise area.

John had considered Candida's welcome to the new arrivals had been ungracious. Her comments on the proliferation of their feathers throughout the garden had been unnecessary. Whilst not the same as having children around the place, an additional presence on the Mulberry Farm estate was proving to be just as noisy. He suspected also that the chickens were just as voracious in their appetites. However, John had been delighted by the sight of his wife's face when he presented the first clutch of eggs retrieved from the coop.

As the sun continued to flood in through the window and consume their naked bodies with its early summer heat, John clutched Candida's hand. 'I know you're right. However, you've no idea how bloody great it is not to have to do *anything* after thirty years of constant activity. This has been the best start to my new exercise regime, far better than any gym!'

'Chop, chop, then!' Candida jumped up from the bed.

The half-hour chime from the old grandfather clock in the hall had been a more immediate reminder that John had been not been totally fixated with his chickens and that he had not been sitting on his arse all day doing nothing. The delay of a few minutes between Bisbury Mean Time and Big Ben was something that would just have to be tolerated. Now that he was not earning, John could not just wantonly sign off the huge expense necessary to have the antique fully restored to its former glories.

'I haven't got time to lie around all day.' Candida abruptly announced. 'I'll be late for my class with Katie Stumple. Come with me! This'll be much better than ninety seconds' exertion in the missionary position.'

Candida determined that the rules of *"Candida Country"* would apply. Whilst she had certainly enjoyed giving in to her own desires, she was not going have her husband collapse on the job due to his lack of physical conditioning.

++++

John knew that he had been right to stay away from the outside world. He had not prepared himself for the intense questioning from the overweight, the skinny and the downright nosey who had lined the way to the back of the Dance Room at the Bisbury Fitness Centre.

'You must be John. We don't get many husbands coming to this class.'

'You must be Candida's husband. How nice!'

'Are you on holiday? You must be very bored to want to come here. Don't you play golf?"

'Yes it is nice that he's with me.' John had heard Candida explain to the grey haired lady in her seventies next to her. 'I

50

thought that he needed a reason to get out of bed. He's retired or at least he's stopped working for the time being.'

'Did he lose his job? How tragic!'

'There's a lot of it about. My husband ......' A lady in her forties on the other side joined in. Candida turned towards her. 'He had to get rid of twenty people a few weeks ago. Now he's been given the chop. He seems quite calm about it. He says it's part of modern day work....'

'Morning ladies. Are we ready to do it?'

Mirrors on the room's walls showed John to be the only man among the group of thirty limbering up before the start of the class. Whilst he could hear the shrill Welsh voice, his view was blocked as the others sorted themselves into regimented lines. Then the petite shape of Katie Stumple appeared through the ranks. Her closely cropped dark hair reminded John of one of the Beatles, he could not remember which. There the similarity ended as he took in her toned shoulders and small breasts wrapped in a red body-hugging singlet. Black tracksuit trousers were further testimony to Roger Mortlock's assessment of Katie's trim figure as she continued the inspection of her troupe. John looked forward to watching her in action.

'Well, well, look who's swung down from his tree? A feller, no less!' Katie's twang was pointed in John's direction. 'You're most welcome, luvvie. It's nice to see a man who wants to keep his body beautiful and supp-el.' As she eyed him up and down, John stood braced for her review. 'I do like the Worzel Gummidge look. Very fetching. Very han-some. Right ladies...and gentleman, Let's start warming up, shall we!'

John was uneasy about his role of the singular Adam among the platoon of Eves. Where was Roger Mortlock? The music from the speaker system started to blare out. He could just make out the image of his own athleticism in the mirror as flailing arms and legs moved to the blast of heavy-base music. The garden trousers with dabs of creosote and a Smiths Screws T-Shirt had not looked too out of place as he concentrated on the moves, gyrating and twisting his body from right to left and back again. The trim, the ample and the shapeless all shimmied to the pulsating tempo. Located where he was, nobody noticed John's inabilities to cope with dance moves. Nobody seemed to care about his trousers riding up and down to expose the bright red socks which clashed with his blue and white deck shoes.

After a few minutes of strenuous work-out, John felt puffed. He paused to draw his breath. Spirits were lifted when the main doors to the Dance Room opened.   Mary Mortlock, dressed in what John could only describe as a bright yellow artist's smock, entered the room, followed by her husband. Roger's white rugby shirt and baggy, black trousers quickly joined into the routine. The white sweatband swathed around his bald head showed that he certainly looked the part of a second row forward, even if the drills and exercises were maybe better suited to pre-match entertainment rather than on-pitch confrontation.

Forty strenuous minutes later, Katie brought the session to a close. 'Eyes closed. Empty the brain. Breathe in and then .....owwwwt.'. John lay on the floor and closed his eyes. Katie's soothing tone drifted in and out as he wrestled against the onset of sleep like a sapper in the trenches. He was woken by a tap on his shoulder. John looked up to see the reddened face of Roger Mortlock towering over him. Beads of sweat oozed from his forehead. The headband had been removed.

'So you've relented then? Or have you just run out of things to do? Don't you feel great after all that?' As John as he got to his feet, Roger stood over him, hands on hips, waiting for answers. Since none came, he carried on. 'After a bout of exercise like this, I find that it's really important to rehydrate.

I'm going across to the Badgers for a swift pint. Why don't you join me? We can have a chat. Talk meaningful bollocks or else just get drunk and then ask our wives to drive us home, as usual. See you in a few minutes, then!'

John watched Roger have a brief word with Candida, before giving her a playful tap on her bum and exiting out through the door. Candida approached him.

'How do you feel?'

'It was hard work but I feel great!'

'It gets easier in time.' Candida's face also looked flushed. 'Anyway, I'm off for my milky weak latte with a covering of cocoa powder. Are you coming?'

John shook his head. 'Your friend Roger has suggested a more interesting alternative.'

'He's not my friend, as you put it! I don't really know him. Mary's my friend really. I've just seen Roger here.'

'Bum-patting is part of the regime here, is it? I thought that he seemed a little fresh, that's all. Anyway, I'll find out more in a few moments.'

'Don't be silly, Johnnie! It's just a friendly gesture. Nothing more. Anyway, bugger off to the pub and talk retirement plans. God knows, you need one!' Candida shouted after her departing husband. 'What shall I tell the chickens? They'll have nobody to talk to this afternoon!'

'They'll get by! I'll have more to tell them when I get back!'

++++

The Badgers pub sat in a prime location on Bisbury High Street. As John passed through the entrance, he was met by the sickening smell of stale beer and a hubbub of lunch time drinkers. He caught sight of Roger sitting in a tall corner seat, clutching a mobile phone to his ear. John ordered a couple of pints of Meon's Best bitter. He made his way over. Roger was still deep in conversation.

'Well that's fixed then, Jack! I must dash, there's somebody here for my next meeting. See you this Friday!' Roger snapped shut the mobile with the smug action of another satisfactory deal done.

'Do you hold many of your meetings in the pub, Roger?' John asked hesitantly.

'All over the place, me.' Roger replied. 'I call it hot-spotting. Anywhere that get's me out of the house. How did you like La Stumple? Isn't she good? Very energising.'

John thought that it would show the wrong attitude were he to confess that he had felt quite ill after the session. Nevertheless, he had convinced Roger that he would be a regular attendant at the weekly work-outs.

'How have you resolved your new work life balance?'

John had never grasped the mumbo jumbo of Work Speak. After taking a gulp of the tepid beer, he replied.

'It's like being on holiday the whole time. There's much to do. None of it useful to anybody else, but me.'

'It took me a few weeks to get used to having my own time.' Roger furrowed his brow as he considered his predicament. 'I've now been away from work for nearly four months and I'm starting to miss something. I can only do jobs around the house for so long. Golf has certainly helped fill the void. Even that's starting to get repetitive. I suppose it's the sense of purpose that's missing.'

'Do you want to go back to work? I mean to get another, paid job?' John asked.

'Good God no! Not *employed* work. Not what I've been doing for the past thirty five years type work. But I certainly want to do something, but I'm not quite certain what.' Roger gulped down the last remnants of his own pint before starting on the one bought by John. 'In the meantime, now that summer's here, I've decided to enjoy the healthy outdoors. So I've taken up sailing again. I used to have a boat when I was a kid. Sailing offers great opportunities to refocus one's energy and get rid of a lot of pent-up emotion. Something I needed after leaving Crosthwaites.'

John knew that Roger had worked in insurance . He had never heard of Crosthwaites. Nevertheless, more intrigued by the pent-up emotions, John asked 'Such as?'

'Oh bloody hell, John.' Roger revved up. 'Where shall I start? I was so bloody pissed off when they asked me to go. The bastards! It still makes me my blood boil thinking about it!' Roger's expression turned to one of embarrassment as he loosed off his litany of grievances. 'There were the normal emotions you'd expect from somebody who believed that he still had something to offer. Anger, obviously, at the rejection. Disappointment, at the waste of my capabilities. Panic, at the thought of what I should do next.........' Roger went silent to give further thought to John's simple question. 'I suppose shame, at being asked to leave rather than going at a time of my own choosing....... It was an awful feeling to be thought...... unnecessary after what I'd done for the company over the years.' He paused for a further slurp of beer. 'now that I'm out, I do feel relieved at the lift of responsibility, ...delighted to be away from the ever increasing rules and restrictions which the insurance business has had to implement in recent years. Transparency and correctness, my arse! Fucking waste of time, if you ask me.' Roger added, after a moment's reflection. 'Sadly, nobody did.'

As John listened, he watched Roger toy with the yellow and red beer-mat that suggested *"Make mine a Meon's"* He sensed that Roger's wound had only been temporarily stitched.

'To cut a long story very short, I was asked to make way for a younger man. A rather odious Hong Kong European, maybe you would call him Eurasian. Gavin Fu-Fing. He lives in Hong Kong ...... and then shags in Shanghai and Beijing. Rather a neat little set-up for a rather dapper man. I sometimes thought that he was gay, the way he minced about the office. Anyway, I mustn't be bitter and twisted. However, it was thought best that our two desks be combined into one under his command.'

John adopted the role of psychiatrist and counsellor. 'It obviously still wrangles.'

'I've mellowed a bit since I stormed out of Alistair Crosthwaite's office in a total red haze.' Roger put down the beermat and sipped on his pint before continuing. 'He did provide me with a very generous package of first class travel to say my farewells to the clients in Hong Kong. It was silly not to take it. All the posh hotels; Mary loved it, even if she knew that it was all a bloody charade.' Roger adjusted his position on the hard seat before asking. 'Anyway, that's enough about me. What happened to force you to join what my wife affectionately terms as the expanding army of "Space Invaders"?'

John then recounted, as quickly as he could, the saga of the last few weeks. 'So Charlie and I said - Stuff it! We'll take the Swedes' money and go! I was rattled off from the factory a couple of weeks ago. It's an old family tradition.'

'What is? Skipping off with other people's money?' questioned Roger. 'Sounds good to me! Was it enough?'

'No, being rattled off!' John wondered whether he should

tell the full story. 'We had some loans and overdrafts that were owing to the bank. The payout, after everything, should be just enough to see me and Candida through.'

Looking at his watch, Roger exclaimed and stood up. 'I've got an idea. I'm going down to the coast this Friday. Why don't you come with me, if you've got the time?

'Time is a commodity I have in abundance at the moment. In spite of being fully occupied, I do sometimes feel that I could cut the lawn with scissors and still have time for a bath afterwards. What are you going down there for?'

'I want to look over a boat. I could welcome a second opinion and a bit of company.' Roger was adjusting his trousers around a stomach that still carried the legacy of too many good lunches with insurance brokers. 'It should be a good day out. Roof down. Spot of lunch. Get out of the ladies' hair. Show a bit of independent spirit.'

'Sounds OK with me!' John announced, gulping down his beer.

'Great! I'll pick you up at nine thirty. I'm meeting Jack Hubbard the broker at midday. Bring your lifebelt. See you then!'

John watched Roger bid his farewells to others in the bar as he made his way to the main door. John liked the idea of a Day Out to the Coast! He would also need to mug up on sailing boats. There would be a lot to tell the chickens.

++++

Chapter Seven

Sailboats ...Expectations ....and more plans

Friday morning, Roger Mortlock braked the white Porsche Carrera outside the front door of Mulberry Farm. He had not seen the place in the daylight and had not appreciated that there was little sign of a working farm. This was more a large manor house with land. As he got out of the car, Roger looked past a line of empty outbuildings towards a wooden caravan-shaped structure in which chickens flapped and fussed. He noted a few cows in the field beyond.

As he looked up at the front of the house, Roger shuddered at the thought of what the place must cost to run. He suspected tall ceilings and stone floors, albeit with corded carpet, were not a formula for cosy eco-warmth. The oak front door opened. John walked out to acknowledge his arrival. Candida followed behind.

Roger had confessed to the blokes at the golf club that he had always felt a slight tingle in his todger every time he clapped eyes on Mrs Smith. As she approached him on the gravel drive, he could only admire the tan riding breeches which encased her with tight keep-your-hands-off protection. Disappointingly, the loose white shirt hid any other provocative curvatures.

'Roger! How nice! You've come to take my husband away. I had no idea about your plans to buy a boat. Mary hasn't told me about this.'

'She knows that I'm taking sailing lessons. My plans for taking things further are still in development and are subject to further discussion.'

'I think that it sounds a great idea. It's good to see somebody who has definite intentions in his retirement.' Candida turned to her husband and kissed him fully. 'Enjoy the sea air! See if you can convince Roger to buy a lovely boat that he can take to the Bahamas or to the Caribbean this winter.'

'I think that you should limit your ambitions a bit, Candy darling. I doubt if Roger can get out of the reservoir yet!'

'Very soon, Johnno. Very soon!'

John climbed into the passenger seat and watched his wife wave her farewell from under the bloom of the wisteria that hung over the front porch.

Despite the grey clouds threatening the early morning blue sky, Roger was determined to drive with the hood down. The dark blue baseball cap with *"Ex exec"* displayed on the front, had been a consolatory present from his oldest son, Jasper. He had read somewhere that black leather gloves provided better adhesion to the steering wheel when travelling at speed.

'We'll be there in about a couple of hours.' John could only just hear Roger over the din of the wind and the accompanying traffic. As the Odd Couple sped along the motorway through the Oxford and Hampshire Downs, John had little idea of where they were headed until he heard Roger mention something about "Lyndhurst Quay" . He was just able to make out Roger's brief description of what he termed " this lovely little place used during the Second World War as a base for landing craft before ....and by Lord Nelson in ....."

After a further few minutes of intermittent chat, both men realised that meaningful conversation was becoming impossible. John resigned himself to the wind buffeting his face, whilst Roger savoured his display of youthful exhibitionism and his eager anticipation of fulfilling a long-held ambition.

The flirtation with boats had started whilst others at school had sought to emulate the football skills of Jimmy Greaves, Danny Blanchflower and other members of the magical Spurs "Double " team of Sixty One. Roger's father had given him a model version of *Endeavour*, the sleek twelve meter J-class yacht that had carried the British flag in its unsuccessful campaign to wrest the Americas Cup from the New York Yacht Club in the Thirties. The failings of the real yacht had been dismissed as irrelevant. A quarter of a century later on, model boat owners still held to the patriotic attitude that *Endeavour* had been the most beautiful yacht in the competition. Roger would take his boat to the pond at Northwood Park, where, under the beady eye of his father, he would carefully set the boat's sail before casting it off on its journey. Man and boy would watch the wind fill the sails of the miniature vessel as it bobbled its way through uncharted waters, past the hazard of resting ducks and moorhens basking in the Sunday morning sunshine, over to the far off shore on the other side of the pond. In sea-lanes busier than the English Channel, these voyages were not without incident. Roger often had had to face the wrath of men three times his age who harangued him for setting his wind-powered boat on a collision course with their more sophisticated, radio-controlled boats.

Roger became immune to this ill-temper from men who should have known better. His enthusiasm grew as he used his pocket money to buy bigger, more complicated wind-driven model yachts. The sight of the fully rigged, four foot high

BY24, based on the design of the victor in the previous America's Cup, scything through the water was infinitely better than that of any insignificant petrol-driven motor boat.

"They aren't very cool, are they?" The dark-haired Valerie Black had sat down next to him on the Green Line bus taking them through the winding hills of North London to Northwood School. She had looked over Roger's shoulder as he studied the latest edition of *Model Boats Monthly* "I mean, they don't do much, do they? It's very boring just watching them float off from one side of the pond to the other."

"The skill is in setting the sails." Roger had tried to explain. "It's very satisfying to set the trim to suit the wind. It's fun as well. What do you do for fun?"

"We, that's Rita, me and Joyce with one or two of the boys from Lower Fifth, we go to the band-stand in the park. We listen to *Pick of the Pops* on the radio. We have a right old party. You could come and join us after you've finished playing with your silly boat."

Roger had thought that Val was quite pretty. At weekends, he had seen her in tight hip-hugging jeans bouncing down the road past his house with other girls from LF, whilst he and his mate Jim Watson prepared the rigging of their boats in readiness for their Round the Pond voyage. Little further encouragement was needed before both boys would skip ashore, park their sloops against the rusting railings of the bandstand and join Valerie and the Gang as they handjived and bopped to the music selected by the enthusiastic Australian deejay.

By the beginning of the summer holidays, Roger had not only ditched his model boats monthly magazine for the weekly *New Musical Express*, but he had also convinced Val that, whilst model boats might be uncool, dinghy sailing on the Beverley

Hook reservoir a few miles away was extremely cool.

By the beginning of the summer holidays, Roger had not only ditched his model boats monthly magazine for the weekly *New Musical Express*, but he had also convinced Val that, whilst model boats might be uncool, dinghy sailing on the Beverley Hook reservoir a few miles away was extremely cool. He had had to demonstrate his sailing skills not just to Val, but also to Rita who would tag along with her transistor radio. It had taken several outings and Rita's lack of sea-legs before Roger had been able to encourage Valerie to accompany him on her own. As they voyaged to the farthest confines of the reservoir, Roger discovered that the combination of sailing a fifteen foot dinghy and exploring uncharted territory with Val was as much as any sixteen year old could want.

When asked what he wanted for his seventeenth birthday, Roger was told by his father that the very idea of a sailing dinghy was out of the question. "You will never get any A Levels if you're out on the water all the time with those girls." Exams and academic ambitions relegated sailing to an occasional pastime. Val moved away to develop mathematical algorithms at Cambridge. Years later, after marriage to Mary Harrington and the arrival of children, Roger had been unable to convince members of his family that the cold sea of the English South Coast was more fun than the warmer waters of the Mediterranean. Consequently, Roger's sailing ambitions had remained unfulfilled until an early maturing life insurance policy and ample time on his hands had enabled him to relearn his old skills with the Brass Triangle Sailing Club.

The stench of seawater and dried mud carried on the breeze told John that they were not far away from the river Lynd. He caught a glimpse of the river over the gorse hedgerow that lined the road. The car passed the sign welcoming him to *Lyndhurst Quay – founded in 1796*. The sun had now burnt away the threatening clouds to reveal a clear blue sky. Roger looked at the clock on the dashboard as he pulled into the car park.

'Two hours and ten minutes. Not bad. There's life in that old girl. Ninety thousand on the clock and still goes like a rocket!'

John had been more intent at looking at himself in the nearside wing mirror and attempting to realign his mop of flailed hair into some order. He watched Roger looking down the hill, hands on hips as he shouted in full voice.

' "Or like stout Cortez when with eagle eyes, he star'd at the Pacific — and all his men look'd at each other with a wild surmise — Silent, upon a peak in Darien." You know, Johnno, Keats got it right. He must have seen this place when he wrote that. Breathe it in! Doesn't it make you feel good to be alive?'

Roger was staring towards the small jetty that protruded out onto the low-lying water of the river Lynd. John could not disagree. The sun's beams played onto the golden shingle of the path as it carved its way through immaculate green lawn past a line of cherry trees in full pink blossom. Yet there was little time to take it all in before Roger was striding down the hill towards the river.

Both men scrunched their way past the squat red-brick cottages which, according to Roger's snippets of travelogue, had once housed burly boatbuilders and Admiral Nelson's squat mariners. The occasional shriek from a seagull swooping overhead competed with the clink and clank of wires beating against the aluminium masts of boats parked on wheeled trailers by the side of the path. As he approached the river, John could only see isolated masts peeking up from the reeds and bullrushes on the dried river banks. With the tide still low, hulls of the boats were hidden from view, yet John could hear muffled chug of an outboard motor from the distance. Soon a

63

small inflated rubber boat turned the bend of the river and approached the jetty. Its bow seemed to be riding perilously high above the surface of the water, its stern heavy with its two crew-members.

Roger had turned off the main path and was headed towards a line of wooden cabins a short distance away from the jetty. He knocked on the door marked *"Jack Hubbard, Boat Broker"*. The red and white paintwork of the sign was chipped and weathered. Not waiting for a reply, Roger opened the door and stepped into the small office. John followed behind. A bookcase with shelves filled with a ramshackle mix of books, maps and magazines stood to one side of the room. A large Georgian-style desk sat in the corner. Two leather buttoned armchairs reminded John of his father's old office at the old factory. Shafts of sunlight flickered through the one window onto parts of the chairs that were not covered by large nautical charts. Behind the desk stood a man whose face had probably been exposed to most conditions known to the Met Office. Jack Hubbard extended his right hand to Roger, whilst his left enclosed a mobile phone into which he was talking. On finishing his conversation, Jack's Hampshire burr sounded genuinely pleased to meet Roger. He turned his gaze towards John.

'This is my friend, John Smith.' Roger explained. 'He has come along for the ride and to make sure that I don't spend too much money.'

'We'll have to give him something else to do whilst you and I talk then, won't we?' Jack smiled at John. 'Although I do think that you've made an excellent choice. What a fun boat she is! You're going to love her. Follow me!'

John hoped that the boat they were about to view was not as damaged as Jack's voluminous knitted sweater with standard issue holes at the elbows. The baggy brown corduroy trousers could not hide the brand new pair of white deck shoes.

'You've seen her details, I presume?' Jack rattled them off anyway. 'Thirty two feet long. Twelve foot displacement. Wooden construction. Standard rig. Two berths. Central steering set-up. Thirty foot mast with crossangle and spinnaker rig. Built twelve years ago by Fred Hunter's yard on the Hamble.'

Roger strode on ahead with Captain Jack along the grey wooden boardwalk of the jetty. John took in the expensive line-up of craft moored in their allotted berths. *Marine Lady - Southampton*, packed with radar beacons and chrome finish, bobbed next to *Beaux Locks – Hamble* , a top-heavy cruiser, more suited to catching shark off the Florida coast. A pair of faded red cord trousers and a torn white shirt hung over the railing of *Tramp of the Seas – Newport IOW*. The entanglement of boats creaked and squeaked their welcome on the tide that was higher than before.

Jack had stopped by one of the smaller yachts in the flotilla and was clambering onto its white deck. Roger eyed up the mast before stooping down for a closer look at the turquoise hull. John had noted the name *Fandango – Lyndhurst Quay*. Roger stepped back towards John and whispered to him. 'Six grand! That's not bad, as a starting point. She does look the part, don't you think, Johnno? This summer we're going to have so much fun!'

Jack beckoned Roger into the cockpit that housed the large wooden steering wheel. The boat bobbed animatedly on the water as Roger jumped the short distance from the jetty to deck. Whilst the others disappeared below, John breathed in the ozone of the breeze and watched other craft processing down river on the gathering tide. It was also quite obvious that Roger's plans were more advanced than he had let on. There had also been the word "we". Was this a signal of co-partnership, of his joining up to Roger's plan?

A few moments later, Roger leapt ashore and came up to John. 'Don't you think she's a beauty?' He asked directly. 'Come and have a look at her. She's just what we want.'

"We" again, John noted, as he stepped gingerly from the jetty to boat. He hadn't a clue what he should be looking for. Coils of rope were all neatly laid out, the mainsail tidily stored within a large white sheath on a pole that lay at a right angle to the mast. He ducked his head to enter the cabin. Jack was sitting at a small table looking at the log-book and other documents that presumably detailed the history of *Fandango*. Beyond him was a small stove with two electric rings on top. John looked further towards the pair of beds that lay either side of the forward bow area.

'I like the inside. It feels very cosy......' John paused. '....now. But when out on the high seas, I'm not so certain.'

'That's so right, John!' Jack said enthusiastically. 'Because when you're out in her, you'll hardly spend anytime down here at all. You'll be up on deck taking her across to the Island or going along the coast, or even going over to France. Stay the night in some little *demi-pension* and make an adventure of it.' Jack was working well, but John was not yet convinced by anything. He went back up onto the deck. Roger was sitting behind the wheel. He summoned John to join him.

'Jack has suggested that, if we like the look of her, we can take her out. Now that the tide is on the rise, we can put the boat through her paces and see what she's capable of. Obviously, we'll need to know where everything is and see if it all works. It seems too good a chance to lose. What d'ya think?'

'One small point, Roger!' John lowered his voice whilst Jack stayed below. 'Are you suggesting that we buy her jointly, as a partnership between you and me?'

'Why not? You've now got the time. I presume that you now have the money. It's not going to cost a fortune. We could learn the ropes together. Christ, I need a change from doing the Sudoku every bloody morning. I need a reason to live.'

Roger's enthusiasm was almost too overpowering. Nevertheless, John was beginning to sense a twitch of excitement. The challenge of a new venture of co-partnership and shared decisions, encased within a swirl of physical energy. All were coming together in a giant wave of child-like exuberance. It would be regrettable not to see where it took him.

It did not take long for all three men to prepare *Fandango* and get her under way. Jack gripped the spokes of the wooden wheel with one hand as he guided the yacht away from her mooring, past isolated boats in mid-river, out into the main flow of the Lynd. The rhythmic chug of the yacht's engine echoed against the river bank. Cows munched on the grass in the fields on either side, showing little interest in the beginnings of the men's new adventure on the water. As the river widened, the cockpit in the boat became alive as Jack issued instructions to his fledgling crew.

'Hold the wheel firmly, John. Aim towards that hut on the bend a few hundred yards ahead! Roger! Pull hard on the jib.'

John gripped the wheel with the rigidity of *rigor mortis* and watched the small white sail at the bow rise up before him. His eyes fixed straight ahead on the course that Jack had set him. He could hear the ratchets of the winch as the blue and white mainsail inched its way up the mast. John responded as best he could to the instructions that flew on the wind towards him. It was great to be busy and focussed again!

'Mind the buoy on the port side! Cut the engine!'

The harsh clatter of the engine was replaced by the more gentle sound of rippling water as the yacht took on responsibility for its own progress.

'Pull in the jib!' The small belly of the front sail expanded as Roger pulled the rope.

'Mind out!'

John had not been prepared for the impact of wind on the mainsail which Jack had tightened. The boat leaned over unnervingly, knocking him off balance and taking the spokes of the wheel out of his grasp. Alive to the momentary change in the boat's direction, Jack Hubbard brushed John aside as he reached for the wheel before correcting their course away from the rapidly approaching river bank. The cows looked on at the minor panic in the river. They had lost count of the number of times they had seen novices making a hash of the art of sailing.

'We'll take her down to the Shallows and turn her round there. ' John followed the direction of Jack's hand towards a large white wooden cross that stood in the middle of the river some distance away. 'Then we'll have to tack our way back up river.'

Having taken over the helm, Roger was also alert to the marker and noted a couple of small boats making their way along a short stretch of water that led out to the main sea. Sea water stung his face whilst he listened to the rush and splash of *Fandango* scything through the water at some speed. It had been a long wait, but this was what it was all about. He watched his partner go below deck.

Despite the numbing cool of the wind, John felt the sun's heat burning layers of skin off his face. He sought temporary shelter in the small cabin and looked out of the small porthole. The cabin had its own language as the water slapped against the hull exterior and a loose ashtray slid from side to side on the small table.

'Ready about!' John heard Jack's barked instruction a few minutes later. Roger pushed hard down on the wheel, turning the boat at right angles from its previous course. John stood at the cabin entrance and looked on helplessly as the sails flapped in an excited frenzy as the wind was denied them. He was not totally convinced by the boat's loss of momentum as she continued to turn on her axis.

'Pull in the sheet! Mind your head!'

As Jack pulled in one rope, he handed another to John which he pulled as instructed. Each man ducked as the boom swung over with some force to the opposite side, whilst Roger set the boat's course to the furthest bank. Thus began the zig-zag course back up river. John pulled and ducked his head when necessary, moving from one side of the boat to the other as *Fandango* made her way back up river past the cows, some of whom lifted their head to acknowledge the improved seafaring skills of Roger and John.

By the time the *Fandango* had reached the marina, the two crew members felt like round the world yachtsmen as both leapt like gazelles onto the jetty to fasten the boat to the mooring. Any early queasiness had long given way to exhilaration.

++++

'Well, Johnno! It looks like we have ourselves a boat. Bargain price. I knew that we could beat him down. The market for second-hand boats is stuffed at the moment, just like everything else. Cash is king.'

With all the relevant registration papers and certificates of sea-worthiness tucked under his arm, Roger was striding back up the path away from Jack Hubbard's cabin towards the car. John was considering the project that he had undertaken.

'Well, now I have a new hobby. Candida has her stables. You have your dream. What does Mary have? '

'Oh you don't need to worry about the wife. She has more than enough. She has her own life!' Roger held the mobile to his ear before bellowing into it. 'Diana? It's Roger Mortlock! How the hell are you? I've been meaning to call you for ages. Look! I want to give you some business. Lord knows why after what Crosthwaites did to me! How is Gavin by the way? Not that I give a shit! That bastard owes me such a helluva lot.'

By now both men had arrived at the Porsche. Roger leaned gently on the roof. 'Look Diana darling! I've just bought a boat and I need it covered. Can you ..... What's that?

John grimaced at Roger's dirty leery laugh. 'No, it's not a bloody tanker! Neither is it a very large crude carrier with deadweight of up to three hundred thousand tons. That's you, darling! Yes, crude carrier! You know what I mean.' Roger turned towards John and mouthed an apology. John wondered whether the knowing winks were being done for his benefit as Roger continued. 'Yep, I just want the usual bollocks, cover against theft, storm damage, loss at sea, man overboard. Fully comp. What was that? About thirty feet.' The cackle boomed into the air again. 'You saucy cow! How's your love life, by the way? Are you still with that bloke from the Operatic Society?'

John moved away. He had no desire to listen in on somebody else's intimate conversation, even if some of it did have some relevance to him. After another few minutes, Roger clicked shut his phone.

'Well, that's the boat's insurance sorted!' John saw a smile of quiet satisfaction cross his face. 'I did think about placing it with somebody else. Then I thought, stuff it! It would be stupid not to use my previous employer. They're rock solid – unlikely to go tits up. Diana Vowlds and I go back a long way. She's given us a good package, maximum cover for the minimum price. So, a satisfactory day's work! '

The two men set off on their journey home in silence, the car roof up, deep in thought at what they had just concluded. John still reeled from the impulsive last few hours. Roger drove up the motorway, comfortable in the knowledge that he had found a partner with whom he could have a fun summer. As he pressed the car's accelerator to the floor, he relished the excitement of forging this new relationship. A screw manufacturer might not be the most exciting ship-mate, but the chief executive of a family business would bring a sense of responsibility and level-headedness which would be a useful sop to Roger's more impetuous and hot-headed nature. He knew that Mary would appreciate the merits of his decision. He remembered a recent conversation one morning as he pored over the Financial Times for old times' sake.

"When the kids first left home, you were still working or away on a trip, I realised that I needed to refocus my own life....y'know , develop new interests.....discover a new regime to my life. You've got to do the same, Roge!"

Roger knew that Mary had been right. Now he had found *Fandango*, he had fuel for his mind, fuel for his body. It would cost a bit. Did he have enough? The boat-share idea had been a bit of a brain-wave. He hoped that the partnership would not come a cropper like it nearly did on the test sail. He had been pleased that John had acquired the basic sailing skills so readily.

The blue motorway sign announced another forty two miles to the turn-off for home. John was sound asleep in the passenger seat. Roger cast his mind back to his recent telephone conversation with the current Director of Claims and Compliance at Crosthwaites. It had been overkill to have called Diana Vowlds to place the insurance cover for the boat. Yet it had given him the opportunity to renew contact after his sudden departure from the company. Whilst Roger's role had been to set up insurance for owners of large vessels, Diana had ensured that details on the contract between insurer and insured were watertight. Their paths joined when cracks appeared in the contract or when subsequent claims for loss or damage were starting to let in water.

"Your client's cargo could never have slipped overboard just like that. The fixings must have been faulty." Diana had stormed into Roger's office one morning. "I don't believe him, Roge! We need to sort this one out. He'll not receive a penny from us until we find out more."

Diana had flicked back the mane of curly black hair over her shoulder, before adjusting the hairclip to keep it under control. She deposited the file back on Roger's desk and turned to leave the glass-walled office. Roger wondered how he was going to face the hard-nosed, large fee-paying client and accuse him of lying.

"We'll obviously need more evidence to prove your case, Diana!" Roger had suggested.

"You give me authorisation to investigate and I'll set my dogs onto it!" Diana stopped and poked her head back around the glass wall. "I'm not going to approve the fucking claim just because a Big Shit Boat Owner tells me that I should. That's not what I'm about or indeed what this company is about!"

Roger had watched the ample figure in a black suit stomp away around the corner of the corridor back towards her office. The subsequent investigation by Diana's dogs into the suspicious claim had resulted in Roger and Diana having to pore over pages of witness statements and experts' assessments of the client's sloppiness. The need to prepare their case before the showdown meeting with the client on the following day had required an overnight stay at the hotel near to the Crosthwaites offices by the Tower of London. During a respite from their intense scrutiny of the evidence, they sat opposite each other in the hotel restaurant. Diana had taken a sip of red wine and then let out a big sigh.

"God, I'm shattered! This case couldn't have come at a worse time for me."

Normally, Diana's piercing eyes could take on an unruly mob of male brokers and break them down with a glowering smile that told them that they were being complete pricks. Roger had seen her banter with the most brazen and leave them flummoxed by her put-downs. Yet, as he had looked on, he began to witness another side to her that had been hidden from public view. He watched tears well up, as the expression on her face fought to keep her unhappiness from taking over.

"It's been a long day. I'm sorry, Roger!' Diana quickly found a handkerchief to wipe the tears away. 'It's just that........my sodding, selfish bastard of a husband has left me for somebody else."

Roger remained motionless as he listened on.

"When we got married, there was always some tension from his family about my not being...... suitable. Class? Religion? My job? His job? I never was able to put my finger on it. All I know is that his mother could never warm to me. I thought Gerry and I were good mates. I knew that he had got bogged down at work. He'd been passed over for promotion on a couple of occasions. Whereas I had been more fortunate, more determined in getting to where I am. But we had our daughter to think about. He was, still is, great with her. Anyway, there is this girl, this woman in his office, younger than me, much younger than Gerry. They'd been having an affair - Well that's what he told me - for the past year. So, a couple of days ago, I came home to find him packing his bags. He'd decided that he wanted to live with her rather than with me. It's all so bloody......humiliating."

Maybe it had been the offer of a consoling hand and the look of genuine concern on Roger's face that made Diana continue her sorry tale. "So, here I am, on the wrong side of fifty and I just feel so ......alone."   Roger remembered her frustration. "Fucking hell!   I'm meant to be all tough and uncompromising at work. When I get home, it will just be me and Charlotte. She was distraught at first, but she's getting used to it. She told me that she wasn't totally surprised. She'd seen Gerry and his ....friend, Naomi, in his car driving away from our house. I'd still been at work. Charlotte was coming back from school.' Diana picked up her wine glass and swilled the remaining wine around in the glass. 'Charlotte's had to put up with a lot. With me to start off with, when I come home and loose off about my fucked up day at work with stupid fucking clients trying to wheedle a fictitious claim out of us. All she wants is somebody to help with her French homework."

Roger's efforts in providing emotional support had previously been dismissed by Mary as totally useless. "What man could possibly understand why their daughter was in tears or why their son was so moody?" He had offered his freshly laundered handkerchief from his pocket as Diana sought to patch up the cracks in her composure. Then he took both her hands and started to rub them gently.

"Your daughter is going to want you. She'll need your love and your attention. You have your job. You have your health." Then he had no idea where the final phrases came from, but he went on. "and there's me. I will help you in any way I can."

The flickering candle in the middle of the table had caught the querying expression in Diana's watery eyes.

"What can you do, Roger? You're married and you have your own responsibilities."

"I can listen. I can advise. I can be there for you." A rush of emotion was collecting inside him, a feeling that he had not had for ages. Here was somebody whom he could help, who might just need him. He had wanted to take her in his arms and bring her close to him. He had wanted to wipe her tear-stained face with his own hands.

Surprised by Roger's comforting gesture, Diana had lifted her hands to take another sip of coffee. "I'm sorry about getting myself into this state, but I haven't told anyone how I really feel. My Mum and Dad don't understand, although they're very cross with Gerry. My girl friends just keep encouraging me to get a good lawyer and get as much money as I can, which is what I'm doing." Diana paused and placed her hand back on Roger's. "I'm glad that you now know. Men are usually pretty useless when confronted by a weepy woman. You and I make a good team at work. It's nice to have a manly shoulder to cry on."

If there had been any attraction between the two, neither had let on. Roger had been taken by surprise when Diana announced outside his bedroom. "I don't suppose you'd mind if we share the same bed tonight? It's just that I don't fancy wallowing in my own self-pity..... on my own." Diana had drawn Roger close to her. "A bit of a cuddle, nothing else. Maybe.... who knows, but I'm not very good at it!' She looked at his perplexed expression. 'Is that being too forward for you, Roger? You did offer to help!"

The presence of two mature adults under the snug of high thread-count Egyptian cotton had at first been sleepy and chaste. The feel of warm nakedness had been consoling and different. Intimate passion had sat, like the solitary rose in the teak vase on the bedside table, unused, unnecessary and waiting to be properly appreciated.

As Diana had lain in the firm clutch of his arms, Roger had tried to dismiss thoughts of his wife's reluctance to adopt a similar position. On the pretext of his bulky presence preventing her from a good night's sleep, Mary's increasing use of the spare room had given her the rest needed to be the active woman she had become, yet denied Roger the release he needed to be an active man. Diana snuggled closer into the embrace. She looked up at him.

"Well, Roger, I know that we have an important day tomorrow. But I can feel that you might be ready for some further study of the facts..."

Roger had needed no second asking. Thoughts of betrayal and doubts about performance were quickly dispelled as he started to kiss Diana's lips with a suffocating intensity.

The secrets of Room 454, with their reminder of Diana's playful grin looking down on him, were interrupted by the insistent glare of the red traffic light at the entry into Bisbury High Street. The warm glow of the subsequent carnal action with Diana two years ago was replaced by the here and now of the still dosing John Smith seated next to him.

As the car pulled away, Roger afforded himself a smile as he recalled the remains of the memory. *"Thanks for being there. It will not happen again."* The message, written on the hotel note-pad, had been lying on the pillow when Roger had woken the following morning. Diana had already returned to her own room. The subsequent inquisition of their formidable client had not gone as well as both Roger and Diana had hoped. The claims could not be proven incontrovertibly to be false and untruthful. Their failure put a damper on the consolatory drink in the hotel bar after the meeting.

"We did our best, Roger."

"I know. They're a clever, conniving company, but their business is very useful to us. I suspect that we might have a problem getting them to renew for next year." Roger had paused. The conversation could not go on without some comment. "About last night, I've been thinking..."

"As I wrote to you, it was a one-off." Diana interrupted. "You have responsibilities. Sailing any closer to the wind has all the bearings of collision course. I don't want you being sued for any damages."

The intervening years before Roger's dismissal had combined the humdrum of work with the occasional lunchtime review of Diana's battles with her ex-husband's lawyers. He enjoyed the spicier tales of her search for more realistic male companionship within the local Operatic Society. However, there had been the satisfaction of Roger and Mary buying a larger bed. Mary had returned to the conjugal bed. Rights had resumed, even if Mary was a willing partner with both her eyes clenched tight as she waited for it all to be over.

After dropping John at his house in the evening darkness, Roger was able to let the hot water from the shower wash away the salt from his exhausted body, but not the excited anticipation of further *Fandango* adventures. The outlook for summer was not so bleak. He might meet up with Diana again, for old times' sake.

++++

Chapter Eight

Beached whale and other animals

'So, tell me more about this boat then! I don't remember this to be in the treaty for *Togetherland*!'

Candida sat opposite her very own Rhode Island Red at the end of the kitchen table. She had not seen her husband's face in such distress. The red-raw visage pierced by white pebbles of his lugubrious eyes, coupled with hair splayed out like Robinson Crusoe, convinced Candida that her husband had finally gone native.

'More importantly, are you going to tell your mates in the Chicken Coop about your new project, Johnnie? They will let you in without a murmur, looking as you do. They will be all ears on this project, as will I.'

John watched Candida as she cleared away glossy brochures displaying new stabling partitions and hay feeders. He had never felt so exhausted. He knew that he had caught the sun, but this was a whole lot more painful.

'Well, it's a joint purchase. The boat will be moored at Lyndhurst Quay. Roger has already passed his basic sailing exams. He will then teach me until I get the qualification. Then we can then battle it out as to who's going to use her when.'

'Sounds like a relationship made in heaven, Johnnie. I had no idea that you were interested in sailing.' She had been pleased that her husband seemed to have found something, finally, that would take him away from the monastic existence of communing with the chickens or sifting through the written ramblings in his family's diaries.

'Well, neither did I!' John replied. 'I just found the wash and the waves of the sea quite exciting.'

'How big is it, then?' Candida quickly filed away the price list for heated stable flooring.

'The boat? Big enough to ride the waves, small enough for us to manage capably. ' John showed her an image on his mobile phone showing Roger and Jack Hubbard on the deck of *Fandango* after their return from the test sail.

'Oh!" Candida was disappointed that the boat seemed to be smaller than she had might have hoped, yet it seemed still large enough to warrant a small measure of scepticism. She continued to sort out a stack of catalogues into order before finally placing a copy of the lease document for Bisbury Stables on top with a definitive pat of her hand as if to remind John of his priorities. She sincerely hoped that a tenancy for five years at a very low rent, coupled with an agreement to upgrade the premises into a proper equestrian centre had not been hijacked by the recent impulsiveness of her husband. The combination of Boys and their Toys can be a dangerous canker unless closely monitored.

The ring tone of Candida's mobile erupted in the stillness of the kitchen. Candida listened to Mary Mortlock's deep breathy voice.

'Well, how's your Captain Pugwash then?'

'At the moment, he's collapsed here at the kitchen table like a beached whale on the mudflats waiting for the tide to come in and sweep him out to sea.'

Mary reported that her Roger had sunk with all hands under the shower. 'At least, he will have a change from the golf club and their silly white balls. I've never understood the point of doing something with others if you never see them until the end?' She needed to expand her premise. 'Sometimes, Roger comes back from his golf, cursing how much it has cost him. Not so much in green fees, but in the betting during the game and the drinks afterwards. Now that they're not earning a salary any more, these men have to live within their means.'

'Buying an ocean-going yacht is not exactly cheap!' Candida replied.

'Men need fresh challenges. That's why this sailing thing does seem a good idea. Space Invaders need to be kept at arm's length most of the time. I do worry that it's a bit bloody dangerous. I had this awful dream the other night. I was at home talking with Roger on the phone. He was on a boat somewhere with the children when suddenly there's a loud crashing roar on the other end of the line. Roger sounded calm as he told me that his boat has been hit by a large oil tanker. The line then goes dead. I woke up in a cold sweat. It was horrendous.'

'No more dangerous than what we do each morning.' Candida sought to reassure her riding companion. 'I'm sure that they'll use the boat as an excuse to motor round to a pub for lunch and chat away putting the world to rights. They're both responsible enough not to want to sail around the world in her.'

'Let's hope so. See you tomorrow at eight. I'm dying to see what you have in mind for Mick's stables. It sounds very exciting!'

Candida turned back to see her husband's head lying on the table, comatose and safely beached at the far end of the table.

++++

The ambition of establishing an equestrian centre in Bisbury had festered in Candida's mind ever since she had grown impatient with the lackadaisical attention offered by Mick Flanders and his team of daft sixteen year old stable-girls. She had seen horses left unattended in all weathers waiting to be ridden off or else to be sent back to stables after a hack. She had become fed up with being provided with saddles, bridles and tack that were so worn or weathered that sometimes they had just came apart in her hands.

She remembered the headline in a magazine article she had read at Carlo's Coffee House – *"Adman jumps first fence in new biz venture"*. She had seen the picture of a slick-haired Smoothiechops who had sold his agency to a French rival for a ridiculous sum at the height of the stock market boom. She had not been impressed by how he had not only left his clients, but also his four bedroom house in Primrose Hill and his wife and two boys – "we wanted different things" – to set up with his new girlfriend in a small cottage surrounded by many acres deep in the hills of the Cotswolds. However, Candida had warmed considerably to his setting up a twenty -box livery centre that catered to the needs of the local riding community. The spark in Candida's mind had been lit. Maybe not twenty boxes, but certainly ten, just to start off with.

As she looked across at her Red rousing himself from his slumbers, Candida completed her list of items that she had wanted to discuss with John and her new business partner. She thought that they would be pleased that she had kept the list to just five pages. Now that June was here, Candida knew that there were only twelve weeks for the work to be completed before the arrival of crap weather and shorter days.

++++

Chapter Nine

Unwanted liabilities

Since the purchase of *Fandango,* John had grappled with the mysteries of weather, navigation and steering as explained in *"Elementary Sailing"* . A beginners' course with Jack Hubbard's gangly assistant, Tristram Harkness, at Lyndhurst Quay had been a considerable benefit as he joined Roger in charting courses beyond the river Lynd, through the Shallows and out into the wider expanses of the Solent. Wind direction and tidal flows were becoming as easy to calculate as the percentage of zinc and copper in the formulation for the new *"Gambit 35"* range of screws which had so attracted Sven.

The arrival of the postman was one of the morning highlights in John's day as he delivered fresh supplies of glossy catalogues of equestrian equipment. Hand -written notes were then piled up on the kitchen table as daily reminders of Candida's spending. The Wish List was turning out to be as expensive as the refurbishment of the new Smiths Screws foundry. The installation of new flooring and partitioning in each stable box suggested that the ten horses would receive enough care and attention to satisfy a major Hollywood celebrity. He had not questioned his wife's decisions. He had enjoyed seeing the delight in her face as her plans evolved. The funds received from Langstrom had seemed to satisfy her ambitions.

Candida reached for the bulging envelopes whilst finishing her cup of green tea. John picked out the few addressed to him. Discarding the offer of a free estimate for double-glazing, John was surprised to open a letter from Ishy Hassan, honey-king and hopper supervisor at the foundry. This was the first contact that John had had with anybody at Smiths Screws since his leaving two months ago. The typed letter announced "the unannamous decision of the Cricket Committee to offer to Mr John Smith the prestigious position of Honorery Chairman of Bisbury Cricket Club". The role offered no executive powers, other than as possible proof-reader and spell-checker of all correspondence.

John was pleased that, whilst he may be gone, he had not been forgotten. He looked forward to putting in a request for further supplies of *"Ishy's Googly Honey"* not for use as a sex-aid, but as a delicious accompaniment to his morning toast. John cast the letter to one side ready for his future acceptance of the kind offer. The envelope addressed to "Mr John Smith - Private and Confidential" had remained hidden from view under the latest issue of *"Fasteners and Screws Monthly"* . He had not received a letter with a postmark displayed "Moncrieffs - London, EC1" since concluding the deal with Sven. He tore open the envelope and scanned the formal typed script.

"Dear Mr Smith,

We would refer you to the arrangement agreed with our Mr Giles Fortescue-Smythe relating to the repayment of the outstanding loans by yourself and by Mr Charles Weatherhead.

We have already acknowledged receipt of the payment for £500,000 received from yourself, for which we thank you. As you

are aware, the terms of the arrangement
with the Bank set out that the remaining
sum of £500,000 be repaid by Mr Weatherhead
within forty five days of the completion of
the sale of Smiths Screws vis. June 15th.

John gripped the letter more tightly as he read on. Candida continued to thumb through her brochures unaware of her husband's gathering turmoil.

"Since this date has now passed, I have
to inform you that no repayment has been
received from Mr Weatherhead. We have
attempted to contact Mr Weatherhead
directly, by letter, by e-mail and by
phone. I regret that, thus far, we have
failed to receive any reply from him.

As you know, the terms of our
arrangement with you and Mr Weatherhead
state that, in the event of non-payment,
the Bank would have to refer the matter
back to yourself as Counter-guarantor of
the repayment. I am therefore writing to
you in this capacity to demand repayment of
the outstanding sum within thirty days of
the date at the head of this letter.
Interest will be levied on the remaining
sum at the pre-agreed rate...."

'Is all well with your mate Giles? We must have him up for dinner or lunch!'

Candida looked towards her husband who was engrossed with the second page. The fancy vellum envelope had aroused her idle curiosity. Anything that had *"Private & Confidential"* merited further interrogation. Her husband's lack of response was forgotten as her attention was drawn to the higher than expected cost estimate for the heated flooring submitted by its German manufacturer.

'I'm off now to make sure that the builders put on the new stable doors the right way round. I told Mick that I would be there in ...oh shit....five minutes. Bye!'

Candida's departure was barely noticed as John skimmed the remaining paragraphs of the letter.

> "I would request that you contact Mr Fortescue-Smythe immediately to discuss the situation in greater detail and that you give this matter your urgent attention. If repayment is not received by the due date, then we will seek ...."

'Oh my God! Oh my God! This had certainly not featured in the Retirement Plan! What the hell was Charlie playing at?

> "We are confident that Mr Weatherhead's actions can be easily explained. Nevertheless, we trust that you will understand our position and appreciate our need to reclaim funds that rightfully belong to the Bank."

John sat at the kitchen table whilst the wires in his brain struggled to make some connection with the time when the loan agreement had been set up. Images returned of the small conference room which had previously housed the portraits of the senior John Smiths. As John's grandfather, sided by his father and his son, looked on expressionless. John remembered that the whole process had been hurried and condensed into a quick few moments before he had had to rush off to a Dinner held by the Hardware Manufacturers Association (West Midlands Chapter) at the Duke of Bisbury hotel. He was sure that Bridget Murphy had witnessed both signatures. John needed to refer to his copy of the document for peace of mind.

John had valued Charlie's down to earth approach to the business and to their customers. It had helped to open doors, forge new relationships and generate orders for the company. He had forgiven the occasional lapses when Charlie had overlooked his responsibilities as his attention was diverted by the excitement of purchasing his apartment in Alicante and the prospect of sharing his future life with the formidable Francine.

With Candida now away to lavish more of his money on her pet project, John needed the next few hours before her return to resolve the matter.   She was therefore spared the sight of her husband rifling through the filing cabinet, fingering folders headed   ...... *Purchase of Mulberry Farm..... Loan from Moncrieffs 1987...... Loan from Moncrieffs 1995......*before arriving at *Loan from Moncrieffs 2003.*

Papers fell to the floor like dead leaves in autumn.   John breathed in deeply as he started to read through the copy of the Agreement which Charlie and he would have signed.   He turned to the last page.   John's signature sat visible and illegible in the specified space,   as did Charlie's.   John sat back in his chair, greatly relieved, as he reviewed the carnage of his office.

Why was Charlie being so evasive? Why hadn't Giles alerted John sooner on what was going on? Why had John counter-guaranteed the bloody loan in the first place?   It was all very well to have these whys after the event, but what was he going to do about them now?

Suddenly, the phone rang.   John grabbed the receiver.

'Johnnie, can you believe it? They won't be here until tomorrow.'

John continued to listen to his wife's tirade with one ear. There was little need to alert her to troubles of his own.   No confessions, yet, about the bloody mess he might be in.   He informed her that he was tidying his study.   She continued to tell him about the stable doors.

'The bloody van has broken down, so they say! I don't believe a word of what they said! Bloody driver was probably hung over from last night! The builders are here waiting to put them in! So we've got to find something else for them to do. Hey ho! It's only money!'

As he put the phone down, John considered whether, the way things were going, he had enough "money" to even buy a bar of chocolate, let alone ten spanking new stable doors with electric locks. He consoled himself that he had experienced similar crises before when the company had suffered alarming declines in sales. However, generous terms from Giles at Moncrieffs, guaranteed by the value of Smiths Screws intellectual property, its very desirable freehold premises and a reasonable-looking balance sheet were not going to be available to him this time. No safety nets, just a bloody great hole in his plans for the future. His mobile phone rang. It was Roger. He sounded, as ever, lively and excited.

'Hey, Johnno, I've just received my Skipper's Certificate. You can now call me Captain! We must have a small celebration. I was thinking that maybe we could take the wives for a *Fandango* adventure next weekend. I've discussed the idea with Mary and she's really keen. What about Candida?''

'I'm not so sure, Roger.' Any type of celebration was not at the top of John's list at that moment. However, maybe he could do with the distraction, let the wind clear his brain, whilst he worked out a clear strategy of how to proceed. He sought to delay Roger with the predicament of his wife being unable to bolt the stable doors.

'See what you can do! It would be great if she could make it. She'd love it!' John wished that he could share Roger's optimism as the house phone rang in the hall.

'Yesss! ' John rushed to pick up the receiver. He did not look at the display panel to see who was calling. 'Ah Giles!' He paused and took in a deep breath. 'Good to hear from you. Hold on one moment.' The few moments to finish his conversation with Roger had given John valuable time to present a more measured mood as he began listening to his old school chum and benevolent banker. 'Yes, I've just received it. Yes, it was a bit of a surprise. More of a disappointment, I would say. I'm sure that there's a simple explanation. Yes, I do understand. You know Charlie's in Spain now. I haven't spoken to him since we left the company. I'll call him to find out what's going on. I'm sure that he'll speak to me.'

John listened patiently as Giles outlined the official bank stance on un-repaid loans. He sensed Giles' discomfort with the matter.

'You must understand, John, that the matter is out of my hands. There's considerable pressure on me to get the money back. In the current climate of Imminent Shit, the bank is getting very twitchy about unpaid loans. So it could be nasty for you if we have to call in the big guns.'

'It would have been nice to have been alerted sooner' John said, knowing that any advance warning of a Shit Attack did not make the Shit any less palatable. 'Leave it with me. I'll see what I can do.'

As John put down the receiver, a pall of sadness wafted over him. Within three minutes, a friendship that had started in their teens at school and had developed into a close and personal relationship based on trust was now under severe pressure.

John suddenly felt alone. If one of your closest friends is now gunning for you, to whom can you turn? Least of all Candida, at this particular moment.

John slowly piled the scattered papers ready to be filed away in the cabinet, before carrying his mug of now tepid coffee out into the garden. John had remembered what his father, John Daniel, had said to him.

"The best way to resolve a problem is to walk it off. Nothing like a good stroll around the hills of the Triangle and you'll be surprised how easy it is to come up with a plan of action; something to do with getting the adrenaline pumping through yer brain."

John continued along the narrow path towards the cows. Maybe they could help him? He looked around at the bush of blood red roses whose first flowers were on the wane and in need of pruning. A robin whistled from a nearby branch. As John opened the gate into the field, several cows backed away as if to say "you're on yer own, mate!" He considered that his offer to Charlie, three years ago, to buy shares in Smiths Screws had been a sensible gesture. Not having enough money himself to purchase the shares outright, Charlie had negotiated a separate loan with Moncrieffs which John had agreed to guarantee. When the Swedes had agreed to buy the company, John had made sure that the value of Charlie's shares would be sufficient not only to buy his love-nest in Alicante, but also to repay Moncrieffs. It had all seemed so watertight. Half a million quid had seemed manageable when the deal was struck.

The robin had moved off, equally mystified by the whole situation. Blackbirds and thrush swooped low into the hedge of thorn and bramble. John listened to the scuffling that came from within as if the birds had met to discuss his predicament. By the time he came back towards the house, John's mind was made up. The issue needed to be addressed urgently. If necessary, he would go out to Alicante and sort out the matter face to face. He remembered the words of Charlie's open invitation.

"When you get fed up with the awful English climate, John, and you feel the need for some hot sunshine, give us a call and get on a plane. Frankie and I would be delighted to see you both at any time."

Because the moment should not be of Charlie's choosing, John decided that surprise and canny planning would be required. There was a lot at stake. Suppose Charlie's evasiveness had been deliberate? John looked through his Blackberry to locate the number for Charlie's apartment. Before dialling, he went into his study and booted up his computer. He looked at flight schedules and the horrendously high fares displayed on the screen. He pulled off a list of hotels; yet more expense! Damage limitation had not been part of his Retirement Plan.

John was about to press the button for Charlie's mobile, when he decided to scroll down further to another number. He pressed Dial. Soon a female voice answered.

'Frankie! It's John Smith. How are you?' The pleasantries continued between the two. 'Guess what?' John came to the point finally. 'Candida and I have taken off for a few days' sunshine on the Costa Blanca. We're staying at this wonderful hotel just down the coast from you. We thought that we would come up and see how you've settled in.'

John sensed Francine's hesitancy as he listened to her reply. 'Charlie's not here at the moment, John.' His heart sank with thoughts of Charlie's disappearance off the face of the earth. '....He's gone to the market. I've got him well trained. You know Charlie and his love of food. He should be back later this morning.'

John had last seen Francine as she had sat at the bar at the Duke of Bisbury hotel with Candida. Both had been waiting for the arrival of Sven, Charlie and John to celebrate the completion of the sale of Smith Screws to Langstrom. The lines on her bronzed face, the fall of dark hair onto her broad shoulders, the strain of her black tailored jacket suggested a woman in her late fifties. The narrow, dark shaded eyes had looked at him carefully as John approached her. The blood red lips had broadened into a smile as she stood up to greet him. The tailored trousers completed her tall elegance. As they chatted over dinner , John remembered her excitement at the imminent purchase of the apartment in Alicante.

"It's been something that Charlie's always wanted. He's worked hard for it over the years, I bet. He said that you were a very demanding boss!"

John had tried to put her right. "More a desperate boss, I would say. At times, the company needed Charlie to boost sales. How did you meet him?"

"On the internet." Francine had replied. "On one of those

dating sites. There was an instant attraction ...from both of us."

John had not been surprised. Francine had had the allure of a gangster's moll. John had thought that she would eat Charlie alive. However, as they had continued to chat at dinner, John had softened his opinion of her. There was a softer side to her as she explained how she was looking forward to caring for Charlie. "He's lost his way a bit after the death of his first wife. He'll need me to look after him. We're good together. We have lots of fun.'"

Months on, John sat in his study listening on to Francine's not exactly thrilled enquiry. 'When were you thinking of coming then, John?'

'When would you like us? We're here for another....'John didn't want to push his luck.

'We've got nothing on for tomorrow.' John sounded relieved. 'Come for lunch. Would one o'clock suit you? That'll give Charlie and I time to come up with something.'

"Yes, like five hundred fucking grand!" thought John as he concluded arrangements with Francine.

'It will be lovely to see you. Tell Candida that she doesn't need to bring very much. If anything...' John could hear Francine's earthy laugh. 'As you know, it's so bloody hot here. Charlie and I are very relaxed about dress code. It'll be like old times for Candida.'

John winced as he put down the phone. The notion of him and Candida wandering around the apartment stark naked with their host and hostess seemed rather appalling.

John realised that he was shaking, the adrenalin now coursing through him like hot lava. He was suddenly nervous about what he had just committed himself to. It might also have been the cost of the fare, which had been nearer to that he had paid to travel to Australia, rather what he had assumed a budget fare with an economy airline to have been.   Nevertheless, he had little else planned for the coming days, so a meeting in the sunshine seemed as good a way as any to sort out the matter. The sooner the better.

++++

'You're going *where* tomorrow?' Candida had asked him when she returned.

'To Alicante, to see Charlie.' John had been braced for Candida's look of astonishment as he proceeded to outline his hair-brained scheme. 'There are some documents which Giles wants that need his signature. That's what his letter was about. I'd forgotten all about them. I've little else to do, so I thought that I'd better get it done sooner rather than later. Why don't you come with me? We could stay in a nice hotel. You could do with some sun. You've been working really hard on the stables. Give yourself a few days off. What could be nicer? ' John kept his fingers crossed. This was a high-risk offer. Plan B could be a more painful strategy, if not a more honest one.

Candida came towards him and smiled. 'It's very tempting. Thirty degree temperature by a hotel pool does sound great......' Candida was reminded of her last conversation with Frankie at the bar at the Duke of Bisbury hotel.

"We have a lovely balcony which looks out over the bay."

Candida remembered her irritation at having to watch Frankie continuously flicking strands of her dyed black hair off her eyes. The full fringe was better suited to the winning dog at Crufts.

"It's so nice to lay out on the sun lounger, a drink by my side, with Charlie not far away and let the heat of the sun play over my body."

Candida had struggled as Francine suddenly lowered her voice to a whisper.

"I feel that I can talk frankly with you, since you was in the business of glamour modelling." Candida grimaced inwardly as Frankie continued. "Sometimes, Charlie likes to use the video camera .... on me, you know......He videos me as I go all provocative ....writhe around, you know.... with all sorts of....... you know....." She then contorted her mouth and whispered. ".... toys........and such like." She then took in another swig from her glass of wine and continued. "We then watch it on the big telly later as sort of foreplay.....you know.....to our lovemaking. It's like what you used to do, I suppose."

Candida had had no wish to compare notes on shedding inhibitions. She suspected that it was far easier to look sultry under a hot Spanish sun than in a grubby photographic studio in February with just one small electric fan heater for warmth. Fortunately, their conversation had been interrupted by the arrival of the three men. She was glad to have been spared any further memories of a career that had happened such a long time ago, when her life had been so different and taking off her clothes had just been the means of earning really good money.

Candida shook away the memory and looked back to her husband. 'However inviting it might be for just the two of us, Johnnie, I think that I will pass this time. There's still a helluva lot to do at the stables. You can take me away, when it's all finished, to somewhere really nice. Winter sun in the Bahamas would do just fine! Something to look forward to, don't you think?'

Candida turned away, secure in the knowledge that she had been saved from her husband's barmy plan to meet up with two over-sexed and overweight holiday companions in some ghastly apartment complex. She was more excited that once the new stable-doors had been securely bolted, albeit a day late, she could start to take in horses of paying owners. Let them enjoy the new heated floor in each of the boxes. Her dream was rushing to become a reality. She could soon set a date for the formal opening of the *Bisbury Equestrian Centre* and the beginning of a new era for the local riding community. Why should she stand in John's way? If he wanted to trot off to see the awful Francine, then so be it!

++++

Chapter Ten

The pain in Spain

Four o'clock in the morning at Birmingham airport had not figured in any of John's Retirement Plans. It was his first brush with travelling reality since his trip to Australia earlier in the year. The drift of families with their piles of suitcases, backpacks and sunglasses was different from the cushioned exclusiveness of the Business Class Lounge. Whilst he waited in the ramshackle queue at the departure gate, John doubted whether any of his fellow passengers would be boarding the plane with the same intent. Any concerns about the hotel room not having a view of the sea or close questioning by the children as to why they were up at such an ungodly hour seemed mild against John's own mission to recover half a million quid.

The narrow one-class seat did nothing to calm his inner turbulence. As the plane gained height into the awakening sky, John thumbed the pages of the in-flight magazine for distraction. An article about Ian Fleming's house in Jamaica took his eye. John likened his own mission to those described in the author's fiction. He just hoped that the outcome would be as successful as that achieved by the fictional Bond, but without the need for a Walther PPK.

'Do you want anything from the bar?'

John suspected that a request for a Dry Martini "shaken but not stirred", even at seven in the morning, would have been lost on the stewardess. She looked too young to be able to buy a drink, let alone sell one. John declined the offer and re-immersed himself in the images of *Goldeneye* and the calm blue of the Caribbean Sea lashing the surrounding coves.

'Any food from the trolley?'

John listened to another stewardess, whose short spiky hair looked in need of a good brush, recite the choices available to him. The beef sandwich, a bag of crisps and a cup of coffee in return for his tenner did little to settle him as he wrestled with the packaging.

'So where are you staying then?'

John had noticed the grey-haired lady settle into the seat next to him before take-off. Through the corner of his eye, he had noted her small hands arrange the crossword puzzle and her pen in readiness for the journey. He had not expected in-flight conversation as he battled with the plastic packaging of the sandwich.

'I'm staying with friends outside Alicante.'

'We love Alicante. We've been going there for the past fifteen years.' The lady lifted off the top of her own sandwich, picked out the slice of tomato and placed it neatly in a tissue. 'Yes, me and my husband, Maurice, we love the weather, the food, the change. It's our second home. We always stay at the same hotel, the *Las Palmas*.'

'These friends of mine have just moved from England. I'm going over to see how they're getting on.'

'We make so many friends when we're away. We keep in touch by the SpaceBook, *Cheryl and Maurice holidays dot com*. My husband spends a lot of time editing the videos and putting them on the Interweb. It keeps him busy in his retirement.'

'I'm not so sure.' John pronounced between mouthfuls of his beef sandwich. 'Social networking online still can't beat face to face contact, especially when there is so much to catch up on.'

'That's all very well if you have the money to travel. It's not cheap any more. My Maurice's pension does not allow us to swan off as much as we would like.'

At least you know how much you've got, John thought as he continued to munch on his sandwich. 'It will be nice to see them again, anyway!' John realised that he had absolutely no idea of how Charlie and Francine might react to his face to face questioning. Would they still be there? He closed his eyes. He needed to be sharp and alert for his mission. He was woken by the announcement.

"Ladies and Gentlemen, we will be landing shortly at Alicante. We would ask all passengers to kindly clean around their seat before leaving the aircraft....."

John wondered why this request had been necessary. The flight had not been that bumpy and he did not see that many passengers had been of a nervous disposition. After the plane had landed, he watched Cheryl pack away her crossword and dust down her seat as requested. John made sure that he had left no signs of his own nervousness.

++++

The captain's proud boast of the plane's arrival seven minutes ahead of schedule was soon annulled by an interminable wait for the bus to take John and his fellow passengers to the main terminal building. John waited yet longer at the desk of the car rental company, before setting off northwards towards the coastal village of *Sant Miguel de Mar*. Having declined the offer of discounted Sat-Nav on the grounds that he did not have any coordinates to go by, John had to rely on the directions offered by Francine in their conversation the previous day.

"Where are you coming from, John?" Francine had enquired.

"We're in this wonderful little hotel, called the Excelsior. Hidden away on a bay near to....."

John detected a certain impatience in Francine's reply. "Why didn't you call us first? We could have told you where to stay. Some friends of ours run a delightful *Pension* in the next village to us here."

"We've stayed here before, soon after we were married. We thought that it would be nice to revisit. Give us some time to relax and chill." John paused for a moment as he came to terms with the ease with which the fibs tripped off his tongue. "Candida's been really busy renovating the old stables. She needed a break."

"A break from spending all your money, I would imagine!"

John had not been prepared for Francine's jocular observation about what was becoming a diminishing commodity. However, his explanation did convince her to provide him with detailed instructions on how to get to *"Apartamentes de Castille"*.

Driving along the wide motorway away from the airport, John pinched himself about the subterfuge he was embarking on. He was about to invade the privacy of somebody whom he had trusted, somebody whom he considered to have been loyal and honest. During the ten years they had worked together, there had been lively debate at times. John had welcomed Charlie's rough-edged approach based on his insight of hard-nosed project managers of building and construction companies. Charlie had more than repaid John's intuition by achieving sales targets for the Smith's *Gambit* range that had exceeded all expectations.

John was relieved to see the sign for *Sant Miguel de Mar* as he steered the car away from the frenetic motorway and the sudden sight in the rear mirror of a car travelling at breakneck speed whilst only two inches from his back bumper. The less hectic pace of the long *Avenida das Palmas* allowed him to notice the red and white oleander bushes that lined each side of the road before they were replaced by a high yellow painted wall on his right side. The battlement-shapes continued until the tongue of a large covered entrance jutted out. John slowed the car to catch sight of the brass name-plate, announcing *"Apartamentes de Castille"*. John looked for any sign of a guard or the threat of burning oil from the turret above. A single barrier across the entrance seemed all there was to keep intruders at bay. He sped past the building and turned the car into a short *cul de sac* . He parked in the shade of tall eucalyptus trees and let the red earth dust of the street road swirl in the gentle breeze and settle. He got out of the car and stretched his body.

Regretting his early-morning selection of thick jeans and check shirt, John wished that he could have taken up his fictitious booking at the *"Excelsior"* hotel. He pulled out his mobile phone, before nervously punching in Charlie's land line number. He listened to Francine pick up at the other end.

'Si, ola!'

'Frankie, it's John Smith! How are you?'

'John! How nice!' John sensed a momentary hesitancy before her voice mellowed. 'Where are you? We're really looking forward to seeing you both.'

John then went into the script which he had rehearsed in front of the magazine article on the plane. 'I'm sorry that you'll just have me to entertain today. Candida got up this morning and was violently sick. I think that she rather overdid the sun yesterday. She's stayed back at the hotel. I'm on my way and should be with you in about twenty minutes.'

John could just hear Frankie whispering. 'He's nearly here. Twenty minutes. No you're not! You're staying here, my love!'

John was much reassured by hearing Charlie's voice in the background, but not necessarily by what he was saying. Frankie came back on the phone.

'Did you hear that, John? Charlie, the daft bugger, has run out of Piri Piri sauce for the Paella he's making for lunch. He wanted to go into the village to get some more. I've told him not to bother.'

'Good idea! I don't like too much heat in my food. I love this weather though. I'll get there as quickly as I can.'

'We're in Apartment Ten on the top floor.' Frankie had announced. 'Come to the Main Entrance and press five four two one. You can park the car in the underground car park.'

John stood for a few minutes and let the breeze blow its cool over his overheated body.. What was he waiting for? Was he expecting to see the two felons shinning down the drainpipe on the outside wall with their bag stuffed full of bank notes? Being on the front foot was the best place to be. He must not lose momentum. It was Showtime! He started the car and drove back to the front entrance.

A sign in the small courtyard directed John towards the dark cavern of the underground car park. John's heart beat a little faster as he shut the car door. The dim light could not prevent thoughts of henchmen dressed in smart suits and Black Bowler Hats lurking behind the concrete pillars. A sudden door-slam echoed loudly throughout the concrete building. The tip-tap of anonymous footsteps made their way to an exit. Two pigeons flapped away from one of the dark corners as John walked smartly towards the staircase to the ground floor. John was still half-expecting to see Charlie and Francine scurrying away into obscurity. He looked to the doors of the lift. No movement showed on the floor indicator. No sound either of scurrying from the marble stairs. Lunch and the midday sun seemed to have closed down any activity in the apartment block.

John took the stairs up to the next floor. The open landing looked over to the swimming pool. One or two bronzed bodies lay on sunbeds amid a landscape of unoccupied white mattresses that dazzled in the summer sun. A pool-boy, dressed in uniform beige shorts and white sports shirt, stood languidly guiding a pool-net in pursuit of errant leaves that had blown onto the water.

His attention was interrupted by furtive glances at the red and white bikini-clad body that lay on one of the sunbeds. John wondered why any sensible architect would have installed the noisy water-feature whose constant rush of water destroyed the peace and tranquillity.

As he made his way up the staircase, John eyed the pool area from the landing of each floor, whilst checking the lift for any movement. As he reached the fifth floor, he heard the lift motor start to whine. He looked at the dial. The lift was on its way down! Bugger! Bugger! Bugger! Had his birds finally flown? He rushed to look over the edge, hoping to see the exit on the ground floor. No sign of anybody. He looked at the dial. The lift had stopped at the first floor. The swimming pool! He rushed back to the other side, just in time to see a man and a woman making their way towards the pool-boy. Both wore sunhats. John could not see any more features. Young or old? Fat or frumpy? A cheat and his girl-friend? He couldn't tell. All he could see was the shimmering heat on the blue sea over the roofs of surrounding villas. John took in the sign that announced *"Weatherhead"*.

John knocked on the door and waited. He could see no movement. How could he have missed them? Suddenly, there was a twitch of the curtain at the window next to the door. The door opened and Charlie Weatherhead stood before him dressed in a pair of bright green swimming shorts. His stomach hung over the waistline. A gold chain with a "CW" medallion nestled among the hairs on his deeply bronzed chest. John was taken aback by his debauched appearance.

'That was quick, John. Then, I remember that you always were a fast driver.' Charlie shook his hand. 'Come in. It's good to see you.'

John followed into the open-plan drawing room. Black leather sofas lined each wall. A glass table sat on the white-tiled floor. Francine approached John to give him a welcoming kiss. He felt the moist warmth of her suntanned face on his cheek. The fringe of her hair had been clipped back off her face to reveal eyebrows that looked at John with a puzzled frown. He noted the butterfly tattoo on her bare shoulder as she turned away.

'I'm so sorry to hear about Candida.' Francine sounded sympathetic as she padded her way out to the exterior balcony. 'Although, if she was dressed like you are for this heat, then maybe I shouldn't be so surprised after all.'

John said nothing as he moved towards the balcony and its view of the sea. He had not really worked out how he was going to tackle this part of the conversation. It was clear that neither Charlie nor Francine were going to make the initial move. John had come to see them. They leaned against the balcony rail and watched him approach.

'What a fantastic view, Charlie. This really is a find, isn't it?' John was starting to wish that he had joined the seascape of small sailboats and jet skis scything their way silently over the water beyond.

'We both like it.' Charlie agreed tersely. Francine had placed one arm on his shoulder. Her flimsy leopard-print shirt did its best to hide the briefest white bikini she was wearing underneath. John wondered whether he had barged in on a video shoot which Francine had told Candida about. Francine lit up a cigarette. Charlie broke the silence. 'Do you fancy a drink, since you're here now? Could you open a bottle for us, babes?'

John watched Francine turn to go out of the room. She seemed unabashed by her state of deshabille. Her shirt fluttered in her wake as she passed him, revealing yet another butterfly tattoo, this time on her fleshy right buttock. John detected a mocking tone to her question.

'I trust that you've brought something more suitable to change into, John? As you know, we're very relaxed and chilled here.'

John could wait no longer. He turned back to face Charlie. 'Charlie. I do need to ask you something first.'

Charlie gestured John towards a wicker seat that sat in the shade on the balcony, whilst he filled the one that was still in full sun. 'Ask away, John!'

'It's more of a simple explanation, really.' John had worked on this part of his opening address. 'Seeing all this, I suppose that it's so easy to forget about everything else in the world. All this sunshine, this superb view and Frankie needing care and attention means maybe that your other responsibilities get overlooked. So I thought the best way of bringing a little reality back to your life was to meet with you directly.'

John needed to keep himself under control. Charlie's face showed a hint of embarrassment. A smile remained annoyingly stuck to his face like a toy mask, empty and valueless. His bloated body glistened under the unforgiving sun as John hesitated.

'You.... may remember the small matter of the loan that you were due to pay back to Moncrieffs after we concluded the deal with Sven. Have you received any letters from the bank... recently? They certainly haven't heard from you nor, more importantly, have they received any repayments from you.' John sensed that his words and the firmness in his tone were becoming increasingly pointless. Charlie's smirk had not moved. 'Since the due date has now passed, Moncrieffs are now expecting me, as the counter-guarantor on the loan, to meet the outstanding sum in full.' John puffed himself up for one last push towards reason. 'So, Charlie, has there been some mistake? I presume that you have made the repayments and that your bank has cocked up by sending the money to the wrong account or whatever.' John paused to give Charlie time to take in what he had just said, as if he really needed it. 'I would love to go back home to tell Giles where to find his wretched money, but not before having sampled your delicious paella..... albeit without the Piri Piri.'

Charlie had got up from his seat and had moved back to the edge of the balcony to admire the view. He then turned to face John full on and sighed.

'I haven't got it, John! It's all gone, mate! That's the simple, honest truth.' Charlie brushed away a fleck of peeling skin off his arm as if there was really nothing left to be said.

The simplicity of Charlie's words hit John's astonished face like a boxer's right hook. He may have sensed that it was coming, but the answer still had him reeling. It was the one he had most dreaded. He sat rooted in his chair.

'What do you mean, it's all gone? It takes some doing to get through half a million pounds in three months. Christ Almighty! Has it been a bottle of Cristal fine champagne every night?' John stood up from his chair to face Charlie directly. 'How can you have spent it all? That's plainly ridiculous. How could you?' His anger was threatening to erupt like oil from a gushing well. Other emotions, like shame and the hurt of being betrayed by a trusted colleague, were lining up behind. A future that had once had looked so sunny and certain was now receding into a shimmer of hazy doubt.

Charlie stood like a sullen teenager, offering only a plaintiff shrug of the shoulders. After a while, he repeated. 'It's all gone, except for about ten grand.'

The pop of the wine bottle being opened sounded from within the house was not lost on John. 'Is that another bottle of Bollinger being opened in celebration of me being made to look a total fuckwit?' John walked away and stared over the balcony out to sea before turning back to face Charlie. 'Surely, there must be something that can be retrieved?'

Francine arrived carrying a tray with three glasses and the wine bottle in a ceramic cooler. 'There you are, boys! I will be back. You look as if you're having such a lovely time. I really don't want to miss out on the fun.' The flash of naked cheek winked at John again as Francine barefooted her way back inside. John wondered how much of their conversation she had heard. Indeed how much did she know of Charlie's treachery? The sound of a scooter accelerating away in the street outside broke the unreal silence that sat on the balcony like a fog.

'Come on Charlie! You owe me an explanation, at least. We've been through a lot together over the years. If there's a problem, then I'm sure that Giles can sort out a new arrangement with Moncrieffs.....'

Charlie began pouring the wine into each glass on the tray. He handed one to John as he listened on. The smirk had been replaced by an expression of resignation.

'I used the money to buy this place. It's all tied up in this.' Charlie met John's gaze whilst gesturing weakly around the room. 'I had to do it, John. I had no alternative. Frankie had very little money of her own. So we needed to fund this place.' He sipped on his wine before carrying on. '....when her first husband died, he left her very little by way of assets and a lot of debts with the bank which she was forced to repay. So, when we met, I had to help her out......'.

John shut his mind to Charlie's rambling explanation. Here was a paella of a very different sort which was about to destroy much of John and Candida's plans for the future. This needed no bloody Piri Piri sauce, it was creating a heat all of its own! John sipped on the cool white wine as he sought to work out a scheme that might force Charlie to change the recipe. Never mind Frankie's bloody debts, what about his own?! John's ears pricked up when he caught a change in Charlie's plea of mitigation.

'......besides, it's not that bad, John! You've made more than enough out of the company over the past years. You don't really *need* this money. Your old man left you well looked after.......'

This was more than John could cope with. The legacy of his father and his forefathers being squandered by an overweight salesman and his unclothed tart was becoming too much. 'So, you think that it's OK just to run off with the proceeds of nearly a century of a family's hard work.' John knew that the central argument had been lost as he gesticulated towards the overstated furnishings and furniture in the drawing room. 'Did you really need to spend as much on all this? Couldn't you have been more careful if you knew that it wasn't really yours to spend? Come off it, Charlie! What you have just done is blatant theft. I could have you arrested.'

John had always felt that he had run a well-managed good business. He had disregarded the encouragements from Giles and Moncrieffs to take out larger loans to fund the purchase of other companies. Through canny planning and good business judgement, John had kept the business afloat for longer than others might have expected. Having worked out a good deal with the kindly Swedes, John was now expected to finance a Love Nest on the Costa Blanca for one of his ex-employees. This was humiliation on a grand scale.

'There has to be a way out.' John volunteered. 'Maybe you could sell up and use part of the proceeds to repay the bank and use the remainder to buy a smaller place....or maybe you could take out a mortgage.......'

'I'm not fucking moving for anybody!' John watched Frankie re-enter the room. Her voice was firm and abrasive. She pulled hard on a cigarette as she headed purposefully onto the balcony towards Charlie. Her long legs were now covered in a pair of white trousers. What seemed to be a man's red shirt hung loosely over her shoulders, the unbuttoned collar highlighting the deep brown tan of her neck. Her dark hair, still wet from the shower, was brushed forward in prize-dog fashion.

John could only acknowledge that Frankie's Best in Show allure was extremely attractive, yet as he tried to regain the high ground, it was also downright intimidating. 'Well not immediately, maybe...'

'Not fucking ever. Charlie and I aren't going anywhere.....' She inhaled deeply from her cigarette. '..... *you* can't make us do anything. The arrangement is with Charlie, not with me. You ask any lawyer if I'm not right.'

John's mood had changed from one of possibility to one of total impotency. 'But he says that all the money has gone!'

'He may be right! To pay for all this was not cheap, neither was it outlandishly expensive. I had a vague idea of how much it was all costing, but the deeds of the apartment are in my name only.' She put her arm around Charlie's waist and looked him in the face. 'I thought that I was shacking up with a man of substance. Have you spent *all* of Mr Smith's money? You daft cock!' She gave his crotch a pinch with her free hand. Charlie gave one of her large breasts an affectionate squeeze and summoned up a modest smile.

John watched their dumb arrogance in a seethe. The ground had been taken from under him and he was left standing on the tiniest piece of it. Frankie had broken away from her husband and was refilling the three glasses.

'We don't normally drink at lunchtime. I find that alcohol makes me ever so horny, but in the heat of the day, it's just too hot to have sex. So we'll just have to have Charlie's paella with whatever hot sauce he still has left!'

Despite the aroma of fish, onions and red peppers coming from within the apartment, John's appetite remained completely uninterested.

'So that's it then, is it? My life's work, my family's life's work....just spent so that the two of you can fuck your brains out all day. You are a disgrace, the both of you! Charlie, I thought that you had more integrity.'

John turned to face Frankie who was now seated inside on one of the black leather sofas. She had put on a pair of sunglasses to protect her eyes against the glare of the early afternoon sun. 'Can you please take off those bloody stupid glasses! I would really like to see whom I talking to!' John could not stop raising his voice.

'John! Shouting at me is not going to get you anywhere. Look, we all need to be calm.' She lifted the sunglasses onto the top of her head and pulled on another drag from her cigarette. She blew the smoke contemptuously into the warm Spanish breeze. She continued. 'Let me ask you something. Who's going to get hurt the most in this situation? As Charlie has already said, you don't really *need* this money.......' John listened dumbfounded as she emphasised the point 'You would *like* the money for the sake of your conscience, to maybe satisfy your sense of family honour which might have been dented.' Francine stubbed the remains of her cigarette in a nearby ashtray. 'Maybe you should look at it another way. Consider that slightly more of the Family Silver has been assigned elsewhere than you'd have liked. Not for fucking our brains out, as you rather hurtfully put it.' She picked up her glass of wine and took a healthy sip as she digressed. 'Although Charlie and I do have fun pleasuring each other, I will admit. I mentioned it to your lovely Candida. Having sex at our age is terribly important. It kick-starts the body and makes sure that we're still alive. Aren't I right, Charlie?' She sipped further on her glass of white wine and warmed to her theme. 'Even at our reasonably advanced years, we need to be able to enjoy ourselves and do things. Not just sit around waiting for death to strike us down. So, Mr Smith, John darling, rather than *turning* in their graves at our behaviour, your family should rest easy in them, knowing that the fruits of their hard work are being shared with those that helped to build the business. The workers at the factory, the managers and the directors, you have all done well out of the deal. You should be really proud of the way the Swedes' money has been distributed."

'But, that's not really the point.....' John tried to butt in.

'Let her finish, John.' Charlie had sat down on one of the other leather sofas, his chest glistening like a heavyweight boxer.

109

Frankie continued to clutch her glass with both hands as she sat seductively on the sofa with one leg folded under her as she continued. 'All I was going to say was that none of your family would want to see anybody starve. I've had to sort out a lot of grief from my ex-husband and also from the useless greedy pensions company who lost much of his money through dodgy deals. So, Charlie and I have been up against it ever since we've been together. We're both too old and too useless to work. So, we needed to make sure that we had enough to last us through.' John's jaw was motionless as Frankie soldiered on. '......lawyers can do nothing about it. You can bleat all you like, but the fact is that Charlie's bank account is almost empty. My account has just enough. You certainly have enough. The Swedes have the business. Everybody's happy. There's much more to life than just money. John. Get on and enjoy it!"

'That all sounds very righteous, Frankie! You've just repaid *your* debts using money that *I* will now have to repay to the bank from *my* own savings. Most people would describe that as theft on a grand scale.'

John stood in the middle of the room facing the two others like the barrister pleading to the jury on behalf of his client whose cause was lost. He summoned up one last gesture of conciliation that might change their minds.

'Tell me how much you really need to keep going.' John's accountant's brain had been working on other alternatives. 'I can go back to Giles, tell him how much that you'd be willing to repay. He can then work out a restructure of the remaining debt. '

Charlie and Francine remained expressionless. There was little sign of reason, even less of recognition that what they had done had been in any way unethical or unlawful.

'All of it, John dear!' Frankie sighed. 'We've calculated that we will need every last penny to keep us going. Look! I am fifty eight and Charlie is sixty four. Neither of us intends to pop our clogs for a good few years yet.'

'Did you not even think to *tell* me what you were doing?' John started to pace the room as the others watched on. 'Did it not occur to you that I might actually *need* this money for plans of my own? Plans that would allow others - of my own choosing, not you thieving little shits – to enjoy.' Panic and desperation were new cellmates in John's mind. He couldn't believe the bile that he was issuing.

'Well, John! We're telling you *now!*' Charlie had stood up and was facing John. He started to prod John's chest with his forefinger. 'Remember this! John matey! Neither you nor your Calendar Girl will be suffering. You will still benefit from other investments that you've made, using the family's cash. This was always just going to be the icing on the cake for you, rather than ordinary bread and butter for the rest of us. Don't give me your rubbish about plans for others to enjoy. This is money for us to *live* on! Don't you understand? Sort it out with your mate Giles. I am sure that he'll be most accommodating. You public school types always stick together. They may have fucked it up for the rest of us, but they've made bloody sure that they won't suffer. So you'll be alright. Trust me! So just bugger off and leave us alone.'

John had never felt so frustrated, so impotent or so lacking in purpose as he did at that moment. After one final prod from Charlie, John's anger took hold. He clenched his fist, drew it back and then delivered it forcefully into the face of his ex Sales Director. Charlie reeled backwards, before stumbling onto one of the black leather sofas.

'You bastard!' Frankie rushed to attend her bruised partner, who was lying prone, gasping for air in a rather theatrical manner. 'Get out, John! Now! Before I do something that I might regret!'

'Well, I'm sure that it's time for Charlie's afternoon nap.' John stood motionless in disbelief at what he had just done. The pain in his hand soon told him the reality. 'That'll give him something to sleep on.'

John turned immediately and made for the door. He had never struck anybody before. The sensation of bone on bone was one that he would rather not repeat. He grimaced as he turned the handle of the door before facing the pair one last time. 'I think that I'll decline your offer of lunch. I would have difficulty swallowing anything to do with you. Besides, I have much more pressing matters to deal with..... like instructing my lawyers to fling the fucking book at you both. You're totally.....'

'You can try, but it won't get you anywhere and it'll cost you.......loads. Get out, you bastard!' Francine moved to the glass table.

John had been standing by the door to take in one final look at the scene inside the apartment. He had failed to notice the ashtray which Francine had picked from the table and thrown at him. Momentarily dazed and surprised by the dull thud of ceramic on forehead, he faced the two who were now getting to their feet. 'Despicable, yes, that's what you are. May you both rot in hell! Charlie, I am really disappointed in you. You'll regret it. I promise you that!'

John stepped out of the front door, but not before stumbling precariously on the raised doorstep. Correcting himself, he stomped out, slammed the door behind him and headed towards the central staircase.

'Don't think that you can get away that easily, you pompous prick!' Francine had opened the door and was shouting down the stairway. 'You haven't heard the last from us either. You've hurt him, y' know! It's called assault......'

The raucous tones of Frankie receded into a blur as John took the stairs. His head had started to throb. He wiped at the tickling sensation on his forehead with his right hand, before looking down at the reddened knuckles which were now coated with smears of blood. He shuddered to think what sort of mess he looked.

The lift pinged its arrival on the fourth floor as he passed by. He waited for the doors to open. A white-haired woman, in her seventies, carrying a parasol came out followed by an older man dressed in a pair of yellow shorts and a white sports shirt. She stopped in front of John as the doors shut behind them.

'Goodness me! You do look a sight. Do you need a doctor? I can ask....'

'No, I'm fine. It looks far worse than it is. I had a bit of a run-in with an ashtray, that's all.' He smiled back and waited for the lift to return.

The couple looked at each other before the lady whispered as they moved away. 'That's what comes from drinking in the middle of the day, George dear; arguments and unhappiness. Did you smell the alcohol on him? Anyway, it's high time for our little snooze, don't you think!'

++++

John's right hand continued to throb as he steered his way slowly along the *Avenida das Palmas* He was oblivious to the horns from impatient drivers behind. Unlike John, they probably knew exactly where they wanted to go and were furious at being held up by some idiot who seemed to have little clue on what he should be doing. He stopped at the traffic lights. Signs directed him right to the beach or left inland to the golf course and tennis centre. Straight ahead, he saw a small *plaza* littered with chairs and tables and lunchtime diners. At the green light, John drove straight on, oblivious of bikers' and scooter-riders' irritation at his slow progress. One thing he was certain of was that none of them had just hit a man deliberately. None of them had a sore head oozing blood. He was pretty certain that none of them owed five hundred thousand pounds to their bank.

John pulled in and parked the car. He looked in the rear-view mirror and dabbed his face with a handkerchief to reduce the bloody mess to an acceptable level so that he could wander the streets without arousing too much attention. The red plastic awning of the *Café de Sol* in the square offered enough shade and anonymity for John to slump quickly into one of their canvas chairs. His sweat-filled shirt clung to him like a damp cloth as he looked around the few tables that were still occupied. He hoped the initial curiosity of the other lunchtime visitors who had seen him arrive would die down, once they had decided that he was neither a tramp down on his luck nor a football supporter recovering from the previous night's brawl. His presence had captured the attention of the two Spanish women at the next door table, who stopped their conversation briefly to take in their new neighbour. John smiled back at their surreptitious looks and watched the waiter continue to ladle the contents of a large copper tureen onto their bowls. The smell of garlic and wine in the fish stew wafted towards John, triggering thoughts that this man of violence, now on the run, was ravenously hungry.

The waiter approached John. 'You want eat or you want drink?' He asked whilst giving the table a cursory wipe with a yellow cloth.

'Both, please.' John replied. He felt a slight embarrassment at his lack of any word of Spanish.

'You see menu?' The waiter continued.

'No thanks. I'll have a beer, some water and the fish stew.' John pointed to the ladies' table.

'Ah Cataplana! Good choice! Very nice!'

The waiter went away after administering a quick flick of his yellow cloth to a sparrow that had perched on one of the neighbouring tables. John was relieved that he finally had found somebody who agreed with his decisions. He sat back in his chair and pulled out the Blackberry from his small leather overnight bag and began texting a message to Candida.

"Good flight down. All is well. Weather hot. C&F send their best."

He thought it wise not to mention that Francine's best had come in the form of a missile thrown with some force. The uncertainty of the meeting with Charlie had persuaded John to book a room for the first night. If matters had been amicably resolved, then he would have been delighted to take up Charlie and Francine's kind offer to stay in their ugly over-decorated penthouse apartment. Whilst he congratulated himself on booking at the hotel *Buona Ventura* in the *Rua da Frederico Cortez*, John had not bargained on the need for a lawyer.

Trawling through Google on his phone, John soon found a listing for *Sr Luis Gomez, Abogados en Civil*, whose office was located in the same street as the hotel. He was reassured further by "English spoken". A single set of directions to the street from the waiter would be sufficient to set him on his way, once he had devoured the fish stew and the beer. He might as well enjoy himself whilst he still had the chance. John put in the call to the lawyer.

++++

Chapter Eleven

Man on the Run

'It will be very difficult, Senor Smeeth. It will take a long time. More important, it could be very expensive.'

John had been pleased that Senor Gomez had been able to see him so readily on the following morning. His initial alarm at the lawyer's boyish face proved unfounded as he listened to his transatlantic tones outlining the complications of his predicament. The air conditioning unit hummed gently in the background, providing much needed cool away from the heat outside.

'It may well be possible to prove that Senor Weatherhead has deliberately avoided his responsibilities in your country. It could be possible to demand his extradition back to your country, but it is unlikely that he can be forced to go.' Stroking the point of his small goatee beard, the lawyer went on. 'It is likely that he will make himself a bankrupt in both our countries. So...' he paused to look up at the resigned expression of John. '........under Spanish law, if you have no money and no assets, then you are worthless. By rights, you should not be allowed to live and you should be dead.' He smiled briefly at his own use of humour. 'However, this Frankie Beetch, as you describe her, will be able to care and look after him without any prior responsibility to you or to the Moncrieffs bank.' He sat back in his chair. 'It is unfair, I know, but in Spain, and maybe in your country, there is the Law, but sometimes there is no Justice.'

'So, Senor Gomez, my situation is hopeless? Is that what you're telling me?'

'Si e non.' The lawyer looked at his watch. 'If you have the time - and the money - then no. If you have neither, then my answer is yes. I am sorry but we have many people, not just from your country, but from many other countries, who are living off the good wishes of their lover or partner. It is part of our service industry. We like them to spend their wealth in our country. We don't ask too many questions.'

The hour's conference had passed quickly. John Smith had handed over the three hundred euros without further ado. As he made his way down the street back to his hotel, his disappointment was forgotten by the chirping of his mobile phone.

'Johnno, it's Roger! Where are you?'

John confessed that he was in Spain. Any further revelations as to the reason for his visit or his feeling of desolation would have to wait. Roger pressed on regardless.

'Guess what! I took Mary for a *Fandango* outing yesterday, just out into the Solent. Not too far! She loved it! You must get Candida to come along next time. I've been looking at the forecast for later this week. I thought that we might see if we can get over to the Island for a spot of lunch. Something a bit different. Are you on, provided you get back from Spain?'

John thought that the plan would be fine with him. He wished that he could have been as encouraging with Candida's message that he had read earlier that morning.

`"Electric doors look great. People really impressed with how the stables are looking. Might need to spend a little more on ....."`

117

John just needed to come to terms with "a little more". The mirror in the hotel room had shown the swelling on his forehead had reduced overnight to be replaced by an ugly-looking blue bruise. He supposed that he had it coming. He had used considerable force on Charlie's jaw. But Charlie's derogatory description of Candida had been totally uncalled for. Charlie knew full well the contribution she had made to the success of the company. Her provocative poses had opened the eyes of many interested customers who in turn had unzipped their order books. How dare Charlie imply her lack of worth to their joint prosperity! More importantly, how was he to explain his damaged face?

John drove out to the airport. He sat in the terminal bar. He had ample time to send off text messages to Candida and to Francine, as well as to take in the continuous captions that streamed along the base of the television screen in the far corner of the bar.

"Breaking News.....Hijackers seek asylum otherwise they will blow up oil tanker...Bankers meet to discuss bail-out options......!"

Now there's an idea! Seeking asylum away from mounting financial commitments seemed a very sensible option for John to consider. He was just not certain of his own ability to hold others to ransom, with or without his own Walther PPK. Who would give in to the demands of a man with a bruised forehead and aching hand?

As John waited for his plane by the departure gate, he looked at the text reply from Francine.

"See you in court too. We also have taken legal advice. It's not over! C. badly bruised".

Not the response John had wanted to receive as the stewardess scanned his Priority Pass at the plane's entrance.

'Welcome aboard, Mr Smith!'

Her smile suggested that she was genuinely pleased to be at his calling for the next three hours. She screwed her face in concern as she looked at John's face.

'That's a nasty bump! Too much sangria last night, was it? Never mind, it's twenty degrees cooler back home. That'll sober you up! Have a nice flight!'

++++

'Is all well with the two lovebirds?' Candida asked as she broke away from her husband's tight clutch. 'Have they got bored with all that sunshine? What happened to your head? Did you squabble with Charlie over whose pen to use for the signature?'

John parried his wife's questions with as much straight-bat as he could. He then thought back to the helpful stewardess on the return flight. 'I tripped on the doorstep at their apartment on my way back to the hotel, head first on the floor. Too much rioja and white wine, I'm afraid. Bloody painful it was then. Now it's not so bad. It'll be better in a couple of days.'

'You stayed at a hotel and not with Charlie? That's a bit steep!'

John hoped that his momentary hesitation was not obvious to Candida as she busied herself with collecting up bills and papers that were laid out in piles on the pine table. 'They only had one spare bedroom which was .....being redecorated. So, they booked me a room in the hotel next door.' The fiction from John's mouth could have been written by Agatha Christie herself as he moulded an alibi like one of her upper class villains. 'They were really sorry not to have seen you. There will be other times, I said.'

'At least you got what you went for? It seemed a long way to go just to get a signature. But when you're retired, you can afford these little indulgences, I suppose.'

'Sort of. Charlie was pleased to see me. Frankie was looking her usual tanned self.' How could John best break the news that he was going to be worse off by the sum of half a million pounds? 'Charlie and I had a good chat. Instead of signing the document,

119

we came up with a rather interesting alternative. How about investing in a small apartment in Alicante?'

'Since when is Alicante in the Bahamas? I thought that's what we agreed, Johnnie!'

John winced at the promise he had made two days earlier. He watched Candida gather up the pile of bills and a cheque book and place them in front of him.

'As long as this investment doesn't affect the stables. Could you just sign these cheques. I'm glad that you had nice time, anyway.'

John's eyes glazed over at some of the sums that he was signing for. A *Fandango* adventure with Roger could certainly help him chart a way through the impending mess.

++++

Chapter Twelve

The Fandango adventure

Roger stood behind the steering wheel as *Fandango* moved off on the morning tide.

'You didn't kill him, did you? I really have no wish to be harbouring a murderer.'

'Badly bruised is all she's told me. I am not *that* callous.' John sat in the cockpit as they motored past the boats moored in the middle of the river. As the brisk breeze blew the yacht through the Shallows into the wider sea, he felt a similar gust of relief run over him after giving Roger a blow by blow account of his red haze.

'I probably would have done the same.' Roger announced after consideration.

'When was the last time you actually hit somebody, deliberately ?' John asked.

Roger paused. 'I do remember hitting a schoolfriend on a skiing trip. He annoyed me by snogging a girl whom I really liked. I saw him outside the nightclub and I hit him to the ground. Not my greatest moment.'

'I never have. Usually, I keep my anger under control, but this time I just flipped. I feel so embarrassed.'

John watched the sails fill as *Fandango* pierced the white horses of the choppy sea on her way to the harbour on the other side of the island.

'You could always spend twenty grand to get your lawyers bring him back to this country.'

'There's still no guarantee that I would receive any money back. Charlie would just file for bankruptcy over here. I imagine that he has no assets. Frankie's the one with the money.'

'They've both done you over, haven't they?' Roger was starting to feel rather sorry for John. He knew what it was like to have been deceived by others and to have been powerless to do anything about it. Whatever his feelings about his dismissal, Roger at least had some degree of financial security. He suspected that John would not be destitute, but half a mill is a very large chunk out of anybody's estate.

An insistent fog horn rent the skies. A container ship loomed a few hundred metres away as *Fandango* crossed in front of her. As both men watched the ten-high stack of containers peeking perilously low above the water line coming towards his yacht, John wondered how the ship would deal with more agitated waters of the oceans that it was about to cross. As Roger steered away from the wash from the churning propellers of *Eastern Carrier, Hong Kong,* he thought that there was a nice little insurance commission for somebody. Both men watched the stern of the vast ship recede into the distance.

An hour later, *Fandango* motored slowly through the entrance to Newlyn harbour towards the Harbourmaster's office on the grey slab wall.   In the office doorway, a teenage girl with long plaited blonde hair gestured to a space on the wooden jetty below for the boat to moor up. John looked up at the line of faces staring down intently as he secured their boat to the mooring.   Soon the young girl's father strode along the narrow jetty towards the boat brandishing a ticket from his little book. Roger handed over a twenty pound note in return before striding off with John in search of a good lunch.

++++

The oak-panelled restaurant at the Newlyn Arms was half-empty. Those at the remaining tables downed the final drops of their coffee, whilst looking through the windows at the busy Harbour-master and his blonde assistant rushing back and forth as boats came and went.

John and Roger sat and savoured their bottle of Sancerre. An aroma of fish, garlic and wine hung over their table like a Scottish mist. Roger looked across at the tureen of John's fish stew and then to the waiter who was crouched nearby, filleting his large Dover Sole with spoon and fork before pouring the melted butter over the glistening white fish.

'You could always send in the heavy mob to sort out Charlie.' The waiter had moved off leaving John to wonder just how seriously Roger was taking his predicament.

'I think that he's taken more than enough punishment.' John had started his stew as if he had not eaten for a week. 'Francine's the one that needs to be worked on. She's the crafty one. Where's the wine?' John topped up both glasses before gesticulating to the waiter that another bottle might be needed. He needed extravagance even if he was about to be cut off at the knees.

'How well do you know your mate, Giles?' Roger asked. 'Is there any chance of cutting a deal with him? The banks are all making so much bloody money at the moment, they don't know what to do with it.'

'Are they? I'm not so sure, judging by the News.' John was reminded of the images on the television screen in Alicante. 'Giles and I have known each other since we were thirteen. We were both sent away to the same school, Myndhams.' John wondered how much he should tell of his school chum's past.

'Where's Myndhams then ?' Roger asked.

'In Mitterne Abbas, a small village locked away in the Dorset hills.' John replied resignedly.

'That's a long way from Bisbury. Where did Giles come from?'

'My dad's idea, apparently. He thought I would learn more away from home. Bisbury Grammar would have done me just as nicely.' John tasted the first slurp of the new bottle of wine.

'I think Giles' parents lived in Delhi at the time. His Dad worked for an English bank. Anyway, Giles arrived at the school a term later than me; something to do with his mother forgetting to send in the Registration Form early enough to catch the winter term.' John was surprised by how much information had come back to him. 'I remember that he was a bit of a prick; always the first to arrive in the lesson; the first in the lunch queue; not the brightest, but no dunce either. I remember that he always received more cards on Valentine's Day than anybody else. It turned out that many had been sent by his mother.' John poured wine from the new bottle into Roger's glass before suddenly announcing. 'He was also very proficient at the House Wankathon!'

John's words echoed around the now empty dining room. The Italian waiter and the remaining lunchtime diners had all left, having had no obvious desire to hear further about quaint habits in English schools.

Roger was more curious. 'If it is what I think it is, then it sounds very painful.' He listened to John's description of the competition designed by pubescent teenagers to relieve their suppressed sexual tensions. Why was he not surprised by the homoerotic antics of public school boys? Which other educational establishment would have their own rules to govern contestants in their aim to complete the highest number of wanks in any twenty-four hour period before the announcement of the Final Result in the Warm Room on the following day?

'Was Giles' success really believed, given his performance with Valentine Cards?' Roger's opinions on the banking profession were being confirmed.

'Well, he sort of came clean, if you'll pardon the pun!' John lowered his voice, embarrassed by the relish with which he was dishing the dirt on one of his oldest friends. 'During an inspection for personal hygiene by the housemaster, Jumbo Watson, Giles was forced to drop his trousers. Jumbo then saw the colouration of his dick before accusing him of overenthusiastic rubbing of the frenulum.' Roger listened on with an expression of mild incredulity as John finished. 'When asked what his score had been, Giles boasted a score of eleven.'

'In one day? Blimey!' Roger had had enough of pathetic all-male macho exhibitionism. 'We just had girls do it for us, much more natural, maybe not as frequently. We all considered it to be part of the syllabus for Sex Education. Facts of life – practical study of male seed.' Roger continued. 'So you've kept in touch with Giles because he's a lying, cheating wanker? Is that it?'

John smiled before issuing his answer. 'When I took over the company and needed to refinance the business, I approached Giles, who was by then working at Moncrieffs. He offered the most affordable solution and continued to do so. So in answer to your question, there is a chance that he might cut a deal with me for old times' sakes. However, he says that there's a lot of uncertainty within the banking business which could make future deals more difficult to arrange.'

Roger was puzzled for a moment until he remembered faint rumours before he left Crosthwaites. 'Oh you mean toxic debt! That's only happening in America. It won't come over to the UK for ages. It's only one insurance company in the States having a problem with providing cover for some loans in the mid-west. There's always one rogue. The London market is much better organised. They've got pots of money. So I doubt if Moncrieffs will be affected.' Roger was busy pressing the digits of his bank card into the restaurant's electronic payment machine before he announced another solution to John's predicament. 'Have you thought about blackmail? Why don't you threaten to reveal Giles' prowess in self-pleasuring to his fellow bankers? That might force him into submission, you never know.'

'Hardly! They're probably all at it! Anyway, Giles was soon knocked off his perch by the Chief's son, Wayne.' John laughed as he continued his story. 'Wayne Oduku outperformed everybody. He was always at it. He was useless academically, so he needed to be better than the rest of us at something. Mind you, he hasn't done too badly since leaving school.'

Both men had noticed the clock in the restaurant. It was the time that the tide chart had suggested they should be leaving. They hurried towards their boat. Quickly casting off the ropes from the jetty, the boat was soon motoring out to sea.

'Tell me about the Wanker Chief? Do you still see him? ' Roger asked as the southerly wind caught the mainsail to take the boat back towards the river Lynd.

'Well, I did keep in touch with him immediately after we left school. Then, I went off to university to study accountancy and Wayne went off to manage a band called the *"The Tribal Chiefs"*. They were quite successful. They had several top-selling albums in the Seventies. Wayne was always travelling with the band. So I lost touch with him. Then it all went tits-up for him. The tabloids had a field day. The band accused Wayne of siphoning off their royalties to finance the family chiefdom of Remanda. I understand that there are quite a few chiefdoms in South East Africa. My geography of that area is not that good.' John drew breath as he poured out the litany of gossip that he had gleaned from various sources. 'I read in a recent copy of the School Magazine that Wayne Oduku, 1961 – 1966, is now pursuing a successful career in the computer software market.'

'So he's keeping his dick in his trousers, so to speak.'

'As far as I know, although the *OM Magazine* is hardly the proper channel for news of old boys' libidinous activities.'

John pulled on another sweater to warm himself against the increasing wind, before looking at his watch. Roger was more intent at watching the small blue and yellow burgee flapping energetically from the mast-top.

'The wind's changed direction, Johnno!' Roger shouted. 'We're going to have to beat into the wind as close as we can. Otherwise we'll have to tack. You take over the wheel whilst I pull in the mainsail. This should give the old girl a chance to get us through the Shallows whilst there's still enough water.'

The slap of the increasing wind in John's face had dispelled any lasting effects of the Sancerre. He clutched the wheel, keeping the boat on the course set by Roger. *Fandango* was moving fast. The coastline was getting rapidly nearer. John's calm was replaced by excitement and exhilaration as the boat sliced through the waves of the choppy sea.

'Head for that buoy straight ahead!' Roger winched in the sail a little more before taking up the binoculars, looking straight ahead, then to the right, then straight again. 'The water in the Shallows still seems to be quite high.' He shouted. 'I can see a few boats going through. I think that we should just make it. It'll cut at least an hour off the journey. What do you think, Johnno?'

John sensed that Roger was fired up for the challenge. *Fandango* was set fair and going like the clappers. It seemed a shame to spoil the party.

'Straight ahead it is, skipper!' John shouted.

"I like your attitude, sailor!' Roger smiled.

Fandango approached the mouth to the strait. Both men saw that the tide had receded, leaving the bank on each side exposed. However, the level on the marker in the central channel still showed over eight feet. Roger looked up to the flag at the top of the mast.

'We're going to have to tack quickly from bank to bank if we're going to get through before the tide runs out.'

John realised that this concentrated strategy was not one that he had had much experience of during his short maritime career. He looked longingly towards the white cross-marker two hundred yards away in the middle of the smoother waters of the river beyond. The start of the run home seemed a long way away.

'Ready about? Lee-o! Now! John! Now!'

Roger released the mainsail. John turned the wheel hard. The heavy boom swung over and the boat set off towards the starboard bank. A few moments later, both repeated the manoeuvre as the yacht lurched onto its other side and headed towards the port bank. Another few tacks and they would be in calmer waters and homeward bound. John could see the marker getting closer. He determined that this zig-zag crossing was far more tiring than Katie Stumple's workout. Suddenly, a gust of wind, far stronger than before, blew into the sail of the *Fandango*.

'Bloody hell!' John shouted as he sought to recover his balance.

'Hold onto the wheel, Johnno! Turn away! Turn away!' Roger was the quickest to grab the wheel. He wrestled to alter the boat's direction. The few seconds of uncontrolled freedom allowed the boat to enter uncharted waters beyond the port-side marker, where the sea was no longer deep enough. The rudder remained fixed. The full sail was driving them towards the bank where rocks flashed their welcome through the waves. The thump and crunch followed by the sound of fingernails being dragged along a blackboard told their own story. The men stumbled as the boat came to an abrupt halt on her new berth. The sails flapped and roared in anger. Waves lapped at the outer gunwales of the beleaguered boat like hungry dogs. John could see water entering the cabin below. His smart new deck shoes failed to prevent the freezing water from numbing his feet as it voraciously covered the floorboards in the cockpit.

Roger released the rope to the mainsail before clawing down armfuls of white nylon which filled the cockpit like blancmange. Having pulled in the last remaining sail and tied up the flapping ropes, both men were coming to terms with the realisation that only a taxi was going to get them back to Lyndhurst Quay that night. The sailing days of the good ship *Fandango* were at an end. Both men sat speechless and watched the waters ebb away, leaving the bare rocks to chuckle at how another hapless boat had succumbed to their wickedness.

Roger surveyed the mess. No other boats had entered the Shallows after them. *Fandango* was high and dry on rocks only some twenty metres from the side of the bank. 'Bollocks and bloody bollocks!' His irritation was tempered by the forlorn expression on John's face. He shouted over the wind. 'Look, Johnno, it wasn't your fault. That gust could have happened at any time.' He wiped away flecks of sea salt, maybe coupled with the odd tear. Like John, he was distraught by the wrecking of his plans. 'It's more of a bloody nuisance, rather than a catastrophe.'

With some carefully balanced walking, both men made their way to dry land and back to civilisation. John took off his soaked socks and shoes and began rubbing his bare feet to restore circulation. Both men noticed people scurrying around a large wooden clubhouse several hundred metres away. Soon, a car was heading towards them.

John looked back at the wide gash in the hull of *Fandango* as she sat discarded on the rocks amongst the seaweed and rock pools. The sails flapped in the wind as they hung uselessly over the side. The dream was in tatters. Sailing days and trips to far off lands had been blown off course by one extreme gust of wind. John felt mightily pissed off. What had seemed a well plotted route towards fulfilment and enjoyment in a new life had been ripped to shreds by a freak of nature beyond his control. John watched a couple of strangers get out of the Range Rover and shout towards him. He felt that he had plumbed new depths of humiliation. He was half a million quid down, out of a job and now out of water. He had just got used to not having to work for a living. He had just got used to keeping himself occupied doing inconsequential things that amused him. He liked talking to his chickens. The thought of having to haul himself back onto the merry-go-round of working life filled him with dread.

'Are you alright?' He could hear a female voice shouting in the background.

'No I'm bloody not!' John thought.

'Would you like a cup of tea?'

A lady in her forties with wild grey hair stood before him. Her hand held a plastic cup into which she was pouring the hot brew from a thermos flask.

'I'd prefer something stronger.'

'You'll have to go to the pub for that, I'm afraid.' She handed a cup to John and to Roger. 'Really hard lines about your boat!   It was a real shocker of a wind. Force Eight. The anemometer showed thirty five knots.'

++++

The relief of dry land, the fug of a warm bedroom and the effects of a large glass of whisky in his hand started to wash over John as he lay, fully clothed, on the small bed in the MacEwan Arms hotel. In the corner, a small television screen showed the early evening news. The image of the blonde newsreader blurred as he closed his eyes, her voice started to resound in his exhausted mind.

Bong!   Two old gits in shipwreck disaster!

Bong! Boat a complete write-off!

Bong! Our correspondent reports live from the scene!

The newsreader's face was now full screen; her eyes looked out with contempt, her brows arched in disbelief; her bright red lips curled in a sneer as she read from the autocue.

'This afternoon, a thirty foot sailing yacht owned by two recently retired business executives careered onto the rocks in the Shallows strait off the Solent. Accident investigators are trying to establish the reasons why the two men so blatantly disregarded standard procedures. If they fail to provide satisfactory answers, the two Know-it-alls could be facing serious charges. For the very latest news, we can now cross to our correspondent on the spot...'

The shrill ringing from his mobile phone jolted John from his nightmare. Sweat dripped from his tired and bruised body as he struggled to deal with the reality of the unrelenting tone. Candida's voice sounded very similar to that of the condemning newsreader on the television.

"Johnnie! Are you alright? Mary's just told me the news.'

As he provided a brief eye-witness report of what had happened, John had hoped for a more sympathetic response.

'You've only had it two minutes. Nice one, Johnnie! As long as you're both alright, then nothing's lost ....'

'Apart from the boat.'

'Yes obviously.....Well, you'll just have to come up with something else then, preferably on dry land. Have a good night's sleep tonight. You'll feel better about everything in the morning.'

John was not convinced as he stepped into the cramped shower in the hotel's en-suite bathroom. He had not bargained for two losses in three days.

++++

Candida had been relieved when Roger Mortlock and *Fandango* had taken John away from his listless existence at home. However, with the boat foundering on the rocks on the South Coast, there was a danger of him reverting to his previous ways.

'It couldn't have happened at a worse time, Mary.' Candida had explained when she had called to compare notes on the two survivors. 'I've spent all this money, well, all John's money, on

131

renovating these stables. Now I need to be there to make sure that everything and everybody works. With the school holidays about to start, we've got tons of bookings for lessons and rides. I can't afford time to devote to my shipwrecked husband. If he starts to commune with his noisy, messy chickens, I will seriously question whether the ex-screw-maker might indeed have a screw loose.'

'Roger had sounded very calm and philosophical about it. It's like riding one of my horses, he told me. You fall off, you brush yourself down, you check for any bruises and then you re-mount and carry on.'

'What if the horse had died in the process?' Candida thought that both Mortlocks were being somewhat cavalier in their post-trauma diagnosis.

'He just didn't see it like that.' Mary continued. 'We didn't talk for long. He said that he had to call the insurance company. Roger can be terribly brisk and organised when he wants. He'll be back tomorrow. Then he'll plonk himself in front of the computer screen and look at his wretched weather charts, even though he's got no boat. No doubt, he'll impress his chaps at the golf club with his tale of heroism during the Wreck of the Mary Deare. He always seems to turn adversity to his advantage.'

After talking to Mary, Candida returned to the large desk in John's study which she had requisitioned as Control Centre to house all papers relating to the stable project. She had looked at the sheet marked *"Bisbury Equestrian Centre – Staff Rota"*. Dealing with horses was one thing, but handling the demands of paying clients was another. She was pleased that the five surly stable girls which she had inherited from Mick Flanders were now halfway helpful and sociable members of staff. She looked at the loose papers and brown files, some marked *"Moncrieffs – loans"* piled in the corner. Old diaries and battered journals were stacked under the window. Why could her husband not just burn the whole bloody lot? Nobody would miss them. She was going to need somewhere to store all her stables stuff. She would give him the project of sorting out all the mess. This would give him some sort of purpose whilst Roger sorted out the boat with the insurance people. Maybe John could go back to Alicante to get some more papers signed? Maybe he should try his hand at the Golf Club as well? She would not dissuade him from buying a replacement boat. Mary and Roger were right. She must not let this setback stop him from doing it again. She was not certain how long it would take for the insurance compensation to come through, but she just hoped that it would be before the official opening of the Equestrian Centre in a month's time.

She had never considered her husband to be reckless or foolhardy. Buying the boat had been one of the more adventurous things he had done during their fifteen years of marriage. She accepted that screw manufacture had required a practical, sensible and safe approach to business. Somebody had to make them, so it might as well be John. She had lived well off it. She looked at the photograph that hung above the desk in the study. It showed her standing between John and the photographer Jeremy King. It must have been during the shoot for the very first Smiths Screws Calendar in 1983. She was dressed in a silk kimono dressing gown, John had just looked business-like in white shirt and tie. It did not show his seeming embarrassment at her state of undress within the inner sanctum of his factory. His face had shown hints of a tan from a business-man trip to Dubai. She had admired his aquiline features and dark hair, but her attachment to the younger, ambitious Jeremy precluded any thoughts that she would end up with John Smith some years later.

It had been Jeremy's energy and eye for the big pay-out that had found her the job in the first place. Over a bowl of muesli and a cup of black coffee, Jeremy had outlined his thinking. "Look Candida luv, the client may not be Pirelli or Lambs Navy Rum! It's more like Unipart, y'know the one which Pat Lichfield does, but without the exotic locations. But, this is the best bit, I've been able to get the same money as they all get. Your future, babe, is Smiths Screws!'

Standing semi-naked in front of the camera had not affected Candida unduly. She had been going out with Jeremy for over three years. His two assistants on the set had been more intent on discussing light exposures and depth of focus, rather than eyeing up Candida's vital statistics. The make-up girl had been more intent on using her portable phone to talk to her mother in London. Windows had been boarded up to prevent any prying eyes from passers-by. So, there had been no embarrassment within the unit as she lay enticingly on a bed surrounded by thousands of tiny bits of brass and rolls of wire mesh looking like Cleopatra eying up Mark Antony. She had responded to Jeremy's encouragement as she presented poses that she thought stupidly clichéd. He had stopped her giggling at what he was asking her to do. She must have sweated off at least half a stone as she stood like Vesta, the Goddess of Fire, in front of the foundry furnace. At the end, thirty grand had certainly been the largest sum that she had ever pocketed for seven days' work. In those days, it was not a sum to be sneezed at.

The request to return for the following year's calendar had taken her by surprise. She had been unaware of the furore that the twelve pictures of the first edition had caused within the hardware industry as repressed males clamoured to obtain a copy of the calendar. She had been delighted that Jeremy had been able to increase the fee. She had been less prepared for the provocative pose and suggestive leer that had been required of her as she sat astride a sundry array of tools and machines that combined semi-decent innuendo with the honest manufacture of brass screws.

Driving away after the shoot, she and Jeremy had travelled through the narrow lanes past small thatched cottages half-hidden behind oak trees and hedgerows filled with yellow and pink summer floral lodgers. The car had slowed to pass a couple of riders on large chestnut hunters hacking down the lane.

"Do you fancy living in the country one day, Jez?" Candida had blurted out.

"Good God, no!" Jeremy had replied, relieved to have finally hit a stretch of dual carriageway. "Too slow. Too remote. In our business, you need to be where the action is. We'd soon be forgotten if we lived out in somewhere like this."

"We've got the telephone and the handheld." Candida had replied. "We can still be in London within two hours if we were needed that quickly. Fax machines can keep us in touch with what's happening."

"Too risky. Do you hear of Bailey or Lichfield living out in the sticks? If I hadn't met the art director for this job at my photo agent's party in Highgate, we'd never have got this gig with the Screws. Don't get me wrong, there's nothing lovelier than the English countryside right now, but not permanently. I'd go bloody barmy, not enough excitement."

"Lichfield's got a castle in the middle of the country. He doesn't find it remote."

"Well, I just don't fancy it, that's all!" Candida remembered Jeremy's dismissive reply.

It would take another two years before Candida would find out that Jeremy, by then her husband, did not fancy her either, having found fresh excitement with a twenty three year old Japanese hand model. Sitting at his desk one morning, fat, bloated and stuck at home waiting to give birth to their first child, Candida had found some photographs of Jeremy and the young model with hands pictured where a model's hands should not have been.

One miscarriage, one divorce and many years later, Candida sat at John's desk working out staff rotas for her very own Equestrian Centre. She suspected that pictures from her current husband's licentious past would be more difficult to come by, if they ever existed.

She remembered her mother's reaction when she broke the news of her engagement to John in the family cottage on the edge of the Yorkshire moor.

"You're lucky to have a second chance. You deserve a bit of good luck. It's much easier for you girls to do new things." Candida had braced herself for a bout of self-pity as her mother continued. "When I was your age, life was about survival. During the war we never had the chance to do our own thing, as you would say. When it ended, girls were expected to look after their men. Can you believe it? So I spent my time following your father from base to base with you and your brother in tow. I never had the chance to plant roots and establish a life, let alone plan a career for myself."

"Poor old Mum! I do know what you mean. That's what's so good about Bisbury; it has a community with its own life and its own pace. Sometimes it's a little dull after London. But after the mess with Jeremy, dull can be very satisfying."

Candida remembered her mother's stare as if questioning her daughter's conviction in her decision. " Don't worry, Mum. John does make me very happy. He says that he has a fair amount of money, which he wants me to spend for him. His house desperately needs a woman's touch. Then I can do what I want."

"But you don't know the first thing about wiring or plumbing. It doesn't sound very exciting, darling!"

"I know something about colour and design. Fifteen years in the modelling game does allow you to know what works and what doesn't. Besides, I think that I've had more than my fair share of excitement. I could do with a bit of stability. He doesn't want children either."   Candida had seen the disappointment in her mother's face as she looked out of the window. "So no more grandchildren, I'm afraid, Mum.   I just can't risk another miscarriage. It'd be too distressing. John says that he would be a crap father anyway."   Her mother turned to   Candida and squeezed her arm gently.

"As long as you're happy, darling. That's what counts. As long as you're happy."

Candida remembered that her mother was never as lucid after that conversation. A tightening in her throat, initially diagnosed as dehydration or some sort of glandular fever, had developed into a dryness and eventual loss of her vocal chords. Before Candida married her new husband, her mother had succumbed to the cancer, but not before whispering to her.

"I'm sorry that I won't be there. John seems charming. He's a keeper.'

Fifteen years on, Mum had been right. Memories of that sad time were suddenly dispelled by the ringing tone of the house phone.

'Hi Candida, it's Giles here! Is John with you? He's not answering his mobile and I need to talk with him.'

'He's away on his boat.' Candida felt that any further information would not be necessary. 'He'll be back tomorrow. I'll get him to call you when he gets back.'

'Fantastic! Thanks, Candida! How's his retirement suiting you? Not getting in your way, I hope. I can't wait until I have to retire. I've got so many things that I want to do, you wouldn't believe!'

'We're both keeping ourselves very busy.' Candida thought her summary was a pretty accurate assessment as she replaced the handset. Having completed the Staff Rota, she thought that a good soak in a hot bath, accompanied by a glass of red wine, followed by a DVD-feast in readiness for the return of her shipwrecked husband on the following day sounded quite busy enough.

++++

Chapter Thirteen

Salvage

After returning from Lyndhurst Quay, it had taken John a while to get over his disappointments. He sensed that it was only a matter of time before lightning would strike him down dead. He had tried to dispel any fear of impending doom when he spoke with Giles at Moncrieffs.

'I've spoken with Charlie. He's asked if the bank might extend the repayment date.'

'Why didn't he reply to us directly himself?' Giles asked. 'It's a bit strange. I think that our Lending people will want to put your name directly in the frame. What you do with Weatherhead will then be down to you.' If Giles was trying to be helpful, then John wasn't quite seeing it as the banker continued. 'It's just that things at the moment are becoming unnervingly hairy. The States is starting to unravel more than was previously envisaged. If the rumours that I'm hearing are to be believed, then it could become Armageddon and not just in the US, all over the world. So the board is desperate to retain its liquidity. So your half a mill, plus interest, is very important. However, because of the history between us.....'

John was reminded of the accusation levelled at him by Charlie about schoolboys sticking together. He could only counter rather petulantly. 'But you banks have been creaming it for ages. Your coffers must be stuffed to the brim, surely?'

'They have also been lending lots as well, which is fine when things are going well. But, it seems that hairline cracks of default are threatening to open quite wide, which could have far-reaching repercussions.' Giles paused. 'Look, John. Here's what we're going to do. We'll re-structure the loan with you being the sole debtor. In return, I'll see if we can extend the repayment date for another six months. We'll do it at three percent over base.' John just sat listening at the end of the phone as Giles made the arrangement seem so straightforward. 'This'll give you time to sort out your mate in Spain. The bank receives a slight increase in the interest on the debt together with proper collateral. You just need to confirm what that might be. Maybe your house? An old family trust? I believe that you still have a small shareholding in the Swedish company who bought you out. Six months should give you ample time to conclude the matter.'

John felt a distinct queasiness as his few remaining assets were pulled out for public exposure. With his money-making days as good as finished, whatever wealth he had accrued would now have to last him out. However, this wealth was being hacked away in uncomfortable chunks as a result of promises that he had made to others. It was unreasonably early to think about selling Candida's Equestrian Centre. She would be devastated and would probably kill him, unless the streak of lightning had not already done the job in the meantime. John listened on to Giles winding-up their conversation.

'Smiths Screws was a good client. So for old times' sake, I'm sure that I can wring out some leniency from the powers that be. I tell you what, why don't you come to the school Old Boys' Day in a couple of weeks' time? I can tell you how I got on and it would be good to catch up after all these months.'

John set off towards the chickens. Most were quietly basking in the mid-morning sun, uninterested in their owner's predicament. He threw a handful of grain into the coop to encourage some movement. He watched the cockerel quickly gobble up as much as it could before the others sensed what was going on. He stopped at the gate and looked out towards the large farm buildings sitting at the bottom of the valley. He closed the gate behind him and tramped around the perimeter of the field. The cows picked at the short clumps of grass, whilst others looked at him impassively, offering little help to the questions going through his mind. One ambled purposefully towards John before providing its own informed opinion by lifting its tail and defecating on the grass. John smartly stepped to one side and continued his tour back to the house. One thing was for certain, Mulberry Farm would certainly not be offered to the bank as part of any new arrangement.

John shook off his self-pity and went inside the house to reality, picking up letters that had fallen on the mat in the front hall. The buff manila envelope showed signs of a spillage of coffee or water on the corner. The letter was written in a scrawl that seemed to have been carried out in haste.

Dear John Smith,

I just wanted to tell you what a wonderful blessing the new stables are. I look forward to working with your lovely wife. It was hard running the yard on me own. I reckon that your money - not as much as I would have liked, but what the hell – will allow us to compete with the other Livery Bastards and take business from them.

Maybe we should put together a calendar featuring your Candida! That would knock their eyes out!! Only joking!! She's a grand girl.

Please excuse the formality of this letter. I like to write down me thoughts

Cheers for now.

Michael Flanders

John folded the letter and placed it on top of the pile of other letters addressed to his wife. It was good that his largesse had at least been recognised by somebody. If only Charlie and Francine had shown similar gratitude, John might have considered their overseas property as an attractive investment rather than as an excuse for daylight robbery.

John's irritation was quelled by the ring of his mobile phone.

'Johnno! It's Roger. How are you coping without our boat? Rather dull, isn't it? Do you fancy meeting up at the end of this week? I reckon that, by then, I would have hit enough golf balls to last me some time. Do you know the Bengal Lancer pub on the Wedlicote road? I'll meet you there!'

++++

In the days following the wreck, Roger had used the time to reconsider his options. He had had little choice but to consider Mary's measured reasoning one morning as he chewed on his alternatives and a mouthful of muesli.

'Be happy with what you have, Roger.' She had suggested. 'Any action against Crosthwaites will just cost money and cause unnecessary heartache. Unfair dismissal is not a sufficient defence for a man of your age. You might be considered old by some, but charities are crying out for men with your credentials. So, stop feeling sorry for yourself. Make yourself useful. Use the time you have left to put something back into society.'

Roger was not yet convinced that he had taken enough *out* of society to warrant his putting anything back in just yet. He did not blame John for what had happened. Nevertheless, the loss of the boat during the prime sailing season had been a bloody nuisance and an annoyance he could have done without. He called Diana Vowlds.

'I'm afraid that I've got some rather embarrassing news.'

'Sorry Roge. I'm in a bit of a hurry. I'm just about to get on a plane to Hong Kong.' Roger could just about hear Diana's shrill voice against the background hubbub of the airport. A pang of envy cut through him as he realised that July was the time for the

141

quarterly reviews. Not necessarily a fun time to go, when the humidity made the place pretty unbearable unless you were inside an air-conditioned room. However, Roger missed the energy of the place. He missed the luxury of staying at nice places at somebody else's expense. More importantly, the July Review always determined his income for the forthcoming year. He realised that he was losing the battle for her attention as he heard Diana being greeted by enthusiastic cabin crew. He stumbled on with the story that he had rehearsed.

She interrupted him. 'Look, Roge. Just put in the claim. Sorry. Call me when I get back. We must catch up. Shall I give your love to Gavin?'

The line cut out before Roger could respond, but not before he heard the beginnings of Diana's distinctive cackle as she dug the knife deep into his still fragile ego. Even if he had not been directly responsible for the boat's demise, there was still the humiliation of having to clear up the mess afterwards. Roger's mantra that age and experience were synonymous had also foundered. Whilst his age accepted the disappointment as not catastrophic, his lack of judgement had let him down. He had been embarrassed by the welling up in his eyes like a spoilt brat whose favourite toy had just been smashed. He had been angry that something so fundamental in the art of sailing, like the wind, had caught him so unawares and so incapable of dealing with it.

Roger could have done without the ignominy of having to call Matt Pissarro, who worked on the PMT Claims Desk at Crosthwaites. Premium Medium Tonnage usually encompassed legitimate claims for sunken coasters and missing iron ore carriers. Roger's details about the destruction of his thirty foot yacht were received with the same equanimity, but with less scrutiny, by the thirty year old West Ham supporter.

'That's cool, Roge. What about salvage? '

'The hull is a complete write-off. The keel is a bit wonky. The superstructure is still one hundred percent intacto. Jack Hubbard is looking after the wreck at his yard at Lyndhurst Quay. You might be able to sell on the mast and the sails to him. They're no good to me, not at the moment anyway.'

'No problem, Roge! I'll get it all sorted as soon as poss. Anyway, how's retired life? I expect that you've had plenty of time to sharpen up your putting skills by now!'

Roger did not like to be reminded of the last Crosthwaite's Open Golf Day, when Matt had beaten him on the last hole with a very fortunate putt from twenty feet.

'You're right, Mattie-boy. I'm ready to take you on any time. Come up here and we'll make a day of it. Want to fix a date?'

Roger put the phone down, comfortable in the knowledge that compensation was on its way, even if it came with the price of a round of golf at Powder Hill.

++++

Chapter Fourteen

Restitution and revenge

The sign showing a bearded Bengali cavalry officer seated on his white charger was in bad need of a lick of paint as Roger walked from his car to the pub entrance. The walls inside still carried a legacy from permitted smoking and fumes from the large open fireplace. The framed black and white photographs of some old aunt's youthful life on the North West Frontier at the turn of the last century combined with the smell of stale beer and the faint stench of cat's pee. Located on the road from Bisbury towards the great metropolis of Birmingham, it had been surprising that the Bengal Lancer was still open for business. For Roger, the pub provided an anonymity away from the claustrophobia of the Bisbury social scene and away from the scrutiny of fellow members of the Golf Club. Mary had always thought that all pubs were just filthy establishments.

As he waited, Roger cast his eyes on the two old men in the far corner contemplating their dominoes on a table between them. One, with full grey beard in need of a trim, sat perched on his chair like a sack of potatoes, the tight red sweater under his brown tweed jacket accentuating his full stomach. His hands drummed the top of his walking stick as he studied his collection of un-played tiles. The other, hidden behind a pair of large rimmed glasses kept together with sticky-tape, waited impatiently for his opponent's next move.

Roger also enjoyed the presence of Valerie the Voluptuous Widow, who owned the pub and whose ample stature usually welcomed customers. As he walked through the door, Roger had had to make do with Valerie's daughter, Bella, whose baby face was half hidden by loose strands of red curly hair. Her bright yellow tee-shirt, emblazoned with her name in diamante lettering, failed to cover her belly piercing as she used both hands to pull on the pump handle.

'Where's your mum?' Roger asked.

'At the Bike Rally with her new boyfriend.' Bella replied as she tipped the surplus beer froth away into the drip tray.

'She should be here with you pulling the pints and pulling in the punters.'

'Tell me about it.' Bella replied. 'I've told her what she needs to do. A lick of paint in this place would also be nice. But she's not getting it. So, I'm left here earning money before I go off to college, which is fine by me, but she needs to do something quick after I've gone. Otherwise this place will go down and she will be out on her arse.'

Glad that his own children were off his hands and earning their keep, Roger moved to a small table by the window. He looked out at the scurrying clouds. Even if he had no boat, Roger had continued his study of the local weather systems. To fill the void, he had begun to check out the weather in other parts of the world to see which continent or island was getting it in the neck whilst he languished in below average summer temperatures.

The white, crisp vellum envelope, postmarked *London EC1*, had arrived the previous morning. Roger had been alerted by Matt Pissarro earlier in the week that it was on its way. Roger checked that it was still safely stashed in the breast-pocket of his shirt. Above all, he was looking forward to seeing the expression on John's face when he opened it. He did not have long to wait before John stooped under the low lintel of the entrance and

145

waited to accustom his eyes to the murky interior light. He came towards Roger.

'This place may not be the Ritz, but it serves a purpose. Are you feeling better now? I've got something that will cheer you up. Pint of Meon's?'

As they settled into their seats by the window, Roger was suddenly nervous as he placed the envelope on the table and gestured to John.

'Go on! Open it!' He said cheekily.

John handled the envelope as if it was about to explode. As he unfolded the letter, a second slip of paper fell out and landed under the table. Roger saw the two Old Codgers looking towards them as John scrabbled on the floor to retrieve it. He was not disappointed by the look on John's face as he studied the errant cheque.

'Blow me!' John said after a few moments. 'Is this for *Fandango*?' He looked at Roger's mischievous expression.. 'But that's nothing like what we paid for her.' John stuttered.

Roger loved John's assumed incredulity. 'That's the beauty of insurance!'

'I know, but normally you just get compensated for the cost of the lost item less the excess.' John replied.

'It's a little different in this case. It's to do with value rather than cost.' Roger had toned down his voice so that no-one would hear their conversation. He noticed that Bella was busy filing her nails. 'Both parties agree on the value of the boat. The owner pays the premium set by the insurer, who in turn is relied on to compensate the owner in the unfortunate event of loss.'

Roger's pleasure in seeing John's perplexed expression was magnified by his own relish at his ability to benefit from a practice which had been second nature to many of his erstwhile clients.

The frustration of being lied to for thirty years in the business had been lifted.

'So, nobody knows what we paid originally?' John asked innocently.

'They don't need to.' Roger was taking delight in exposing the seeming innocence of a business that governed so much of modern day life. 'As long as we pay the premium, the insurer is not bothered.' Roger looked across as John finally took in the reasoning in his argument.

'Well, it's their misfortune, as well as ours.' John said finally. 'I'm very happy with the extra. I'll take anything that'll help my cause.' John took a sip from his glass and turned towards Roger. 'Given what Candida is spending on Mick Flanders' stables, the hole is threatening to be wide as the one on *Fandango* and I could be under water in no time. It's all very embarrassing and not what I had planned at all!'

'I can see that.' Roger sensed that the time had come to load the bait onto the hook and drop it into the water so that it could be sniffed and nibbled at. 'The other piece of good news, Johnno, is that Jack Hubbard has found another *Fandango* for us. I've arranged for us to go and see her next week.'

The bar had filled with a few more lunchtime drinkers. Bella was doing her best with the Meons pump. John had not expected things to move so quickly. 'I hope that we're going to use her for recreational purposes. I have no desire to freeze my arse off again.'

'This time we'll be more sensible and less hasty.' Roger knew that he could carry out what he had in mind equally well on his own, yet, it would be more fun if he had a partner to work with. 'We'll use her like we did before.' Roger looked straight at John with a smile. 'I don't know about you, Johnno. I still feel that I've so much else that I want to do with my life. I can knock off the Sudoku puzzle in fifteen minutes. I've had enough of reading the opinions of know-it-all journalists and ineffectual politicians

147

pontificating about how they'd make the world a better place. Mary insists on having somebody in to do the garden. So I'm a bit buggered with nothing serious to do. I'm a man of action and decision. I need something to excite me and to turn me on.' Roger took another sip from his pint. 'That's why we need to master this boat and then some.'

'Some what?' John was puzzled by Roger suddenly dropping his voice.

'Then some fun, Johnno! You and I, we've made a little at somebody else's expense. You've gone a bit over the top by hitting someone, which some people might consider to be assault. You could be wanted by the authorities in Spain. Now you're party to fraud. Neither crime has been reported, so far.' Roger emptied his glass with one final gulp.'Let's have another drink to celebrate.'

'Celebrate what?' John asked before finishing his glass.

'The start of a new chapter in our lives.'

Roger watched for John's reaction as he went on. 'I've got some ideas which could be a nice little earner for both of us. It would certainly give us something to fill our days, to occupy our still active minds.' He was not surprised by the look of blank astonishment on John's face. Here was a man to whom making screws had not required treading far from the road of innocence and honest toil, whereas, Roger's path at Crosthwaites had been lined with potholes created by cheating bastards. He knew how he had been worked over. It was time to reverse roles.

'What's it to be, Johnno? Another pint of slop?'

John sat in silence for a few moments. Realisation of his true predicament was slowly dawning on him. He had no choice. If whatever Roger had in mind would help his parlous situation, then he had little choice but to follow.

++++

Chapter Fifteen

Boats fast and furious

'They've come back for another go, Tristram!'

Roger noted the wry smile on the face of Jack Hubbard as he shouted into the interior of his hut near Lyndhurst Quay marina. John noticed that the sign on the front door had been repainted in an authoritative red against a light blue background.

'Can we trust these reckless people to take out *Dreamboat* ?' Jack's exaggerated conversation with his tousled-haired assistant was not lost on John. Enjoyment of the men's discomfort was uncalled-for, although not unexpected. Tristram Harkness beckoned John and Roger towards the line of boats tied up at the jetty.

The deep blue hull of *Tara's Dreamboat* bobbed gently on the high tide. John looked at the gleam in Roger's face as he cast his eye up the mast and reviewed its collection of wires and stays.

'Of course, we'll change her name.' Roger stated as they approached the boat. '*Fandango Two* maybe?'

John nodded, even if familiarity with the boat's layout was undermined by the memory of her predecessor. He was just content to move to calmer waters and to leave behind the flotsam of painful memories.

Tristram had undone the sail covers. Roger had checked that there was sufficient petrol in the tank. John saw that there was sufficient depth of water to motor out into. Soon ropes were cast off.

'Only one owner. She's been well looked after, although when she came to us to sell, she reeked of hash.' Tristram announced, above the noise of the motor, with a grimace of embarrassment. John immediately eyed up Roger, wondering whether drug dealing was another ingredient in Roger's package of Extra Fun. 'The smell's gone now.' Tristram continued. 'The owner said smoking had helped him pass the time whilst carrying out boring maintenance on the boat. That was until his wife came down one day unannounced and found him scrubbing the bottom. Unfortunately, it wasn't that of the boat! It was that of his wife's best friend!' Tristram's words were being shouted out. 'Now they're getting a divorce. They've asked us to get a good price for the boat.'

The open section of the river Lynd was exposed to the full brunt of the chilly east wind. Roger assessed the area of mainsail needed to combat the Force Six breeze. John cut the engine as the boat progressed down river towards the ill-fated Shallows.

'So this is where you came unstuck, is it?' Tristram asked as Roger took over the helm. 'Did you keep the middle course for the Cross Trees?' Roger nodded towards John.

'I suggest that you ask him. He was steering.'

John was not in any frame of mind to discuss his errors with somebody obviously far more experienced. Tristram's smart-arsed smugness was beginning to annoy him.

'We were doing really well.' John replied. 'It was just one big gust. Knocked me off balance.'

John watched Roger steer the boat confidently through the Shallows into the choppy sea.

'This is more like it!' Roger shouted, pulling the bright red waterproof over his head.

'She seems to go pretty well. I think that she's ideal for our purposes. Mary's very keen to come out for a spin in her. What about Candida?'

John did not answer.

'Time to take her home?' Tristram was becoming bored. He had showed them quite enough. He was relieved at how well the boat was being handled by the two men who had been such novices the last time he demonstrated a boat to them.

An hour later, they pulled into the marina. Tristram threw the bow rope up to Jack Hubbard who was waiting on the jetty.

'So, Tris, have you sold these gentlemen your Dad's boat then?' John and Roger looked at the reddening face of the young lad as Jack made fast the rope to the mooring.

'I think so.' Tristram replied uncertainly.

'So your Dad broke the eleventh commandment?' Roger placed a consoling hand on Tristram's shoulder. 'Thou shalt not get found out!"

They all walked back to Jack's office. 'It's a bit of a shitcase, if you really want to know. Stupid buggers!' Tristram's face remained stoic despite the inner turmoil that he obviously felt about the split in his family. 'That's parents for you!' Shrugging his shoulders, Tristram went on. 'Well! I hope you have better luck with this boat. Mind you, if you sink her as well, just let us know. I'm sure that we can find plenty more for you!'

John and Roger remained stony-faced.

++++

The tables in the small Snug Bar of the McEwan Arms were empty. John and Roger laid their waterproofs over the chairs.

Roger pulled up one and rested his feet on it. 'I suppose you've heard nothing further from Spain?'

'No. For all I know, Charlie maybe dead.'

'You'd have heard by now if he was and you'd be awaiting deportation.' Roger was glad that his partner's crime had still remained unsolved. 'So what are we going to do now, Johnno? We've spent four and a half thousand. We need to pay for the insurance. So there's something left in the kitty for ....ventures.'

John turned to Roger. 'I know that you've got some ideas. I also have one or two of my own. I've started to edit my father's diaries. I might need some investment if I were to publish them.'

'That won't make you serious money.' Roger sensed that there was no going back. 'What if we got another boat?'

'.....and then charter her in the Caribbean ...or the Bahamas?' John considered the suggestion for a few moments. 'That's a great idea! Candida would love it. Do we really have enough for that?'

Roger realised that he needed to spell it out. 'I'm not suggesting that we buy another of Jack Hubbard's boats. I'm not suggesting that we buy another real boat from anybody. However, this does not stop us *owning* a boat ...or two.'

Roger waited to see if his partner would catch on. He knew that he was asking him to enter totally uncharted territory.

'...and then insuring them with your company. Am I right?' John eased back in his chair and stretched himself. 'Now that I've seen how easy it is to own and insure a boat, why hold back?'

'Exactly, Johnno! One real boat is quite enough. We just pay for the cover for others, based on the valuation which we provide the insurers.' Roger was relieved that his plan was being treated seriously.

'So the first one, let's call her *The Spirit of Meon*, is based here?'

'I was thinking somewhere further afield...like the South China seas, maybe the Philippines.'

'That's a bit far, difficult to arrange?'

'Difficult weather conditions certainly.' Roger's sales pitch continued. 'I know it's taking advantage of other people's misery, but, believe me, we won't be the first nor will we be the last to do it.'

'How do you know?'

'Trust me, Johnno! I'm checking the weather charts every day. Mary thinks that I'm totally barking. She sees all these maps strewn on my desk and on my computer and wonders what I'm up to.'

'At least Mary can see that you're actively doing something. She may not necessarily understand why. I daren't tell Candida a thing. How can I? Luckily she's been so preoccupied with the stables.' John shuddered a little at what the future might hold. 'When we're down to using one candle in the kitchen, she might notice that all is not well. Then what do I say? "Sorry darling, but we've used all the money to buy your stables, a villa for my ex-colleague's lover and a fleet of boats, only one of which is fit for the sea. The rest don't actually exist. By the way, could you lend me a tenner to feed the light meter?" It doesn't look good, Roger? '

'That's why we need to think outside of the box, Johnno. We've spent our lives being ruled by others' regulations and obligations.'

'So this is your retirement plan, Roger? Revenge?'

'Sort of. The combination of your man in Spain and Crosthwaites fucking me over makes an interesting cocktail, don't you think?'

John nodded. 'Do you know, Roger? Strangely, I'd never thought about it like that! Here I am, prepared to rearrange my pension, if necessary; maybe dig into the family trust or even sell the house. If that doesn't work, then I could rely on the wife to support me or as a very last resort, I could live on state benefit. However, I'd never thought of *stealing* for a living. How naïve am I?'

'Hold on, Johnno! That's a bit harsh.' Roger was unsure about John's state of mind. 'We're not stealing *per se*. This is about taking money that is already assigned to be paid out to *bona fide* claimants. It's just that we may not fulfil all the correct criteria to receive it.'

'But it's still criminal and against the law.'

'What's the law done for you recently, may I ask?'

'Made it very difficult to get my money back from Charlie.'

'Exactly, people have been abusing the law ever since Cain killed Abel. We're not planning to murder anybody, although...' Roger's eyes looked out of the pub window towards a group of young children playing on the Green outside. '........if I met Gavin, I'm not so sure'

'I hadn't banked on a life of crime, but when circumstances change, plans have to change with them.' John was feeling queasy as Roger went on to justify his scheme.

'In my view, limited use of the truth, bare-faced lying and deception are all part of modern life. During my time at Crosthwaites, there were times when I knew that the firm was being conned. It's just that I couldn't prove it. The company was contractually locked in to pay out in the event of a loss and so it did, albeit through gritted teeth.'

'I'm sure that there were times when you were able to prove it and not pay out?'

'Sure, Diana Vowlds and her Claims and Compliance team were very sharp. She was tenacious and had no problems with going after false claims. But sometimes we took the bigger picture. A paying client is better than an absent one. You paid out, but you made damned sure that you increased his premiums for future years!'

John was warming to Roger's patter. He was beginning to see the attractions of how personal ambition can be taken over by the need for revenge and restitution.

'The challenge obviously is not to get caught.' John volunteered after a moment's reflection.

'We've already got away with it once.' Roger's tone was firm. 'We've bought another boat with the proceeds. In the next few weeks, we might be owning a fleet of .... Phantom *Fandangos*.'

'"Fleet" was not a word that had even entered John's head. Roger's intentions were obviously far bigger than he had envisaged. Thoughts of Coastal Command in the bunker came to him. Prim young Wrens dressed in straight skirts and starched white shirts push markers around the large map of the world displayed before them. Their commanding officer awash in gold braid looks down from the balcony, as he sucks on his pipe.

'We've lost Fandango Seven in the Philippines, sir!'

'Poor show! Carry on, Smith! Send in the Claim Form.'

'More bad news, sir! Fandango Twenty has gone down in the South China Seas.'

'No problem, just send in the Claim. Be sharp about it!'

'Aye Aye, sir!'

'So Johnno! What do you think? Or do you want to buy the John Bull printing kit for your grandad's diaries?'

'If you think it will help me find a way out of my mess.'

Roger's eyes shone. 'Good man! I've already arranged cover with Crosthwaites for *Fandango Two*.'

'And what about the *Spirit of Meon?*'

Before Roger had time to answer, John's attention was distracted by his mobile phone. He looked at the message that filled the screen. It was from Francine.

```
"C and me have had think. Wld come to meet u
in UK, but cash bit tight. Suggest u come to see
us.  No flying ashtrays. Promise."
```

'Well, well!' John announced. 'Things are looking up. The Weatherheads are crumbling! They want me to meet them in Spain. About bloody time!'

'I'm off on my travels too!' Roger grinned. 'I told you that our venture needed careful planning and skilful implementation. I'm presuming that my esteemed ex-colleague in Hong Kong, Gavin Fu-Fing, will be very keen to increase his book of insurance premiums. He'll have been told by London to seek increases of twenty percent or more, which will suit him. The bigger the book, the more commission he'll get. He'll take on whatever comes his way.' Roger produced a sheaf of folded papers and placed them on the table in front of him.

'Roger, you have been very busy!' John realised that this plan had already had a long gestation period.

'He'll barely notice the addition of these boats.' Roger rifled through the pile of papers on the table. 'Smith has a wonderful aura of anonymity about it. I've got Jessica, Barnaby, Charles, Daniel and William. I've given them fictitious addresses mainly in Kowloon and Manila. There is one in Bisbury.'

'Only the five?' John asked with a certain panic in his voice, although he should have been pleased that his father's strategy of obfuscation was now being used by his son.

'At the moment. More would be better. However, I need to make sure that all the registrations are correctly lodged and quickly. So I thought it useful if I caught up with one or two contacts in Hong Kong. So I've booked a flight to go out there tomorrow.'

'Isn't that a bit excessive? Can't you do it online? '

'If we are to succeed, then we need to be thorough and professional, which brings me on to corporate structure. I think that you and I need to set up as consultants.'

'For the perpetration of fraudulent claims? From what I hear from you, many do quite a good job themselves, Roger! Besides, when we used consultants to advise us on market trends or whatever other bollocks, few of them had a clue what they were talking about. Also they were very expensive. Is that what you have in mind?'

'That's exactly what I do have in mind! Unlike most men of our age who set themselves up as consultants, we will expect that nobody will want to use our services. Nobody will be requiring our outmoded expertise. We will be fully aware that once we have left the building, any possible value to a client leaves with us. There will be no danger of our being contacted by ex-colleagues. Yet, that will not prevent us from setting up *BDN Consultants*. Busy Doing Nothing seems to encapsulate the lifestyle of the nation's retired, don't you think, Johnno? It can cover a range of different ventures. Roger sipped contentedly on his beer whilst John smiled at the obvious need for the venture.

'Is Mary going with you to Hong Kong?'

'What do you think? She thinks that I've been invited by my ex-colleague to sort out a charitable venture which he has set up on the main island in Hong Kong. I presented it to her as a sop generously offered to me by Gavin. She seemed genuinely pleased for me.'

'Candida keeps telling me how much Mary does for charity. Always off to meetings or seminars. I can understand why she would approve of your mission.'

'She does love to organise, whether out of a genuine desire to help or just to feel better about herself, I'm not certain' Roger replied. 'She's currently arranging a Ten Kilometre Run for one of her pet charities. She's even got me to join in. However, I've selected another charity that's very close to my heart. Mary'll get enough money from the other participants. People sponsoring me will be donating to the BDN charity where all expenditure will be vetted by me and spent by me personally.'

'Like your plane ticket to Hong Kong?'

'You catch on very quickly, Johnno! I knew that I'd made the right choice in selecting you. Another drink?'

++++

Chapter Sixteen

The Old School tie

John's car coasted down the drive past a row of mown cricket pitches. The lush green outfields, where he had once patrolled the long-on boundary with youthful keenness, defied the overcast grey of the July day. The gothic towers of Myndham House loomed at a lesser height than he remembered. John followed the procession of cars towards the back of the Upper Field. A team of boys, their high-visibility yellow vests hanging loosely on their puny bodies, directed him with frantic waving to park within the white lines marked out on the grass.

The opportunity to meet up with Giles for the first time in months had been sufficient incentive for John to join the melee of Old Myndhamians as they walked towards the main building. Candida had also suggested that John should "network more". As he waited to register, he looked around for any familiar faces worth networking with. How would he recognise any of his fellow "termers"? Moreover, did he really want to meet any of them again? He felt uncomfortable about any future conversation. "Hello Smithers! What are you doing with yourself these days? Oh really, that sounds very useful. Me? Well, I'm actually on the run from Interpol and about to become a serial fraudster!" What was there to share with the red haired man, dressed in a green baggy corduroy jacket, who stood in front of him in the queue? Could he have been the spotty red-haired thirteen year old who had been compelled to clean John's army boots to mirror perfection as punishment for daring to scoff down an unequal share of Bread Slice coated with beef fat before evening prep? Giles' response to John's predicament had better be good to warrant this visit.

John had dismissed any idea of bringing Candida to his old school. This was Man's Territory where recollections of shared suffering and the long-winded process of growing up had to be limited to participants alone. He was amazed by the number of wives, girlfriends or partners that were tagging along with their respective OM. The flimsiness of their brightly coloured dresses was being put sorely to the test as they waited stoically in the wind swept stone-floor hallway. Two women, wrapped in thick wax jackets and pink pashminas, seemed to take ages scouring sheets of names before handing over a name badge. Finally, John was sufficiently equipped before moving towards the large white marquee that stood on the Headmaster's Lawn.

'John Smith, Hamilton House. That's a name to conjure with, I bet !' The headmaster stood outside the tent and shook him by the hand. 'Jack Kingsford-Jones. How nice to meet you!' The name badge proved useful. 'Sixty one to sixty six,eh? A lively time, I bet? Allowed you to get up to all manner of tricks, I bet!'

John was shocked not only by the firm grip of the headmaster's hand, but also by the sight of his slicked dark hair tightened into a ponytail trailing over the black and burgundy academic hood. 'Lots of rock and roll, a little drugs, but probably not enough sex!' John replied as both men struggled to find any further common ground.

'Rock on! We must chat some more.' The headmaster gestured towards the entrance to the white interior of the marquee. 'You'll find that there are lots of Baby Boomers here today. So I'm sure that you'll find quite a few who were in your year.' He then turned to welcome the next in line.

John entered the large tent, passing a table lined with glasses of red wine ready to be offered by a team of sixth form girls. Behind them, two boys struggled to master the corkscrew. John picked up a glass of local beer drawn from a large wooden cask that balanced precariously on the next table. He moved towards a large notice-board and began to scan the list of other members of his table. He felt a hand clutch his shoulder. He turned to look into the boyish face of one of his closest friends from school. The warmth in Giles' smile seemed genuine, maybe a hint of embarrassment lurked in his eyes.

'Well, finally here's one face that I do recognise!' Giles Fortescue-Smythe embraced John in a half hug and shook him by the hand. Both men were determined to use the old school reunion as an excuse to overlook their business differences.

'I vowed that I would never to set foot in this place again.' Giles confessed. 'However, in these difficult times, I've been told by my boss to use all social contacts at my disposal to go out and push the good word that is Moncrieffs. Banking is not going to be one of God's chosen professions over the coming months.' John's ears pricked up. 'That's why I've had to be so firm with you, John. The bank is desperate to call in all outstanding loans by their allotted date. It's good to see you again.'

John had seen the news, probably too much of it over the past weeks.

'So, no chance of my loan being reclassified as toxic sub-prime, then?'

'No, John, I'm afraid that you are a cast-iron "Triple A" creditor. Giles had added puffily. 'If we reclassified all our clients' loans, can you imagine the amount of unpaid debt that we'd have? Besides, how else am I going to receive my bonus? That's what we rely on.'

'It would be better if it was honestly earned.' John had never liked the transition of the banking system from one peopled by

161

dull housekeepers with safe hands to one run by greedy bastards looking out for their own ends. John still considered Giles to be a member of the Old Guard who had stuck by him.

'However, now that I've got you here, let me just tell you that I've been able to work a bit of magic with my people on your particular situation. I've got them to agree to my suggestion. Next February....six months should give you enough time to work things out with Weatherhead or to retrieve funds from elsewhere. I can do no more, John. After that, you're on your own and at the mercy of our Debt Retrieval people.'

'I'm going out to see Charlie. I'm sure that it can all be sorted.'

Giles' gaze had moved and was scanning the new arrivals shaking with the rocking Headmaster. 'Hello, there's a face that looks familiar. I'll leave him to you. I've noticed somebody else I must meet. Big landowner in Somerset. Could be useful. See you at lunch.'

John had noticed the name *"Mr Wayne Oduku, Hamilton House 1960 -1966"* on the Seating Plan. As one Wankathon champion retreated , so his successor of forty years ago headed towards him. Wayne Oduku extended a smile of joyous warmth which contributed to an impression of swaggering ebullience. His dark handsome face looked creased and lined. The extravagant orange-frames of his glasses and his gleaming smile could not divert John's eyes from the three women who stood behind him. The vivid colours of their full-length silk robes provided a curtain of extravagance around Wayne that overshadowed the sombre suits and sensible summer dresses of their fellow guests. As he shook each girl's hand, John was taken aback by their statuesque beauty, heightened further by their turbans that dazzled under the lights of the marquee.

'Hey, my old chum, John Smith! You look well, a little on the thin side maybe, still in need of a good meal!' Wayne's bulk showed no sign of the same malaise. His thick set shoulders seemed to engulf his neck like a vice.

'Wayne, you old rogue! What a pleasant surprise! I thought that you'd been locked away for good after the business with your band.'

John had been one of the millions of people who had bought albums by "The Tribal Chiefs" in the Seventies. He had reggaed to their chart-topping "Walking with my Lady" . He had read about the break-up of the band amid rumours of royalties and payments being diverted to a small state in East Africa to sort out domestic squabbles.

'It was all just a misunderstanding; a case of misrepresentation of the true facts. That's all behind me now. As you can see, I'm in rude health.'

'And these are your personal health consultants, then, Wayne?'

John guessed that they might be too old to be Wayne's children, but quite young enough to be his escorts. Wayne gestured to the tallest. 'Hey Jackie, meet the only guy I know who ever received a cake through the post. It would arrive flat and in crumbs, but John would still pull it out from the envelope and offer us a piece. I've never forgotten that!' Jackie smiled sympathetically as Wayne went on. 'I think that I was jealous that somebody's mum was sending extra food to their child.' Wayne's cackle resounded throughout the tent. 'My mum's attention was more devoted to the salons in Paris and spending my dad's cash.'

John had forgotten the treats sent by his mother in her attempts to either fatten him up or to overcome the shortcomings of the school's cooking. He realised that secrets that he had hoped would remain buried for eternity were likely to resurface as school memories were ritually exchanged.

'So how are you, Wayne? Still pleasuring yourself ?' John had lowered his voice knowingly. 'Or do you get your staff to do it for you?' Jackie and the girls were looking around the tent as they fended off the glances of curious fellow-guests.

'Not so much now!' Wayne grinned. 'You could say that the tank is running low. However, sperm donation is a lively market! We have our own website *"Fertility for you dot com"* ' John nodded intently as Wayne continued his sales spiel. 'We receive requests from all over the world.' John was taken by Wayne's seriousness about the subject as he listened on. 'God knows how many children I've fathered personally. I can think of at least eight pop stars whose mothers have received my stuff. In my country, masturbation is considered a sign of weakness, not very virile. Over here, it's business. All our donors are checked thoroughly.' Wayne turned towards his entourage. 'These are my Hand Maidens. Jackie is my partner. Patience and Comfort run the clinic. They have hands like velvet!' Wayne winked as the team giggled amongst themselves. 'I thought that they would enjoy coming to see where it all started.'

Comfort stepped forward clutching her glass of wine. 'We think that the clinic does great things for humanity, bringing happiness to those that have been denied the chance to conceive naturally. Do you have children, Mr Smith?' The Welsh twang was at odds with her ornate ethnic dress.

'No. My wife and I ......'

'That's a shame. Every family should have children.' The gloss on Patience's lipstick dazzled under the chandelier overhead, as she continued. 'We could have helped you.'

'There were no problems. My wife had lost a baby in her previous marriage. It was a conscious decision of us both not to have children. Thank you for the offer.'

'So the family line stops with you? That's a shame!'

'Maybe, but it suits us. I don't think that either of us would have been good parents. We like doing what we're doing too much. Too selfish!'

Sensing that the sales pitch was falling on disinterested ears, Wayne gestured to his troupe to follow him outside. 'Come and see the grounds, girls! They're amazing. We must talk further, John Smith. I look forward to catching up on your past forty years.'

Heads turned as Wayne and the Maidens moved off. John watched their head-wraps carve their way through the sea of grey, balding heads and specially-prepared hair do's.

John's eyes fell on Giles who was in earnest conversation with the man in a light green baggy jacket who had been in front of John as they waited to register. Giles' boss at Moncrieffs would have been pleased with his employee's efforts.

'We'd love to help. These are tricky times. It's our view that America's barely scratching the surface of its debt problems and that it could come to affect the UK. The Bank of England thinks that it'll all pass over, but if you want my advice.......'

The Jacket had a badge "James Monroe, Hamilton House: 1968 - 73" He looked perplexed. 'My broker tells me that it's a minor correction. My mother just tells me to do something with it before it's too late.'

'I tell you what! Why don't you come to our offices for a spot of lunch? ' John watched Giles and the Jacket pocket each other's business cards. He listened to Giles continue on. 'I can arrange for my people to tell you more about our Safe Haven strategy. Give me a call and we can fix something. It was lovely to meet you!'

John wondered whether the Moncrieffs' safe haven was really any safer than that of any other bank. Surely, that was what banks were for? A receptacle for their clients' money.

'Might I ask you whether that was the Wankathon champ you were talking to a moment ago? ' A tall, willowy man with eager eyes had approached John. His name badge announced "Charles Spunner: Hamilton House, 1970 – 75" 'My brother told me all about him. The contests had rather fizzled out by the time I got to the school.'

'Oh you mean Chief Wayne Oduku - or King Onan as some others called him' Why was John unable to stop himself from replying? He had not come back to school to talk about the antics of horny schoolboys! 'We did very silly things when we were young.' John felt that to labour on the topic much longer was becoming unnecessary. 'Nowadays, I imagine young boys are much more sensible. They don't have the same needs.'

'I am sure they do! It's just that their needs are more properly channelled.' Spunner's eyes darted to John's lapel badge. 'You must have been here at the same time as my brother, Miles.' Spunner continued. 'He's very big in oil. I have my own diocese in Clapham.'

'Spunner? Miles Spunner?' John just could not picture him. His mobile throbbed in his jacket pocket. Reverend Spunner remained standing next to him whilst John looked briefly at the small screen before turning off the call. 'Business partners always think that they have a divine right to call you at any time.'

'But you don't have to answer, do you, John?' Spunner had replied calmly. 'The mobile phone is the very devil in today's world. They're contributing to the breakdown in our cultural behaviour, don't you think? Personally, I don't own one. If people need to speak to me, they can leave a message at home and I will call them back at a mutually convenient time.'

John quickly determined that, short of confessing to the Reverend that his own moral behaviour might provide him with cause for further reprimand, there was little to be gained by continuing their conversation. The dinner gong sounded. John arrived back to Table Seventeen at the same time as Wayne and his Hand Maidens. John watched them settle into their seats.

'Come and join us, John Smith!' John followed Wayne's gesture to a seat between him and Jackie.

'You can tell me what you've been doing since we last met.'

As sixth formers attempted to pour wine into each guest's glass, John started to unleash the opening salvo of his thirty years of Smiths Screws.

'That's a really cool name, isn't it?' Jackie interrupted. 'It's so wow. Y'know what I mean? It's so what you're going to get when you get a Smiths Screw. I love it!' John had been surprised that her accent was more New York or Chicago, rather than Africa. He had expected a little more sense, however.

'Easy, darlin'!' This man is a genuine manufacturer. It's a dying art in this country.' Wayne gestured to John to carry on.

'That's about it really. We battled on. We produced a good product which a Swedish company wanted. We sold out and here I am today, retired, finished and looking for what else life might have in store for me.'

'So, no more screwin', then?' Jackie's ribaldry caused great giggles amongst the other two girls. Patience looked around her to make sure that their antics were not causing too much consternation among guests at other tables.

'Not of the brass kind, no!' John chose to disregard the suppressed laughter and turned to Wayne. 'So, now that you say that your tank is empty, what's keeping you going, now?'

'Software, John!' John was still finding it difficult to accept Wayne as a computer geek as he listened on. 'All types. PC Games, SMS text messaging, intranet systems. Compiling, debugging, interpreting. Systems design.' The techno-jargon rushed from the cultivated tongue of Wayne. 'Links. Downloads. Cloud file storage. Homomorphic encryption. Data transfers. You name it, Oduku Systems does it. Our latest client is a major international bank.' John wiped the piece of lettuce from his chin and turned up the interest quotient.

'Banking, eh? That is interesting! Have you talked to him?' John gestured towards Giles, who was deep in conversation with Comfort on the other side of the table. 'Maybe I could talk to him

167

about Moncrieffs taking one of your systems, on your behalf?' Earning legitimate money would certainly ease his problems.

'Why not?' Wayne said thoughtfully. 'It could be good for both of us. You obviously have the time. D'you know him well?'

'He and Moncrieffs helped me at Smiths Screws. I like to think that we are still good friends.'

'I just love that name! Yes sir!' Jackie swallowed the final dregs of her red wine before reaching for the remaining bottle on the table.

'That's probably enough, Jax!' Wayne took hold of the bottle from Jackie's hand and placed it out of her reach before continuing. 'Mister Smith and I are discussing business. Maybe, Giles might be interested in our brand new *SpeedyTrans* system. I've had a team working on it for the past twelve months. It's cost me a fortune, but I think that they've finally cracked it! We just need to get it to market.'

'Tell me more. Why don't I come to your office in London? You can show me how it works. I can tell you what I can do to help. I could do with something to get my teeth into.'

'Good idea!' Wayne placed his large hand on Jackie's thigh. 'Don't mention it to anybody, John. Otherwise, I'll have to put one of my tribe's spears through your heart!' His deep cackle boomed out over the table.

A few moments later, there was a hammering from the Top Table. The guests were called to order by the Master of Ceremonies.

'Ladies and Gentlemen! Pray silence for the headmaster of Myndhams School, Mr Jack Kingsford-Jones!'

The Rock Head stood up to speak. John watched Jackie stroke the top of Wayne's hand as they all listened to the rallying cry for donations to the Myndhams School Memorial Appeal. John determined that he had given away enough of his money for the time-being.

++++

Chapter Seventeen

Work in progress

'How are you getting on now that John has retired? Bloody hell! The word makes him sound so old!'

Candida considered her reply as she looked towards Persephone Muldon-Jones, owner and chief executive of Perse Publishing Limited. Both had settled at their table in Carlo's Coffee House after battling through the clutter of three-seater buggies and car seats to reach their table. The light briskness of Mozart's clarinet concerto area underscored the hushed gossip of mothers and their babies enjoying the warmth away from the mid-morning grey outside.

Candida had always liked Perse ever since the two naïve, eighteen year-olds had shivered together in a freezing small studio in Leeds waiting for the hung-over photographer to turn up for a catalogue fashion shoot. They had shared much since. Shabby dressing rooms, rushed visits to beaches on the Portuguese and South African coasts –"to get the best light" – and a nice two bedroom flat in a posh part of Leeds.

Yet, it had been the image from some thirty years ago that still haunted Candida the most -   Perse's eyes that were seeing nothing, the white motionless body lying on her bed, only just breathing. She still remembered the shivers of fear, panic and then relief as she watched the ambulance-men fight to restore her to being the liveliest, bestest friend in the whole world. As she admired her friend's fab roll-neck black sweater and her newly purchased beige poncho, Candida was greatly relieved that the life-threatening combination of pills and whisky had now been replaced by a weight-threateningly large piece of carrot cake and a large pot of green tea.

'It has certainly taken some readjustment.' Candida replied. 'He has his...second.... boat, his troop of chickens and now ......this book. It means we still have our own interests. It's nice to have him around.' She then started to giggle as a thought entered her mind. 'We've certainly had more sex!'

'Good for you, darling! I've no time for that sort of thing.' Perse picked at the last remaining crumbs on her plate as she continued. 'John's Diaries could be very interesting, if he were to hurry up and finish it. There is a market for this type of book, especially at Christmas.' Perse's enthusiasm sounded genuine. 'We call them G and G books, for Granny or Grandpa. When all inspiration on what to give has run out; when panic sets in at lunchtime in Christmas Eve, people settle for a G & G book.'

'My dad used to call them Loo Books.' Candida smiled. 'Books of Giles cartoons, old copies of Wisden Almanacs, *"Butterflies of Great Britain"* lined the shelf. They were never read, but still they needed to be dusted!'

'When is John likely to finish this book?' Perse shot out the question from under her bob of red hair. Candida had not expected such positive interest from the publisher.

'When do you need it?' Candida replied casually. 'I think he's only just started it. But he could do with a kick up the arse.'

'By the end of January? ' Perse shifted her tall frame in the wooden chair. 'That would give me time to sell it at the Book Fair in late March.'

'It will be done. He'll be so excited that you are so interested.'

'Anything to help out a friend. We might make us both a little bit as well. Anyway, you must keep him at it, my love. Now have I told you about my meeting with this cabinet minister? She's recently retired as well. No more flunkies to flap around her. No more late-night help from ambitious male researchers wanting to tinker with her speeches. Now she's writing about it, although she's calling it a novel.'

An hour of London tittle-tattle mixed casually with Bisbury tales before Perse stood up to depart for her appointment in Birmingham.

'I must be off to meet Madam Red Box. She is a bit dull and so I'm not very hopeful about what she's written. I might need to get a ghost in to spice it up. The History of a screw-manufacturer is much more honest.'

Candida's smaller frame was enveloped within Perse's hug. She assured Perse that she would keep prodding her husband towards finishing his book.

++++

The Headmaster's blatant begging at OM Day was a distant memory. Even the excitement at Perse's interest in the Family Diaries could not match the anticipation of the opportunities offered by the Chief's son as John entered the offices of Oduku International.

Jackie stood up to shake his hand. The national costume displayed at the OM Day had been replaced by the cool of Notting Hill; the collar of her white shirt filled with a profusion of brightly coloured silk scarf, her long legs tightly wrapped in black jeans.

'Mr Oduku's expecting you. Can I offer you one of our wonderful refreshers whilst you wait? Or maybe a Hazelnut Energy bar?'

John looked to the glass panel on the wall behind her, to the display of logos and company names that constituted Wayne's empire. Oduku Systems, Bobby Records, Fertility for You.com competed with others unknown to John - Mother Nature's Drinks, Remanda Foods, Tribal Chief Events, Chief Bobby's Childrens Home...

'You choose for me.'

John's attention was briefly diverted away from Jackie to the large television screen in the far corner. A po-faced blonde mouthed silently, whilst subtitles told their own story.

"USA Mortgage company goes bust. Federal bailout ...... "

Maybe Giles' warnings were not so unrealistic after all, John thought, as Jackie returned with a bottle of Mother Nature's Mango Delight.

'John!' Wayne's voice boomed out from the corner of the reception hall. This was his home patch. The gaudy gold of his oversized watch and the heavy neck chain dazzled in the morning sunlight.

John followed Wayne into his large office. The large window looked on to tall oak trees and green rhododendron bushes in one of London's oldest Victorian squares. Through the leafless branches, he could see players hitting a ball across the net of the tennis court. He followed Wayne's gesture to the large purple sofa that lined the back wall. Three mobile phones and a gold Blackberry sat in a line on the glass table in front. Wayne sat down in his armchair opposite.

'Moncrieffs would be ideal for us to run a field trial for *SpeedyTrans*. It would not only make their ForEx business more profitable and more efficient, it would mean also that you could something out of it as well, John.'

'That'd be great, Wayne. How does it work?'

'Foreign currency transactions will now take a fraction of the time to process. Each transaction usually takes up to one working day, that's eight hours, to complete. With *SpeedyTrans*, this can be done in minutes, automatically, with the minimum paperwork.

The bank can capitalize on the fast movements in the currency markets without having to take an age to complete all the formalities.'

'This presumes that the currency rate is always on the rise. What happens if...' Sipping on his overly sweet drink, John was relishing the chance to use his skills to assess Wayne's continued explanation.

'No problem! If in the four minute slot, the rate starts to slip, then the transaction is terminated.' Wayne's explanation was interrupted by a familiar melody coming from one of the phones on the table. John recognized the opening bars of the hit by the Tribal Chiefs.

As Wayne's muffled conversation on the phone continued, John contemplated what he had just heard. Here was something that could go some way towards clearing his debt with Moncrieffs legitimately without the devious excitements of BDN. Giles would be delighted of any opportunity for his bank to benefit at a time when dark clouds were hanging over it.

'Well Wayne. You know that your system will be subjected to the most stringent checks and double checks.'

'We look forward to it.' Wayne leaned forward towards him as he continued. 'Our business is focused on making everything safe, hacker-proof and virus protected.' He paused as another of his mobile phones flashed on the table between them, before dismissing the caller with a casual press of the off-button.

'You must meet my business partner, Roger Mortlock. He could be very useful.' John announced. 'He and I have set up *BDN Consultants.'*

'To consult on what?' Wayne's immediate response took John by surprise. 'Who's BDN?'

John hesitated before replying. 'Insurance business, so far.' He hoped that the vague description would sound legitimate enough. 'The name is the mantra for the retired man, Busy Doing Nothing.'

'Good name. I'd like to meet your partner. He could be useful with his insurance contacts.' Wayne's attention was being distracted by phones flashing on the table before him. 'Anyway, let's get Moncrieffs sorted first. Why don't you call Giles whilst I deal with these?'

John brought out his own phone and moved to the window. The tennis players were packing away their racquets whilst he waited for Giles to pick up the call.

'My diary's pretty filled up at the moment, John.' Giles sounded distracted. 'There's some fuss about a UK bank that's been caught up in the US mess. If you've got any cash in Allied Castle, I would just check that it's still there.'

John replied that he didn't. He looked to Wayne for confirmation that the date in a couple of weeks was good for him and his team. Wayne nodded.

'You don't have any money in Allied Castle, do you Wayne?' John asked after calling off from Giles.

'Why, is there a problem?' Wayne moved to his Blackberry smartly. His face wore an air of fixed concentration as his pudgy fingers tinkered with the minuscule keys of the device. 'I did have until a few moments ago.' Wayne sat back with an expression of relief. 'I hadn't heard that anything was wrong.' He then laughed. 'We Africans are the last to hear about anything useful. We're not often taken into the world's confidence.'

'It's not what you know, but who you know, eh Wayne?'

'You're so right, John.' Wayne patted him on the knee. 'Good old fashioned trust built on English public school principles, very alien to African ones of distrust and deceit!'

++++

175

Chapter Eighteen
Foreign travel

John watched the waiter pour out the opening glass of Montalcino red wine as he sat across the table from Candida in the *Pasta Palace* restaurant in Bisbury. It had been her idea. "Nothing fancy, a bowl of this or that and a bottle of wine. You sound as if you're really busy. The stables have been *really* busy."

John listened to his wife's de-brief about her chat with Perse the Publisher. He felt it only fair to tell her that writing was not as easy as it is cracked up to be. It was useful to be able to get at least one thing off his chest as she faced him.

'You mustn't let flogging the computer stuff to Giles stop you completing your Family Diary. Perse wants to publish it next year. So no dilly dallying, Johnnie!'

'I'm doing my best. But I'm just having a bit of writer's block.'

'For God's sake, Johnnie, you're just writing down other people's words! What's so difficult about that?' Candida's outburst took John a little by surprise. 'It makes the work more genuine, more true to life. Nobody wants to read your fluffy writing. It's all there for you!'

John now knew how Byron or Fitzgerald must have felt as they struggled with the same affliction. He had not yet succumbed to the need for drugs or drink, although he might get through another bottle of the Italian red before the night was out. He resolved to get the book done by Christmas. He was also relieved that his investment in Mick Flanders' stables was proving to be so worthwhile. He was just happy that Candida seemed happy. It was a good time to tell her about his intended visit to Spain.

'I spoke to Charlie the other day and he says that he wants to show me one or two villas that we might invest in.'

'At least, it's not another bloody boat.' Candida munched on a piece of tomato and basil leaf from the Bruschetta that had been placed before of her. 'What happened to our plans for the Bahamas? Winter sunshine is much more interesting.'

'This is nearer. It's also cheaper.' John thought that a bit of realism would sound more responsible, even if neither proposition was remotely realistic. 'Anyway, I said that I would go tomorrow just for the day. Early morning flight, site visit, a brief fling with Charlie's cooking over lunch and back to your loving clutches in the evening.'

'What does Charlie get out of it?'

'He would manage the place for us, for a fee. You know, make sure that it was well maintained, cleaned and in sparkling order at all times.'

'OK Johnnie! But this time you don't commit to anything until I've had a look as well. I would've come with you tomorrow, but one of the girls is sick and so I've got to muck out instead. It's a shame. I could do with the rest. Find me a nice remote island, surrounded by calm blue seas this winter. So, in the meantime, just you hurry back tomorrow night and I'll be waiting for you in my best negligee.'

John breathed a sigh of relief.

'It's quite like old times when you dashed off for meetings at some ungodly hour.' Candida brushed her hand on John's cheek as he started on his small bowl of Pasta Ragu. ' It's good that you're keeping busy, Johnnie. It suits you.'

John hoped that his sheepish smile and his gaze into her eyes gave nothing away.

++++

The promise of a reduced debt was sufficient inducement for John to leave his house in the hush of the early morning dawn, even if it meant bracing himself for the hurly-burly of the school holiday rush at the airport. John had been relieved by Charlie's tone on the phone a couple of days previously.

"John, I'm very glad that you've called. You were obviously very cross about my letting you down. Then I realised that, if it hadn't been for you, I don't know where I'd be. You gave me the chance to prove myself. I'll always be grateful for that. Frankie and I have had another look at the figures. I think that we can repay some of the money. However, it would be much better if we could discuss it face to face. So why don't you hop on a plane. I'll cook you the best paella you've ever tasted. Let's work out a solution that suits everybody. I mean it, John. Life's too short to be harbouring grudges. I'll meet you at the airport."

With the seat next to him on the plane unoccupied, John stretched his legs and luxuriated in the limited extra space. As the plane soared up into the cloud, he opened the draft copy of the first chapters of his family history.

"Chapter one

It is a common conception that essential items, like the screw, the nail, the paper clip, just happen. Like fruit on a tree, it is assumed that screws appear each year, to be harvested by an army of East Europeans, packed and despatched to hardware stores and DIY superstores throughout the land." Not bad! Still awake, just!

Candida's occasional pencilled comments written in the margin encouraged and depressed John in equal measure as he read on. He was pleased at least that the content of the collection of leather-covered journals and tattered school exercise-books had been compiled into something halfway readable.

"In 1586, the introduction of the first screw-cutting machine by Jacques Besson, court engineer for Charles IX of France, paved the way for more innovations. Designers and makers of scientific instruments like microscopes, clockmakers and gunsmiths led the way in screw-cutting machine technology. How interesting!!!

"Researching and writing can be very therapeutic." John thought back to the comments which he had volunteered to Bill Salmon at the Powder Hill Golf Club after a rare appearance in a club competition. "After the cut and thrust of running the company, I've found it vastly enjoyable to cast back to the very beginnings of the company."

"It sounds bloody hard work, if you ask me." Bill had replied. "I did all my writing when I was working. Bloody waste of time, most of it; hours of research and preparation, skimmed by some in minutes and forgotten by the rest within days." Bill had just brought back a couple of beers from the club bar. "My best memories are here in my head. Mind you, John, if you're writing stuff that people, like me, want to read, there must be lots of serious shagging and heaving breasts in it." John had tried to bear Bill's advice in mind. Disappointingly, he had found the dry text of his forefathers provided little lascivious content. Any narrative that might include the story of the Chief Executive falling for the Calendar Girl would be considered far too soppy.

After accepting the offer of a cup of coffee from the in-flight trolley, John continued reading.

"In 1761, two brothers from Burton on Trent in Staffordshire, Job and William Wyatt, filed a patent for the first automatic screw-cutting device. Their machine could cut ten screws per minute and was the acknowledged forerunner of the mass production machinery that is used today...." Oh really?

"In 1916, Archibald Smith started the family company......" Ah that's better!

Despite Candida's encouraging notes, there was still much to tell; three months seemed long enough in which to tell it. Concern about Perse's deadline was overtaken by the plane's arrival at Alicante airport. Whilst fellow passengers hurried to passport control and onwards to pick the best at the car rental, John was in no desperate hurry. For the first time in ages, no meetings booked, no anticipation of a big order for the *Gambit Seven* from a new customer, no bag to collect amid the huddle of expectancy of the motionless baggage carousel. Reconciliation would just have to take its time.

As he left the air-conditioned cool of the terminal, John was at least better prepared for the full force of the midday heat outside. The cotton sports shirt and light trousers made him feel more comfortable than during his last visit. He scanned the faces of waiting relatives and bored taxi drivers lined up against the barrier in the Arrivals Hall. Two Guardia Civil in flak jackets stood by a pillar near to the exit. Their machine guns rested in their crooked arms. A tall man in his twenties suddenly stopped directly in front of John as an equally tall, blonde girl rushed towards him and threw her arms around his neck. John stepped to one side to allow the couple to continue their passionate kiss.

'John! John! Over here, mate!' Charlie Weatherhead was waving his white hat. Another man, shorter, with a black moustache followed behind. John saw that there was no sign of Francine.

'That's the man, senor! ' Charlie had turned to the man, who was dressed in a brown lounge suit, his tie loosened. 'This is Mister John Smith.'

'Meester Smeeth! I am Inspector Calculzia of the Alicante National Police. Will you come with me please?'

'What on earth ......leave me alone!' John tried to wrench his arm away from the clutches of the policeman. 'Where are you taking me? Charlie, what's this all about?'

'It's about this.' Charlie pointed to his jaw. 'It's about a cracked face. It's about weeks of discomfort since you hit me. It's about your thinking that you could just walk away from it.'

'You should have told me, Charlie. We could have sorted it all out amicably.' John was shouting over his shoulder as the inspector led him by the arm toward the Main Exit from the airport.

'In Spain, it's called *asolto*. They don't like it. It's against the law.'

'Charlie! Come off it! If this is a joke, it's wearing pretty thin.' He turned to the inspector who was now gesticulating to a black car that was parked up the road. 'Please let go of me. This is too much!'

'Meester Smeeth, please get inside.' The inspector opened the back door of the car.

John folded himself into the small back seat, he shouted. 'Charlie, for God's sake...' He looked back through the window as the car moved away from the pavement. He saw Charlie give him a cheery wave. He turned to the front of the car and asked. 'Can I call my wife? Can I call a lawyer? Do I have any legal rights?'

'At this stage, you have not been arrested. We just need to ask you some questions.' The inspector sat in the front seat. The sickly sweet perfume in the car could not overcome the stench coming from the sweaty body of the uniformed driver. 'You will be able to make calls once we have arrived at my bureau.'

John sat back in fearful silence. Should he make a bolt from the car as it stood stationary at the traffic lights? Instead, he just assured himself that he would wake up soon and find that he was still asleep in the comfort of his bed with Candida snoring quietly by his side.

The car pulled up outside a white brick building. The wall carried a small plaque *"Comisaria de Alicante Nord"* The inspector held the door open for John to get out. The bright light of the lunchtime sun dazzled. John looked around. Charlie was nowhere to be seen. The nightmare continued as John entered a side-door of the police station.

++++

Chapter Nineteen
The rage in Spain

The clack of hooves echoed in the yard of the Bisbury Equestrian Centre. The cacophony of clanking buckets and swishing brooms preyed too loudly on Candida's ears as she shut the door of the last of the stables. She wiped a bead of sweat from her brow as the momentary image of her husband sitting by the side of a swimming pool, basking in the lunchtime sun, passed through her mind. The image was only alleviated by the thought of Charlie and the busty Francine lying on neighbouring sun-beds. Maybe mucking out the stables was not so bad after all.

The first bars of the William Tell overture sounded on her mobile. She looked at the display - "Johnnie" She could only just hear the muted voice at the other end.

'You are where?!' She closed her eyes as she tried to comprehend what she was hearing. 'What the fuck for? ....Is anybody with you? ....Where's Charlie? ...... He's done what?' Incredulity washed through her, blood drained away as anxiety took hold. 'Don't worry, Johnnie darling. There has to be some mistake!   I'll take the next plane out there.'

Her husband's terse demand that she should stay by the phone did nothing to quell her concerns. Candida felt a mix of embarrassment and anger when she called Mary with her news.

'He's being held in some sort of remand unit in Alicante. Something about him being sued for assault.'

'Does he have a lawyer out there?' Mary's wisdom could not still the mix of panic and anger that raged within Candida.

'It's so unlike him. I'd never seen my husband as a man of violence'

'You know some men when they go abroad. Drink does funny things to them.'

'But John's not a bloody football hooligan!'

Subsequent conversations with John determined that Candida would fly out to Alicante the following morning. This would give her time to talk to somebody who was much more of a street-fighter and knew about being held in a Spanish jail. She called Persephone Muldon-Jones.

'Look Candy darling. He's only been detained. The case will not stand up in court.' Perse did not like to get overexcited.

'But he's admitted it. He's guilty as charged!' Candida wiped the tears that had started to stream down her face as she unscrewed the first available bottle of Cabernet Sauvignon that she had found in the wine cellar.

'Unfortunately, the legal process in Spain likes to take its time.' Perse continued. 'Some of my druggie friends admitted their guilt in the hope of getting out of jail quickly. No such luck! The Spaniards like to keep their cells full. So, John will just have to treat his remand like an extended holiday.'

Candida had seen the film "Midnight Express". That was no bloody holiday. Visions appeared in her mind of her poor, stupid husband being subjected to the most horrendous indignities, even worse than those endured at the most barbaric of English public schools.

Perse went on. 'If you're going out there to see him, take him a pencil and notebook. Tell him to keep a diary of each day of his stay at the remand centre. Very marketable. The Sundays love to publish tales of unfair imprisonment. So, he mustn't be in a rush to get out. He'll have more time to edit his other diaries whilst he's at it.'

'No Perse, I can't just have him stuck in some awful little cell on his own. I want him back here, as soon as possible. I've got the Grand Opening of the stables in a couple of weeks. Any jail stories will have to be for another time.'

++++

John sat with Luis Gomez the lawyer, as Inspector Calculzia rattled on in his native tongue.

'It is best that you stay here whilst the matter is investigated further.' The youthful looking Gomez translated the Inspector's demands. 'They just need to have Senor Weatherhead's injuries reviewed by an independent adjudicator. In our country, any costs for repair are awarded against you. The matter can be settled quickly. It is unfortunate, but if you have to hit somebody, just make sure that they don't get injured. Otherwise he has the opportunity to lodge a civil complaint.'

'Even if the reasons for the injury were justified?'

'As I said to you before, your problem with Senor Weatherhead is not a matter for Spanish law.' John sensed his lawyer's growing impatience at having to deal with yet another Englishman believing that he can abuse local laws with impunity. 'The loan was agreed and the money handed over on British territory.'

'How long will this farce take?' John asked plaintively.

'Who knows?' Luis replied honestly.

John started to panic as he wondered how he would fill his days. He walked around the small courtyard that offered some respite from the incarceration of his small room. He wondered where he might start digging his tunnel.

++++

185

After a night's sleep on a bed more uncomfortable than any school dormitory, John woke and looked out of his room's narrow window at small puffs of white cloud floating across the deep blue sky. From his small balcony, he could see a crowd of men and women, dressed in singlets and running shorts, assembling in the Municipal Park on the other side of the street in readiness for their early Sunday morning run. The high wall topped by a roll of barbed wire prevented John from joining them.

As he prepared himself for Candida's lunchtime arrival, John wondered which was the greater crime, the unprovoked attack on a duplicitous bastard or the lying deception of a gorgeous, loving wife? Judgement from Candida was going to be considerably worse than that meted out by a lowly magistrate in a hot courthouse at some date yet to be fixed. There was a knock on the door. He liked that. At least, he was being given some respect.

'Your wife has arrived. She is downstairs in the Reception. She is a little upset.' The female guard, Silvia, a robust lady in her forties dressed in a light blue shirt and dark military trousers, had always shown a muted sympathy towards John since his arrival. Her near perfect English had come as a surprise. "I was au pair with a family in Godalming before joining the army. I am Black Belt at Judo and Kick Boxing. This job helps me to keep up my English, since we have many of your countrymen coming through – drunks in the summer, petty thieves in the winter coming for the sunshine."

John looked at himself in the mirror. He had used the trickle of warm water from the only shower in the building to wash away some of the stench of anxiety and shame that had consumed him since his arrival. He followed the stout shape of his guard as she unlocked the array of doors on their way to meet Candida. The temperature in the small stuffy Interview Room rose as Candida engulfed her husband with both arms and tears streaming down her face. The chic of her turquoise pashmina, loosely wrapped over her white t-shirt, and her pale blue layered skirt lifted his despondency as he savoured their tight embrace. She would just have to put up with his rather smelly polo shirt which he had worn since he had left home about a century ago.

'What in heaven's name have you done, Johnnie? You stupid, stupid sod! When you said that everything between you and Charlie was alright, I believed you! Why couldn't you tell me the whole story?'

John noticed Luis Gomez standing in the corner of the room watching Candida's tirade. Silvia was by the door ready to thwart any desperate escape. John took the moment to hug his wife tightly, to remember her smooth skin that he had cherished only two nights ago. He inhaled the sweet perfume that hung about her.

'I couldn't bring myself to tell you that I had been so bloody stupid ... so naïve to think that Charlie would willingly carry out what he had agreed to.' John was pleased that the first part of the speech had been well received. They both sat down on either side of the table.

Candida blew her nose and listened on to her husband. Why are men sometimes too proud to face up to their problems? Then again, why hadn't she sensed what was going on? Why hadn't she questioned her husband more thoroughly about why he was going on a jolly to Alicante?

'I can only say how truly sorry I am about getting into this mess.' John looked into her eyes.

'Yes I know you are.' Candida replied, beguiled by her husband's look of acute discomfort.

'Ten more minutes, Meester Smith.' Silvia announced.

John did not know that visiting times were so limited. The lawyer stepped forward to join the Smiths at the table.

'I have placed a deposition of mitigation with the court for their consideration.' He announced. 'It means that you might get away with a warning and an award of damages against you, but at least you will be free, John, if I may I call you that?'

John tried to look positive, unsure what bloody good Gomez' action would do, except to rack up the legal costs. He watched Candida closely, clasping her hands in front of him, before announcing. 'So, my darling, for a little while, money will be a bit tight whilst I sort out matters. At least, you have the stables. I might just have to break up one of the family trusts if necessary. But ...'

'You could always get a job.' Candida suggested. 'You still have contacts in the business, don't you?'

'Who would want to employ me now?' John wiped a dried tear from Candida's cheek. 'I'm over sixty. I could never work for somebody else.' John sat back in his chair to stretch his legs. 'That's why Roger and I call ourselves the Unemployables. Nowadays, work is all about youth and teambuilding and sitting in front of a computer all day.'

'Ees time, Meester Smith!' Silvia interrupted.

John drew close to Candida. 'Look darling, much as I love you, there is little point in your coming here each day to discuss my life inside this place. So go back home. You've got much more to do in Bisbury. I'll be fine here. I expect that the medical report will come through in a matter of days. They can have their hearing and then I'll come home. We can forget all about Spain and think about the Bahamas.' He looked towards Gomez who nodded, although not very convincingly.

'You're forgetting that Charlie still owes you half a million bloody quid, Johnnie. That's not right!' Candida stood back to admire her champion. 'I'm going to start a campaign to get you released. I'll take a leaf out of Mary's book and set up a petition.'

John was startled by the gleam in her eyes. She had re-adjusted her sun-glasses to keep the long tresses of auburn hair off her face.

'I'm not going to stop until you're free, Johnnie! My mind's made up. This is all bloody ridiculous!' She looked towards Luis and then turned back to her husband before saying. 'Senor Gomez and I will find a way of getting that bitch Francine to reconsider.'

'So no birthday cake stuffed with an iron file or a duplicate key for me then?' John tried to be positive about the next days without Candida's presence. 'I suppose I can sit outside under an old sunshade and catch up on my reading. There's a man from Bagshot in one of the other rooms on my corridor, who keeps trying to sell me shares in an apartment complex that exists only in his mind. He has produced a very impressive looking brochure.'

'Hang on Johnnie. We'll have you out of here in no time. Be strong.' Candida hugged him tight before she made for the door.

'Dinner will be served at six o'clock.' Silvia the guard announced as she led John back to his room. 'Don't be late. They're doing paella tonight. Very good. Better than Wimpy, I can tell you.'

'When does the bar open?' John asked with a smile. He could have murdered a cold beer. Silvia smiled back.

'You English always like your joke.'

Silvia left the door to his room ajar as she left. John was not totally deprived of his freedom. He just was unable to go outside into the street to follow his wife home. Instead, he walked onto the narrow balcony outside his window and breathed in the afternoon air. He had another hour before paella time. What a waste of life.

++++

Chapter Twenty

Lost boats and just causes

"If I remember correctly, you said Gavin was a jumped up little C.U.N.T.' Roger was surprised by Mary's accurate account of his irate description of his ex-colleague. 'Why on earth do you want to have anything further to do with him?"

'He's asked me to come. He's paying my fare and he says that there might be some other work for me to pick up whilst I'm there.' Roger replied, hoping that an invitation by an old colleague to discuss his involvement in a charity project in Hong Kong had carried sufficient credibility.

'It's about bloody time that they offered you something besides free travel. Why do you want to go?' Mary asked, as she scraped the half-eaten pork chop off her husband's plate into the dog's food bowl.

'Hong Kong is very active.' Roger replied. 'There might be something for me to pick up whilst I'm out there.' Roger felt comfortable with the explanation, even if only half of it was true.

'See if you can find yourself a directorship or a consultancy. There must be somebody looking for people with your expertise and contacts.'

++++

Roger sat in the window seat of the large Boeing as it made its final approach into Hong Kong International airport. Despite his wife's blandishments, Roger had written down *"Leisure"* as the purpose of his visit on the Immigration Card. He did not consider that *"Filling One's Boots"* would be accepted as proper *"Business"*. Previous visits on *"Business"* had only been to the top floors of buildings designed by extravagant European architects for egocentric property magnates. He was looking forward to seeing more of the colony as he set about launching his fictitious armada.

Over a couple of whiskies and a dollop of beef goulash in a foil container, Roger thought back to Alastair Crosthwaite's mantra. "The Insured is there to be compensated in the event of sudden damage or accidental loss. Luckily, the instance of this happening is comparatively rare and when it does, the Insurer will be recompensed by increased premiums and continued good fortune."

The thump of tyres on the tarmac and the reverse thrust of the engines snapped him out of his reverie. A tingle of excitement ran through him. The planning and the anticipation were at an end. Implementation and execution were about to take centre stage.

After the plane docked onto the gate, Roger waited impatiently for those in the expensive seats to exit the plane amid the chorus of jubilant farewell from the cabin staff. As he waited, his attention was taken by the glimpse of a familiar face. Surely not? Blimey! The unruly strands of black hair had all gone! The dishevelled look of the close-crop style revealed her handsome face rather well. The pink shirt would be easy to pick out as Diana Vowlds disappeared out of view. Roger felt a hefty nudge in his back as he hesitated for a moment. He should have realised that Diana's path might have collided with his. At any other time, he would have rushed up to embrace her. This meeting, however, needed a more evasive strategy.

Roger's light blue shirt clung to him as the thirty degree temperature in the airport building engulfed him like a tight hug from an overenthusiastic aunt. The temperature was compounded by a nervousness that now welled inside him. So far, the "Phantom Fleet" had been a game played in the virtual arenas of his mind and his home. Now the enemy was suddenly real, living in pink, and in front of him.

Roger felt comfortable as long as he could see Diana in front of him. As she disappeared into the Ladies' loo, Roger sought refuge by the glass-fronted dispenser of cans of ice-cool Coke. As soon as she came back into view and joined the melee, Roger continued to follow. He had never considered Diana the most elegant mover, but he was starting to enjoy the angry sway of her hips. He considered that the well-cut black trousers were holding in a slimmer shape. The curve of her body seemed more accentuated. It was not difficult to pick out her dark hair and pink shirt that bobbed like a buoy amid the sea of travellers making their way to passport control.

Roger had not bargained for infiltration by the enemy into his plans. Where would she be staying? It had only been habit that had made Roger book into the Park Lane Hotel on Kowloon without a second thought when he clicked onto their website a few days ago. The hotel, with its early morning view of workers in Victoria Park going through their Tai Chi exercises, had been the principal choice for all Crosthwaite's staff. It was too late for him to change his reservation now.

Roger lurked behind a pillar as he watched Diana lift her large suitcase off the carousel before wheeling it away to the taxi rank. Why do women always bring so much? Then he remembered that September was the month for reviews when a girl needed to look her best in order to justify the twenty percent hikes in premiums to all clients. If they were to be sharing the same hotel, Roger determined that taking the Airport Express would be a faster, as well as a cheaper option. Whilst he did not relish the chore of wheeling his suitcase from the station to the hotel, nevertheless an inconspicuous arrival without the bustling greeting of bellboys might be good if his evasiveness strategy was to work.

The journey from the airport along the lower deck of Tsing Ma suspension bridge to the Kowloon peninsula gave Roger ample time to think. He needed a Plan B. How is a retired out of work executive going to justify his presence in the same hotel, at the same time as his ex-business colleague? Roger surfaced from the air-conditioned metro station at Causeway Bay station into the stream of home-going commuters. The ten minute walk along Gloucester Road towards the hotel exercised his still aching joints as the fresh air accustomed him to the seven hour time difference. He declined the offer of *"Freshly made Dim Sum"* from the stall on Paterson Street. He disregarded the sign for *"bespoke suits made in a day. Saris and kimonos in a range of colors and sizes."* He quickly dragged his suitcase out of the way of a rickshaw intent on carrying two wide-eyed Gap Year students, on their tour of the city. He was relieved to see the palm trees bordering Victoria Park come into view. He knew that he was close to the hotel.

'Good evening, sir. Welcome to the Park Lane Hotel.' The doorman in the brown tunic opened the glass door to Roger, whose clinging shirt and the weight of his case were getting to be a bloody nuisance. Thoughts of a cooling shower were quickly dispelled by the sight of Diana already waiting in the queue to check in. Preoccupied on her mobile phone, she did not notice Roger turn tail back through the revolving door back outside.

'You want taxi?' The smile of the other doorman suggested that Roger's arrival moments earlier had not been registered as Roger made his smart exit. 'Have a nice evening!' Neither doorman seemed perturbed by Roger's frequent glances through the glass doors into the hotel interior as he checked on Diana's progress. He was not ready to face any inquisition; a few points in his fiction needed further research.

Finally, Diana strode away from Registration and disappeared into one of the lifts. Roger charted her upward journey as the display panel showed stops at the twenty fourth and the twenty eighth floors, before descending again to the lobby.

'Do you have a room on a low floor?' Roger asked a small round faced Chinese girl at the reception desk. 'I'm not very good with heights!'

The girl's fingers scurried over the keyboard like mice after the cheese. Her eyes stared intently at her screen before replying with a high pitched American nasal twang.

'We have nice room for you on the twentieth floor.'

'That'll do fine.'

++++

The strain of the journey washed away under the shower, Roger stood in his white towel in front of the mute television set. The Weatherman in a green blazer was gesticulating against the background of a meteorological map of the city and outlying areas. Lines of isobars, arrows and computer generated images on the screen told Roger what he needed to know. The icon *T1* suggested that winds were still some distance away.

The phone by the bedside rang. Roger froze. Back home, why would Mary interrupt her busy day? He picked up the receiver nervously.

'So, you've arrived safely?' Mary's voice sounded almost apologetic. 'I just wanted to know that you got there in one piece.' Roger was surprised by Mary's new-found concerns. Over the years, his travelling had seemed a matter of totally indifference to her.

'I'm fine. I was going to text you. Is all well at home?'

'You know us women. We get unsettled when their out-of-work husband buggers off to meet up with an ex-colleague who took over his job. If I'd called you on your mobile, you could have been in Timbuktu, for all I know. Now that you really are in Hong Kong, let's hope Gavin makes your trip worthwhile. His school for expats sounds such a very worthwhile project. Charity is so rewarding. You'd be very good at it. '

'We'll see. Gavin's collecting me tomorrow. He's going to show me the school on........'Roger hurriedly picked up the tourist magazine lying on the coffee table which had fallen open on a map of the city. He picked a location at random. '......Discovery Bay. Anyway, I'm off for a stroll in the park. I'm sorry that you're not here with me, but you'd probably find it all rather boring. It's also stiflingly hot.' Roger thought that any additional information on weather conditions might cause undue alarm.

'Well, have a nice time. Make sure that Gavin lavishes his expense account on you. I hope that his school project works out. I'll need to know all about it.'

Roger sat back in the sofa and looked vacantly at the television screen. Maybe he should actively explore the opportunities for a school offering an English-style education? He thought back to the limited ambitions of his own school and their objectives of finding apprenticeships for the boys at the large aircraft factory a few miles away, whilst the girls would be prepared for the typing pool until they succumbed to marriage and motherhood. University education was considered to be available only to super-intelligent scholars. He determined that he could tell pupils a lot about the university of life.

Roger threw on a golf shirt and a pair of light trousers and made his way down the emergency stairs of the hotel out into the street. He refused again the doorman's offer to provide a taxi, preferring to cross over the street into the park. The trees flapped chaotically in the gusty wind. Roger made his way to the edge of the park and looked out over Victoria Bay. In the evening darkness, singular beams of light from junks and dhows criss-crossed the water. Roger watched the kaleidoscope of garish neon beaming their messages from giant buildings along the shoreline. The subdued cackle of traffic provided the backdrop to his thoughts about the Phantom Fleet and to his meeting with Stanley Henderson in the morning.

Roger had found the business card when clearing out his desk on his last day at Crosthwaites. *"Stanley Henderson - Boatsforfun.com"*. A visit to the website had shown pictures of brown Chinese junks and offers of *"Liveaboard"* boats. However, it was the memory of a large blustery man, originally from Hull, that had stuck in Roger's mind. Henderson had been master of the *Ocean Amethyst,* a small freighter which had reportedly sunk in a heavy storm in the South China seas six years ago. Subsequent investigations by Diana and her team had discovered that the ship had struggled into a small port in the Philippines, its cargo of iron ore severely tainted by bad weather. Roger and Diana had confronted the ship's owners to irreparably hole their claim for the ship's loss. Henderson's Master's License was withdrawn after a hearing in London by the governing body. After the hearing, Roger received his business card. "You never know when you might need me."

Judging by the address on the card, Henderson had not suffered unduly from being deprived of his livelihood. Roger presumed that the ship's owners had seen to his welfare in return for his taking responsibility for the owners' crass decisions. Recent e-mails and phone conversations had confirmed that the duplicitous qualities of his new good friend Stanley were ideal credentials for the local representative of *BDN Consultants.*

Roger tucked into his bowl of steaming hot Dim Sum on the bench of the a favoured street restaurant which he had found a few streets away from the hotel. He watched debris of scraps of newspaper and cardboard cups swirling in the street. Maybe the game was about to start in earnest.

++++

Eight thirty the following morning. Roger listened to the Geordie accent of Stanley Henderson on the other end of the phone announcing his arrival in the lobby.

196

'I've just seen your former colleagues in here a few minutes ago, Roger.' Stanley Henderson was now standing by the Concierge Desk as he greeted Roger. 'You know, that Vowlds woman with the mess of hair. She's cut it off now. That little shit Fu-Fing was with her. I don't think they saw me. I was able to hide behind this.'

Roger noticed the folded copy of the *South China Morning Post* and the tell-tale red circles around some of the runners and riders at the evening's meeting at Happy Valley. Roger had already scanned the form of the guests in the descending elevator to make sure that there had been no sign of his particular favourite.

'I should have known that it's time for the quarterly reviews.' Roger shouted as he made his way towards Stanley's white Mercedes SL. The leather trim of the two seats was crinkled and worn. The interior smelt of stale cigarette smoke. The driver looked no better. A face that once had been handsome and authoritative was now craggy. The eyes looked tired. Wisps of long grey hair blew in the wind as he drove away from the hotel down Gloucester Road.

'It's no problem. They won't notice you're here. Hong Kong is a big place.' Stanley pulled down the pair of sunglasses to shade him from the bright sunshine. 'I've already heard from Robin Song, the broker......'

'How is old Crusoe?' Roger exclaimed as he toyed with the memory of a small chubby chap with National Health spectacles who used to arrange cover for a whole range of craft that plied their way across the busy waters of the main harbour.

'Robin may be a bit odd, but Gavin still trusts him and takes on all his crazy clients.'

'What about our claims in that typhoon down the coast?' Roger asked.

'He's put them in already. Cheque will come along soon.'

Stanley turned towards Roger and offered him a conspiratorial smile. Roger was not impressed by the irregular set of yellowing teeth that was revealed.

'That's quick!'

'Many people lost their livelihoods in that storm. They need to buy new boats quickly, so that they can get out to sea again. A few more sailboats going down in the same storm were not going to make much difference. Crosthwaite's are good like that. They don't hang around unless they really have to.' Stanley turned towards Roger and raised a disparaging eyebrow.

'You were just unfortunate that the claim for the *Amethyst* was suspiciously high.' Roger needed to move on. 'Have you placed those that I listed in my last e-mail to you?'

'Most of them..... in the spots that you suggested. I'm not sure when they might be sunk.'

'I've seen the depression forming further south. We might have a result sooner than we think, Stanley.'

'There'll be other storms, Roger, even if this one doesn't hit where we want it to.'

'We can't afford to waste the opportunity. I hope Crusoe recognises this.'

A thirty minute drive through the Cross Harbour Tunnel onto Hong Kong Island suggested to Roger that he would be away from prying eyes. The car stopped on a narrow side street in front of a graffiti-covered steel door. The door rolled upwards to reveal just enough space for the car and not much else. As the door closed behind them, Roger followed Stanley through the small doorway at the rear before climbing the rickety wrought iron steps into an office.

Whilst Roger looked through the window onto the lines of market stalls in the street below, Stanley busied himself with stacking assorted papers and magazines that had previously been strewn on his battered Victorian mahogany writing desk. Roger stood transfixed by the activity below where animated traders and customers haggled over the cost of chickens, either dead or alive, and bunches of green vegetables. Stanley moved to a tiny kitchen and filled the kettle from a small tap.

'Tea? I think it's a little early for a Scotch, don't you?' Stanley gestured Roger to a plastic garden chair in front of his desk. 'Have you had any further thoughts about my suggestion to you?'

Roger paused. 'Buying a real boat to keep out here? Yes, sort of. It just seems to be a rather expensive venture to me.'

Stanley placed the two cups of hot tea down on the desktop. He slipped a beer mat under each to prevent any further indentations to the already stained red leather. 'Not necessarily. We both know that Gavin likes to spring spot-checks to make sure that boats he's insuring do really exist and that all details are correct. We just need to be prepared.'

'I get that.' Roger took a sip of tea. 'Tell me more about your *BoatShare* option.'

'Let me introduce you to the *Kowloon Queen* and the *Serenity on the Seas.*' Stanley pulled out the contents of a large buff file and laid them out on the desk.

'These are enormous.' Roger examined the colour pictures of the two boats. The first losses of the Phantom Fleet in the recent storms that had flattened the Sebastian Islands in the further regions of the South China Seas had been no larger than the *Fandango*. Roger had not expected boats whose dimensions were more in keeping with that used by Sinbad the Sailor. 'Haven't you got anything smaller?'

'You needn't worry about size. Placed in the right locations, they can be just as vulnerable. They also have a higher value and therefore a better return on the claim.'

Roger's nose twitched. He let Stanley carry on.

'We have alternative schemes where a client can own a boat either solely or in partnership with others. Whichever way, my company will manage all the income derived from it. If I were to make a recommendation, I would suggest the *Serenity*. The owner is a nice lady in her early fifties, whose husband died a few years ago. He had a big electrical shop in Nathan Street on Kowloon. Mavis Ng uses the boat to commune with his soul. Very peaceful. Lots of Zen. She's done it up very nicely.'

Roger could see the benefits of owning one real boat which could adopt any name to satisfy any inspection by Gavin's marine surveyors. He also liked the idea of larger returns from Crosthwaites. He needed more convincing about the idea of shared ownership

'Why don't I show you the boat this afternoon?' Stanley had seen Roger's face.

'After you've dealt with Robin Song first.' Roger suggested tersely.

Stanley agreed and picked up his mobile.

++++

Roger watched the cityscape of glass and concrete recede as the blue and white ferry pulled away from the Central ferry terminal.

'Lamma Island is the third largest island in the colony of Hong Kong.' Stanley shouted over the rush of wind and the splash of sea. 'It's very popular with the ex-pat community.'

The ferry bucked the choppy seas of the Harbour before turning into the calmer waters of the West Lamma Channel. Roger scanned the shoreline, spotting the occasional lone fisherman looking to catch the family's dinner from a jutting rock, before the ferry turned into a small bay. Roger could see a line of coloured awnings at the end of the bay. The wooden jetty approached as did the aroma of stale cooking oil and post-lunchtime smells from the squat buildings that lay beyond.

The absence of cars on the island made progress along a paved path away from the ferry terminal easy for both to stride along. Soon, a small marina came into view. Through the forest of ship's masts, Roger noticed an ugly-looking craft at the far end of the harbour. The superstructure of two levels of deck piled onto a low-slung hull was radically different from a single level, thirty foot yacht, which he had been used to. Roger could see a small figure standing on the balcony of the upper deck. Stanley offered a cheerful wave as both men approached. Roger's sailing ambitions had not expected to include mastering what appeared to be a motorhome plonked onto a boat.

Stanley hurried ahead, stepped onto the gangway from the jetty and disappeared inside. Roger viewed the flowery script on the stern announcing *"Serenity on the Seas – Hong Kong"*. Moments later, Stanley reappeared on the exposed section of the lower deck, a small, slim woman, dressed in a bright red tunic top and a pair of black trousers, followed behind him. Both waited for Roger to come aboard. She extended her hand towards him.

'Hello, Mister Mortlock, I'm very pleased to meet you. People call me Mavis.'

Roger was rather taken aback by the broad East End cockney and her cigarette-husky voice. He stretched out his hand to greet her. The softness of her small bony hand was at odds with her manly face. Her narrow eyes, heavily plastered with mascara, bore into him.

'So you wanna buy a bit of *Serenity*, do you? Well, come have a look around her.'

Roger followed Mavis through the low door into the interior. He was not prepared for the large double-bed that took up the full space of the cabin. The embroidery of pink orchids sat proudly on the deep maroon bedcover. He followed Mavis around the edge of the bed to the doorway on the other side.

'Who sleeps here? Is this the principal bedroom?' Roger asked.

'It depends.' Mavis smiled slightly, looking directly at Roger. 'It could be for passengers or for crew. It depends who's on board.' Mavis continued. '*Serenity* is very versatile.'

'Is this where you commune with your husband's soul? Stanley has told me about how you use this boat.'

'When I'm on my own, that's true. This was his favourite room. For Family Weekends, this bed is stowed away and table and chairs are put in its place. However, for our Crewed Weekends, this is the Recreation Room for use by guests and crew alike.'

Mavis and Roger had climbed the few steps up to the upper deck. Roger viewed the steering wheel and the display of instruments equivalent to that of the cockpit of a jumbo jet. Dial competed with dial in order to provide data on weather, current position, speed and what was on the menu for dinner. Through the window of the bridge, distances to the bow of the boat and down to the lapping sea looked unnervingly far away.

Roger did not fluster easily, yet he felt his hands begin to sweat as he contemplated what Mavis'definition of versatility might be.

'So, if this boat already has ongoing business, why do you want to involve me?'

'Because, Roger, new partners bring new business.' Mavis was staring hard at him.

'Your UK connections could be very useful. Many people from London would love our packages, do you not think?'

'It's a long way for them to come. Although what seems to be on offer looks very attractive to .....lots of people looking for....'

' a bit of excitement....something different.'

Roger watched Mavis heave herself up into the high seat behind the wheel. Her small hands coyly played with the pearls of her necklace, whilst her legs perched on the rest under the seat. She watched Roger as he calculated the merits of investing in something that was radically different from what he had intended.

She could not take in Roger's questioning of himself on how had he got himself involved with such a fruitcake venture.

'If you join up with Mavis, not only will you be helping her out, but also she could be very useful to your other enterprise.' Stanley had joined the two in the wheelhouse. He leaned against the wall, watching with amusement as Mavis and Roger sounded each other out.

'When my husband passed on, he left me with one or two..... commitments that I have been unable to shake off.' Mavis continued to fidget with the necklace as she continued her tale of woe. 'Some so-called associates have been very persistent and unsympathetic to my situation, making demands that I am unable to meet, unless......'

Roger had not been prepared for the glistening in Mavis's eyes. 'unless you sell this boat.....or part of it. Is that it?'

'Exactly. It is all most unfortunate.' She wiped her face with a handkerchief.

'Let me ask you about your needs. Stanley says that I can help. How? '

Roger sensed that she already knew the answer. He turned towards Stanley standing by the entrance. Stanley nodded that secrets would be safe within the windowed surround.   Roger proceeded to provide a brief summary of his requirements.

'Surveyors!' Mavis cried. 'You don't need to worry about them! I know many of the good ones. Everybody has his price. We can move this boat to wherever any surveyor wants us to. As you can see, Serenity is very adaptable. She can become anything we want. Let's move back downstairs.'

The cushions of the armchair in the forward lounge were deep and soft as Roger sat down opposite Mavis. Whilst she might be relieved to have found somebody to get her out of trouble, Roger was less certain about how this new investment might be greeted back home. Both knew that decisions needed to be made quickly. Mavis broke the uneasy silence

'Roger! If you and I share this boat, then Stanley will make sure that the paperwork for your expanding fleet is correctly placed. Your Mr Fu-Fing will see his insurance portfolio build nicely. I'm not so certain whether the forecast for the oncoming typhoon season will be so favourable towards him.'

'I was hoping for smaller, more susceptible craft to make up my fleet. Not these bloody great gin palaces!'

'I can guarantee that Stanley and I will place lots of them around the area as you have requested. But, in the eye of a storm, these gin palaces, as you call them, are not as robust as you think. A good ninety mile an hour wind can flatten these as well. There's a lot of wood in their structure.'

'You make a convincing case, Mavis!' Roger replied. 'It is a higher price than I had expected to pay to get Stanley and now, it seems, you to help to further my own cause.'

'Do we have a deal, Roger?'

Roger considered the proposition. Cash from smaller losses in the Phantom Fleet could go towards splashing out on more extravagant craft whose fate would be the same. A part share in the versatile usages implemented by Mavis and her crew would not come amiss either. As Roger shook her boney right hand in agreement, he was surprised by a sudden searing pain as he felt her sharp fingernails pierce his palm.

'We do understand each other from now on, don't we Roger? We're now partners in the *Serenity Plan*. I trust you.' She grimaced as she increased the pressure to his hand. 'and you trust me, yes?'

'Ouch!' Roger took his hand away quickly. The reddened imprint showed that he had been inducted into an inner sanctum from which there seemed no turning back.

Chapter Twenty One

Meeting with the enemy

Roger lay sprawled on his bed at the hotel. Two miniature bottles of Jack Daniels from the mini bar sat empty on his bedside table. He downed the last drops in his glass as he considered his new associate. Had he been too reckless in acquiescing to Mavis' ball-breaking charm? Probably! Would the association produce more than he had previously anticipated? Hopefully! Was it more fun than he had wanted? Certainly! Considering also that he had done well to enter the hotel after dinner without encountering any members of the enemy, it had been a good day.

The soundtrack of the movie from the television could not dampen the shrill ring of the hotel phone. Roger looked at the clock on his bedside table. Ten thirty at night in Hong Kong meant that Mary had something serious to talk to him about in the afternoon at home. He picked up the receiver to expect news of a broken washing machine or a request for money from one of his children.

'Hello old girl, what's the problem?'

Roger put the pause at the other end of the line down to old-fashioned delay on the satellite link. He waited for the rasping voice of his wife to respond.

'So it was you that I saw!'

Roger sat down on the bed as he recognised the voice. 'Who's this?' He bluffed on pointlessly. 'Do you have the right room? This is room twenty twenty three.'

'This is Diana Vowlds in room twenty four thirteen. What are you doing in Hong Kong, Roger?'

'Diana! What a surprise! How lovely to hear from you. How did you know that I was here?' He kicked himself as he realised that he had forgotten the script.

'I saw you hurry into the lift before I had a chance to catch you.' Diana explained. 'Are you here on your own?'

'No! ' Roger was soon back on-message. 'Mary's here with me.'

'How nice!' Diana sounded genuinely impressed. 'We must hook up. Perhaps we can meet for dinner? I could do with some relief from Gavin's people.'

Roger sat down on the bed to evaluate the situation. He carried on blindly. 'That would be great. Not tonight though, Diana. We're both completely wiped. We're both lying here in our dressing gowns ready for a good night's kip. It's been a long day for ....us.'

'Lots of sight-seeing?' Diana's questioning had to be answered as truthfully as possible.

'This afternoon we went over to Lamma Island. Mary loved it.' Roger felt better about muddying the line between fact and fiction. 'If you get a moment before you go back, you must ask Gavin to take you over there for lunch.'

'Some hope' Diana replied. 'You know what it's like. Wall to wall meetings all day.'

Roger chuckled to himself. 'Anyway, why don't we have a drink in the bar tomorrow night?'

Diana agreed and called off. Roger picked up the remote control for the television and started to flick through the menu of channels. The Man in the Green Blazer was pointing to the image of thick white cloud amassed in the south east corner of his weather map.

'We calculate that the eye will be over here within the next forty eight to seventy two hours. On your screen, folks, we have upgraded the storm to T3. So, the advice from the Hong Kong Observatory is that all journeys be cancelled unless they're essential. The airport will close some time tomorrow ......'

As Captain of the Phantom Fleet, Roger reviewed the situation. He was pleased that at least he would not have to go down with his ships. The more familiar ring tone of his mobile phone sounded from amongst the clutter on his bed. He looked at the small screen. He had not expected a call from Candida Smith.

'Roger! I'm glad that I've got you. Mary said that you'd still be up. Has she told you that Johnnie's in jail, in Spain? Did you know about the problem with this Weatherhead bloke?'

Candida's voice sounded tense, but in control. She was not really interested in any reply that Roger might have provided as she reported further on his business partner's detention at the La Laguna Remand Centre.

'So, he's not been arrested then?'

'As good as! He can't go anywhere until the medical report on this Charlie's condition has been submitted to the magistrate. It's all utterly ghastly and so ridiculous. I'm going out to see him tomorrow, to take him a fresh supply of clothes as well as giving him a fucking great kick up the arse. You'd have thought that retirement would have quietened him down, not make him want to hit people. When are you coming back? I might need your help. He might listen to you.'

'I don't quite know.' Roger replied, realising that he should text Mary with the news of imminent bad weather. 'They're about to close the airport. I might be stuck here for a bit longer than I'd planned.'

Roger pressed the off switch. The pressure was building, not just outside but inside as well. An impending date with the enemy and his partner's incarceration in a Spanish dungeon would not be easy bedfellows as he switched off his bedside light.

++++

"Can you repeat that, Stanley? It sounds as if you're obviously talking to me from the top of a mountain........what?' Roger could hear the wind on the line. " From the top of a mountain......Yes, that's better! You were saying that Crusoe has lodged cover applications where?" The roar from a gust made it difficult for Roger to listen to Stanley's update on the day's progress. "The cheques have been what? OK ! Got it! ...lodged with Gavin. That's good. What's that? The spread of the locations was ......a challenge for Crusoe? Well, that's what we pay him for, Stanley!" The faintness of Stanley's voice was forcing Roger to raise his own as he sat in the Riva Bar on the twenty seventh floor of the hotel in the evening as he waited for Diana. Luckily the bar was almost deserted, yet he had no desire for any unwarranted attention. "I'm glad that everything is in place, Stan! I've got to go. I have an important meeting. No ...not with Mavis....." The line had gone dead. There was no point in battling the turbulent weather outside.

Roger put his phone back in the inside pocket of his jacket and looked through the window onto the full expanse of Victoria Harbour. The silhouettes of high rise towers lurked behind the coloured neon lights burning into the evening darkness. Pinpricks of navigation lights sprinkled the dark waters of the harbour as ships moved silently between Hong Kong Island and Kowloon. He had arrived early to stake a pitch from which he could watch people come and go. Easing back into the leather armchair, he sipped his scotch and contemplated his conversation with Stanley Henderson. The game was well and truly afoot!

So far, activity on the Phantom Fleet had been restricted to claims on boats supposedly lost in the storm on the Sebastian

Islands. He was glad of the inspiration of his co-conspirator, John Smith, when he had mentioned his wife's interest in the Bahamas. Neither had ever heard of the island of Everson. Its National Bank seemed a most suitable haven for the compensation cheques. So far, no blood had been spilled. Roger would enjoy the spoils of his exploits in due course. He gained a certain pleasure from being able to help his partner to resolve his problems, even if they hade been of his own making. Yet, Roger needed to be careful, not to become over-confident, not to slip up as he watched Diana Vowlds enter the Riva Bar. The long silk jacket made her look taller as she walked past the girl at the reception desk. Here was a stylish elegance that Roger had not seen in the office. He liked the glass coloured beads that nestled within the open collar of her white shirt.

'Well, you certainly look different from the last time I saw you!' Roger stood up and kissed her on both cheeks. 'You look wonderful!'

Diana was pleased that she had made the detour to the silk shop near Crosthwaite's office. She had not expected the need to glam up, having only packed the dowdy and the sensible. 'Where's Mary?' she asked as she sat down in the chair opposite Roger.

'I'm afraid that I've done her in!' Roger hoped his apology would be sufficient. 'She's stayed in the room. I think that we overdid the sightseeing today. It's entirely my fault. Despite the number of times I've visited, there is just so much of this place that I have never seen. So we dashed around trying to pack them all in. She loved every minute of it, but it's taken its toll.' Roger thought that the predicament of his Phantom Spouse sounded quite feasible, as did Diana.

'Oh that's a shame.' There was genuine disappointment in her voice. 'Two full days of man talk is more than enough for one girl to put up with. I was looking forward to a bit of girlie chat.'

'Mary can dash around like a mad thing at home. However, the sultry climate, the time difference and the sheer pace of the city have taken their toll. The winds have not helped either.' Roger sensed his nose lengthening with every word. He must not overdo it!

Diana brought out her Blackberry from her handbag and put it on the table between them. 'I know! We're braced to take a bit of a beating over the next few days.'

Roger remained impassive as a brainwave hit him. 'It's not that serious. It's only "T3", at the moment, but Mary's not one for sitting around. So, I've booked her onto the flight out first thing tomorrow morning to Singapore. She's been really lucky in being able to pick up a flight to London from there.'

'Why aren't you going with her, Roger?' Diana had taken the first sip of her white wine. 'Or is it women and children first? What a chivalrous fellow you are!'

Roger knew that Diana's scepticism should not be underestimated. He smiled at her before continuing. 'I would have gone with her. It's just that I'd made this plan to meet somebody tomorrow who hopefully is going to offer me some work. Mary was only going to mooch around the shops. So she had no desire to be cooped up in the hotel here being buffeted by the winds. So she decided that it would be better to get out whilst she had the chance. More to the point, why aren't you leaving whilst there's still the chance?'

'I just think that the storm will blow over quickly. Like you, I have commitments that need to be finished. It's a bit weedy to retreat at the first sign of trouble.' She looked at the small screen on the table for any signs of activity. 'London is getting twitchy about being sucked into this sub-prime business. A lot of American debt was re-insured in London. So, it's important that all our clients maintain their relationship with us.' Diana sighed heavily. 'So, in this instance, I'll be brave, like you, and stay behind.'

'Oh well, a couple more days being a Bloke won't hurt. Alistair will be very impressed!'

'You've no idea how nice it is not to have stilted client conversation.' Diana sighed as she finished off her wine. 'If I have to bang on any more about the new compliance legislation, I'll do my nut.' She was not finished. 'I know that all you men want to talk about is sex, football and gambling. When they're faced with a woman who's not really interested, they become tongue-tied. In order to keep things going, I launch into quasi-intellectual debates about how we, the insurance industry, are the guardians of modern life and not the controllers, etcetera etcetera......' She stopped herself and looked towards the window. 'It's very tiring and....'

'... very boring.' Roger suggested.

'Quite probably. Where's the waiter? I could do with another drink.' Diana gesticulated to him before turning back to Roger. 'Clearly, these topics held no problem for you? '

'I was alright on football and gambling. Sex, I was a little hazy on. Too personal. As to the notion of the insurance industry being the guardians of modern life, I would have had to mug up on that one beforehand.'

Diana asked the waiter for another round of drinks. Roger was on his guard. Another scotch might make him forget everything he had carefully thought through. The very real possibility of being found out banged in his head like a drum.

'So Roge, how are you enjoying your retirement?' Diana asked as the waiter deposited the fresh set of glasses on the table.

'It's certainly been very different.' he replied. 'After the initial shock and anger at my departure, I realised that, as long as I had enough money, there were other things that I could do with my time. There have been days of insufferable tedium when I missed work, missed being involved in something away from home. I've certainly missed the lunches! However, as time has gone by, I've found other things to get involved with.'

'Lucky you! I'm dreading the thought of stopping work.' Diana looked at him full on as if she was confessing something that she had never revealed before. 'After Gerry left me, I've got used to living on my own. Also having my daughter around has been great. Not that I see her much, what with work keeping me so busy. She goes round to friends' houses.   She'll be off in the next year or so, provided that she gets good results. It's an important time for her. After that, I really will be on my own, for the rest of time. That really does frighten me. Unless I can find me a man pretty darned quick, it'll be crochet and needlework.' Diana paused to take a sip of her wine. 'Why am I telling you all this, Roger? I'm sorry.'

'Maybe you've nobody else to tell?' Roger replied. 'Because it doesn't matter if you tell me, since it won't pass any further?' He had been surprised by Diana's resigned grimace and slight shrug of her shoulders.

'Tell me about your sailing! No more accidents to report, I trust?'

'None at all!' Roger replied. He hoped that his reply had not been too quick. 'I was just really unlucky. Freak wind!'

'Sailing is an unpredictable business, very expensive, but bloody good fun. My ex-husband had a boat which he kept on the Hamble. He used to take me.....'

'In the biblical sense or just sailing?'

'Both, if you really want to know. A bonk in the cabin or on the deck under a moonlit sky can be very enervating. Christ, I must be pissed!' Diana checked her Blackberry for messages and let out a shriek. 'Gavin's just asked me whether I would like to stay at his apartment if I have to stay longer because of the storm. Can you believe that? He'd already asked me out for dinner tonight. Just the two of us! I reckon that dinner was not the only thing on the agenda. I may be single, but I'm not that desperate! He's not really my type. He's far too suave and cocky.'

'He's certainly a trier!'

'He's certainly doing a great job, drumming up a lot of business from wealthy bankers and hedge-fund boys. Very expensive boats demand very high premiums. Excuse me whilst I reply.' Diana sent a brief message to Gavin before placing the Blackberry back in her bag. She sensed that there would be no further need for it. She turned to see Roger looking at his watch. Would it be pushing her luck if she was to suggest dinner? She remembered the wife in her room before she carried on. 'I'm sorry to say this, Roge, having a younger man in post has been very good for business.'

Diana had meant well. Roger dismissed her comment by acknowledging that testosterone-charged thirty-something bastards had never been his favourite clientele.

'Gavin was always ambitious. It's good that he's been able to attract other more lucrative areas of insurance.' Roger decided to go on the front foot. 'My departure has had its plus points for me also. I'm very excited about this new venture which I'm seeing somebody about tomorrow.'

'Tell me more.'

'There's not much to tell. It's still very early days.'

'Oh, come off it, Roge!'

'I'm sworn to secrecy.' He looked into Diana's eyes. There was so much that he wanted to tell her. 'OK! Not a word to anybody else! We're starting a school.'

'Do you have a name?'

'The Royal Northwood.' Roger had no idea where that came from. However, it had a certain ring of academic authority.

'That sounds brilliant. Who are your partners over here? '

'I really can't tell you, Diana, much as I would love to.'

'I understand. Code of the Mandarin, eh?'

'The nice thing about the project is that it will give me a reason to come out to Hong Kong. This is still such a vibrant place. Things get done.....in spite of the noise and the mass of people.'

Diana's attention was waning again. Would she have to faint with hunger before anything happened? She looked to Roger and asked. 'Shouldn't you call Mary to see how she is? She must be wondering how long you're going to be? This is her last night in Hong Kong after all. You should be with her.'

'She's probably asleep. She has an early start tomorrow.' Diana raised her eyebrow at Roger's lack of concern.

'I know that I would love my husband to call me to see how I was. Go on, give her a call. I need to check my e-mails.' Diana picked up the Blackberry from her bag. Roger drew out his mobile phone, not certain whether to conduct a conversation with the Speaking Clock or with a mystified hotel receptionist.

'I'll text her.' He decided. Mary would be surprised by his unusual expression of concern for her welfare, as he tapped in his message. The whisky tasted good as he waited for the reply.

'How nice! All well here. Hope not enjoying yourself too much.'

Roger showed the message to Diana.

'I presume she doesn't know about our fling?'

'Of course not!'

Room 454 might have been a momentary lapse, yet Roger had missed the tenderness of a woman who enjoyed his company as a man. As he sat opposite her, Roger could not fail to see the undone top buttons of Diana's white silk shirt. The glass necklace around her exposed neck could not hide the rise of her breasts and the sheen of her tanned skin.

Roger sighed. 'It was probably a mistake – an enjoyable one all the same.'

'Was it? I do remember that I was a bit miserable at the time.'

'You were not at your best. Are you hungry?' Roger asked. 'I think that I've got time for a quick bite before I go back to the room'

'What did you have in mind?'

'Shall we try the restaurant next door?'

Diana sighed. Dim Sum, a glass of wine and then e-mails and income projections. Sir Alistair should be really impressed.

++++

The warmth of a close hug and a chaste kiss on both cheeks had stayed in Roger's mind as he took the lift down to his room after they had finished in the restaurant. He let out a huge sigh of relief as he travelled down. He had desperately wanted to brag to Diana about his full portfolio of mischief. She had tried one more time to get more info on the Royal Northwood School.

"My balls would be ripped from me if I uttered anything indiscreet."

"I understand." Diana patted him on the hand. "A man's balls are very precious! He does a lot of thinking with them." She smiled mischievously and then changed tack. "I think it's great that somebody of your age still has the energy for a new project like this. I'm sure that Mary must be delighted."

"She's been on at me to do something purposeful in my retirement. She will be very pleased if it all comes good! She had probably hoped that it would be nearer to home, but better to have this than nothing at all!"

The mix of food, reminiscence and chat of future plans swallowed down with a bottle of the house wine was going to ensure that Roger would sleep well. The memory of Diana's

215

delicate strokes of his hand, as she had chided him, would stay with him until he dropped off to sleep. He just wished that he had found a more unfriendly foe. The e-mail light on his phone flashed. It was from Candida.

"J in reasonable shape. He needs visitors. Might you be able to see him after your return from HK? It is all so bloody!"

All in good time, Roger thought as he undressed. There was still work to be done here in Hong Kong He was in no rush to see the inside of a jail anywhere!

++++

Chapter Twenty Two

The rage in Spain - continued

As Candida was driven away through the back streets of Alicante, she determined that her first visit inside a prison would also be her last. The stench of male sweat had been overwhelming. The distant shouts from beyond the walls had had an eerie sound of desperate insanity. The list of restrictions handed out by the prison officer at the Reception had made frightening reading. There seemed little difference between those for the innocent and those for the convicted. She was appalled by the whole thing.

Her husband had been right, it would be more sensible for her to return home and take up the battle. She would treat his absence as if he was away on business, yet with one major difference. She would start to be a bloody nuisance to those connected to his case. She would instruct Luis Gomez to contact the British Consulate to let them know of John's presence in captivity. A visit from a man in a dark suit would reassure her that her husband was being treated properly and that he would have a recent copy of an English newspaper to read.

Luis had booked a room for Candida at the Hotel Las Palmas. She had not stayed in a hotel on her own for ages. The shock of her ordeal took hold as she collapsed on the bed and sobbed loudly for a few minutes until reason and the lack of any more tears took hold of her.

'We have many, many cases of British tourists who have become entangled with Spanish law and who have left free men. I am pleased to tell you. Others receive what our laws demand. They do very good tapas here. I have ordered an interesting selection.'

Candida had joined Luis for dinner in the hotel. The array of terracotta dishes displayed on the table did little to whet her appetite as she listened to Luis' reassurances. As she picked at a slice of Tortilla with red peppers, she was not yet convinced that her husband would be treated any differently from drug dealers and property shysters who were locked up with him. She forced herself to listen to the lawyer's polite rationale of why her husband's freedom was being contained within four crummy walls.

'Civil Assault is the most popular way in our law of bringing somebody to court and to seek compensation. Medical insurance companies demand that every attempt at restitution should be made through the courts. So being held on remand is seen as a just way of holding the assailant until a decision can be made about how to apportion blame or costs.'

'That's all very well, Luis. We cannot escape the fact that John did knock the lights out of the deceitful little shit! It does not look good.'

'We will see. You go back to England.' Luis instructed. 'I like very much to live in England. Very green, very cool, very pretty villages. Stratford upon Avon, I liked very much. You contact Spanish Embassy. Anything will be good to force the Magistrate here to realise that this whole mess is ......' he hesitated for a moment as the bill was presented by the waiter. '..... *tempestad en vasa da agua.*' The Spanish don't understand tea! Paint your banners. Have your march through the streets like we do here in Spain.' Luis stopped to consider his next phrase. '*Free my husband!* Yes! I like it. *Free my husband; he has done nothing very wrong!* It sounds good. I will continue to use the channels of Spanish law.'

'I might just do that, Luis! I need to do something.' Candida shook his hand after dinner. He may have looked twenty one, but his advice had been that of a fifty year old.

On the return flight back to Birmingham Airport on the following morning, Candida sat in her seat and considered her role as campaigner and activist. Whilst many of her fellow passengers would be preparing to show pictures of their holiday to long-suffering friends, Candida would be presenting her friends with a Petition Sheet and asking for their signature. She tried to recall crusading campaigns organised by women to free their loved ones who had been guilty as charged, yet who had somehow got off scot free. Her mission would be to garner support for a man who had had no alternative but to take the law into his own hands. She thought of other women in history who had done what she was about to embark on. Joan of Arc? Possibly, although Candida had no intention of getting that carried away. Emily Pankhurst? Certainly, although perhaps she would fall short of any hunger strike. Candida remembered being impressed by the story on the television news of the woman who had broken into her neighbours' house and destroyed their hi-fi with a sledgehammer, just because it had been making too much noise at three in the morning. There had been *The Guildford Four.* Now, John Smith would become *The Bisbury One!*

She would employ all the usual weapons of democracy, letters to the Spanish Ambassador, to the Bisbury Echo, to her local MP, whoever he or she was , and of course the Petition to be delivered to the Prime Minister at Number Ten. John Smith was an Englishman whose altruism had known no bounds! A man who had allowed his wife to spend his hard earned cash on the regeneration of a decaying set of stables! A man who had been driven to extreme measures just to combat the deceit of others!

Candida sensed that she needed an alternative back-up plan as well. As she walked briskly away from the Arrivals Hall at Birmingham Airport, Candida began drawing up plans for a subsidiary campaign. *Screw the Weatherhead Two* would need cunning and guile. There was woman's work to be done as she sped away from the car park back towards home.

++++

Chapter Twenty Three
Diana and winds of change

Roger woke early. He opened up his laptop and began scanning the weather charts for signs of threatening weather systems. He checked with the television weatherman who was excitedly plotting the progress of Typhoon Harri up the coast four hundred miles away. The next stage of the plan would be a bonus if it could be executed quickly and accurately. The Fleet could benefit from some reinforcements. He called Stanley Henderson to meet him near the hotel.

Roger walked out of the hotel doorway into the small forecourt where a line of Mercedes and their drivers waited under the swirling branches of the palm trees in the hotel forecourt. A couple of smart female executives did their best to retain their composure as the wind tugged at the skirts of their black designer suits and ruffled their coiffed hair with carefree abandon. He scrolled down the messages on his phone. Diana had not wasted much time as he read her note to him.

"Good to catch up last night. Hope Mary got off to Singapore OK. Clients' dinner called off tonight because of the storm. Can you help a lady in distress? Dinner?"

Roger strode around the corner of the nearby street towards the small coffee shop and sat down at the table opposite Stanley.

'With some of the Claims money, Robin has bought cover on a few leisure craft in Lap Dong province.' Stanley struggled on through the breathless wheeze of forty years of cigarettes.

Roger passed a sheet of paper across the table. Stanley's cough caused him to spill his coffee onto the list.

'Ask him to register some more in these areas.' Roger said quietly. 'I think that you'll find these will prove to be quite interesting.' Roger wiped the surface of the paper to make sure that the names on the list were still legible.

'Bloody hell, Roger! It's not like putting money on the Two Thirty at the Track.' Stanley leaned forward as he continued to study Roger's notes. 'Submitting insurance applications takes time. You know how it works. All that paperwork.'

'Limited timelines never stopped Robin in the past.' Roger's eyes targeted the spluttering Stanley. 'As long as Gavin and Crosthwaites have their money, the cover will be in place. You and I know that, Stanley, as does Robin Song!'

'There are quite a few here on your list.' Stanley studied the details on the sheet more closely. 'Some are quite some distance away from here. What do you know, Roger?'

'The time for questions is not for now, Stanley. We need action. Contact Robin as soon as you can.'

'Mavis also wants to talk with you about her Crewed Weekends.' Stanley reminded Roger. 'You're going to have a busy time before you go back.'

Roger thought for a moment. 'I'll call her now.' Both men downed their coffee before standing up in readiness for their day.

Roger watched Stanley shamble his way into the street. He could see him speaking animatedly into his phone. Roger hoped that the Phantom Fleet was about to become a more Global Armada, although Stanley's possession of a rolled-up newspaper in his other hand suggested that the Two Thirty at Sha Tin was also on his agenda. It would take more than just wind to cancel the afternoon race meeting. Roger tapped a message onto his Blackberry.

"Gavin turned you down this time? Will try to re-arrange my meeting for 6pm. I could be hungry by 7.30pm."

Roger contemplated the darkening skies outside the coffee shop, whilst contemplating the fiction of his evening meeting. There were times when he himself believed that the Royal Northwood International School and its mythical housing of forty children from the well-to-do in Hong Kong really existed. It sounded a bloody good idea. In the meantime, it would serve to shape the reality of the number of boats in the Phantom Fleet. Roger knew how long and protracted some client meetings had been. He was not surprised to receive Diana's text.

"Having lunch with Gav and Choo Carriers. Will book table. Crosthwaites' treat."

The red light on his Blackberry flashed again and again as messages pinged back and forth.

"Rooftop closed. Have found Lotus Garden at ground level in street near to hotel. See you there at 7.30pm."

"Meeting should finish by 6.45pm. Come for drink in downstairs hotel bar first?"

"Good idea. Hope meeting goes well"

Roger called Mavis. 'I gather that you want to meet up. Are you free to meet for a drink tonight at the hotel? There's something I want you to do for me.'

He explained further before calling off.

++++

The Lobby Bar on the ground floor of the hotel was not as crowded as usual. Visitors and guests, normally attracted by the buzz of its prominent location and smart black furniture, had been deterred by the warning from the Hong Kong Observatory. Roger and Mavis were seated near to the front which looked on as guests sought to check in to face the oncoming winds or to check out because they were the only ones sane enough or lucky enough to have somewhere else to go.

'All Crewed Weekends between now and Christmas are fully booked. My girls are going to be very busy.' Roger was impressed by Mavis' matter of fact update of the affairs of the Serenity of the Seas. 'I just need to find some good looking guys for the Hen Parties.' Roger admired the black dragon print on her magenta tunic dress. Her dark painted eyes looked towards him as he attempted to offer help for her cause.

'All the men I know are retired and married.'

'and straight.' Mavis wondered why Roger had wanted her dressed like an aristo as she watched people rush before her. 'I'm looking for men with more......'

Roger needed to know no more as his intuition was confirmed as Diana Vowlds approached, a good ten minutes ahead of schedule.

'Diana! How nice to see you.' Roger stood up and brought over another chair. 'May I introduce you to Mavis Ng. She is one of the Trustees on the project I was telling you about. She's having a meeting with them tonight and so she was filling me in what my role might be.'

Mavis did not move from her seat. She extended her hand to Diana in formal greeting..

'I hope that I'm not interrupting anything.' Diana was a bit flustered that her intrusion was uncalled for. 'I will go and sit elsewhere.'

'No, we were just finishing.' Roger looked for the waiter, who was already hovering in anticipation of a fresh order.

Mavis lifted her hand. 'I will stick with what I have. I need to be on best behaviour tonight. I need to keep my mind clear. I understand that Roger has already taken you into his confidence about our little project. I've ticked him off. He says that he trusts you and so I hope you understand the need for discretion.' Her previously passive face let out the hint of a friendly smile towards Diana.

Roger looked on. Mavis seemed to be relishing her role. Even the cockney had been replaced by a calm Chinese terseness as she continued. 'It's just very early days. We can't afford others to hear about it and ruin our plans. Costs would then shoot up and our business model will be in pieces.'

'Absolutely! My lips are sealed.' Diana sipped her wine. 'Anyway, you have a very good man here to help you. It sounds very exciting. If you need help of any sort, Roger knows that all he has to do is contact us.'

'My fellow Trustees are all very well connected. However, we could be looking to the UK for help in all sorts of ways.' Mavis turned towards Roger. 'English education has a very good reputation in China. We appreciate their very high standards, both academically and socially. Is this your first time in Hong Kong, Diana?'

Diana had read about diminutive women who wielded considerable power in Hong Kong society and seemed to know everybody. She watched Mavis take a sip of her Coke and place the glass delicately back on the table. As she relayed details of her previous two visits to Hong Kong for the umpteenth time during her stay, Diana looked for the chance to open up her own line of questioning - like where Mavis's fantastic dress had come from or how much her fantastic drop earrings had cost. She suspected that exclusive chic in Hong Kong was just as expensive a commodity as it was anywhere else.

Mavis looked at her watch. 'Goodness me! I am late!' She took another sip of her drink, stood up and wrapped her silk scarf tightly around her shoulders. 'Not that they will start without me. Others will be late besides me. Top businessmen and leading academics are notorious for their lack of punctuality. It makes me very cross.' Mavis extended her hand to Diana who had also got up. 'Maybe we will meet again, Diana? We will certainly be needing insurance.' She turned to Roger. 'It was very useful to have our little chat. I will talk to you tomorrow. Now where is my driver?'

Diana had sat down again. She watched Roger tower over the slight Mavis, as they both walked to the front door of the hotel. She noticed a man with wisps of grey hair under a peaked chauffeur's cap open the back door of the silver Mercedes for Mavis. She turned back to watch the hurly-burly in the Lobby Bar. Her brain was whirring. The chauffeur's face had looked vaguely familiar.

'How far do we have to walk?' Roger had re-entered the bar and was finishing off the remains of his scotch, whilst Diana put on her overcoat.

'Ten minutes, I was told'

++++

'Mary was lucky to get away this morning, wasn't she, Roge?' The Lotus Garden restaurant was empty as Diana looked out of the window. A street trader across the street was busy closing up his stall. She turned back to face Roger. 'Mavis seemed very impressive. Where did she spring from?'

Roger chewed on his mouthful of Red Crab curry. The stabbing heat of the chilli provided a few vital extra seconds for him to prepare his answer. The two waiters in the corner reading the evening paper just wanted him to hurry up so that they could get home.

'Well, she found me, actually! Mary works tirelessly on various charities, one of which is a school...... near where we live. It turned out that Mavis knew one of the others on the Board and had asked

226

her to find somebody who could help her on this project.' Roger braced himself for another mouthful of curry. He was annoyed that he had not been prepared for the question, but hoped that the answer was being accepted. 'I was sounded out and asked if I'd like to get involved and, bingo, here we are! She even paid for our tickets.' Roger was pleased by how lies can be repackaged so easily.

'Well, you may have found yourself a rather good little number. She seems very determined. I wouldn't like to cross her. Those steely mascara eyes, Bloody hell! Tough as old boots, I'd say! Did you notice her chauffeur?'

Roger finished his curry. He sipped on his glass of white wine. 'No, I can't say I did. Was he a friend of yours?'

'I don't befriend chauffeurs.' Diana refilled her glass. 'It was just that I thought I recognised his face from somewhere. I can't think where or why.'

'It could have been anyone, Diana. You're such a busy woman. You're meeting people with recognisable faces all the time. This is delicious food, by the way!' Roger knew that any further help in identification could end up as Hari Kiri. 'Anyway, tell me about your meeting with Mr Atti Choo.'

'The lunchtime topic today was Chinese nervousness that Western capitalism was about to come apart.' Diana replied. 'Will China be expected to come to our rescue? I reassured him that Crosthwaites have not been as irresponsible as many of our American counterparts. The morose old bugger was not convinced. Is there any more wine?'

'So, no football or gambling chat with Mr Choo, then? I do remember that he was more hard work than a lot of the clients. Sex was a definite no-no, as I remember!'

Roger filled Diana's glass from the bottle of Sancerre. He was disappointed that Diana's white shirt of the previous evening had been replaced by a pink silk blouse whose buttons kept her breasts chastely hidden from view. The smart necklace from the previous evening hung down over their outline.

'Goodness no! With him? I think not!' Diana smiled back as she finished her wine.

'You talked about your need to learn crochet last night. What happened to your auditioning the bass line at the Operatic Society?' Roger could not stop himself. 'Or have you moved on to the tenors?'

'Roger, how dare you? I may be Director of Compliance, but it only applies to my work! I'm not that desperate. I'm rather enjoying my singular status.'

'It sounds like too much work and not enough play to me!'

'Crosthwaites does keep me very busy. Charlotte is starting her final year at school. I've been helping with her revision. It's not easy for someone in my position. The role of Executive Slapper is not one that I aspire to.'

Roger looked out through the rain-spattered window of the restaurant. A stray white T-Shirt, ripped from the sales rack of the street trader opposite, lay in one of the large puddles that had collected on the pavement. The street was empty. 'As long as you're happy, Diana.'

'For now I am.' Diana had seen what Roger had noticed. 'Anyway, Roger, I meant what I said to your Madame Butterfly. Anytime you need anything, just let me know. I'm sure that I can get Gavin or one of the others in the office to help out.' She summoned the bill from one of the waiters. His colleague had already turned off some of the restaurant lights. 'In the meantime, I think that you and I need to get back to the hotel before it gets any worse out there.'

Roger hoped that the amount of local aid would be considerably more than Diana may have envisaged. As they gathered themselves in the outside porch of the restaurant,

Diana's positive assessment was the only one in town. 'It's only a short walk back to the hotel. The air will do us good, Roger.'

Roger encased Diana within his own coat against the driving rain. As they approached the wider pavements of Gloucester Road, Roger noticed that few cars and even fewer taxis were on the street. The locals had run for cover and any visitors stupid enough to still be out in the weather would have to fend for themselves.

'This is slightly more fresh air than I had bargained for, Roge!' Diana volunteered.

Roger had liked the closeness of Diana's warm body burrowed next to his as they battled their way against the wind. He could see the lights of the hotel entrance a few hundred metres away. As a car splashed its way past him, Roger realised that joint cover was not proving very effective. 'Come on, Diana, it's each one for themselves and we'll be back in no time!'

Roger's mind was filled with images of Hurricane Katrina in New Orleans. The wind that was blowing across Victoria Harbour seemed as vicious. It had not been a sensible idea to be out in it. As they reached the hotel, the two hotel doormen rushed towards them in a futile gesture of protection as the wind promptly turned their umbrellas inside out.

Roger and Diana shook off the worst of the rain in the lobby. Roger caught a glimpse of them both in the mirror as they waited for the lift. The ragdoll next to him looked as if she had already been immersed in a bath of her own as he suggested. 'Do you want to come to my room for a whisky and a hot bath?'

Diana seized the offer for warmth and safe shelter without a moment's hesitation. She had only witnessed seriously high winds from the safety of her television screen. She had never before been subjected to the buffeting and the struggle to make progress down the street. By rights, she should have been livid as they travelled up in the lift. She had seen her image with her newly styled hair caked around her face in a bedraggled mess. Her expensive coat had failed to protect her silk shirt which now clung to her body like gluey wallpaper. The legs of her smart-cut trousers were sodden, her feet frozen inside the thin black leather of her ankle boots. With less far to travel, Roger's suggestion had seemed to be an entirely sensible option as she entered the blissful warmth of his room. She had not been on her own with a man in his bedroom for at least a year. Yet, now was not the time to query her decision. The whistling through the windows and the occasional shudder of the room had decided the matter. Her shivering hands, still numb and powerless, fiddled unsuccessfully in their efforts to undo the buttons of her coat. She looked helplessly towards Roger who seemed less affected by the wet and the cold.

'Let me help you, Diana.' Roger walked towards her and undid the remaining buttons of her coat before placing it on a hanger. He noticed that she was still shivering and returned to give her a hug.

Diana responded to the warm tingle as Roger's hands reinvigorated her back. Whatever the after-shave or bath gel Roger had used was providing a sweet comforting fragrance as she decided on how she should reciprocate. Roger would not have thanked her for clasping him in an embrace of ice cold, yet an inner glow started to course through her. Her hands, now restored to working order, were stroking and caressing him in return. She closed her eyes. She could hear Roger breathing more quickly. She hugged him tighter. She looked into his face which was reddening. Oh God! Was he about to explode either from embarrassment or from the effects of her ministrations? She wasn't particularly bothered. She was enjoying the physical presence of a man who hopefully was enjoying her just as much.

'Bloody hell, Diana, we must stop this. I'm so sorry! I haven't felt like this for ages! I shouldn't be ....' Roger tried to pull away from her. Diana held her hands tight around his waist, a wicked smile crossed her face.

'Dear old Roge! Quite like old times, eh?' She moved her hands and started to unbutton the rest of his shirt. She stroked the golden hairs of his bare chest. She moved her face closer to his. She kissed his cheek gently.

'Diana, I'm a married man with children and responsibilities.' Roger looked at her with an ironic smile.

'Roger, at this particular moment, you're just a man who's looking after a woman who needs to be warmed up.' Diana moved her fingers and dug them gently into the small of his back. She kissed him gently on the lips, smiled and then went on. 'Your attention to duty has surpassed all expectations. So much so that not only is the woman warmed up, but she is now ready for even closer attention. Are you going to turn down a lady in distress?'

Roger's response to the posed question was quick, awkward and determined. His hands were already working on Diana's silk shirt; any attempt at teasing technique long forgotten as buttons pinged to the carpeted floor like hailstones.

'Hold on, Tiger! This shirt cost me two hundred quid from Harvey Nichols. Control your urges and respect the lady's clothing.' Diana liked the idea that she could manage the proceedings as she unfixed the remaining button of her shirt, before throwing it wantonly onto the floor. 'You go and run the shower and warm it up for me.' Roger moved away, discarding his own shirt onto the floor as he went.

Diana stepped out of her soaked trousers. Underwear soon followed onto the pile with her damaged shirt. She caught a glimpse of herself in the mirror. Whilst her naked body may have matched Marilyn Monroe's dress size, the contours may not have. The breasts were less fulsome, the hips a little wider. What the hell! She was excited enough not to care. She hoped that Roger felt the same. Whatever his performance, they were going to have some fun.

As she approached the bathroom, a hand extended from behind the door bearing a white hotel dressing gown.

'Oh come off it, Roger. This is no time for modesty. I hope that this is about wanton depraved sex!'

She put on the gown so that it hung with a seductive looseness that hid part of each breast, yet revealed more than she had shown anybody else for the last year. Roger appeared from behind the bathroom door and tried avert his eyes.

'Come off it, Roger ! You've seen it all before.' Diana looked at the faint tan of his exposed chest, the rest of his body covered by a large white bath towel. He stood in front of her, his face flushed, taking in deep breaths. Diana panicked for a moment. Christ! Was he going to have a seizure? She had forgotten that he was nearly sixty. Maybe, she should quell her ardour and stop the show while he was still alive. She let him go past her as he moved to the mini-bar. He pulled out two miniature bottles of whisky.

'This'll warm us up even more.' Roger extended a glass to her.

Diana smiled as she downed the spirit in one. The fire inside her began to mix with playful mischief. She retrieved another bottle from the fridge and emptied the contents into her glass. As Roger moved towards the sofa at the far side of the bedroom, Diana ripped away his towel. The milk white flabbyness of his lower body glared in the harsh light of the room.

'Do take your bloody socks off, Roge!'

Having stripped off the last items of clothing, Roger stood totally naked, his slightly bloated stomach pulled in as best he could. He could hear himself breathing more quickly. He moved towards Diana and peeled the dressing gown off her back.

'Adam and Eve, naked as nature intended, eh! You look gorgeous, Diana! Would you care to join me?' Roger was pleased with his coy announcement as he gestured to the long wide sofa. They both sat down and Diana nestled into the crook of Roger's arm as she stroked the hairs on his chest.

'No Viagra for you, then!' She chuckled.

'My libido has certainly not left the building I'm delighted to say. Sex with Mary is a rare occurrence these days.' Roger replied. 'She just has other preoccupations. You might just have to refresh my memory about what happens.'

Diana watched his eyes close as her hands moved downwards.

'Oh Christ, Diana, Stop!' Roger jumped up. 'I've left the bloody shower running for you. Do you want to use it first?'

'Do you know something, Roge? Cleanliness is the last thing on my mind right now. Just turn off the bloody shower. I will head for the bed.'

Diana felt that a provocative pose among the marshmallow nest of white pillows on the bed should greet her Casanova on his return from attending to the shower. Roger's own taps were still very much turned on. Within seconds, he was kissing her enthusiastically. She felt his hands playing over her body in search of whatever they could find. She pushed him away. Why was it that men were always so bloody unsubtle and so impetuous? There was nothing gentle about Roger. Diana drew breathe as she took another sip of whisky from her glass. A flash of lightning outside the window confirmed that there were not many better places for her to be at that moment. 'That's one helluva storm going on outside, Roge. I feel one of our own brewing inside. So show me what you've got!'

Flashes of lightning lit up the passion. The curtain of rain across the window hid the sight of the couple locked in intensity as they stroked and fondled towards the ultimate climax of desire. The constant rage of the storm muffled Diana's sighs of inner pleasure. A respite in the wind matched Roger's quiet relief that he had still been able to do it.

++++

Roger looked at Diana lying next to him in the darkness of the room. He could see that one eye was closed, yet the other looked

233

towards the eerie light coming from the television as captions blazed their way across the screen.

"Widespread floods hit Guandong Province... Harbour winds reach 130kph... winds lash coast... much damage..."

'Look at that bloody weather! Poor sods! ' Diana sounded reconciled to the situation. The screen was showing a chart that identified the location of the eye of the storm. 'This is going to be costly.'

Roger smiled to himself as he continued to watch the weatherman relate excitedly about the level of storm damage that had affected the region. He remained impassive to Diana's reaction.

'I know it'll depend on how many claims we actually receive, but it looks as if we could be in for a real tanking. I've seen enough, Roger!'

Roger had not seen three o'clock in the morning for some years as he moved closer to the warm front next to him. It was not every day that he was able to enjoy the presence of an attractive woman willing to give herself to him so unrestrainedly. With the extinguishing of the television, Diana's hands gently rekindled their passion. The glow from the street lights filtered through the curtains found Roger crouched behind Diana in what the Kama Sutra might have termed "wondrous congress of man to woman from rear". Suddenly, the hotel phone rang.

Roger's passion dropped like coconuts from a palm tree. Arousal was replaced by irritation. It could only be Mary. Remember, she's in Singapore? Would she have arrived? Telephone lines can be very inconsistent even in this day and age. Stay calm! Act naturally!

'Hello old thing!' Roger tried to sound sleepy and distracted. ' No, we're...I'm fine. .....Yes, it is rather blowy. I'm in safe hands at the hotel. Where are you? .... Still in Singapore? What a bore for you! You've seen the pictures of the storm? Sorry! What was that? The line's breaking up. I can hardly hear you. Call me when you get to England. Have a safe journey! Bye!'

Roger disconnected the line, cutting off Mary in mid-conversation, stemming her concerns after seeing pictures of the storm on the Ten O' Clock News. He hoped that she would be reassured by the sound of his voice, even if what he had said would have made little sense. He turned back to Diana.

'After all that, she's still in Singapore, at the airport, can you believe that?

'Roger, I'm willing to believe anything. I really don't care. There's some unfinished business which is far more important.'

'Diana! You're insatiable!' Roger looked at the prostrate nakedness of the Director of Compliance and Claims for Crosthwaites Marine Insurance.

'Now where were we?' Roger lay down beside Diana and kissed her.

Diana wanted to enjoy the last moments of her lack of restraint before she returned to her own room. The busy schedule of her final day in Hong Kong was about to become even busier. The likely losses from the storm would certainly run into several hundreds of millions of dollars. A night with Roger Mortlock was as good a panacea as anything before the maelstrom of forthcoming claims engulfed her.

++++

Roger was woken by the menacing buzz of his mobile phone. He could not restrain himself from looking at the message.

'Have spoken with J. He looking forward to a visit next week. Needs cheering up. C'

Roger sensed that his good cheer would provide John with just the fillip necessary.

He looked back towards the sleeping shape of Diana; a bare leg protruded from under the sheet. Fault lines of smudged mascara, faint traces of make-up remained on her comatose face. An occasional snore interrupted the stillness within the room. Sleeping with the enemy was a reckless strategy. It was not that Roger had fallen in love with her. This was just sex with an attractive woman, expressions of lust and desire as described in romantic novels and countless top-shelf magazines, although not necessarily in Yachting Monthly. The Royal Northwood International School would continue to be the smokescreen that would cloud all else.

Roger turned on the television again and watched the News Channel silently as the caption *"Storm – Breaking news"* hung over frenzied scenes of people wading knee-deep in muddy water inter-cut with those of palm trees being threshed by the wind. Then, the "money shot" that Roger had hoped for, an entanglement of wrecked sailing boats in a small marina. The sickening pictures of the devastation of people's possessions and the ruin of their livelihoods were countered by the elation of his correct reading of the meteorological charts. The Phantom Fleet in South China had sunk with all hands. He had seen enough. There would be considerable good cheer to brighten even the darkest of prison cells when he visited his partner. In the meantime, he needed to extricate himself from the warm clutches of Diana and the battered, wetter ones of Hong Kong.

++++

Chapter Twenty Four

The Waiting Game

John lay on his bed listening to the contented cooing of pigeons amid the flaking plaster of the courtyard walls. What he would not have given for a bit of early morning rumpy-pumpy with Candida at that present moment!

John had not received any visitors since Candida's quick exit back to Bisbury. His Blackberry having been confiscated, he had been allowed access to the one telephone in his block where Candida had updated him with news of her campaign for his freedom. John still held the memory of their final embrace and the receding sight of her shapely figure, tightly wrapped in a skirt more suited to a Ladies' Lunch in Bisbury than the ugly confines of a Spanish Remand Centre.

Day had followed day with monotonous similarity, whilst John waited for his lawyer or for the man from the British Consulate to bring him news of his case. Most mornings, John would sit in a state of disbelief on one of many plastic chairs strewn around a small courtyard. He asked himself repeatedly how long it took to prepare a simple Medical Report on Charlie's bruised jaw. In the absence of any answer, John resorted to measuring the distance travelled by a snail that had attached itself to the base of his chair which he had claimed as his own. John had marked its shell with a coloured pen bought from the small shop near to the block's only telephone. He had then monitored its progress in the courtyard over the following days. By the end of the fourth day, the shell had moved no more than fifteen feet. The following morning, John had found a squished mess a little further on. He just hoped that this was not going to be how the Spanish legal system was going to treat him.

The change of clothing and the bottle of suntan lotion brought by Candida had stood him in reasonable stead. A dollop of lotion had been traded with some fraudster from Bagshot for a copy of the previous day's English newspaper. John had been less keen to enter into a deal for a pack of mints with the man from Melton Mowbray, whose crime had been to drive his hired car into a wall after consuming an excessive amount of Sangria. The stink of alcohol and peppermint still hung on the man's breath like last week's fish.

There had been moments which John had put to more constructive use. Not only had the draft of the Family Diaries been scoured and read no less than three times, he had also taken up Perse's suggestion which Candida had passed on during one of their short phone calls. By the tenth morning, John's written notes were making increasingly gloomy reading, suitable only for those wanting to take satisfaction in other people's hardship. As he struggled to think of any upbeat phrase or indeed any coherent sentence, Silvia knocked on his door.

'Si!' John replied, expecting the butler to come in bearing a silver salver.

'There is somebody to see you.' Silvia had not brought the man's visiting card. 'He is an Englishman with not much hair. He is bringing a bag with him. We have searched it. There is nothing of interest except a laptop computer.'

John walked into the Reception Room to be met by the ebullient face of Roger Mortlock. He wondered, for a joyful moment, whether Roger's bright blue shirt, khaki shorts and sandals might have been the result of a special dispensation allowing the men to go to the beach. John stayed within Roger's manly hug for a few extra moments.

'Hello Johnno! You look really well. Lots of healthy sun, I would imagine. Are they feeding you properly? Not just gruel or bowls of plain rice?'

John watched Roger tinker with his laptop. The screen filled with images from the outside world. Did all his visitors need to remind him of what he was missing?

'Candida told me that you needed cheering up.'

'The only thing that's going to cheer me up is to get out of here.' Looking at Roger's straight face, he continued. 'Oh I get it! Are you in charge of the break-out? ' Silvia stood in the shadows by the door attending to her nails. John lowered his voice to a whisper. 'I'm afraid the tunnel committee have failed miserably, Roger! Lack of wooden beds! '

'Nothing like that, Johnno. There's an awful lot else that I can report to you. I thought that we'd have a Board Meeting of BDN to bring you up to date.'

'You can't hold a Board Meeting here! Are you quite mad?'

'Hold on, Johnno! Just be patient! ' Roger grabbed John's arm. 'You're about to see something that will really put a smile back on your face.' Roger then tapped the keys of the laptop.

A page showing the Red Diamond logo of the National Bank of Everson flashed up.

'Where is this?' John asked.

'Bahamas. Everson is one of the small islands. It's very pretty. Very peaceful. Three hundred miles from the Florida coast. We've been depositing the cheques from Crosthwaites in an account which we've opened there.'

'For the four boats that we've insured? That's seems a long way to go for four measly cheques.' John had not wanted to sound too ungracious at Roger's news . 'I suppose you didn't bring any post for me?' News of a more legitimate nature from Wayne or from Moncrieffs would be much more welcome. He could not look at Roger's screen any more, melancholia was taking greater hold. 'You know that Candida's threatening to ride through Bisbury as Lady Godiva as a stunt to promote my case? It's so demeaning!'

'I did hear something about that from Mary. She said that it would be like old times for Candida!'

'Not outside, in the cold! She's never done that and I hope that she won't have to do..... ever!' John saw the devilment on Roger's face as he looked again at the computer screen. Oh God, what else has he been up to? He braced himself as Roger clicked on to the next page.

'Actually, Johnno, you'll be very pleased to hear that our losses have been considerably more than four. As you can see from the bank statement on the screen, the typhoon season in the South China region was been very active. There was quite a storm over the Sebastian Islands a few weeks ago which left quite a trail of damage in its wake. It took not only our first four, but....'

'You mean, there are others? Bloody hell, Roger!' John looked down at the computer screen. The list of payments filled the page. The total at the bottom filled him with horror!

'Roger, close down the computer!' John panicked. 'Have you taken leave of your senses? If anyone sees this, we'll end up in prison! This time, it'll be a proper one! '

'That's precisely why I'm here, Johnno!' Although he had checked previously that Freedom of Speech within prison was sacrosanct, Roger lowered his voice in case any secret microphones in the room were active. All private conversations should remain completely private.

'There are probably cameras all over the place looking at ......that! ' John gesticulated angrily at the screen. 'They'll arrest you when you leave here. You've really overstepped the mark this time, Roger.'

'I thought you'd be pleased.' Roger's smile was still plastered over his face. 'This will go a good way towards filling the hole left by your Charlie, surely?' Roger's enthusiasm could not be dampened. 'The Sebastian Sea storm was nothing. Just you wait for the Typhoon Harri! I was there, Johnno! I tell you the place really shook! I just couldn't let the opportunity pass without Gavin's book of business taking a real pasting. So, I instructed our local man to place boats in the regions that I thought would be most affected.' Roger's eyes were ablaze. 'We've put in for claims on quite a few yachts of varying sizes, two pleasure junks and two small motor cruisers in total! Crosthwaites should be paying out quite a tidy little sum. Mind you, it's not been totally plain sailing.' John wondered why Roger had scrolled onto other images on the screen before settling on a picture of ugly looking motor cruiser. 'I've found a very useful partner who has been terribly helpful. What's more, she's let us in on a very interesting investment opportunity.'

'That looks enormous! Roger, what have you done?'

'Pleasure cruising around the islands of Hong Kong is very big business. That's Mavis, our partner, with one of the boat's skippers.' Roger explained'

The picture of a short Chinese woman being towered over by a tall dark-haired girl in her late twenties did little to reassure him of the merits of the investment. The girl's peaked cap with gold braid and a bright red swimsuit did not seem the most suitable uniform.

'She looks very attractive, Roger, but can she handle a boat? Is she wearing standard issue uniform?' John sensed that Roger had charted a highly irregular course.

'That's the uniform for moving out of harbour. When they're out in the open sea, dress code is much more relaxed.' Roger smiled. 'The *Serenity on the Seas* is tremendously popular with bankers and insurance executives. They all have more money than they know what to do with. My thinking is to let those bastards put some of their riches our way. Come boom or bust!'

John walked away from the table and stared at the wall. The money had gone to Roger's head. In the excitement of his success with Crosthwaites, he had got totally carried away, frittering away money on madcap schemes like this floating brothel. He needed to be controlled yet John felt totally powerless whilst he was cooped up inside his stupid little cell.

'How much has this investment cost, Roger?'

'A few thou....not much. Mavis has been very reasonable. She has other.......'

Both men stopped as they heard a knock on the door. They watched Silvia disappear outside. She returned a few moments later.

'Excuse me , Meester Smeeth! There is another man to see you. He says that it is quite urgent.'

John saw Roger's face go blank for a moment. John had been right after all. It had all been far too good to be true. Every word of their conversation had been bugged. The computer images had been secretly recorded. Future board meetings would certainly have a regular location, in a prison cell. They had been victims of the most naïve of honey-traps. He saw the familiar shape of the lawyer, Luis Cortez, appear in the doorway. That was quick! At least John was being afforded proper legal representation from the outset. He waited for the burly figure of Inspector Calculzia to enter the room to be followed by somebody from Interpol and the State Executioner. None appeared.

Roger had closed down the computer and was packing it away from the prying eyes of the not unattractive guard. He was unsure what was happening. Should he unleash his speech about his and John's human rights? Maybe, it had been a little fanciful to push his luck. Scarpering was certainly not an available option. He watched the man with a small goatee beard pull out a sheet of paper from his briefcase before presenting it to John.

'OK Luis! What does it say? Have they been listening in? Where's the inspector?'

'Listening to what, my friend? The inspector has gone home. You are a free man, John!' the lawyer announced. 'You can go back to Bisbury. The charges have been dropped. It is good, yes?'

John sat back in his chair in a state of shock as the news sank in. He started to breathe again as he saw a faint smile appear on Silvia's face.

'Come on Johnno!' Roger was placing his computer in his small overnight bag. . 'I'm taking you home to mother.'

'Before you go, Meester Smeeth.' Silvia was brandishing a form and a pen. ' You please fill in Comment Card. We need to get Feed-back from all detainees. How can we improve the service we provide our guests?'

'Yes, I'll fill it in. Not enough space. Too many doors locked at night. No clear access to the outside world.'

John snatched the card from Silvia's hand and rushed to the phone-box. He called Candida. 'The bastard's dropped the charges. Remorse finally got the better of him, I suspect.'

John listened to Candida's sigh of relief at the other end of the phone.

'Maybe, Johnnie, maybe. Anyway, just come home. Don't get into any more fights! Go straight to the airport with Roger. He's sensible enough to keep you out of trouble.'

++++

Chapter Twenty Five

The Return of the Bisbury One

The flight back to Birmingham had given John and Roger ample time to catch up on what the other had missed.

'This Everson place sounds a great place for a holiday, Roger. Coral sands, turquoise seas, I presume, and a few shops. Just the ticket for Candida and me.'

'Very exclusive, very upmarket, Johnno, and just one bank. What could be better? ' Roger had remembered the island's website . *"Everson always! You'll not regret it!"* Hidden away in an archipelago of small islands, Everson seemed ideal for secretive archiving of funds. 'although, Johnno, I would wait a few weeks until the big depression over Haiti heads away. Not much sun at the moment, I'm afraid.'

'So the Fleet has now expanded to the Caribbean?'

'I arranged this Squadron some weeks ago. It was only a matter of time before the Caribbean would be affected. I think that we've a few in the right position.'

'So, where else then?'

'Eastern Seaboard of the United States, maybe? There are still storms in the Philippines. I'm very hopeful of another strike in that area before the end of the season. So tell me about your arrangement with Giles.'

On leaving the Remand Centre, John had welcomed the opportunity to re-acquaint himself with his Blackberry. There had been a stream of unread messages which would require his attention when he reached home. The one from Giles Fortescue-Smythe had been the most welcome.

'The bank very keen to develop this SpeedyTrans system for their foreign currency department.'

John had been glad to impart some good news of his own into the extra-ordinary board meeting of BDN at a height of thirty seven thousand feet. 'They're on the look-out for any non-debt products that will make them some money.'

'So are the insurance companies. They're looking for anything that will enable them to offset the losses brewing with this toxic debt business. Maybe, I could meet with the Chief's Son to discuss opportunities?'

'Good idea! I'll sort it!'

The plane landed. The two men made their way through Customs and out into the freedom of the arrival hall of the airport. A shriek rent the air as they came through the doors. Mary Mortlock rushed forward to embrace both her husband and his newly released charge. Candida stood her ground. She noticed the white linen jacket hung more loosely on her husband's shoulders. The tanned face failed to conceal the tired eyes and the drawn expression of a man who was badly in need of a good meal. Whereas other passengers were wheeling their luggage trolleys laden with suitcases and the occasional sombrero, John came towards her with just his small leather valise and the air of a naughty schoolboy after detention. He fell into the clasp of her open arms.

Candida had decided that any waving of banners welcoming home *The Bisbury One* would have been excessive. She had winced at Mary's expression of joy. Her rush through the tide of new arrivals to greet both men as if they had emerged after years of captivity with Al Quaieda terrorists seemed excessive. Candida was just pleased to have her husband back and to have been saved the ordeal of riding down Bisbury High Street in a flesh-coloured body suit. She had not relished a return to her days of exhibitionism even if the motives for it would have been totally justified. She just looked forward to lying in the same bath as her husband and to washing away the odour of stale clothing and the ghastly memory of the past ten days.

As they both strode away from the terminal building at the airport, John used his phone to call Giles.

'Welcome back! Did you have a good holiday?' John was glad that Giles knew nothing.

'It was great! So great in fact, that I stayed on for longer than I intended. That's one of the benefits of retirement, you can adjust your plans at a whim. It's good news about *SpeedyTrans*.'

'I know. We're going for a wider field test. Wayne's people are working closely with our IT and Currency people for a very quick roll-out. It's good to provide something that our customers really want!'

Candida steered the Volvo away from the airport. John sat in the passenger seat amid the faint stench of horse and the leather bridles that were stacked in the back of the car. Anything was a welcome change from the smell of incarceration and male recklessness that had permeated La Laguna. Whilst Candida fretted behind a slow-travelling truck that was impeding her progress, John contemplated why Clive Hunt, the ex-Works Convenor at Smiths Screws, might have wanted to call him during his absence. He pressed in the number.

'Who are you calling now? You've only been back three minutes and you're on the bloody phone again!'

'I'm calling Clive Hunt.'

'Y'mean old Whattock? You don't need to bother about him. He and I have had some lovely chats whilst you've been away.'

Candida braked suddenly as she took in the fact that the car in front had slowed to a standstill. John's call was already ringing at the other end.

'Gaffer! It's good to have you back! No lasting aftershocks from your stay in Spain, I trust? Has the Missus told you everything?'

'Not really. What's to tell?'

++++

'So, my release has been a victory for good old fashioned campaigning amongst the Great British Public?' John playfully squeezed the sponge down Candida's face. He was relishing the heady mix of hot water and fragrant bath oil as she sat nestled against his chest in the large tub in their bathroom.

'Not really! Rather one for gentle feminine persuasion......' Her hands washed a froth of soapy bubbles over the hairs of his bronzed arms. She then turned to look back at him. '....but with a bit of additional help.'

John kissed her on the forehead and caressed her. He sensed her smug satisfaction at having her explanation being gently teased from her.

'Not from Whattock Hunt? Surely not?'

'He showed me his album.'

'You mean his snaps of his walks in the Yorkshire Dales?'

'Some of those and also some of his work colleagues.'

'Oh God, not the Ramblers Club? He was always trying to encourage me to join. It would be good for my health, he said. It would keep me vibrant and fertile for the younger wife, he said!'

'No worries there, Johnnie!' Candida looked back at her husband, the recent memory of energetic expressions of physical love and emotional release in the bedroom still fresh in her mind.

She then stood up to reach for her towel. 'These were pictures of Charlie and.....'

'Not ...' John let out a yell as cramp gripped his left leg. His curiosity was dulled as he jumped up on his operative leg and let out a cry of anguish. Candida watched her Tarzan, without the loincloth, hop about as he tried to ease the paralysing pain. She rushed to massage the affected leg to soothe his discomfort.

Moments later, John continued. 'You mean that Clive got hold of those photos that Francine told you about.' His mind was racing. Not only was Charlie a thief and a bare-arsed liar, but now he was now pushing porno pictures of his voluptuous partner. After the ineffectiveness of *Ishy's Googly Honey*, John perhaps could understand Clive's need to search for alternatives to spice up his sex life with the authoritative Daphne.

'Absolutely!' Candida was brushing her hair. 'Apparently, Charlie used to show them to the foundry lads after work down at the pub. He was quite proud of them. Clive didn't tell me whether he and Missus Hunt ever applied the techniques illustrated.'

'Did he show you the pictures?'

'Not all of them. Only the ones of special interest.... of Charlie totally unabashed. It was not a pleasant sight at ten o'clock in the morning over a cup of tea and a biscuit, I can tell you, Johnnie.'

'These were taken by Francine, presumably?'

'Actually no! Neither was she in front of the camera either. Instead, Charlie was enjoying the company of two women I'd never seen before.' Candida's face lit up with a beguiling smile as her tale took its mischievous turn. 'Clive and I agreed that these were quite clearly Charlie's property and that they should be returned to him and to Francine PDQ. So, I called Charlie at his apartment which you have so kindly provided. I mentioned that I had these photos in my possession.' She slipped on a white sloppy T-shirt over her bare dry body. 'I really milked it, Johnnie.

You'd have loved it!' She pulled on a pair of tracksuit trousers as John sat on the edge of the bath, transfixed by her tale of intrigue.

'Charlie hadn't been surprised to hear from me, but he was rather taken aback by my revelations. He suggested that he would prefer that Francine not be offered the opportunity to see the pictures. Since the villa was in her name, he did not relish being chucked out to sleep on the beach.'

Candida was shouting to John as she finished brushing her hair. 'I said that I fully understood his predicament. So I then asked if he would do one small thing for me in return to prevent me sending on the pictures directly to Francine by courier.'

As she looked at herself in the mirror, Candida was relishing the memory of the conversation. It was still fresh as ever. She had worried that Charlie might have laughed off her proposition with dismissive claims that he and Francine had an open relationship and that the photographs were taken such a long time ago as not to matter any more. She had waited nervously for Charlie's response. The unexpectedly short time that it had taken for Charlie to call her back and the obvious unease with which he delivered his explanation had certainly brightened her day.

"I've spoken with the *Justicia*, Candida." Charlie announced. "I've asked them to drop the charges against John." Relief had flooded through her as she listened to Charlie's pathetic excuses about frolics at the Screws & Fasteners Conference in Stockholm some years ago. Yet, there had been no apology, no acceptance of the crime that Charlie himself had committed. Whilst she had enjoyed the satisfaction of forcing an objectionable and untrustworthy man into submission, Candida had decided that no stone was going to be left unturned.

"What about repayment of the loan, Charlie?"

"Francine and I have talked about this. We've made some calculations and we think that maybe we can just about afford a repayment of five thousand euros a year ......" Candida had been gobsmacked by the reply. "We've decided that we'll leave the villa in our wills to you and John when we both snuff it. We've nobody else to leave it to. Let's get on with the rest of our lives, eh?"

'So, he gave in just like that?' John asked innocently as he approached her. 'Candida, my darling, you are terrific!'

'More or less.' Candida replied. 'Do put some clothes on, Johnnie. I really can't go through the whole sex thing again, however alluring you may look with your bricklayers' tan.'

John looked in the mirror and saw the white flesh of his upper chest contrast with his bronzed arms and neck. 'I've found a great place for us for Christmas.'

'A villa in the Maldives? A large estate in the Bahamas?'

'Nearly! Have you heard of Everson? It's one of the smaller islands in the Bahamas. It has a small landing strip, a long coral beach, turquoise sea. There are some great houses there. We can just relax.'

The tale was at an end. John knew as much as she did. Her work was nearly done as she looked at his undernourished shape.

'Time to feed you up! Then you must visit Clive at the pub he's just opened. He's very excited about it! He can then show you all his sleazy pictures himself!'

++++

'When you say ambassador for the school, what does it mean, Roger? Do you have to wander around in a cocked hat with a plume of white feathers looking, like a silly bugger? '

'No, Mary! The Board of Trustees wants me to represent the interests of the Royal Northwood School here in the UK.'

The questions had not really stopped since Roger had sat down at their favourite table at their favourite restaurant in Bisbury. Mary's inquisition had been interspersed with swigs from her gin and tonic. Roger's sixtieth birthday had crept up on him. He was being treated by Mary to a friendly, intimate dinner at the *Il Pirata* restaurant. Husband and wife sat at the corner table where the subdued light hid the effort each had made to glam up for the occasion. Roger could not decide whether the large silver hoops dangling from his wife's ears were meant to look like spare curtain rings. The long flowing burgundy cardigan and black trousers had certainly given her an elegance that he had not seen for some time. Roger had put on one of the new shirts he had bought in the Duty Free at Hong Kong airport during the long wait for his flight home. He was pleased that his further involvement with the Royal Northwood International School Appeal Fund was standing up to the close scrutiny of his wife.

'Does your ambassadorial role also cover Singapore?' Mary asked after giving her order and handing back the menu to the waiter. 'When I spoke to you on the phone, I couldn't understand the bit about Singapore.'

'Not at the moment.' Roger had wondered if the arrant nonsense in his hotel bedroom had been picked up. 'I don't remember mentioning Singapore. Maybe because the line was so clear, you sounded as if you were actually in Singapore. I can't honestly remember. All I do know that it was very blowy.'

'Oh really! My end of the line certainly sounded rather crackly. It cut off halfway through the conversation. Never mind! If there's a chance of your going to Singapore, then I'm coming with you. I've never been there.'

'The way things are looking at the moment, there may not be much travelling.' Roger needed to head Mary's idea off at the pass immediately. 'Whilst this debt crisis is on, everybody's a bit more hesitant about the venture. They still want me to help them, but for the next few weeks, maybe months, they'll wait and see how it goes.' Roger's explanation had seemed credible.

'I don't really understand what's going on. Whenever I watch the News, all the totals are so enormously high; they're like pretend-numbers to me. All I'm concerned about is making sure that I get enough people to do the Fun Run next weekend. You're still going to do it, aren't you Roger?'

'Absolutely! I have a page on my website with lots of people sponsoring me.'

'I'll pass on the address to you where the money should go. It's a new charity I've found. Anyway, happy birthday, Roger!'

The couple clinked glasses and looked towards each other with a momentary affection. Roger savoured the Montalcino red with an appreciation of its light mellow flavour served at the right temperature amid a relief that he had successfully jumped the obstacles planted by Mary. The waiter brought a light salad with walnuts for Mary and a bowl of hot steaming minestrone for Roger as both tucked in.

'Is this the Children's School in Africa where you think we should visit this Christmas?' Roger seized his moment. 'Now Mary old girl, I've told you about my school. Tell me more about this place.'

'Well, Roger. I found it on the internet....'

++++

Chapter Twenty Six

Roger's progress

'Three Lagers - Three plasmas – Three Topless barmaids (only joking!)
Stop by and see them!'

The message handwritten in luminous yellow paint on the blackboard beckoned John as he pulled into the small car-park of the Golden Parrot. Formerly a station on the "Workmens line" to Longbridge and Birmingham, the two storey building was not just the only pub for miles around, it was the only building that stood on the winding rat-run from Bisbury to Birmingham. John noticed the small script above the doorway "*C. Hunt, licensed to sell beers and spirits.*" He stepped inside and was disappointed to see that the outdoor invitation had proved only partially successful. Where hundreds had once waited to be transported to the assembly lines at the car factory a few miles up the track, now the erstwhile ticket hall housed only a few drinkers at tables littered around the room. Tuesday lunchtime perhaps was not the most suitable time for a good attendance by thirsty customers. Nevertheless, two screens were ablaze showing anonymous football games, the third featured a blonde newsreader mouthing silently, as captions rushed along the base of the screen announcing the increase in the price of oil and the weakening of the dollar. The topless barmaids were absent. Only the faint sound of Dusty Springfield's strident voice and giggling from two girls in the corner broke the silence.

John heard the rustling of a newspaper in a nearside room and the faint footsteps of somebody approaching the bar.

'How do, gaffer!' Clive Hunt appeared from a room behind the bar and stood proudly in front of the parade of beer taps.

John was impressed. Dressed in a white shirt and bright blue tie, his ex-Works Convenor, Factory Foreman and sometime pain-in-the-arse looked better suited to sell John a new car than to pull him a pint of Meon's Best.

'This one's on the house! It's not often that we receive someone who has returned from being interred in a foreign land.'

'Interned, Clive! They didn't bury me in Spain.'

'Whatever! It's good to see you back. That Weatherhead was a right pillock who should not have done what he did.'

'I did hit him, though.'

'But you had your reasons. If you borrow money, then you have to pay it back. It stands to reason. Charlie should have been straight with you.' Clive handed over the beer. 'That Francine, she's a right minx. I never trusted her.'

John savoured his first sip of beer in the same way as he had his first moments of freedom. He closed his eyes and let the chilled hoppy brew remain with him for a few seconds. In the days since his return from Spain, John had stayed within the cosy confines of Mulberry Farm Cottage. Candida had been busy at the Equestrian Centre. The phone messages had remained on the answer machine. The Blackberry had delivered e-mails. The answers would be provided in due course. As he took another swig, John reckoned that liberty was worth drinking to. At the moment he was enjoying the peace.

'You didn't last long with Sven, did you?'

'Once you'd gone, Mister John, it was not the same place. Langstrom Dynamic Fasteners was always going to be different. Then Sven brought in a fellow named Gustav to manage the place.

He was all very businesslike, offering us incentives and targets in return for the introduction of multi-skilled practices. It was all bollocks to a lot of us, who just wanted to do an honest day's work for good pay. It all cultivated when Gustav came in and said that there's a reception coming on and there would have to be cutbacks.'

'So, the recession has resulted in you taking more of Sven's money by way of a redundancy package?' John had given up trying to correct Clive, but he was not surprised by his news.

'I look at it another way; that he has invested in my future with this pub. By the way, there's a bloke waiting for you in the corner. We want to encourage businessmen like him to come here for a quiet meeting, curtively without anybody intercepting. ' Clive gestured to the sight of Roger Mortlock crouched over his laptop. John decided that Clive needed a bit more attention first.

'I'm very grateful for your help, Clive.' John went on. 'I'm amazed that Charlie gave you the pictures in the first place.'

'You mean these?' Clive had brought out a buff envelope and had begun to lay the contents out on the bar. 'I nicked'em from him. I thought they might come in useful during our wage negotiations.'

'With me?'

'Just in case I needed to apply pressure over something. Y'know, a bargaining chip.'

'Thank goodness it never came to that. You'd have placed me in a very difficult position.'

'I know. That's the art of labour relations.'

John had not realised how effective blackmail could be as he made his way to the corner. He passed a notice-board promoting *"It's all happening at the Golden Parrot!"*. Having established that Tuesday night was good for Domino players, his eye was caught by a small poster inviting him to sign the petition to *"Free John*

Smith, the Bisbury One". John counted four illegible signatures and a scribbled comment at the bottom of the page.

"If it would help, you can swap my husband, the cheating bastard, for the innocent John Smith!"

Roger lifted his head as John sat down next to him.

'You'll be pleased to hear that Everson is still standing after the storm. Other islands have experienced more severe problems.'

'That's good news for me and you; bad news for the Phantom Fleet, presumably?'

'I'm afraid so! About half of the squadron placed on the Dominican Republic and South Florida has been lost. Another that we placed in the Philippines is undergoing a severe battering as we speak. I'm not certain how many we will have lost there. We've been very fortunate with the weather.'

'I think that you're being too modest, Roger. It should be minuted that a vote of thanks be extended to the meteorology division of the company.'

'That's very generous of you, Johnno. I'm touched by your kindness.'

Both men lifted their glasses in acclamation of the Board's sentiment.

'Gentlemen!' A voice boomed from around the corner of the pub. 'That's where you are!'

The giggling girls in the other corner had looked up from their conversation to take in the bright red jacket and open-neck white shirt as Wayne Oduku approached.

'King Onan, I presume?' Roger whispered before John stood up to shake Wayne's hand.

'You must be Roger, then.' Wayne's smile beamed across his face. 'John's told me all about you I.....insurance, wasn't it? A very interesting business. Badly managed , but full of potential.'

Wayne sat down in the remaining armchair as Clive appeared with his order pad. Disappointed that distribution of his company's Mother Nature range of non-alcoholic drinks had not reached the more remote parts of the Midlands, Wayne was pleased by the landlord's acceptance of his offer of a sample pack to try out on his customers. He was less certain about his choice of Mrs Hunt's home-baked beef and apple pie. Since the others had opted for it with their beer, he was willing to give it the benefit of the doubt with an orange juice and a cup of coffee.

'Moncrieffs are delighted.' Wayne announced, as Clive walked away with the food and drink order. 'They're currently handling something like five thousand transactions a day. In the first six weeks of operation, they've recorded a fifteen percent increase in foreign exchange turnover, year on year.' Wayne's enthusiasm could not be stopped. 'They've taken on a number of new clients. Giles is convinced that this success is due to the faster service provided by the *SpeedyTrans* system.'

'That's terrific, Wayne.' John saw that Roger had closed the lid of his lap-top and was taking closer interest in Wayne's detailed analysis.

'Many of the transactions are small, like restaurant and hotel bills. Yet, other transactions have been far larger.'

'What do Moncrieffs get out of it?' Roger needed to join in the conversation.

'A handling fee for each transaction plus a small margin on the sale of the currency.' Wayne took a sip from the orange juice that Clive had brought him.

'What's their turnover been since the test started?' Roger asked.

'I don't know precisely. Maybe, two hundred million sterling? That's in six weeks.'

'So maybe four million for Moncrieffs?'

'Sounds about right. Moncrieffs are quite tight-lipped about it. All that I know is that Giles is planning to introduce the system into their operations in southern Africa. He has asked us to work on integrating an enhanced application to a separate account in their Johannesburg office.'

'So we need to review our arrangement with you, Wayne.' John was pleased that the bank statement in the Bahamas would be boosted by income from his own efforts.

'Very happy to.' Wayne said. 'Whilst other banks are being bailed out by the government, Moncrieffs see the situation as an opportunity to grab market share. I rather approve.' Wayne's quiet chuckle coincided with Clive's arrival with the men's order of drinks, plus Wayne's coffee. 'So whilst Giles and his people go after new business, it means that he's having to rely on my company to ensure that their control and compliance systems function properly. They should be doing it in-house, but it's such a lengthy process to recruit the extra staff necessary. So they've asked us to do it in the interim. I don't mind, as long as they're happy to pay for it.'

Roger leaned forward. 'I can think of many insurance companies who would love to get a better return on their foreign currency dealings.'

'I'm sure. Many are in as much of a mess as the banks are.' Wayne pushed his glasses onto the top of his head and stared at Roger. 'At this moment, Oduku Systems is working flat out. We just cannot cope with another new major client, more's the pity. When I see the wastage and inefficiencies within Moncrieffs, I'm not surprised by what's going on. My Dad was right when he said that bankers were lazy and arrogant.'

'Your father used London banks?'

'Sure, he had many investments in this country.'

John was glad that Wayne had accepted his invitation to meet Roger. He had been fairly sure that both would get along. He was also glad that his own contribution to the BDN partnership was beginning to bear fruit. He wondered whether the juice might be squeezed a little more. 'Wayne, as the system rolls out into other markets, maybe we should review our financial arrangement with you.'

'My thinking as well, Johnno. ' Roger had drawn up his chair closer to the others. 'What if we were to base our consultancy fee on your turnover? '

'John, I can see why you wanted me to meet your partner.' Wayne drained his cup of coffee as he contemplated his reply.

'We find the clients and....' Roger continued. John's attention was diverted by the vibrations of his phone in his jacket pocket.

'We do the work. Is that it?' Wayne leaned back in his chair as he contemplated Roger's suggestion. 'It sounds sensible, but I would need to recruit more staff. It could be very profitable.' Wayne watched John move away to attend to the call on his phone. Any extra moments, resulting from John's absence, to consider further the *SpeedyTrans* project were soon denied as Roger drew closer to him.

'This sounds a very exciting project; Wayne. I think that we can be very useful to you. Whilst we have a few moments to ourselves, tell me about your Dad. Did he have many interests in London?'

'He certainly knew a lot of people in the City of London. He also hated a lot of people in the City of London.'

'Why was that? Not that I blame him. There are lot of people in the City of London to hate.'

'He said that they stole his money that he had deposited with them. This was in the late Seventies.'

'This was money that he had earned?' Roger asked casually.

'Well, he said that it was his allowance for running Remanda. During his reign, the state became very rich from nickel mining and from gold. His people did very well. So did Daddy.   He trusted the British banking system to look after his money wisely. They advised him to invest in commercial property. Within two years, the values had fallen through the floor.   He was a very angry man and much worse off when he died.'

'I know the feeling.' Roger saw that John was still talking on the phone. There may not be many moments left.

'What feeling?'   Wayne enquired. 'Being angry, worse off or being dead?' His laughter boomed throughout the room.

'The   former,   if   you   must   know.'   Roger   smiled   in acknowledgment. 'There is much to be done before I experience the latter and I am looking to avoid the middle one altogether.' He saw that John was still talking by the entrance to the pub. 'That's why   I   was   wondering   whether   you've   considered   ways   of ....enhancing the *SpeedyTrans* system being used by Moncrieffs?'

'My   people   are   constantly   looking   to   improve   the   system. Oduku Systems is a very professional company.'

'Have   they   thought   about   ...providing   added   value   to   the package?'

The two men lowered their voices to a whisper until John returned to his chair.

'What have I missed?' John asked. 'Has Wayne offered us a revised package that's going to make us lots of money, Roger?'

'Hopefully and lots for him as well, Johnno.' Roger replied. Wayne remained silent and preoccupied with tapping the keys of his mobile.

'Oh good!' John had dropped his voice. 'Nothing like an honest buck, say I!'

Wayne   explained.   'Roger   was   just   pointing   out   how *SpeedyTrans* would be snapped up by the insurance market. A new customer means another finder's fee for you, John, plus....'

'Well, that's much better news! However, you might have to do it all without me, gentlemen, for the next few weeks at least.' John had stood up, his eyes lit like light bulbs. 'I'm going to be rather busy myself. I've got a book to finish!'

'Is this your family's diaries, still, Johnno?' Roger did not want to sound too relieved, but he was excited by having sole access to Wayne for those few weeks. 'I would've thought that a diary of your time in a Spanish jail would be far more interesting!'

As Wayne chewed on the piece of apple in his pie, he took in the unexpected revelations about his two new partners; one fair and innocent with good connections, the other more determined and imaginative and with equally good connections. After swallowing the remains of his juice, he announced. 'Gentlemen, there seems to be a lot to celebrate. A glass of champagne?'

The others agreed that a glass of bubbly would not go amiss. Clive Hunt just hoped that the Italian sparkling wine bought from the Cash and Carry would satisfy their needs.

++++

Chapter Twenty Seven

Roger's Enhancements

The drab grey morning could not dim Roger's spirits as he entered Wayne's swanky office in Notting Hill. A tall African girl in tight jeans and a body-hugging, high-necked blouse stood up from behind the desk to greet him.

'Mister Mortlock, welcome to Oduku House! I am Jackie Mzimba, Wayne's personal assistant. Unfortunately, he is running a little late and asks that you wait here a few minutes. Can I get you one of our Cooler Drinks? Watermelon or perhaps a new flavour we have just launched, Passionfruit and Ginger? Very good for you if you have high blood pressure.'

Roger thought that the Passionfruit would be the most suitable as he watched Jackie teeter on dangerously high heels to the chilled cabinet in the corner to retrieve a bottle. He sat down on the sofa in reception and looked at the collection of logos on the wall behind her. Amid those for Oduku Systems and other brands of healthy-sounding foods and drinks, Roger noticed a name that he recognised. Surely, Mary has mentioned it at his birthday dinner? *Chief Bobby's Children's Home* had featured on the webpage she had shown him when they reached home. Roger would enquire further.

'Were you also at school with Wayne and Mr John Smith?'

'No, I was more fortunate than them! I missed out on the rigours of corporal punishment and the cosiness of all-male environment by going to a co-educational school near to where my family lived.'

'I understand what you mean.' Jackie said. 'Wayne recently took me and the girls from the office to his School Reunion. What a strange place! So remote and so cut off from the outside world. I was surprised that Wayne put up with it all. But that's what his Daddy wanted for him, a good education. Your Mr John Smith was very cool, a very interesting man.' A smile crossed her face before a buzz came from the telephone on the desk. 'Wayne is ready for you now. Please follow me.'

Roger followed the clack of stiletto heel on wooden floor as the statuesque Jackie led him along the corridor to an empty glass-walled conference room. As he waited with her, Roger replied.

'I'd never thought of John as cool. I suspect that Wayne is much cooler.'

'Both cool in their separate ways. Here's the man of the moment. I'll leave you to it.'

'Roger! Welcome to my world!' Wayne burst into the room, carrying his laptop and sat down. Jackie left, closing the door behind her. 'Have we had fun with this baby? Roger, I'm telling you!' Wayne laid out a couple of spreadsheet pages on the table in front of him. 'Your suggestions tripped the wires in my people's heads like never before. They've been buzzin' with all manner of wicked thoughts. They've loved it!'

Roger was mesmerised as he looked for anything that he might comprehend amongst the algebraic formulae of letters and figures on the two sheets in front of him. It was soon apparent that he would have to rely on others not only to identify the recipe, but also the ingredients for his mischievous concoction.

'So, is it really possible?'

'Sure! It's taken a bit of time to work out, but my people have got there. These are the algorithms and the protocols that'll enable the system to do what we want.'

Roger marvelled at the patience and ingenuity of Wayne and his team of skilled computer geeks, many of whom he suspected had not seen daylight for at least a year. He listened intently as Wayne's detailed explanation of the enhancement process threatened to overcook his brain.

'How long will this nano-diversion take?'

'We've worked on ten seconds. The African version can be a little slower, since my countrymen don't work at such a fast rate. The overall transaction time requested by Moncrieffs will remain unaffected. Their customer will still receive their money within the required time-frame.'

'Has it been tested in real time?' Roger asked tentatively.

'We went live last week for a few days and nobody noticed a thing.' Wayne's face broke into a little grin. 'If they had, then we'd have passed off the discrepancy between the two figures as a glitch in the upgrade process.'

'So, when will the bank in the Bahamas receive payments?'

'Not every day, not all the time, however tempting it may be. We have keyed in specific times for the enhancement process to kick in. All the deductions will be held on a secure postle within the system. Then we will transfer the total amount to our bank. The trail will be very difficult to track and almost impossible to relate to any specific transaction.'

Roger's appreciation of the procedure was more or less complete. 'You've been able to ensure that the bank will pay more for the currency than they need to. It's important that the nano-deduction does not merit the scrutiny of even the most dedicated of auditors?'

'They will not notice such small amounts.' Wayne's cackle held a quiet satisfaction.

'Do you think that your father would have approved of what we're doing?'

'He would have been delighted. Let me show you something.'

Roger watched Wayne summon up the website for the National Bank of Everson on his laptop. Soon, a page for a different account appeared. Roger leaned forward to look at the figures displayed on the laptop's screen. Was his confidence in bank staff's lack of scrutiny about to be confirmed? A gleam appeared in Roger's eyes as he focussed on Wayne's screen, his smile could have stretched across the office.

'How many days' transactions are shown here?'

'Four days. A very busy four days, it would appear. It's not a bad total is it?'

Both men looked at each other as they assessed the potential for further mischief.

'I think that we should keep this quiet, Wayne, at least for the time-being, until the system is proven to be robust and effective. I call it the Code of the Mandarin!'

'It's not the same as the Code of Myndhams, but I'm happy to go along with it, Roger!'

'Before you go, Wayne, tell me more about your Children's Home in Remanda.'

++++

Roger could hear Mary let out her usual sigh as she stopped briefly at the entrance to his small study. He hoped that, by now, she might have accepted that his constant attention to weather maps in all parts of the globe was something that kept his mind busy and himself sane as she announced her intentions for the day.

'I'm just off to the meeting of the Local Riders Association. Then I have a regional seminar of CCRAP early this evening. Have you signed up for the Christmas Volunteer Programme at the Childrens Centre in Remanda? You said yourself that it would be very rewarding. I'm definitely going. You can do what you want, but it would be nice if we were together over Christmas, even if the kids won't be. Let's talk about it tonight, although I may not be back until late. You know how these things go on.'

Mary's involvement with the Community Council for Rural and Agriculture Protection and other worthy organisations was becoming annoyingly time-consuming. He reflected that he and she had spent more time together when he had been working. They at least made the effort to go to a concert or a play in London or to do something together at the weekend. Yet, as he sat in his chair and scrolled away from the weather map for the Indonesian Coast, Roger had never felt so invigorated, so charged by what was going on under his control.

It had been over a month since Roger's visit to Wayne's office. It had been twenty trading days since *SpeedyTrans* had been instructed to divert funds into its awaiting postle.

The November cold could not infiltrate the warmth inside him as he reviewed the Bahamian bank statement on the screen. The sizeable sum now deposited in the account was more than just pleasing and certainly more than he had expected. Whilst Moncrieffs' clients had still benefitted from the faster service, it had cost the bank a little more than it should have done. BDN had certainly benefitted by more than it should have done and it had not cost them a penny. The screen had shown how the nano amounts had added up. It wasn't about the money. It just showed what a little purposeful thought and creative mischief could do.

Roger could not deny that it had been a brilliant stroke by John Smith to bring him and Wayne together. Yet Roger determined that their association must not affect BDN's legitimate arrangement with Moncrieffs. The finder's fee and Wayne's promise of further riches must not be put at risk, even if the noughts to an off-shore bank account were not to be dismissed. He changed from gleeful counting of his riches to the more mundane everyday communication with his business partners.

`System being tested in Johannesburg office before Christmas. Enhancement already in place. We've set up a new account with the Royal Bank of Remanda to receive the proceeds.'

Roger was glad that Wayne had found an opportunity to replenish his country's exchequer with repatriated funds. He continued his trawl of messages before stopping at the most recent from Mavis Ng.

"*Serenity* is now fully booked. I have found another boat to cope with increasing demand. Will contact again soon. Maybe you visit again and come see for yourself."

A message from Stanley Henderson informed him that more compensation payments from the South China storm had been received with others to follow. ".... Robin says that there's a helluva lot of claims to process, which all takes time."

He determined that there would be little point in putting John Smith off his stroke until there was really good news. The shrill ring of his mobile phone interrupted the stillness of the afternoon. The display screen announced a text from Diana Vowlds.

`Roger! We need to meet urgently. Need your advice.'

++++

Chapter Twenty Eight

Longueur and Chicken feed

"Guess what, John? *Fasteners Monthly* wants to include extracts from your book in their January and February issues! Isn't that fab? There's not much money in it, at this stage. "

'What about the movie rights, then? Have you spoken with Spielberg yet?' John had been irritated at being called away from the conversation at the Golden Parrot with Wayne and Roger. He had watched the two men lean closer towards each other as they carried on talking without him. He had always felt confident that Wayne's expertise would complement Roger's extensive business contacts. However, as he stood by the pub's front entrance, listening to Perse banging on about the project giving him profile from an accredited business magazine, John felt that any discussion on the possibilities of an honest solution to his problems would have been preferable to the definite talk of peanuts to be received from a trade magazine with a small, eclectic readership.

"It's just a matter of time, Johnnie." Perse had continued. "Start small with the pennies first and, you know what they say, the pounds will follow. If not Spielberg, then I'm sure that we can find somebody who would be interested in making your story into a pantomime...or adapt it into a show on ice. There are lots of possibilities."

John had appreciated Perse's irony as she responded to his own deluded thinking. It was good to know that his toil of the past weeks was going to receive some approval.

"That's very good news, Perse!   I'd better finish the last few chapters then!"

"You better had, John. See you in a month!"

Not only did John have to complete his masterpiece, but he also had to decide on its title. "People don't respond to anything risqué or to double entendre." Perse had advised during a chase-up call. "So nothing about screwing or screws fit for use with Rigid Tools. Yours is a genuine story of honest endeavour. *Smiths Screws – a family business will do just fine.*"

John had winced at Perse's words as he continued his description of the honest endeavours of his forefathers. Simple beginnings with a small foundry in a field in the small village of Bisbury progressing to a larger foundry on a large industrial estate outside the considerably larger town of Bisbury did not rest easy with the current activities of the great great grandson!

In the weeks since the conversation with Perse, John had blocked his mind to Current Deceits and had concentrated on the Past Good in the Smith family. Autumn leaves had fallen from the trees in the garden to be replaced by the chill sparseness of winter. As he walked back from feeding the chickens, John thought that he had done as much as he could. Comments from Candida were no longer necessary.

"You need to get to the point more, Johnnie, which, in poor Jacob's case, was that he had been the one who had started the fire. You need to tell the reader why the bugger wanted to torch the place. It was a pretty vindictive thing to do."

"He was drunk. My grandfather had just sacked him for something. It was never explained."

"It's up to you to provide the explanation, Johnnie! Make it up, if needs be!"

He had been glad of her input. He had appreciated their chats on matters other than the Equestrian Centre and the productivity of his chickens. He had responded to her encouragement to dig deeper into the diaries for family motives.

The hundred and fifty pages, securely bound inside a black file, sat on the table at the Bengal Lancer. The computer disc with the manuscript was already stashed safely in Perse's large leather tote bag. The heat from the burning logs in the open fireplace warmed them both after suffering the damp outside.

'These photographs are fabulous, John!' Perse exclaimed as she leafed through the collection of sepia photographs portraying doughty, rugged men with bush moustaches standing in front of the brick kiln. 'When you see the conditions that these guys were forced to work in, it makes you wonder how they survived.'

'Some didn't, as you will read in the book. There were some horrendous accidents.' John felt quietly satisfied that he had been able to satisfy his publisher. He had limited the choice of pictures to those of burly men standing in front of the furnace. The inclusion of any from the company calendar would have forced the Bisbury Bookshop to place the book on the top shelf rather than lining up with *"Railways in the West Midlands – a history"*. John watched nervously as Perse thumbed through the plastic covers of photographs. At least she hadn't flung the whole lot onto the fire.

'Do you think that we'll sell any copies?' John asked.

'Who knows, John? The content could be of real interest to industrial historians.' Perse buckled her bag securely and finished off the remains of her tomato juice before turning to face him. 'Now John, now that you've finished this, when can you give me your piece about your ten days of hell in a Spanish prison? I'm sure that Spielberg would certainly be interested in your tales of incarceration.'

John paused before giving his reply. 'There's not that much to tell. It was just very....boring, sitting around with a load of fellow unfortunates waiting for the Spanish legal system to complete its long-winded procedures.'

'Didn't you meet any terrorists, drug barons or bank robbers?'

'It wasn't that sort of place!'

'No fraudsters?'

'Only a man from Bagshot with awful bad breath.' John's expression had remained impassive as Perse threw her bright red scarf around her neck. He watched her walked huffily out into the street.

'That's really disappointing, John! If you suddenly remember something, then do let me know. The Sundays and the Red Tops are always on the look out for tales of personal hardship and they pay well.'

'I think I'll try fiction next time.' As he watched Perse climb into her black Audi sports car, John was convinced that nobody would accept his latest tale as Fact.

John returned to his study at Mulberry Farm and scrolled up the National Bank of Everson website. He saw another payment had been received from Crosthwaite Marine. He was staggered by how Roger's mischief continued to produce results. There were still no further payments from Wayne or from Moncrieffs, since the first one. John had been out of contact for too long. He needed to find out what was happening. He looked for his mobile. The shrill ring from inside his jacket told him where it was. He pushed the On button.

'Gaffer? It's Clive Hunt speaking?' The voice sounded hesitant, almost reluctant to continue the conversation he had started. "I've some bad news.' John was braced. Maybe the photographs of Charlie Weatherhead were proven to be false. Was John to be extradited after all? He listened on. 'It's about our bruv,George. He's passed on.' John listened, in relief, as Clive recounted the demise of his twin brother.

++++

'It's good of you to come.' Clive Hunt stood outside the small chapel at Bisbury Crematorium as John and Candida shook his hand. 'Jani, that's his wife over there with her two boys, Alfie and Raj, and Our Bruv had been right impressed by Lady Diana's funeral and by the procession of close family behind the coffin. So we thought that we'd do the same. Would you care to join the cortage?'

Clive's lexicon was still his own. There had been little time to consider the suggestion before John and Candida were being lined up behind a tall stout lady, dressed in a royal blue silk sari. She gestured to her two teenage boys whose hands peeked out from the sleeves of their oversized suits. Clive's suit carried several badges pinned on the lapel. His wife Daphne smiled briefly to John before Clive called her to take up her position next to him. John felt a twinge that the procession was incomplete as the group started to walk slowly into the white-painted chapel. He watched the display of white lilies wobble precariously as the dark coated pall-bearers shouldered the oak coffin towards the front. Muted strains of organ played in the background as the procession passed pews of mourners. As everybody stood, John noted the sombre suits with shirts that cut into the neck, the more flamboyant coloured saris and the occasional hat, all contributing to the confusion of culture and emotion.

John drew in a deep breath. Not only was he about to make yet another speech, but he hoped that funerals were not about to become the principal highlight of his social life as friends and associates dropped off the Tree of Life. George Hunt had been only sixty five, for God's sake!

Candida had wrapped a maroon silk scarf around her neck. The full length coat bought during an irrational shopping spree in London could not quite hide the tips of her riding boots that protruded from beneath the hem. She just hoped that her dress code would be seen as further demonstration of her grasp of fashion, rather than one of expediency caused by a last-minute problem at the stables which had prevented her from being properly dressed for the occasion.

John watched the coffin being lowered onto the catafalque. Two large black sound speakers stood either side as if in vigil or in readiness for karaoke. Candles burned strongly at each end of the altar. In the centre sat a glass bowl containing jasmine flowers and orange marigolds. The spray of red roses behind was ample display of a relationship that had defied ecumenical divides for over thirty five years.

The organ died down. The family members shuffled into the front pews amid a few seconds of solemn silence. Clive Hunt then stepped forward and spoke into the microphone.

'We are all assembled here to remember, to celebrate the life of Our Bruv, George Hunt. There will be no prayers, no psalms and no lessons, just music and a few memories.' Clive's voice sounded strong and resolute as if he was at the monthly Management Works Committee Meeting. 'This first song was one of his favourites. You have the words on your service sheets. It reminds us of the many happy holidays that we spent together as a family when we were growing up.'

John looked down at the printed programme as the organ launched into the familiar opening bars at full volume.

"I do like to be beside the seaside...I do like to be beside the sea....." Clive's tenor voice could just be heard as the organ bellowed its encouragement to the congregants to join in. John winked at Candida as they both shrugged their shoulders as they went *"on the prom, prom, prom, tiddly om-pom-pom"* with as much gusto as an ex-boss and his wife could muster.

John should have known. The Hunt brothers had never been ones to conform. The service continued as Clive and then a member of the Bisbury Veterans' cricket team offered the sixty congregants their memories of the deceased. As the final strains of *"Return to Sender"* concluded, John went forward and turned to face everybody. Clive handed him the microphone.

Candida hadn't heard her husband speak in public for some time. In the early years of their life together, she had reluctantly accompanied him to various official dinners whose starchy formality had provided little amusement. She had half listened to speeches that he had been forced or asked to make in his capacity as owner of an engineering company. She suspected that this might be his last speech in public.

'To me, George Hunt was family. Thirty six years of loyalty to our company shows selflessness, a sign of contentment even.' John looked up from his notes and saw the faces of one or two others who had also given the company similar commitment. 'As long as George received a good wage sufficient to provide for Jani and the boys, then he was happy. I'm proud to think that George felt that he did not need to move on, that he was comfortable that our family was his family. I will always remember that he was the one on whom I could rely to do the extra shift, if production was getting behind. He was the one who would sort out his brother if the company needed to change work practices or introduce new methods. As I sat down to write these few words......'

Candida was thinking that the few words were starting to become too many. She issued a muted dry cough. Enough was enough she thought.

'Every company needs a George Hunt to make sure that new ideas actually happen, to ensure that the order of *Gambit Tens* comes out of the foundry with the proper coating and to the right size, to make sure that the customer receives the best that we can provide.'

John could hear shuffling and nose-blowing. He sensed that the congregation was growing restless and perhaps tiring of the eulogy about a man whom they just called Suchack Hunt. Turning to the last page of his notes, John continued on at a slightly faster pace as he caught sight of the sound engineer setting up the next item, listening through his headphones.

'So let us enjoy our memories of George. We shall miss him. Our sympathy goes out to Jani and to all members of the family. When we are at work, we all plan for the sunny day when we no longer have to work, when we can attend to those dreams or tasks that we never had time for whilst we were at our desks or in the foundry. The sadness is that George was taken before he had had the time to enjoy many fruits of his retirement. When I retired .....'

Candida's ears pricked up. She wondered where John was going with this.

'....I found it quite difficult at times to get going, to find a reason for getting out of bed each morning. George had little chance to discover what lay ahead of him or to achieve his plans. So, I say to you all, take note of George's circumstance, take each day, love it and enjoy it. God bless you, George!"

Candida watched John put away his notes and return to his seat next to her. Suddenly, a singular handclap sounded from within the congregation. She looked up to see where it had come from. Before either she or John could establish who was responsible, others had responded and soon the walls of the small chapel echoed to the sound of loud applause.

John felt Candida's tender squeeze of his hand. He smiled into her eyes that glistened towards him. He looked down in mild embarrassment at the service sheet.

The applause died down as everybody watched Clive take up the microphone and announce the next instalment in the service. "Many thanks to the Gaffer! I had always wondered why Our Bruv got a bigger bonus than I did at Christmas. Now I know!" A snigger of nervous laughter permeated throughout the room. John was not certain about the vengeful eye that was cast his way by Clive.

John became aware of vibrations coming from the Blackberry in his pocket. He knew that it would be unwise to cast even the most furtive of looks at the phone. Instead he listened to Clive's final announcement.

'As you know, the game of cricket was very close to Our Bruv's heart. Having stood as umpire and acted as scorer for many matches at Bisbury and elsewhere, he loved the game. So please be upstanding as George Sydney Hunt finally leaves us."

The sound man pressed the button. Two male voices started to speak from the large black speakers. John turned to Candida's perplexed expression as the crisp modulated tones boomed out into the chapel.

"Botham could not quite get out of the way......Yes he failed to get his leg over..... he was out for forty nine......then ....." John smiled as Johners and Aggers, the two commentators, struggled to maintain their usual calm demeanour as schoolboy innuendo gripped them both. *"....... Do stop it, Aggers!"* Their summary of the day's play at the Test Match had degenerated into convulsions of suppressed giggles. Recognising the notorious clip of radio history, the congregation joined in the contagion of restrained giggling. John looked around to see everybody with smiles stuck to their faces. He turned to the front just in time to see the oak coffin disappear behind a red curtain. John had always considered George to be a rather serious man. Would he have been consumed by the smiles that creased the faces of his fellow colleagues?

After a boisterous rendition of *"Jerusalem"*, John followed Clive and the immediate family down the aisle into the crisp air outside. He had not been convinced by the expression on Jani's face. Her husband's departure had been not so much a laughing matter, more one of extreme irritation that he had left the family without her permission.

John and Candida were soon joined outside the chapel by fellow mourners as they exited from the chapel. Some came to shake him by the hand. Ishy Hassan congratulated him on a "well-crafted oration." John thanked him and asked after the family. Bridget Murphy asked John after the welfare of the chickens had how well they have settled in their penthouse accommodation. A few minutes later, people moved away to their cars for the drive to The Golden Parrot to sample Jani's home-cooking and Clive's hospitality. Candida grabbed John's arm and pulled him away from the throng.

'I don't want to be there long.' She insisted. 'You've done what you were asked to do. You're no longer their employer. You're not even their friend either. Your responsibilities to them are over, Johnnie! It's just you and me, now.'

John knew that Candida was right. He had no further wish to be reminded of his own mortality. There was still much to be done before he followed his ex-employee. He pulled the Blackberry from his pocket to see who had wanted him. Two texts from Roger told their own story.

"We need to meet urgently. We have some decisions to make."

"Can you do *Fandango* tomorrow morning?"

John wondered what necessitated taking the boat out in a fresh November wind. However, he would go regardless. He had nothing else planned.

++++

Chapter Twenty Nine
The Crossroads in the park

There had been no disguising the urgency in Diana's voice as she went on. 'This is serious, Roger! I'm about to go into a meeting with Alastair. The shit is flying all over South China.'

Roger's heart beat more quickly as he listened to Diana's terse instructions.

'Did Gavin see us? Is he insanely jealous?'

'No, he is very annoyed. His book of business has taken a hammering.'

'You said that he might have been a bit too keen in taking on so much.'

'I think that he may have got a little carried away taking on business from some dubious characters. You'll know one or two.'

'I probably recruited them.' Roger's initial alarm had eased. Maybe genuine claims did need further explanation which he was the only one able to provide. 'I'm coming to London next week, why don't we meet....'

'Tomorrow afternoon's fine with me! I'll text you where and what time.'

Diana called off. Roger sat back, a little disappointed that she had not wanted to add other matters to the agenda.

The suggestion by text on the following morning to meet by the Serpentine Lido in Hyde Park had come as a surprise. After reading so many spy novels, he half expected the park to be teeming with people talking to their coat buttons whilst others listened to enigmatic conversations from nearby ice-cream vans. Having arrived half an hour earlier, Roger watched from a distance as Diana got out of her taxi and walked with her usual purpose towards the edge of the lake. A bright orange scarf wrapped high around her neck was not hard to miss among the assembly of mothers or nannies with push-chairs gathered to feed the attendant ducks. Crosthwaites' Director of Claims and Compliance then sat down on a green wooden bench and put her face towards the glare of the watery sun. After a few moments, Roger approached her.

'Do you come here often?'

Diana lifted the sunglasses off her face momentarily before replying. 'Only when I'm pissed off and angry.' She craned her neck to accept Roger's gentle kiss on her cheek.

Roger sat down beside her and clasped her left hand. 'Like that duck who's had his bread nicked?'

'Possibly. Although he seems happy enough to let it go. However, he's probably muddying the water for the fish swimming underneath.'

Both sat in silence for a few moments watching other mallards and drakes waddle along the bank of the lake before entering the water to paddle out of harm's way.

'So, Diana.' Roger opened. 'What's with Naturewatch? Which duck are we looking for today? The lesser-spotted Crosthwaite? The outrageous plumage of the Fu-Fing?'

'There are quite a few and ...' Diana paused, wondering whether to continue the Le Carre-style conversation or whether she should break cover and take up what she had rehearsed in her mind on her way from the office. '..... and most of them are men.'

'Mallards, you mean.'

'What?'

'The male duck. They're the ones with the green plumage.'

'I know perfectly well what mallards are! Don't mock me, Roger. I'm not in the mood. This is serious'.

'Is it? Is it really that serious?' Roger thought a friendly arm around Diana's shoulder would provide a certain reassurance that life was not as bad as she was making out. 'What's happened, Diana?'

Diana broke away from him, before looking straight at him. 'Did you know a mallard named Robin Song?'

Roger paused. Diana's Claims people were not as blind as he had thought.

'Yes. I knew him. He was more the shadier breed of broker, like a moorhen, busying among the reeds of the riverbank rather than being out in the main stream with the rest of the guys.' Roger was warming to the George Smiley routine. 'Everybody called him Crusoe. He specialised in the small fry of the Leisure and Pleasure market.' He watched real moorhens squabble over pieces of bread that were being gleefully strewn by a little old woman wearing grey woollen mittens and a long winter coat that scraped the ground. 'He was one of Gavin's team of brokers. I didn't have much to do with him.'

'Oh really?' Diana sat back on the arm of the bench. 'Are you certain about that?'

'Absolutely! I haven't seen him for well over two years. Maybe longer. Why do you ask?'

'Well.' Diana drew in a deep breathe before continuing. 'Going through the Green Claims file, my team have noticed that his name featured in many of the claims in the typhoon.'

'But that's not surprising, since South China was Crusoe's patch. It was quite likely that many of his clients were going to be affected. After all, that is what he's paid to do, to bring in business for the company. It was inevitable that he.....'

'OK!' Diana interrupted. 'Let me release another mallard for you to shoot at. Stanley Henderson.'

Roger paused to prepare his reply. The silence was broken by aggressive quacking from those left unfed by the Woman in Grey. 'Stanley Henderson?' He was a little irritated that the name had been unearthed so easily by Diana's beady-eyed team. 'That does ring a bell.'

'You could say that he's another who likes to keep hidden in leafy undergrowth, this time away from the eagle eyes of Loss Adjusters, together with a small cargo carrier laden with rusting iron ore in a small bay in the Philippines.'

'Oh him! That Stanley Henderson!' Roger watched Diana's stony expression before going on. 'I haven't seen him since he was struck off the Masters' List. That was a long time ago.'

'Well, he's back and now owns leisure craft all over the place. Many succumbed in the recent storm.'

'Nothing surprising there - that storm covered a pretty big area. When we were watching the news in bed together, you said that many clients were going to be affected.'

'I said a lot of things during that storm. It was an emotional time.'

'But fun and enjoyable, if I remember correctly.'

'That's as maybe.' She started to gently massage Roger's hands. 'But...'

'So what's the problem?' Roger looked towards the face that had teased and toyed with him in the hotel room in Hong Kong, any hint of expression hidden behind her dark glasses. 'Are you suggesting that Song and Henderson were in cahoots together? I think that's pretty unlikely. I just don't see them as likely business partners.'

'Let me try another one on you, Roger! This one's closer to home.' She paused as Roger's face remained impassive. 'Mavis Ng, the trustee of your so-called Royal Northwood School? Very important lady in the community, well connected, you said.'

'What about her?' Roger saw Diana's eyes glaring straight towards him. He moved to clasp her hands. 'Did she suffer as well? I wouldn't be surprised if she didn't own a boat or two. As you saw, she's a wealthy woman. I must ask her if she suffered in the storm.'

'Come off it, Roger!' Diana moved her hands away as if Roger carried the Plague. 'Stop poncing about! You know what's going on here. We've found at least forty boats in the names of people whose reputations are well known to us as being dodgy.'

'Are you telling me that Mavis is in with Henderson and Song as well?' Roger needed to hold on for as long as he could.

'Gavin tells me that she's another with .....questionable plumage, as you might say.'

Yep, Roger thought, Gavin would say that. However, he doubted whether Gavin would have divulged the full story to his Director of Claims and Compliance. Mavis had been fairly certain that he had been entertained on one of her Crewed Weekends. There was little time for a response before Diana carried on.

'OK, Roger. Try these. Johannes Schmidt? Jean LeFebvre? Jan Schmitz? Do these mean anything to you? '

'Unfortunate Europeans who, I presume, have filed claims for their loss?'

'And Ja Wang? Jo Tan? Ji Xing?'

'Never heard of them! I don't know everyone on the Crosthwaites client list. They sound very common names.'

'Exactly my point!   Did you not mention that you have a business partner named John Smith?'

'So what?'

'All these names have a very similar denominator. They're all variants of John Smith.'

'That's a little far fetched, don't you think?'

Diana sank back into the corner of the wooden bench. She was never going to receive the answers she wanted to hear. She had to continue with her assumptions. 'You've been having a laugh with us, Roger, haven't you? Playing games to get back at Crosthwaites, isn't that it?'

'Come now, Diana! I think that you're imagining things. It's been a rough time. I can understand......'

'As you know, it's my job, Roger, to identify claims that have a nasty smell to them. Believe me, these stink, big time!'

Roger stood up. 'Let's walk. The sun will soon be going in and we're going to freeze if we just sit here. There's still much to talk about.' He took Diana's arm as he led her along the path along the water's edge. 'Let me ask you something. Is it just your job that's causing you to ask all these questions or is it something more fundamental?'

Diana was glad of the inner lining of her expensive coat. The draught of the cold breeze caught her as they walked under the road bridge away from the warmth of the sun. At the far end of the short tunnel, she could see the bronze sculpture of Peter Pan surrounded by a small crowd of admirers. She wondered how long it would take for Roger to admit his own childish antics to her as he clutched her arm.

'Both...probably....I'm trying to do something which I'm paid to do.... to the best of my abilities. Why do you ask?'

'Because I think that you're doing it all wrong. Your job is to minimise the claims, not to stop them altogether.'

'That's all very well for you to say. So far, Crosthwaites are in for just under seventy million dollars and there are many more claims to come. I can't just rubber-stamp every one that comes in, especially when the toxic debt business from the US is looming as well. I tell you, Roge, it's not just the winds. There's a whole lot of heavy pressure of a different kind that's going to wreak havoc. It's a very scary time, I can tell you.'

Diana knew that her presence by the Serpentine was as reckless as when she had sought shelter from the storm in Hong Kong. The memories of the warmth and the presence of somebody who had cared for her were being eradicated by the demands of Alistair Crosthwaite to reduce the company's exposure and she didn't like it.

The pair walked along in silence as a couple of sweaty joggers puffed their way towards them. Roger sensed that a sense of proportion was needed.

'It's not the worst loss suffered by Crosthwaites, neither will it be the smallest. Seventy million is not a lot of money. I doubt if the Old Man will be cancelling his shooting weekends as a result of it.' Roger continued his pragmatic approach. 'Gavin's the one who'll need to worry a bit. He'll need to shift his attentions to larger boats that can withstand the weather.'

'He's not had much luck with that sector either. A twenty thousand tonne freighter called "Eastern Carrier" has disappeared into thin air. At least, Gavin's got his surveyors looking into that one!' Diana sighed. 'This one's a left-over from your book, I believe. Owned by our good friends, Choo Transport. You may remember that I met the very unsavoury boss during my last trip.'

'His was the last large tonnage vessel I covered before leaving the company.' Roger thought back to closing the deal with a man whose face had resembled one of those dangerous toads seen on nature programmes about the forests of Borneo. 'I suppose that I've always liked large tonnage!' Roger looked directly towards Diana and brought her closer to him.

Diana punched him gently in response to his jest. She did not see herself as particularly large tonnage. Nevertheless, she had been flattered that her five foot eight, size fourteen, pear-shaped frame had been sufficient to incite Roger into some passionate action during the storm. She needed to bring him into harbour.

'You were questioning my motives. What about yours, Roger?'

Roger had not been prepared. 'They're still the same as ever. I know what's wrong and what's right. I know what's fair and what's just. I know that this relationship between you and me is immoral, but I also know that it's right.... for this moment.'

'Do you think that retirement has changed you?'

'It has certainly made me think about what I do and what I've done.'

'Do you think that what Song and Henderson and others have done is fair and just?'

'What have they done?'

'You know exactly what they've done, played some Greek Scam, claiming for loss of boats that never existed.'

'How do you know that their boats never existed? You can't prove it.'

'There are enough coincidences to make me realise that their claims are suspect.'

'What makes you think that I knew what they were doing?'

'I thought that I had spelt it out quite clearly to you already. Do the names *"The Bisbury Belle"* or *"Mary's Daydream"* mean anything to you?'

'Nothing at all.'

Diana changed tack. 'Tell me more about Lamma Island? You know, the place you suggested that Gavin should have taken me to.'

'Shit!' Roger's felt his shoe squelch into some softer matter as he sought to come to terms with Diana's question. She grabbed his arm as if to hurry him along.

'You were seen, Roger. You were not with Mary, though.'

'Are you sure that it was me?'

'One of Gavin's surveyors says that he recognised you and Mavis Ng whilst he was assessing another boat in the marina. There was another man, European, with you. I presume that would have been Stanley. The guy knows Robin Song and he told Gavin that there was no sign of him.'

'Still not a totally reliable source then?'

'Maybe not enough for a court of law, but enough to tell me about the company you keep. I may have got it all wrong, Roger, but I don't see Stanley becoming Head of Geography for your new school. It was him that I saw at the hotel acting as chauffeur for Mavis to take her to her meeting with fellow trustees, wasn't it? Well connected, Roger? You could have made me look so stupid.'

Roger felt a few beads of sweat appear on his brow. He thought that he had escaped, but his world was now showing some fault lines that were threatening to collide.

'Proof is everything, Diana.'

'Don't I know it? If I had the time and the resource, I'd be able to prove what's going on and that all of you were in it up to your necks. That's what I'm finding so unsatisfactory. My job is becoming increasingly pointless. The task of establishing fraud or deception is so costly and time-consuming and for what? So that, by not paying out on claims, Sir Alistair and the Board can become fatter and richer. I think that I've reached a time in my life when I either need to make a real difference to something or else make an awful lot more money than I currently am.'

Crumbs! Roger marvelled at her ambition.

'Yesterday's meeting with the Claims Committee made me think about my life, my career, my future.' She then turned her gaze to Roger. 'Even about you!'

Roger gulped. He had hoped that the subject of their relationship would have fallen under the category of Any Other Business, the last item of the agenda, not right at the bloody top.

'I've nobody else to talk about it with. My mother, bless her, just says that I should do whatever makes me happy. I can't really confess to her that being a Director of Claims and Compliance is becoming a load of bollocks. My girl friends and man friends just tell me stuff that they think I want to hear. They're a bit scared to tell me home truths. I just want someone to be honest with me. So in spite of your association with Stanley and Mavis, I think that you at least.... '

Roger tensed as they stopped walking. He turned towards Diana and grasped both her arms.

'So that's my role? To tell you that you're slightly overweight, your face could do with some toning and that your breath really does smell. Is that it?' Roger's sarcasm brought a smile to Diana's severe looking face. 'Let's cut to the chase, Diana. What has happened that's made you so ...so unlike you? You look sad, a bit confused.' He suddenly had a flash of impending doom. 'You're not pregnant, are you?'

'Hell no! I'm past all that!' Diana carried on walking with her arms folded in an expression of self-sufficiency. Her smile to Roger was full of warmth, full of if onlys. 'I'm told by my boss to limit payments only to those people whose claim can be obviously justified. I must fight about the veracity of the other claims. The re-insurers are proving reluctant to step up to their responsibilities. Then there are people like you who are trying......'

'Hold on, Diana! You don't know anything for definite! Why would I want to be embroiled with these people?' Happy that at least half his fleet had been passed as justifiable claims, Roger listened to Diana's raised voice.

'Because you no longer have responsibilities.... except to your wife and to your family, possibly. I suspect that you're a bit of a loose cannon, Roge. I'm thinking that you've had enough of toeing the line. You're thinking that it's time to explore new opportunities.'

The couple had reached the head of the lake. Roger could not detect whether Diana's more insistent tones were due to the need to make herself heard above the roar from the Italianate fountains or were as a consequence of his straight-bat obduracy. Light droplets of spray helped hide the perspiration that still remained on his forehead. He needed to direct Diana's suspicions away from the hurly burly of the noisy traffic in the nearby Bayswater Road onto a more peaceful pathway of the park.

'Let's head over towards the Palace.'

'Maybe, now it's my time to explore new opportunities as well?' Diana looked across at the expanse of dead-brown grass and the leafless oak trees that stood stark against the darkening afternoon sky. I'm responsible for a department which is about to pay out millions of dollars on losses brought about by natural calamity. Now I suspect that I may have to contend with other liabilities caused by the reckless arrogance of people who blatantly disregarded the basic rules of risk in their greedy pursuit of riches. I don't feel that I'm in control of anything.'

'You shouldn't. You can't control the uncontrollable. People, wind, turbulence. They're all forces of the indeterminate.' Nice one, Roger! If wise counsel was needed, then who better to provide it?

'I realise that.' Diana replied. 'However, knowing that you're being rolled over does not appeal to my sense of moral conscience. So......' Diana entwined her arm with Roger's and increased the pace of their stride away from the cacophonous roar of traffic and falling water. '....... I've put out some feelers with headhunters, executive search consultants, to see what jobs are around that might appeal to me.'

She'd be brilliant working for a benevolent charity, Roger thought, distributing money to worthy and justifiable causes. There would be little difference from what she was currently doing; only the funds would be delivered with a more sympathetic smile of encouragement rather than with a begrudging reluctance. He listened on.

'I've had chats with one or two people. Many have liked my CV. There are several interesting options for me, which has been a relief.'

Roger's mind began to consider whether there might be a bar nearby for a quiet celebratory drink.

'There's one in particular; a small private bank; net cap of half a billion sterling; predominantly dealing with client wealth management. They have interests in Africa and the Caribbean, amongst other places. They're looking for a Head of Compliance.'

Roger's inner core stilled for a moment. He felt distant rumblings.

'Can you tell me who they are? Or are you sworn to secrecy as I am with my school in Hong Kong?' Tremors were building within him. He just hoped that the outer core would hold.

'This is a real bank, Roger, with real people.' Diana stared hard at him. 'Have you heard of Moncrieffs? I must admit that I hadn't.'

Fuck, fuck and quadruple fuck!! Lava was spitting inside Roger like Vesuvius. The outer core was holding fast, just. Why couldn't she be talking to other banks? Why did Moncrieffs have to ruin the party by wanting to tighten up their controls? Surely Crosthwaites would fight to hold on to Diana's assiduous sense of responsibility?

They stopped on the pathway to pass judgement on a large black statue that was silhouetted against the setting sun. Physical Energy by George Watts portrayed a naked man looking into the distance astride his frenzied horse. Roger knew how the horse must have felt bucking under the uncertain control of its rider. Perceiving his own predicament to be just as ugly as the bronze sculpture, Roger was relieved when Diana moved on, more intent on examining her own situation.

'It's between me and another man. It's a new role. So whoever is appointed will have to make their presence felt within the bank, no doubt ruffling a few feathers in the process.'

Roger's mind was racing, more concerned about the trim of his own feathers. His inner turmoil would remain hidden under the outer skin of avuncular counsel and gentle persuasion. This would have to do until something better came up.

'Presumably, it's well paid with a good package? A position on the board? It's a big opportunity. What's the problem?'

'The package is fine. There's no board position for the first twelve months. Then it would be reviewed. I'm comfortable with that.'

Roger watched a young couple break away from their full-on kiss in the shade of a large oak tree that lined the path. He sensed that any such approach to Diana would have been unwelcome as he continued his questioning.

'What's holding you back? Don't you *want* to take it? Is this what all this is about?' Roger stepped to avoid another turd of dog mess that lay like a land mine on the gravelled footpath.

'That's just it, Roge. I knew you'd understand.' Diana replied. 'I'm not certain that I really do. Yet, I've worked bloody hard over the last couple of years, for what?'

'Money for you, for your daughter's education? To bring good into the world? To ensure that your employer can continue to provide for all his employees?' Roger watched Diana raise her eyebrow as he went on. 'This new role sounds very demanding. Setting up all those controls and checks wouldn't appeal to me.'

'You do surprise me, Roge!' Diana's smile shone in the half-light of the orange sunset settling over roof and chimney top of Kensington Palace.

'I suppose that somebody's got to carry on knitting the whole lacework of rules and regulations of our everyday existence. That's one of the main legacies of the Baby Boom Generation.'

'Oh don't talk such tosh, Roger.' Diana riposted. 'The Baby Boomers have provided a lot for mankind. They've built on the initial ideas started by their fathers and have made them infinitely better. The car, the plane, the telephone have been developed beyond all expectation.' She was enjoying the cleansing of her muddled brain as they both headed for a bench that sat at the top of the hill. She looked towards the lightshow below as darting beams of car headlight combined with illuminated interior of double-decker buses moving along the busy high street. As she sat down and tugged her coat tightly to her, Diana considered Roger's sweeping statement further. 'You're right in one thing. Policing has never been so important, yet never so difficult to enforce.'

'Maybe.' Roger was less certain about sitting down. He'd had enough of conversation in the murky dusk. 'Come on, Diana, let me buy you a drink. That's one thing the Baby Boomers have done nothing to ruin.' He went to grab Diana's hand.

'Wait a moment, Roger! This is not easy for me' Diana remained seated, gesturing Roger to sit down beside her. 'What you don't understand is how tired I am of living in a world of scepticism, where suspicion of others has to stay with me all the time. I'm surrounded by lies and deceit. Everybody's at it and much of it I can't prove.' For a moment, her eyes began to fill. She turned to Roger whose face was hidden in the gloom of the orange light hovering above. She needed reassurance that she was not going slightly batty. 'Would you ever tell me the truth, Roger?'

Roger looked back into her eyes. There was so much that he wanted to say, yet he remained silent.

'There you are; a chasm between us. It's something that I'm not enjoying. I don't think that's good enough any more. I'm looking for something to control that would give me enjoyment. In the same way, I'm still looking for some body to enjoy.'

'Like your daughter, maybe?' Roger felt that Diana's dagger of accusation needed to be replaced by one of his own.

'Ah! Charlotte!' Diana sighed and breathed deeply. 'Poor kid! On the whole, she's done amazingly well. She's got on with her life in spite of everything. Luckily, she's got a great group of friends, who have all been very supportive. I must admit that there have been days when she has felt like a stranger to me.' Diana was pleased that Roger was there to listen to her outpourings. 'It is getting better. You're right, Roge, if you mean that I need to be a good parent again, before it's too late. I think she still wants me to be there for her. I want to help her achieve her potential, to sort out her own uncertainties. I'm not so sure all that would be possible if I were to join Moncrieffs.'

'But two hundred grand plus perks is not to be dismissed lightly.' Roger needed to find the chink in her armour.

'One twenty with driver, dress allowance, private health, pension contribution. It's a very good package, as I've said, and they seem a nice enough company.' Diana watched Roger nod as he considered the merits of the package. 'The bank does have some interesting ideas on how to go forward. They're well positioned overseas in places that will make a nice change from Hong Kong. Maybe you could set up a Royal Northwood School in Mauritius or the Seychelles? We could meet up to review syllabuses.'

Roger pressed on regardless. 'Do you think that you might regret not taking the bank job, if they offered it to you? '

'I know that I would be very scared if I were to take it. It would appeal to my pioneering spirit of wanting to break down the walls of egocentric male complacency. But.....' Diana paused. '....there's that word again. Do I really want to change the world? Would I not just be bashing my head against a brick wall? '

'Maybe now is the time for you to change tack and try something totally different. Have you thought about work in the charity sector?' Roger needed to steer carefully.

'That's going to another extreme, there are far too many women. I like the idea of a woman being Head of Compliance. I understand that Sir Gerald Moncrieff does not quite trust female senior employees. Maybe he thinks like you, that a woman in her fifties is a liability. She will become pregnant immediately and then demand full pay whilst on maternity leave and ask for a continuous supply of disposable nappies! My fear is that I would be paying lip service to the gender balance. I would be patronised and told by other directors what a great job I'm doing, yet nothing will fundamentally change, unless I'm prepared to fight tooth and nail to get my own way.' Diana realised that her rant had long run its course. 'Anyway, what did you mean totally different? Like what? Become a traffic warden?'

'Setting yourself up as a consultant is one option.' Roger's internal volcano was being calmed by cool, clear thinking. 'When will Moncrieffs let you have their decision?'

'Before Christmas, I've been told. Sir Ian is busy shooting in the Highlands. He's obviously not worried about the mess over sub-prime.' Diana looked at her watch. 'Bloody hell! I must rush home to recover my daughter from her lack of parent, as you have so wickedly pointed out.'

Roger's smile of satisfaction was hidden by the darkness. He sensed that time was running out. There were still questions needing answers. 'If Moncrieffs were to offer you the job tomorrow, Diana, what would you do?'

'I don't know, Roger. I really don't know.' Diana paused to take stock. 'Consultancy? Is that what you describe yourself as?'

'It covers many bases, Diana.'

Roger could see Diana looking at the lit-up screen of her phone and tapping in a quick message. He felt that his time was running out as well, yet he needed to provide context for what he had in mind.

'My partner, John Smith, and I are building a very nice little business. BDN Consultants is involved with .....

'I know......fabrication, deceit, flights of educational fancy......what else?' Diana had put away her phone and was gathering herself to move off towards the nearest underground station.

'We have a disparate range of interests. Financial services, computer software systems and the leisure industry. So, Diana, if it's money, control and a nice lifestyle that you want, have you .....' Roger had no option but to come out with his budding idea. '.....have you ever thought about Non-Compliance as an option?'

Diana could only see the shadow of Roger's face in the dim light. 'What on earth do you mean, Roge? That's what I'm dealing with all the time.'

'This would be completely different.' Roger went on as they started down the hill. 'I think that you could be extremely useful to us.'

The arrogant snarl of a sports car threatened to interrupt Roger's sales pitch to Diana as it accelerated past the couple. She grimaced as its low-slung shape roared away into the general din of the home-going, theatre-coming, dinner-dating throng. As they made their way towards Gloucester Road underground station, Roger's boisterous voice continued to outline his suggestions for her future. Diana was able to hear enough to appreciate that it all sounded quite credible, even attractive. Coming from anybody else, the package might have been really interesting. Roger

Mortlock was a man with a vivid imagination and warped ideals, albeit with an awkward manner that was somehow alluring. Oh bloody hell! There would be a lot for her to think about on her journey home.

++++

Chapter Thirty

The price of everything, the cost of nothing

As John approached the car park in Lyndhurst Quay, he had noticed a sleek silver sports car driving away in the opposite direction. The drophead roof had been lowered. The dark blue baseball cap and white scarf draped around her shoulders prevented identification of which Hand Maiden was behind the wheel. He therefore wasn't surprised to see her boss waiting to greet him, although he was taken aback by the display of gold on Wayne's dark blue jacket as epaulettes dazzled in the morning sun.

'This is the Number Two uniform of Admiral of the Fleet of the Remandan Navy. Pretty neat, eh? I used to wear it on the large cabin cruiser when patrolling the coast on the lookout for pirates and smugglers.'

John locked the door of his car as he reviewed the two flamingos on the blazer badge and the gold buttons on the cuff of each sleeve. 'It's slight overkill for a humble outing on the river Lynd, isn't it Wayne?'

'I only use this on special occasions. This seemed to be one.' Both men had started to walk down the hill towards the jetty. 'I wonder what Roger wants that necessitates us coming down here in such mystery?'

'I haven't the faintest idea, Wayne. But it's not a bad day for an outing, is it?'

Both men walked along the wooden jetty towards where Fandango Two bobbed on the high tide. The icy wind was doing its best to spoil the warmth of the bright morning sun. Roger was gesticulating to them as they approached.

'We haven't got much time, gentlemen. There is a lot to talk about. So, for complete privacy, what could be better than a meeting on the high seas, followed by a good lunch?' Roger inspected Wayne at closer quarters. 'I hadn't really bargained on fancy dress for this trip. Luckily, I've brought something more suitable for you to change into once we get under way.'

After guiding Fandango Two through the early reaches of the river, John winched up the mainsail as Roger set the yacht's trim, his frown now focussed on the course ahead. Wayne had needed no second invitation to retreat below deck into the comparative warmth of the galley and a couple of thick sweaters.

Roger and John watched the eager waters of the Shallows approach as they sailed past the white marker and into the strait. The memory of their earlier misfortune could not quite be eradicated as Fandango Two took on the force four wind before entering the chop of the Solent. A sigh of relief and a couple of hours' sailing would take them to a welcome bowl of hearty fish stew as they headed towards Newlyn Bay. The sting of ice-cold water on John's face was made bearable as he contemplated his announcement.

'I also have some very good news.'

'Don't tell me, Johnno! Your book is a number one best-seller? Pull in the jib! Make yourself useful!'

'Not yet. Although I did receive a very nice letter from the editor of *Fasteners Monthly*, congratulating me on the content of the early chapters.' John could not restrain himself. 'This news is much more satisfying. It came from my lawyer in Spain.'

'Has Charlie found some spare cash from somewhere? Is he going to pay you back? I hope that you're not going to say that all our efforts at restitution have been wasted, Johnno?'

'I'm afraid not. The good news is that he and Francine are in even deeper trouble. Apparently, their apartment block is under review. There's a suspicion that it's been built on land that did not belong to the developer. The bad news is that the money cannot be retrieved from the developer. Charlie came to see my lawyer, Luis Cortez, almost in tears, to ask his advice.'

'Well, that doesn't surprise me. So much land in Spain has been filched over the years. Land that should have gone to a proper cause has just been ripped off and taken by unscrupulous developers.'

'Talking of unscrupulous, Roger! Can you just tell me why we're all here?'

Roger had not seen Wayne appear at the entrance to the cabin. The brash uniform had been replaced by the sweaters encased within shoulder straps holding up high-cut oilskin trousers. His expression suggested that the Admiral was not used to the stinging spray from the sea.

'Ready about..........' Roger shouted as the boom clattered from right to the left, tilting the boat so that the sea sloshed along the lower decking. John winched in the slackened rope as the boat settled into a more comfortable angle. Wayne clutched the hatchway door. He had never experienced leaning at a forty five degree angle during his outings on patrol on Lake Oduku.

Roger outlined his recent conversation with Diana. John and Wayne remained silent throughout.

'That sounds like rather good news.' John said finally. 'I was always concerned that her role at Crosthwaites might catch up with you.....or us. When does she start with Moncrieffs? She could be incredibly useful to us, don't you think?'

'She hasn't been offered the job yet, Johnno. There are still small details to sort out.' Roger looked straight ahead, unwilling to look John in the eye.

'The sooner she leaves Crosthwaites the better, I say.' John carried on. 'I promised Candida that her days as prison-visitor were over. She'd certainly never come to see me in Dartmoor.'

'Diana was just chancing her arm when she met me. She knows that she can't prove anything conclusively.' Roger needed to be reassuring. 'Furthermore, she has no real desire to go to such lengths.'

'How do you know that, Roger? If she's a sensible, intelligent woman with all the tools of investigation at her disposal, why wouldn't she shop us? That is her job, after all?'

'It's more cost-effective to go after larger fish!' Wayne interjected. 'What you've done is such small fry.'

John stared directly at Wayne. How much did he know? Has Roger fully briefed Wayne about the adventures of the Phantom Fleet? Had Roger now placed a flotilla along the Remandan Coast? Did Roger not realise that deceit is a fragile commodity that offers an increased chance of discovery, the more partners there are involved? Memories of the hot airless courtyard at the La Laguna Remand Centre flashed before him. Roger was getting carried away.

A low-pitched blast of fog-horn rent the air. Roger turned to see a gigantic container ship a few hundred metres away bearing down on the yacht. The threat posed by the immense bow and its wash was not quite as daunting as that possibly to be presented by Diana Vowlds. Nevertheless, Roger decided that the wind might not be sufficient to carry their boat away in time. He turned on the yacht's engine to speed away from any danger. The other two men seemed to be more concerned by what he had just told them.

'Giles did tell me that he was recruiting somebody.' Wayne watched the huge container ship tower over him as she went by.

'I suppose two contacts in the same bank could be good news for us. To start off with, your lady will be involved with mainstream business. She won't be touching foreign exchange, not for a while anyway.'

'Surely, that's what we want?' John couldn't understand why his enthusiasm for another income stream was not shared by his partners. 'She can direct us to other parts of the bank where your people can weave their magic, Wayne.'

'That's what concerns me.' Wayne looked to Roger.

'Why?' John asked. 'What's wrong with pitching for other parts of Moncrieffs IT work. We know that Giles is very pleased. He'll put in a good word, I'm sure.'

'I agree. I'm sure that we'll get more work from the bank.' Wayne turned to Roger who was looking up at the burgee at the top of the mast. 'Is she going to be well paid, Roger?'

'That's certainly one of the attractions.' Roger felt the wind was now on their backs. He adjusted the wheel to let the sails fill as *Fandango Two* headed for Newlyn Bay.

'Why should that matter to us?' John asked. He was determined not to be blown off his course of questioning. 'What concerns do you have about weaving your magic in other parts of Moncrieffs, Wayne? I thought that's what software design is all about?'

'It's also about bringing..... added value to an ongoing project, Johnno!' Roger interjected. The moment had come. '...which might not necessarily be what Moncrieffs had in mind when they asked Wayne to install *SpeedyTrans*.' He went on to provide John with a fuller explanation of Wayne's magic and the benefits that it had brought to *BDN Consultants* bank account in the Bahamas.

'I can't believe it, Roger. You are unstoppable! Both of you are out of your bloody minds.' John realised why the meeting had been held on the yacht. He listened in a stupor of incomprehension as Roger continued. He saw Wayne's face light up with a cheeky grin.

'Isn't it brilliant? It's turned out to be one of the most remunerative systems we've come up with. The HPI, I mean the Hidden Postle Installation, was a brilliant brainwave. We've been looking for ages for somewhere to place it! ' His face was beaming at John's expression of disbelief.

'So how do you know that this so-called "postle", which you say you have embedded into the bank's system, cannot be discovered?' Not only was John floundering in the choppy waters of Wayne's computer jargon, he realised that he was being sucked further down into Roger's whirlpool of mischief. Anger and irritation tried to bring him to the surface. 'Where is the bloody thing? Is it stuffed up Giles' arse? The next time I see him, I must ask if he's been feeling a bit uncomfortable recently. This is pure madness, Wayne!' John turned to the helmsman. 'Roger, I suspect that this has your fingerprints all over it?'

'My fingers have been nowhere near Giles' arse, I can assure you, Johnno! I merely suggested to Wayne that if this HPI thing was possible, then BDN might be interested in pursuing it, that's all. Besides, may I remind you, Johnno, that you are half a million quid down and that this might just get you out of trouble! You should be grateful, not furious.'

Wayne sensed that a bit of Remandan realism was needed. 'I'm not saying that somebody smart will not discover it. It's just up to us to make sure that they don't. That's the challenge. Isn't it great?'

'Take a look at this, Johnno!' Roger pulled a sheet of paper from the pocket of his high necked storm jacket. 'This'll put things in perspective for you.'

John noticed the Red Diamond logo familiar from Roger's laptop screen unveiled in the room at the Spanish Remand Centre. He studied the figures on the statement. He was reassured that the

"Finder's Fee" from Oduku Systems had finally come through. Sums from Crosthwaites Marine continued to surprise. However, the figure from Fandango Consultancy was nothing short of astounding.

'How long has this been going on for, gentlemen?' John's reproach would not have disappointed his old housemaster at Myndhams.

'About three months, Johnno!' Roger replied. 'We would have told you sooner, but you were busy doing much more worthwhile things.' Roger smiled. He sensed that he and Wayne probably looked like a couple of naughty schoolboys about to be punished, yet quietly proud of their misdemeanour.

'Roger, let me take over for a bit. I need to think this all through.' John grabbed the helm. He could see the harbour wall of Newlyn Bay in the distance, yet he decided that he needed to steer a wider course to enable time for further questions. 'All this doesn't really answer the question about what to do about Diana?'

'She's quite clearly a bit disillusioned by the way things are going at Crosthwaites.' Roger was relieved by John's change of approach. 'She's certainly looking for a fresh challenge. I suspect that she might be quite keen to earn a lot of money without the bother of having to work so hard for it. The right sort of criteria for a position with *BDN Consultants*, I thought.'

'Have you mentioned already BDN to her?

'Of course, it's a legitimate company, which with Wayne's help and that of our other global partners, has outstanding prospects.'

'Have you offered her anything, Roger?'

'Well, yes I have, actually.'

'You're a cool one, Roger. I'll say that for you!' John's sarcasm could not be controlled as he motored the yacht past the Harbour-master's hut to the mooring assigned to it.

'I've not asked her to become a crook, Johnno! I'm not that daft!' Roger jumped ashore with the lead rope and fastened it to an iron ring hanging from the stone wall. He tested the strength of the anchor-bend knot. 'Far from it, we would be using her knowledge of compliance systems to enable Wayne's people to, as you put it, weave their magic for clients.'

John decided that he needed to hear his partner out before finally getting him to walk the plank. 'Is this not just plain foolhardy! She'll cotton on soon enough to what's going on, surely?'

Wayne sat in the cockpit and listened to the Odd Couple battle it out. There would be definite repercussions on his own plans and he was not certain what to do.

'She's never going to agree to it.' John jumped onto the shore.

'Everyone has their price, Johnno!' Roger said, extending his hand to help Wayne onto dry land. 'Diana Vowlds is no different.' Roger and Wayne had hurried away up the small hill to the Newlyn Arms discussing their varying levels of hunger.

John considered his own appetite as he followed on behind them. What would be the price necessary to lure Diana Vowlds away from what she's doing? Would money really blind her to the devious magic of the Hidden Postle and its nano-diversion? Were Roger and Wayne themselves not becoming blinded by their success? How far would John allow himself to go with them? He was still out of pocket by several hundreds of thousands of pounds. Obviously, his share of the spoils held in the Bahamas would be immensely useful in helping him out his mess. Maybe answers weren't as important as actions.

As he sat down with the others at the lunch table in the restaurant, John knew that his answers and actions would need to tally with those offered by Roger and Wayne.

++++

'Employing the services of Diana Vowlds as Director of Non Compliance will enable us to infiltrate banking and insurance systems quite legitimately.'

Roger leaned forward and grasped the half-empty bottle of Sancerre. The waiter busied himself with clearing away the detritus of John's fish stew and the remains of the others' Dover Soles. The dining room in the Newlyn Arms was empty. Wayne emptied the contents of his Watermelon Cooler into his glass to show that there was still unfinished business. John watched Roger pour the remains of the wine into their two glasses.

Wayne's eyes were alive to the range of possibilities being suggested by Roger. He folded his arms on the table as he continued Roger's theme. 'Like the story of the Trojan Horse, she would look pretty and engage the client, whilst my men would secretly work on the enhancement implementation.'

'You mean planting your postle?' John rejoined.

'Exactly. It is important also to remember why we're doing this, gentlemen? It's not just for the money.'

'It's certainly helped, Wayne.' Roger expounded. 'But you're right. Men of our age need challenges. Nobody else will provide them for us. We need to engage our restless minds. What else are we going to do, Johnno?'

John supposed that he hadn't really given much thought to the question recently. He had had more than enough to do over the past months, none of which had been planned. So how could he be expected to provide an informed answer? However, there was need for some hard-headed realism in the discussion. 'As I see it, Diana must be headed away from her current position at Crosthwaites if the Phantom Fleet is to continue to sail. We need to make sure that she doesn't rush off to the Serious Fraud Office to report her suspicions. If she's as sharp and conscientious as you say she is, I'm surprised that she hasn't contacted them already.'

'If she is to be bought off......' Wayne stated. '....the financial package has to be bloody amazing, one too good for any woman or man to pass up.'

'I think we can, Wayne.' Roger had absent-mindedly corralled crumbs on the table into a small pile in front of him. 'I think that we can give her almost everything that she wants.'

John was still not sure as he turned towards Wayne. 'This presumes that your people can continue to develop the right systems.'

'Rootkit algorithms, backdoor systems and false trail-setting are useful bi-products of what Oduku Systems does. My people would love to work with somebody who has intimate knowledge of setting up procedures and protocols.'

'Diana certainly knows where to look for scams and deceits.' Roger added. 'If we use her right, then I'm sure that we can reap the fullest rewards from the seeds that she will have sown, albeit unwittingly.'

'Have you got something on her, Roger, which she is keen to keep hidden?' John was reminded of Candida's powers of persuasion with Charlie Weatherhead. 'Being a lady of a certain age, does she not have secrets stashed away which you've somehow got hold of?'

'No love children. She has an eighteen year old daughter by her divorced husband. No predilections to dominatrix tendencies or to lesbian lovers as far as I can tell. She was certainly confused by my suggestion when she left me at the underground station the other night. She said that she would sleep on it.' Roger was pleased that neither John nor Wayne had detected any disappointment in his voice as he remembered the tight hug from Diana as they had parted. 'She said that she will know more before Christmas.'

Wayne pulled out his Red Diamond credit card to pay the bill for the meal. 'Let's hope that Moncrieffs offer her the job quickly.

My technical people could do with something to tax their geeky minds.' He stood up and brushed down his Admiral's jacket. 'Anyway, gentlemen! I'm off! I've had enough sea for one day. I'm taking the short ferry ride back to the mainland where Jackie is going to collect me. Keep me posted on developments.'

The three men shook hands. Whilst Wayne went to his waiting taxi, John and Roger walked towards the harbour.

'So it's BDN or Moncrieffs?' John heard the beep from his phone.

'I'm not certain.' Roger led the way whilst John looked at the text message from Candida.

'Candida's just told me that she's received a credit card from the National Bank of Everson.'

'Tell her that it's her spending money for use on holiday. That's how we're going to pay ourselves. Tell her that it's all totally legitimate. No need to panic her with any complicated explanations.'

Roger and John were back on board Fandango Two and had cast off from the mooring. The sun had retreated behind dark grey clouds. The icy wind remained as it blew into Roger's steered out into the sea. The blast of cold air failed to diminish his enthusiasm. 'Y'know, Johnno. By presenting a sizeable amount of cash to a woman, they'll find every opportunity to spend it, quickly. You look at Candida. No sooner was your business sold than she was off to buy new stable doors and the like. Mary has found a new cause to donate her time and her cash to. She wants me to go out with her this Christmas to oversee it all. Diana will be the same. If she's not working as hard, she'll have time to spend. She won't feel the need to ask questions after a while. She's been spending all her life asking questions. She'd like a change.'

'All the same, I'd like to meet her before we go much further.'

'I think you should. I've been thinking about that.' Roger wiped the sea salt from his face. When are you leaving for the Bahamas?'

'The week before Christmas.' John replied, hoping that there would be ample time to arrange a meeting with his prospective extra partner.

'I'm not sure that you should meet her until she's decided what to do.' Roger's tone sounded wary. 'I can't have you expressing your thoughts on corporate honesty and dishonesty with her. You must remember that she is experienced in sussing out feckless people. So far, I've kept her onside. She's the key to untold riches, Johnno, and I can't have our efforts over the past months jeopardised by your suspicions. You do understand, don't you?'

John nodded, stomped the floor in the cockpit and clapped his hands, not just in agreement, but also to restore long-lost feeling to his frozen feet and hands. Roger's intentions were now abundantly clear. As the bitter east wind blew the two men and their yacht homewards,   John began to tingle with excitement as questions that had hung in his mind like heavy grey clouds were beginning to open up with answers. As the occasional darting ray of late-afternoon sunshine pierced the cloud, so did opportunities to take hold of his own destiny begin to present themselves. If Wayne and Roger needed guidance, who better to give it to them?

++++

Chapter Thirty One

A questionable future

Diana stepped out of the taxi at Heathrow Airport and paid the driver. She watched him depart leaving her and her suitcase to face the teaming hordes of Christmas travellers on the pavement outside the terminal building.

It had been some weeks since she had frozen half to death in the shadowy dusk of Kensington Gardens. Walking down the steps of the station to her train, her mind had reeled at what she had given, at what she had learned and, more astonishingly, at what she had been offered in return. The intervening days had fuelled her confusion with a barrage of such emotional intensity that it was a surprise to her, above all, that she was still standing. Volleys of rejection and approval, normal and abnormal, kindness and beastliness had soared back and forth over her, subjecting her to a final state of pummelled submission.

She made her way towards the Bag-Drop Desk, brandishing her pre-printed Boarding Card. This was to be no departure to Hong Kong to refill the coffers of Crosthwaites. Neither was this a Christmas Break for a cutesy snow-capped break with Charlotte. This was Diana's retreat from the ravages of calamity, her escape to a continent to which she had never been, her last-minute acquiescence to a ridiculously far-fetched offer of calm that would offer her time for measured thought amid an alien surrounding.

She had always vowed that she would never travel over the Christmas Holiday. She had lost count of the number of stories of hardship, delay and rank inefficiency that she had had to assimilate over the years as claims for missed flights, overbooked hotels and lost luggage were assessed for veracity and cost. She had seen enough pictures of departure lounges bursting at the seams with people desperate to seek out peace and quiet as offered by airlines, hotels and holiday brochures, topped up by their own fanciful desires.

Giant red, silver and green balls hung down from the steel roof of the terminal building in their salute to the Festive Season as Diana placed her bag next to the bag-check desk.

'Good morning Madam!' The generous smile from the neat thirty something woman behind the Business Class desk beamed as if genuinely pleased to be attending to Diana's travel needs. 'Dar es Salaam! Dar is lovely. Great beaches. Great markets.'

'Are there? That'll be nice.' Diana replied hesitantly. Uncertainty was not her usual travelling companion. 'Shame I won't be there long enough to enjoy them. I'm only there to change planes, before going on to .....Remanda? Do you know it?'

'I can't say that I've been there myself!' The woman replied. 'What happens there? Christmas on Safari? How exciting!'

'Not quite!' Diana replied as she watched her large Mulberry suitcase wobble its way along the rubber runway before disappearing into the mechanical clutches of the baggage handling system. She had no doubts about seeing it at Dar. The worry was where it was going afterwards. 'I'm meeting some friends and we're all working in a Childrens' Home as volunteers.'

'Now, that is exciting! Good luck with it. Here's your voucher for the Premium Lounge. D'you know the way? Happy Christmas!'

'Yes, I have been there before.' Diana had liked the snobbery of the exclusive Lounge on the first floor. On previous trips, she had felt that the formal comforts and the lack of tell-tale bustle were just rewards for working her buns off for Crosthwaites. This time, even though her mission was entirely different, Diana felt that any cosseting was merited.

She placed her passport and boarding pass back in her large leather handbag. She saw that the three letters she had received in the past week were also there. She looked forward to having the time over the coming days not only to parse every sentence, but also to work out a suitable response to each.

Diana sank into the comfort of one of the lounge's soft armchairs. She sipped on the whisky that she had poured herself – at eleven thirty in the morning?! The tentacles of recklessness had squeezed out all breath of reason, for Christmas at least. The television in the corner was repeating news that was fresh to those not already shell-shocked by the collapse of a couple of American banks, the bailout of another major insurance company and the subsequent demise of a lesser British bank. To Diana Vowlds, the news was old hat and of little relevance. One of the envelopes containing six lines written in Sir Alastair's large ornate script, on vellum from his personal stationery, gave eye-witness testament to what had happened.

Diana had been prepared for admonishment for the losses in the South China Sea. Yet the revelation of the true state of Crosthwaites had hit her with the same force as the typhoon itself.

For two hundred million dollars to have been described as insignificant in comparison with what was heading the company's way as a result of the demise of one of the largest insurers in the western world had knocked the very stuffing out of her. That she should somehow be seen as one of the sacrificial turkeys to be slaughtered in the days before Christmas had come as a complete shock. Being made to suffer for the misdoings of others seemed both grossly unfair and worthy of heavy litigation on her return to the country in the New Year. Discovering how people had been creaming off something from the top or from the bottom or from the middle for their own gain made her assessment of Roger's activities seem ludicrous and harsh.

Diana looked around the lounge as others eagerly studied their laptops for news from the office or for the start of the downloaded movie. Normally she would have been logging on and sending e-mails just as voraciously. However, her new laptop was empty of just about anything. She had at least asked Charlotte to download some episodes of the TV series about an American firm of undertakers which she had missed and promised herself to catch up on.

Charlotte's announcement that she intended to spend Christmas with the lugubrious Jake and his mother had also taken her by surprise. It had showed parental responsibility of a sort to condone her request. She should be with somebody of her own age, even if the tattooed work on the upper shoulder of the nineteen year old boy was better suited for display in a small art gallery. Any semblance of "Christmas with the family" had been replaced by the sight of the mother seated in the lounge knocking back her whisky, catching up on the latest magazines before buggering off to do good for others in a village in Africa. Diana consoled herself with the thought that not many mothers would have been fired from their well-paid job ten days before Christmas. Even fewer would be carrying two letters with job offers in their fake designer handbag bought in Hong Kong. The short sentence scrawled onto a card was succinct, *"Eligible at all good banks, including Moncrieffs!"* The enclosed Red Diamond Credit card was more enigmatic. The embossed letterhead in black and red ink, attached to ten pages of legalese outlining her rights as *"Executive Director – Compliance"* was more self-explanatory.

Diana had never heard of the National Bank of Everson. A quick look on their website showed that the bank had the right credentials to look after other people's money. She was chuffed to bits that her abilities and credentials had stood up to close scrutiny by Moncrieffs and had withstood the misogynistic views of the noble knight himself. It was good to know that the world had not ended for her just short of her fifty third birthday. She had liked the people at Moncrieffs who had interviewed her. Giles Montague-Smythe seemed to be safe and trustworthy, somebody with whom she could work. Moncrieffs seemed not to have the aspirations of self-serving greed that was rife in many other banks. There had been almost a brave naivety in their desire just to lend money to those who could afford to repay. Their ambitions to extend their services into other areas seemed measured and controlled. The ethos was one that she could work within.

As she toyed with the plastic card, Diana was forced to accept that Roger's rogue-like behaviour was not without its attraction. She had enjoyed his close attentions in Hong Kong. She was reminded of their conversation a couple of days following her meeting with Alastair Crosthwaite. Roger had been his usual calming self as they walked again along the anonymous paths of Kensington Gardens.

"This Christmas, Mary and I are off to work at a Children's Centre in a village in Remanda, wherever that is! We wondered whether you might like join us. Call it Christmas compassion or seasonal concern for the plight of others. It might be a good opportunity for you to sort yourself out."

"Why would I want to work with other peoples' children, when I can't do a proper job with my own? You have a mean sense of humour, Roger, after your assessment of my parenting skills!" Diana had not been able to contain herself. "I do presume that this is a real school you're going to and not one contrived in your head, like Royal Northwood?" She had listened to Roger's encouragement. As her plans of femme fatale, whose favours could only be bought for a high price in a nice hotel, started to wither on the vine, she had responded with encouragement of her own. "I suppose that this is your way of putting something back into society, as your wife has often suggested. After what you've taken out recently, Roger, I suspect that you're going to be a busy man!' Diana recognised that Roger had caught her when she was feeling at a low ebb; any offer to take her away from her current plight sounded attractive as she heard herself reply. "I would like to come with you, thank you!" The bing-bong of the public-address system brought her back to the here and now.

"Would Miss Diana Vowlds come to the Information desk. Miss Diana Vowlds, please!"

The breathy pronouncement was reminiscent of nineteen forties elocution lessons. As Diana walked to the desk, she half expected to be greeted by a lady in a tweed suit and a jaunty black hat from Swan & Edgar. Instead, the lady, dressed in a smart navy blue, pointed to a man standing by the desk.

'Miss Vowlds? Miss Diana Vowlds?'

The man seemed to be in his late fifties. His face was bronzed. His hair brushed straight back. The dark suit looked smart and well tailored on his tall frame. The blue shirt and red tie provided a picture of debonair.

'That's me! Who are you?'

Diana inspected the picture on the man's warrant card before looking up at him.

'The spelling is different from what I've been used to recently, Detective Inspector'

'I'm sorry? What have you been used to, Miss Vowlds?'

'It's just that I've come across many variants of the name recently. It's all very confusing.'

'Spelt with a Y and an E makes it a little different from the ordinary Smith, I always think.'

'That's true. Anyway, inspector, what do you want? You'd better hurry. I'm due to catch a plane in twenty minutes.'

'I'm well aware of the timing, Miss Vowlds.'

The man seemed too well dressed to be a copper. Then Diana remembered that her Dad had looked quite dapper in his final years with the Kent County Constabulary. His expression remained impassive as wild thoughts started to race through her mind.

'I hope that this is not about my daughter.' A sudden panic hit Diana. How could Social Services have found Charlotte abandoned so soon? She had sounded fine when they spoke on the phone in the taxi. How did this policeman know where Diana would be?

'No, it's nothing to do with her!' Inspector Smythe gestured towards a door in the Lounge. 'I just would like a quick chat. It shouldn't take more than a few minutes. Please follow me.'

Diana looked around for signs of a camera crew or of a giggling crowd who would be in on the joke as she entered the windowless room. She heard the door shut behind her as she sat down at the small brown lacquered table and waited for an explanation.

'My department OL12 at Scotland Yard have been asked by our counterparts in Hong Kong to help with their investigations.' Smythe had settled into the other chair facing Diana. 'They're a little concerned about your leaving the country and they want me to ask you one or two questions.'

A gentle hum from the heating unit in the corner interrupted the uneasy silence as Smythe studied his notebook.

Diana looked at her watch. 'Can we get on with it, Inspector? I don't want to miss my flight. I'm meeting a friend ......'

'Roger Mortlock. Yes, HKPD have told us a lot about him. How well do you know him?'

'We were work colleagues. He sold insurance policies and I made sure that they were all proper and legitimate. We also worked together on fraudulent claims.'

'So you had a close working relationship? Have you seen much of him since he left Crosthwaites?'

'We have met once or twice recently.'

'In Hong Kong, for instance?'

Diana breathed in deeply. She wondered who had leaked that piece of information.

'You are well informed, Inspector. Yes, we did meet up, strictly by chance.'

'Really?' The inspector looked down at his notebook. 'You were staying at the same hotel, I gather? More than just coincidence, wasn't it? Did Mrs Mortlock know about this?'

'Yes, I believe she did, although we didn't meet. She left early to avoid the storm.'

'Ah yes the storm!' Smythe turned back a few pages in his notebook and paused. 'We'll come back to that in a moment. You're going to meet Mrs Mortlock tomorrow, I gather?'

'Yes, Roger and his wife have taken pity on me, I suppose. It's all rather humiliating, if you want the honest truth. They knew that I was facing a miserable time over Christmas and so they suggested that I join them. Mrs Mortlock has a very charitable streak in her.'

'I believe she does. I presume that she doesn't know about your sharing the room with her husband after she left?'

'That was because I was frightened, Inspector! What has that to do with ......'

Before Diana could finish, a phone chirped. Smythe answered in a rather hushed tone. 'Yes sir. I'm talking with her now.' Diana could hear sibilance of a voice speaking at the other end of the line. 'I will, sir. Absolutely sir.... I understand. I will let you know.' Smythe closed his phone and turned to Diana. 'That was my boss at OL12. He's got to report back to Hong Kong before he goes home tonight. So I will get to the point. Tell me about the South China claims you were working on before you left

Crosthwaites. We understand that some of the more dubious ones had a possible connection to Mr Mortlock. Can you confirm this?'

'There were certainly some submitted by dubious people who were known to Roger.'

'How many might there have been? Four? Fourteen? Forty? Four hundred?'

'From memory, I think that there may have been about ten.' Diana sensed that her own suspicions needed to be tempered. Roger was a friend after all.

'Is that all? The HKPD suggests that the figure was far higher.'

'Could very well be! But my department didn't have the manpower to verify every claim that was lodged with us.'

'Was it lack of manpower or.....was it a lack of willpower that held you back, Miss Vowlds? Was it not easier to pass each claim and send out a cheque, regardless of the justification of the claim?'

Diana remained silent for a few moments. What tricks had Gavin Fuck-Face been up to? Why would he want to discredit her? Africa was becoming an even better place to be than she thought. She looked at her watch and then stood up to leave. 'As you may know, Inspector, I no longer work for Crosthwaites. I think that you should direct your questions to them.'

'We are, Miss Vowlds. However, they have asked for our help. Please sit down!' the policeman consulted his notebook again before looking up. Diana sat down again as she listened to the Inspector's further questioning.

' So, you don't consider that your controls were maybe a bit lax?'

'My Compliance and Claims team did their best with the resources available to them.'

'You think so? What if I were to say that your team was not as stringent as it should have been in assessing dubious claims....that somehow you were complicit?'

'That is utterly preposterous! I've worked bloody hard over these past two years. I'm not the sort to bugger it up for the sake of.....'

'....money, MissVowlds? A lot of money, if the figures are to be believed? ' Smythe threw down his book onto the table. 'Let me ask you this! As a professional investigator, does it not seem strange to you that a person in your position is going away on holiday with somebody who is suspected of fraudulent activities?'

'Rash, maybe, inspector! But nothing has been proven. There was insufficient evidence to show that Mr Mortlock did receive monies from Crosthwaites to which he was not entitled. Deceit is very hard to pin down, as I'm sure you know. As for holiday, I'm more inclined to think that we'll be working quite hard at the Children's Centre in Remanda.'

'That may well be. Nevertheless, we're becoming increasingly concerned about the proliferation of white-collar crime. There are people who think that helping themselves for their own ends is fair game, as long as nobody gets hurt. It is our job, Miss Vowlds, yours and mine...' Smythe pointed to Diana. '.....as responsible citizens to stop them'

'*Was* my job, Inspector. I have to remind you.' Diana looked at her watch. She should be boarding the plane and settling in her seat. This whole conversation had Gavin's fingerprints all over it. One man's scorn was far worse than that of any woman. To think that Diana had swallowed Alistair's reasons for her dismissal! She had been duped by his suave good looks, battle-scarred by lines of emotional shock and professional embarrassment. She had certainly not expected to be a suspect in her own investigations! Yet, she could not just storm out and leave the country under a cloud of any sort. It would not suit her future prospects to have any hint of suspicion that might affect her position with Moncrieffs.

'I presume that you are planning to return to the UK?'

'In two weeks' time! With Roger and Mary Mortlock, as far as I know.' Diana rustled in her handbag for a tissue. 'Will that be all, inspector?' She watched Smythe flick through the pages of his notebook.

'One last question, Miss Vowlds! You said that you have recently come across quite a few people with a similar name to mine. There is a particular John Smith about whom my colleagues are interested to find out more. He comes from Bisbury. He used to own a screw manufacturing business. Has Mr Mortlock mentioned him to you at all?'

'Roger has talked about him, but not with reference to insurance claims as far as I can remember. It wouldn't surprise me if he was involved in some way, but there's no clear evidence to prove it.'

'Have you met him? Are you working with him at this school over Christmas?'

'No and again no, inspector.' Diana breathed a huge sigh. 'Can this not wait until I come back after Christmas?'

'I do understand your impatience, Miss Vowlds. All in good time! As we continue our investigations with Crosthwaites, we're bound to uncover more about these claims. So we'll need to talk to you and to Mr Mortlock in the New Year.'

Diana had had enough. She was about to go off to do good at Christmastime. She was not having her crazy plan destroyed by one overly inquisitive policeman. She gathered up her bag. 'That's fine by me, Inspector!'

'Hopefully, we might have spoken with Mr Smith in the meantime. Anyway, Miss Vowlds, you have a plane to catch and I have a report to file. Thank you for your time and a Happy Christmas to you!'

She shook the inspector's hand and rushed out of the Lounge in search of the departure gate for her flight. Suddenly Diana felt liberated. A veil had suddenly lifted. From now on, she realised that there would be no more questions, no more lies, no more deceits. Diana could look forward to some plain uncomplicated living, albeit with a swarm of sneezy children! *"Paging the last remaining passenger for the flight to Dar Es Salaam!"*

The announcer sounded annoyed and impatient. Diana ran as fast as her legs could carry her. The bright yellow gate number got larger as her future became more uncertain. She didn't really care as she eased her way into the window seat in the front section of the plane.

'Welcome aboard, madam. A glass of champagne?' The stewardess extended the tray towards Diana. The mix of whisky before lunch and a police interrogation on an empty stomach made their own uneasy cocktail. The champagne could wait. Diana sank into the cushioned seat and listened to the large exit door thump behind her. Within minutes, she could see the sights of the airport recede as the plane taxied towards take-off. She could breathe easy as the cabin crew were instructed to close doors to automatic and cross check. Whatever was going to happen from now on, she was going to enjoy it. She bloody deserved it! Where was that champagne?

++++

Chapter Thirty Two

Adjusting course

The stewardess was older than other members of the cabin crew. Diana sensed that she was one of the last of the Old School "Trolley Dollies" when the position had a glamour and an aura of luxurious stopovers and handsome pilots. The red and yellow scarf rested neatly in the collar of her white shirt like a floral display in a vase. She stopped by Diana to refill her champagne glass as the plane continued its climb to its cruising height.

'Going away for Christmas?'

Diana knew that the stewardess had meant well. A woman on her own tucking into the champagne can be a sorry sight. She treated the comment with equal respect as she outlined the purpose of her trip.

'Isn't Remanda one of those small places on the sea in Tanzania? I think I've been there, when I was married. Great landscapes. Marvellous views, if I remember correctly. Anyway, I must move on. If there's anything you want, just press the call button.'

Glad to have made a new friend, Diana eased back in her seat. The champagne was combining with the earlier whisky and the excitement of her chat with the police inspector. She looked out of the window onto the powder-puff of cloud outside and allowed her eyes to close out all recent memories.

Diana didn't know how long she had nodded off before she felt the gentle tap on her shoulder. She opened her sleep-filled eyes slowly and looked up at the hazy shape hovering over her. She sat bolt upright as she took in the Cheshire cat grin of Roger Mortlock.

'What on earth are you doing here, Roger? I thought that I was going to meet you in Remanda.'

Diana pressed the button in the panel above her head. She needed a refill as she reconciled herself to Roger's explanation. It had sounded perfectly plausible. The fates playing with her life having already drained her of most emotions, there remained just enough supply of suspicion and irritation.

'This is quite a dramatic change of plan, Roger. There was I expecting to meet Mr and Mrs Mortlock at a small airstrip, ready to travel into the bush to administer great works to the poor and the needy, ready to combat my low level of compassion fatigue with the chance to really make a difference at the front line. Now, all I see is Mr Mortlock in the Business Class section of my plane, clutching a glass of champagne with the mischievous look of a cat who's got the cream. Bloody hell, Roger! What's going on? Am I that gullible?' Diana was aware that she had started to raise her voice. She changed her tone as her irritation continued. 'Have I just been prey to the worst sort of entrapment that a girl of my mature years should be most wary of? You have some bloody cheek if you think that I will just ......'

'Just what?' Roger didn't catch the reproachful look on the stewardess' face as she refilled both their glasses; a woman travelling on her own can be vulnerable prey.

'I don't know.' Diana looked flustered. 'It's just that I hadn't quite expected.....'

'Expected what?' Roger seemed genuinely taken aback by Diana's uncertainty. 'I certainly hadn't planned for this to happen.

I was looking forward to displaying my football skills and playing Pooh sticks with the school's kids. I've been forced into this.'

'By whom?'

'By Mary! This is her plan.' Roger leaned across so that Diana could hear his explanation above the gentle roar of the plane. 'We were lucky to get tickets in the first place. Mary was booked to come out earlier than me. Wayne, the owner, had previously suggested that she would be really useful in helping prepare the Centre in readiness for the Christmas holiday. I was due to travel out yesterday. However, two days ago, Mary calls. She told me that there was a problem with the accommodation. Available space was very limited and there was really nowhere for you and I to sleep. She also made a comment that our coming to the Children's Centre might hold things up and prevent her from getting all the work done. She was quite definite.'

'So no thoughts of telling of *me* beforehand, then?' Diana looked towards Roger, easing her irritation as she took in his story. 'The sight of a Business Class ticket to Africa would be enough to entice me away, was that it?'

'Well you're here, aren't you?' Roger looked around the cloistered seclusion of the cabin for any response to Diana's indignant outburst. 'It's not that bad! Fortunately, Wayne is quite influential and put me in touch with the owner of a very nice thirty five footer with a cabin that sleeps four. It will be an adventure! We can rent it for as long as we like.'

'Who's going to steer it for us? Your captain's log is a bit chequered, Roger, if I remember correctly. Do you know your way around these waters?' Diana paused and considered the suggestion further. 'Oh, I know what happens next. You're going to sink the bloody thing and then put in a claim on the insurance, again. Am I right? Lucky for both of us that I know how to sail as well, don't you think, Roger?'

'I knew that you'd love the idea, Diana, once I'd explained it to you in full! It'll give you the chance to recapture your old skills.' Roger smiled towards her. 'The Swahili Coast has very easy seas to sail in. I've been told that there's nothing to worry about. There are lots of coves and beaches. Somebody has told me of some great places to eat.'

'Mary's OK with this? Christmas is all about the family, or so I thought. It sounds a bit strange that she's banished you. Banishing me, I can understand.'

'I think she's flipped, if you ask me. It's a sort of mid-life crisis that women of her age go through and then come out the other side after a few months.'

Diana finished her champagne. Then she asked. 'Do you *really* have a wife, Roger? This is the second time that I don't get to meet her. I'm starting to believe that I've been consorting with a complete fantasist. Does this school really exist? '

Diana saw Roger's face break into a smile. 'Of course, they all exist! It would take a very vivid imagination to make this up.'

'Good, that makes me feel very comforted by the state of the Mortlock mind.' Diana was reconciled to her fate. 'I shall look forward to relating Bosun's Tales of my own about policemen named Smythe – with a Y and an E. Quite good-looking, but rather unpleasant. He seemed to know a lot about you and a fair amount about me. So there'll be lots to discuss when we splice the mainbrace together on the high seas.'

A nudge from the male steward pushing the food trolley to the front of the cabin had been a good sign for Roger to return to his seat. He needed to contemplate not only the future of his marriage, but also what the policeman named Smythe had been playing at.

As she tucked into her first slice of peppered steak, Diana considered whether she had brought the right clothes for a crummy little yacht. As she browsed through the in-flight magazine, she determined that there were many worse things than enjoying the sea breezes on a turquoise sea under a hot sun. Besides, there would be more time to quiz Roger Mortlock. What would be her role as *"Systems and Diligence Consultant"* at BDN Consultants? How come DCI Smythe knew so much about her investigations of Roger and his cronies? Which was port and which was starboard? She at least knew the answer to that one.

++++

Chapter Thirty Three

Advent of Christmas

In the days since they had motored away from the jetty in Remanda Town, Diana had become accustomed to the sound of the Indian Ocean lapping the hull of the *Voyager of the Seas*. She had been impressed by Roger's capabilities at keeping the yacht stable and upright. She had forgotten the exhilaration of the open sea. She had marvelled at the shift of wondrous blues as it stretched out before her. She had revelled in its embrace as she swam off the boat. She watched the coastline change from bare sand to crowded mangrove as the local KazKazi winds blew the yacht southwards.

She had been greatly relieved that she had been assigned her own quarters, although she was disappointed by the limited wardrobe space available within it. The springy mattress, new sheets, albeit with low thread count and the brash orchid embroidery of the bedcover had enlivened the limited space. Her new daily routine had been as regular as the one so unfairly denied her by Alistair Crosthwaite. The timetable had been just as measured. Swim at sun-rise in the warm waters of a cove away from the busy Ocean; breakfast of mango and a cup of coffee; sails-up to catch the mid-morning KK breeze; taking the *Voyager of the Seas* down the coast ; mooring up at a rickety jetty; lunch at a small wooden cabin on the coastline of coral reef; a doze in the afternoon sun. However, the agenda had been fluid and the content wonderfully slothful.

Seated on plastic chairs that were in dire need of replacement from the hardware store in Remanda Town, Diana would watch the parade of dhows motor their way past her out to the open sea. Three days of hot sun and sea spray in the hair had allowed Diana to drain down her brain and clean out all thoughts of others' misdeeds. Plates of *Ugali* mush, deep-fried white fish or stewed goat, served at bare wooden tables, had become easier to swallow as had the sweet-tasting beer. They made a change from the exotic overpriced fare served up by the sandwich bar near to her office in London. She had got through the seven hundred pages of how a serial killer in Rotterdam was finally brought to justice by a plucky woman investigator; the first time in ages that Diana had reached the end of a book. Taking over the tiller herself had presented challenges that she had never faced, even sailing along the Hamble coast.

As the first demonstration of Christmas cheer, Diana let out a whoop of delight as she steered their yacht past the Oduku Bay Hotel on its way to the calmer waters within. With Christmas Day only six hours away, Diana was pleased and surprised by the gaudy neon of Santa Claus and his reindeer lighting up a squat brick building that stood at the entrance. She closed down the engine and waited for the yacht's anchor, thrown overboard by Roger, to take hold on the seabed.

In the orange glow of the evening sun, Diana scanned the stretch of white sand that carved its way around the bay, a thick sprawl of trees shadowed their protection from the silhouette of cliff behind. The ensuing silence was interrupted by the swish of a couple of large winged birds flying overhead on their way to their overnight stop in the trees inland. She watched Roger approach with an armful of chilled beers retrieved from the amply-stocked fridge in the galley. His bare chest still showed signs of over-consumption of Crosthwaite lunches, but the suntan had started to paint over these excesses and provided a healthier picture than the ghostly white that she had confronted in the Hong Kong hotel a few weeks previously. Invitations to visit the Captain's cabin had been refused on the grounds of inadequate physical comfort and a lack of emotional well-being. The heat of the sun and the freedom of the sea had filled the void in the meantime.

Roger had identified the hotel's position on the chart. Wayne had mentioned that it was a good, if not the only, option for Christmas lunch on the following day. Roger was just happy that the winds of the Indian Ocean had been kind and had not presented excessive challenges to his sailing skills. He was also hugely relieved that Diana had been equally accommodating as she adapted to the change of course set by Mary. As he dropped the anchor over the side, he offered a cheerful wave to a small fishing smack as it tooted a Christmas greeting on its way past them towards an inlet in the far corner of the bay. He could make out a posse of children gathered at the water's edge either in anticipation of Christmas presents or of the evening's dinner.

It had been a relief that the small fridge had worked beyond its call of duty to chill the stock of beers and bottles of a very acceptable Moroccan wine which he had found at the *Chief Bobby Supermarket* in Remanda Town. He was pleased that Wayne's conversations with Mavis Ng had been so productive. Crewed Weekends along the Swahili Coast could be a useful addition to the BDN portfolio.

'So skipper, what's the schedule for the morrow to celebrate the birth of Christ?' Diana had settled on the deck and was leaning against the foot of the mast. 'More fish or shall we look for somewhere with a shower and a hair dryer by way of a change?'

'We've just past it.' Roger pointed back to the lights that now shone more brightly in the failing light. 'That place is owned by a friend of Wayne's. It has a couple of bedrooms with bath and all mod cons. I've reserved us a room for a couple of nights.'

Diana shuffled her bum to allow some space for Roger to share the few centimetres of space next to her. 'So no more stinky fish for a while?' She rested her arm on Roger's crooked knee.

'Talking of which, Diana, tell me more about your conversation with the copper at the airport. You said that he seemed to know rather a lot about your stinky claims in Hong Kong.'

Roger was just getting used to the presence of a crewmate who was no longer an ex- work colleague, but one who could be a potential partner in his enterprises. He wondered how she might respond to the absence of any corporate discipline in *BDN Consultants*. . Already the strict formality of smart chic had been replaced by the dress-down code of white linen shirt and half-length trousers. The faded tan that had lain uninhibited on the hotel bed in Hong Kong had been refurbished to a nut brown. Her nakedness modestly covered by an orange bikini had further brightened his day. The glow in her face, so lacking on the flight from Heathrow, had returned as her eyes sparkled in the fading light. Nothing had been revealed, however, as to what her response might be to his offer of considerable wealth. He listened attentively to Diana's assessment of DCI Smythe's interrogation skills.

'I suspect that Gavin has been feeding false information in a desperate bid to defer any responsibility for his over-enthusiasm in building up his book of business. He certainly knew a lot about you and your contacts.' Diana concluded.

'He won't find anything.'

'You're being very cool, I must say, Roger, with two police forces gunning for you.'

'What about you?' Roger sensed that the conversation needed to be steered closer to home.

'They won't get me, because I've done nothing wrong!' Diana exclaimed. 'Whatever Gavin may say!'

'What about our offer to you?'

'Ah! ' Diana paused 'You can't really mean it, Roge? It's not a proper job. You know that!'

'My colleagues and I are deadly serious. *BDN Consltants* has a lot to offer. As our *Systems and Diligence Consultant,* you could provide an invaluable service to clients whose compliance operations are in complete meltdown at the moment. They'll be needing your …. and our help.'

The job interview was under way. The Familiarisation section was at an end. The Q and A session had begun. A glass of chilled Serengeti Lager was certainly different from the cup of tea and a biscuit presented by a starchy PA within the anonymity of the Moncrieffs boardroom.

'What happened to *"Director of Non-Compliance",* Roger, which you offered me in Kensington Gardens? Aren't you going to make a dishonest woman of me? I was beginning to relish the role of being your moll!'

'Wayne's team is supremely well qualified in the implementation of software that'll rectify flaws and enhance existing control procedures.' Roger could not stop his Office Speak. 'You would help identify the weak spots, Oduku's people would devise systems and programmes to plug them accordingly.'

'So, this is you, me, the Chief's Son and anybody else?' Roger's association with some of Wayne Oduku's business interests had taken Diana by surprise. She had heard good reports about Oduku Systems. She considered that she didn't need to know about the merits of *Fertlity 4 U.*

'There's my other partner, John Smith. He's already brought in one client, who trusts us implicitly and is delighted with the service that we're providing.'

'Inspector Smythe was less certain. He sounded quite suspicious of this Mister Smith.'

'He *was* floundering in the dark, wasn't he?' In the gathering dusk, Roger had stood up to light a couple of oil lamps that swayed gently in the light wind. He wanted to see how genuinely Diana was treating his gentle persuasions. His attention was momentarily deflected by the lights of a small boat that had entered the bay from the ocean.

'Was he, Roger?' The flickering light caught Diana's quizzical expression. 'His name did show up quite a few times during our investigations. Who's the lucky client who loves Mr Smith so much?' Diana could just see the smile appear on Roger's face as he leaned forward to give her another beer. She carried on gamely. 'OK! The Code of the Mandarin, is it? One of these days, Roger, you and I are going to have so much to talk about! God, you have more secrets than Tutankhamun! '

'This is a critical time, Diana, for banks and insurance companies. They're going to need the likes of us.' Roger sat down again at the foot of the mast. 'We could start with our previous employer. They'd be really impressed by your initiative, your willingness to start with a fledgling company.'

'With you, Roger, and your history? They'd think that I was barking bloody mad!'

'You'd be doing Alistair a favour by offering him our *SpeedyTrans* foreign exchange system.'

'I'd only contemplate it if I knew that it was going to make me some real money.'

'We might not be able to match the Moncrieffs package, but it would certainly be more than just beer, stinky fish and sunbathing.'

'This is all magical and lovely, isn't it? I think that Charlotte would have liked all this, although she's not too keen on stinky fish.' Diana took in another gulp of the new beer. 'I can't afford to lose her, Roger! I have to be there for her and to give her what she wants. At the moment, I think she feels sorry for me. She says that

I've been sucked into the corporate whirlpool, fuelling the needs of big beastly bosses.'

'Then look what they did! She does have a point.'

'I don't normally drink this stuff.' Diana had stood up and was staring at the level of beer that remained in the bottle. 'I'm normally a white wine girl. But this is going down rather well. Cheers, Roge!' Diana had noticed the dark shape of the motorboat. Its interior cabin lights showed up anonymous shapes of maybe three crew members. She gave them a cheery wave and was pleased by a reciprocal wave from one of the crew. She turned back to Roger. 'When I announced that I was coming out here to work in a Children's Home, Charlotte did express some surprise. She didn't really know what to say. I think that she was rather impressed ...or maybe she just thought that her mother had lost it, totally.'

'Maybe she was angry that you chose to come to the school, rather than stay with her. Yet more rejection, but you probably need this time to sort out what you want to do when you get back.'

'She made the decision to go with Jake first! But you're right! Maybe I should have fought for her more, if that doesn't sound too melodramatic.' Diana downed the remaining beer in one swallow before she announced. 'I think that it's time for a swim before supper, don't you, Skip?'

Trousers and linen shirt had already been removed to reveal the orange two-piece. Roger did not really have enough time to take in the joyful release of bra and bikini bottom before being enveloped in Diana's tight embrace as she whispered in his ear.

'Permission to jump overboard, Captain! Maybe you'd like to join me?' Diana's mermaid silhouette made its way to the edge of the boat and dived into the moonlit water.

'Be careful of that boat!'

Roger's warning fell on submerged ears as he watched Diana's head surface a few yards away. The moonlight showed animated ripples playing around her. Suddenly, his attention was taken by the sinister outline of the motorboat as it gently moved towards the bow of Roger's yacht. He could not see Diana, but he could just hear her splashing above the muted gurgling of the other boat's engine.

Roger shielded his eyes from the spotlight that was focussed directly on him. Thoughts of local villagers returning from last minute Christmas shopping in town or of tourists being ferried to witness the arrival of Christmas Day in exclusive seclusion on the beach were soon dispelled. The dazzling glare prevented him from seeing who was driving the boat or whether Diana had been caught up in the boat's propellers.

Suddenly, a shadow jumped onto the bow of the yacht and attached a rope loosely to a cleat on the deck. As the figure made his way towards Roger, the red sports shirt and black trousers seemed innocuous enough. The peak of his baseball cap hid most of his face. The Remandan features that were visible suggested that he was probably not looking for directions to the local supermarket. What was blindingly obvious was the very serious and very lethal-looking machine gun that was pointing directly towards Roger.

'Happy Christmas, gentlemen!' Roger had no idea where that had come from. His heart beat like a jungle drum. He had never seen a gun brandished with such intent, let alone towards him. The sweat on his forehead felt chill in the light evening breeze. His offer of good cheer did little to avert the gunman's aggressive pose with his front foot firmly forward. Roger noticed movement from beyond as another shadowy figure stepped onto the yacht and approached him. The man had removed his hat to reveal a mop of unruly grey curly hair. The toothy grin was not a pretty sight. Whilst the sunglasses may have hidden his motives, the grizzled cheeks and bushy moustache suggested that he was older than Roger. The camouflage shirt and trousers showed that he was more prepared for confrontation than Roger, even if the pistol remained stuffed into his leather belt.

'Happy Christmas to you, too, sir!' The cut-glass poncey accent was not what Roger had expected. 'May I ask what you are doing here?'

'What business is it of yours?' Roger asked. 'We're not doing anything wrong, are we?'

'I don't know. That's what I'm trying to find out. I will ask you again.'

'Let me ask you something first. Who the hell are you?' Roger was not impressed by the dark blue cravat which clashed with his khaki garb. The silver stripes on the silk scarf suggested the livery of an English school. He was not sure which.

'My name is ......'

The heads of all three men were turned in an instant by the sound of splashing from the other side of the yacht. The Grey Hair and his mate drew their guns ready to repel whoever had swung over onto the deck in the darkness on the port side. The beam of light moved round to catch Diana's nakedness in full view.

'What on earth is going on, Roger?' Diana had retreated back into shadow. 'Pass me a towel, quickly! You didn't tell me the hotel was sending out a Welcome Party.'

The gunman had moved towards Diana and, between unintelligible grunts, was gesticulating for her to come forward. As she came out, she let out a muted shriek. 'Oh my God, what is that?'

'It's a bloody gun, Diana, and I don't think that he's just been given it for Christmas.' Roger moved to wrap the towel around her shoulders. Diana was shivering. He brought her close to him to reassure her that he was only slightly less scared than she by what was happening.

'So now you will tell me what you are both doing here.' Grey Hair had stepped forward to restrain the gunman from any further bullying of the soaking wet Diana.

'You haven't told me who you are and why it is any of your bloody business.' Roger's belligerence did not go down well.

'My name is Frederick Magumba. This is my home.' He gestured towards the lights that shone through the trees on the beach. 'I intend to find out why you are trespassing.'

'The charts say that these are open waters. So, if you don't mind, Freddie, we have our own plans for dinner tonight. So maybe you would just bugger off to your place and we'll get on with knocking up the remains of the goat stew we had last night.'

Magumba stood immediately in front of Roger and shouted. 'Please do not be difficult....old boy! Why are you spying on me and my fellow officers....old boy?'

'We haven't seen a thing, Freddie.' Roger replied, wiping the spray of spittle that had shot from Magumba's mouth. 'We only arrived an hour ago. Did you see anything, Diana?'

Diana had towelled herself down. 'Not a thing, other than the small fishing boat that......'

'You see! You have been noticing movements in the bay. Who are you working for?'

'This is ridiculous!' Diana felt that it was time for a strategy of feminine belligerence. 'We've seen nothing. I'm freezing my arse off out here! So maybe you'd allow me to put on some dry clothes and brush my hair, whilst you two carry on swopping boat numbers. I'll just go to my cabin and then, maybe, I'll put on the kettle. Do you take milk and sugar with your tea, Mr Magumba?'

'Stay where you are, missus!'

Roger decided on one last attempt at reason. 'Look Freddie, old boy. Let's pull up our anchor and steal away into the darkness. We won't tell anybody about our meeting. You can then carry on with

334

whatever you're doing. That'll be the end of it.' As he turned away, Magumba barked out an order in a tongue that he did not recognize. The gunman let off a hale of bullets into the sea.

'Don't make me really lose my temper, old boy! Next time, he will aim the bullets straight at you.' Magumba had moved towards Diana. 'Ladies first, always, in our country. Just think of the mess that she would make to our wonderful turquoise sea if we were forced to throw her overboard. So I suggest that you both do as I ask. The lady may put on something more suitable for where we are going. Contrary to what you might think, not all our womenfolk wander around bare-breasted. My man will be watching for any false moves.'

Diana disappeared below deck, followed by the gunman. Roger grabbed a shirt that had been lying in the cockpit. It was clear that Christmas Day was promising much more than an exchange of presents.

Roger clutched Diana close to him as they watched the *Voyager of the Seas* recede into the distance, whilst the lights in the trees on the shore became brighter. A few children still remained at the shore's edge. He had not been prepared for Diana's clear mind as she whispered to him.

'When I last looked, Roger, I didn't see Crosthwaites'normal travel insurance policy include K & R, did you, Roger? There's not a much call for it in Benidorm. So we're on our own, Roger. I'm sure that they wouldn't want to kill us, would they?'

'They wouldn't dare! We're much more valuable alive. There's been some misunderstanding, Diana. I'm sure that Christmas Day with Mr Magumba and his family will be a very pleasurable experience. They might not run to the provision of a hairdryer or shower, however. ' Roger hoped that he sounded convincing.

++++

Chapter Thirty Four
Christmas - present

Within minutes of John and Candida's arrival on Everson Island, colours had abounded everywhere. Any fears that the yellow and white clapboard *Coral Beach Cottage* would bear little relation to the images on the website were quickly proven to be unfounded. Subsequent mornings of bright sun and clear blue sky streaming through the white slatted shutters reassured each that their presence on the island was very much fact and not some dream fiction, from which they would wake up in a cold sweat. Aquamarine stripes overwhelming a single yellow band on the giant Bahamian flag flew proudly from the flag pole in the car park on Main Street in Everson Town. Next to it sat a blue and white dolls-house building, the principal and only branch of the *National Bank of Everson*. Mr and Mrs Smith felt very much at home.

Whilst Candida had had to cope with mid-morning phone conversations with Mick Flanders about the late delivery of horse-feed and with frantic e-mails about the non-appearance of one of the stable girls, there had been a news blackout on John's chickens. He was satisfied that their daily diet of organic corn pellets would be greatly enhanced by selected leftovers from Clive Hunt's pub menu.

Candida had got used to the feel of bare feet and to the undemanding rig of straw hat, long T-shirt and beige shorts. She clung to her husband, kicking at the fine powder sand, as they ambled back to the cottage from Christmas lunch at the nearby hotel. The rush of the sea reverberated inside her head as the effects of the wine began to take hold.

'Happy Christmas, darling!' She put her arm around John and kissed him on the cheek, squeezing his arm gently as she tried to maintain her balance. 'I'm just amazed that the project with Moncruft's has been so remuneraful, Johnnie. Banks are obviously very generous with........ other people's money!'

The Christmas Special lunch "with all the trimmings" and a share of two bottles of Californian red wine lay heavy on John's stomach, as did the bill for three hundred and fifty bucks. He had regretted that the statement on the Red Diamond Card had been found open on the kitchen table back home. He considered that some things were best left hidden from view. As he reached the gate of the cottage, John determined that there was no point in ruining the tranquillity of the late afternoon and the possibility of a good snooze with explanations of the mysteries of insurance cover and the secrets of the Hidden Postle and the nano-diversions. He entered the cottage to scan his Blackberry for any messages, away from the rigours of any inquisition.

Candida moved to one of the sun beds that were set up on the beach in front of their small garden. She idly watched a small army of black and white plovers and sandpipers patrolling the water's edge in search of riches left by the receding waves. As she let the sun warm her face, Candida banished the need for news of the stables. Thoughts about what extra work might be useful in order to improve the stables when she returned home had occupied a little place in her mind until her husband approached bearing a couple of glasses of sensible Bahamian water. She noted that her own Rhode Island Red was assuming a much more acceptable Bahamian Bronze, so much healthier than the pretend stuff which he had coated on at the airport. She watched him put away the Blackberry into the pocket of his trousers.

'Who are you expecting a call from?' Candida asked. 'You complained about *my* addiction to the phone. Now you're at it. Just relax, Johnnie. It's good to do nothing once in a while. You've had a busy year. Remember you're retired now. You should be slowing down.' Candida took a sip of water before lying back on the soft mattress and pulling the sunhat over her eyes.

'I thought that I might call Roger. Y'know, wish him and Mary a happy Christmas. Find out how they're getting on at the school. See what the weather's like. Usual Christmas stuff.'

Realising that his hastiness was perhaps unnecessary, John hesitated before sitting down on the edge of Candida's sun bed. He started to brush sand off her legs as he addressed her straw hat. 'You're the one who deserves this the most, you know, after what I've put you through. I'd certainly not reckoned on all this in my retirement plan.' John moved to stroke her hand. 'I'm so glad that we found this place.' he paused as he considered how best to describe his reasons. 'If Roger hadn't suggested that we place some of the BDN money off-shore, I don't know where we'd be.'

Candida lifted the rim of the hat to squint directly at her husband.

'Some? You mean there's more, elsewhere? Blimey, Johnnie! Mary and I have been really impressed how the two of you have taken to your retirement so positively and been so ......productive. Neither of us had a clue on how well you've done. It's just rather a long way to come to take money out from that diddy little bank.'

'That wasn't the main reason. It's always good to meet the bank staff. You never know when you might need their help. Besides, we did need a holiday and you had been banging on about the Bahamas.'

Candida's sunhat had returned to its original position. 'However, Johnnie, I've also been thinking.'

'Stop right there, Candida darling!' John took his hand away. 'You mustn't get too carried away. I know that you've seen the statement, but you must realise that the money's not just yours or mine to spend. There are others to think about.'

Dismissing her husband's caution, Candida carried on. 'I was just thinking how the addition of another ten boxes to the stables would be such an excellent business proposition. I'm sure that Roger would approve.'

'Listen darling, let's not rush things. We need to work out these projects together, sensibly and methodically.' John hoped that his voice of reason would somehow curb Candida's blue-sky enthusiasm.

'Now seems as good a time as any to ....review all options, as you put it. However, I need a refill; this time of something more festive. Do you want a glass? ' Candida lifted herself up uneasily from the sun bed and waited for the blood to circulate to all the right places before finishing off the contents of her glass. 'A girl can get used to this life very easily.' She stood up a little shakily before stomping over the sand towards the cottage.

John watched one of the world's most shapely arses walk away from him. He lay back on the adjacent sun-bed and closed his eyes. Yet he could not sleep. The after lunch snooze would have to wait. The call should have been through by now. John hoped that he had not miscalculated the time zones. A flock of tern squabbled and shrieked overhead before swooping down to catch innocent sand crabs going about their normal business. The cry that suddenly came from the veranda was more piercing, more urgent.

'Johnnie! Come quickly! Something awful has happened! It's on ..... It looks like...' Candida was shouting from the veranda before she disappeared back inside.

John had forgotten that he had left the television switched on in the living room. Even on Christmas Day, he had been unable to deny his addiction to television news, having overdosed on it over the past weeks as much of the world's banking system unravelled into crisis amid displays of extravagant largesse from government. The tone of Candida's voice suggested that he should move smartly to see what she had seen. He half ran, half stumbled over the sand to catch the pictures of the Pope giving his Christmas Blessing in St Peter's Square, whilst a caption continued across the base of the screen.

".....location of abducted British couple still unknown....."

Candida was leaning forward on the cream sofa, her arms resting on her knees, her hands cupping her chin as she looked intently at the television. 'The newsreader was talking about a couple in East Africa. Then they showed blurry photographs of the two. I didn't recognise the woman, but it certainly wasn't Mary.'

'You mean the other was Roger? Are you really sure?' John was more alert.

'I'm pretty certain, but there was nothing about poor Mary.'

'She should be with him at this place in Africa.'

'Why was there no picture of her? Oh God, Johnnie, something awful has happened. Do you think that she's been killed? Who's the other woman then?' Candida continued to stare at the screen. She felt so helpless as news of one of her best friends remained so scarce.

'They'll tell us in a few moments.' John sat down beside Candida on the sofa. 'That's what rolling news is for. To tell us the same bloody thing time and time again. Breaking news followed by News Update, followed by the Headlines, followed by "News if you haven't been paying attention"'

'Shut up, Johnnie! This looks really serious.'

'I presume that they must have got Mary as well. They just don't have her photograph.'

John's Blackberry still nested in his pocket as the distinctive text tone rang three times. He pulled the phone from his pocket and read the message. He began to consider his reply.

'This is just so awful. Johnnie.' Candida's attention was still focussed on the screen. 'Stop using that bloody phone! Call Roger's mobile. You never know he might still have it on him. I'll call Mary on her phone. She's bound to have it with her, if it hasn't been confiscated. If she's still alive! Oh God, it's all so dreadful!'

John composed his short reply and pressed the "send" button. Candida was having less success. 'No reply. It goes straight to voicemail!'

++++

Chapter Thirty Five

Christmas - passed

Wayne Oduku closed the door of his apartment and walked down the steps out into the gardens of the *Chief Bobby's Children's Centre*. A row of newly planted violets lined each side of the red ochre pathway. As he ducked under the overgrown branches of the tall acacia trees, he was reminded of just how much work still needed to be done. He walked past the gardeners, who stopped sweeping to allow Chief Bobby's son to go by.

'Jambo, Oduku Bwana!'

'Jambo, gentlemen! I hope that Christmas Day was good to you! You're doing a goodly job here.' It had been over twelve months since his last visit. The lexicon of Swahili had not rushed back to him and it had taken some while to attune his ear to the local dialect.

In the meantime, the white flowing kaftan with the Remandan Flamingo crest emblazoned on his left breast would have to command the respect and recognition for his position as Life President of the Centre. Swishing the strands of his fly swat from side to side, he approached the gleaming newly-painted walls of the first buildings in the compound.

Wayne could see the improvements as he passed the open doors of the Year Four and Year Five schoolrooms. He smiled as he listened to the shrieks and yells of children in their new green uniforms volunteering to recite their Seven Times Table or to read out-loud extracts from their daily diary about their excitement of the Christmas Lunch on the previous day.

The display of plastic Christmas trees and inflatable Santas still decked the balustrade of wooden poles and walk-boards that hid the faded walls of the next building. Wayne had been pleased that the festive trappings from another world had found favour with the children as they had paraded into the Main Hall for the Christmas Day Carol Service. As he looked up at the team of painters dressed in blue overalls applying their paint, one or two turned to acknowledge Wayne as he walked past.

'How was the Christmas day for you, my good people?'

'Jambo, Oduku Bwana!' was the choral reply. Wayne did not expect much more.

'The walls are looking excellently fine!' Wayne swished a valedictory wave and walked on to the next, yet to be painted, building. He turned through the door marked   *"Internet and Communications Room"*.

Inside, the room was airless and without windows. A fan hung down from the ceiling, its rotating large blades cooled the air as best they could. Along the far wall sat a line of four computer screens and keyboards. In front of one of them sat Mary Mortlock.

'Ah Wayne!   I'm glad you're here. I was about to come and find you.' Beads of sweat covered her face as she turned from the computer screen to greet Wayne's arrival. 'There are some issues that need to be addressed. First of all, the dormitory for the seven year olds is in an appalling state......'

Wayne listened on as Mary breathlessly outlined her list of achievements and intentions. Her bright yellow smock had not only brightened the grey walls of the *Comms Room*, but her rasping voice and boundless enthusiasm had ignited the whole Centre with a renewed energy. The children had loved her as she ordered

343

them to form an orderly line before dispensing plates of roast goat at the Christmas Lunch. The staff seemed to have warmed to her. Wayne's annual gesture of using volunteers willing to give up their time over Christmas had worked better than expected, even if it had forced him to make some last-minute rearrangements.

'The twelve new mattresses that I ordered before Christmas will be delivered from Town in two days' time. Anyway, I've used your Red Diamond Card to pay for them.'

Wayne listened on as Mary went through her list of how some of the proceeds from the BDN venture could be put to good use.

'......and there is just one last thing, Wayne.......'

Wayne was beginning to wonder whether the BDN riches would be sufficient to cover everything on her list when the black bakelite phone rang on the nearby desk

Mary picked up the receiver and listened to the voice of the secretary from the main office before handing over the receiver to Wayne. 'She says that it's important.'

'Oh good, I've been waiting for her call.'

Mary could hear the secretary talking excitedly down the line, whilst Wayne listened. After a few minutes of two-way conversation, Wayne rattled off what sounded like executive instructions before putting down the receiver. Mary watched him approach her with his arms outstretched.

'Mary, my dear, if I may call you that, I have some bad news...' Wayne paused before carrying on . '..... and also some good news.'

Mary froze as she braced herself for the bad news. 'Oh God! What is it? Has something awful happened to the children?' She wondered whether the whole idea of coming to Remanda had not been ill advised. Then she thought nearer to home. 'Has Roger sunk your boat?'

'He has run into a little local difficulty with one of my fellow countrymen.'

'Oh my God, no!' Mary leaned forward into Wayne's embrace, tears welling up in her eyes, as Wayne summarised her husband's predicament. 'Trespass? What a stupid bugger he is! Roger's always poking his nose into other people's business! ' Mary searched for a handkerchief to dry her eyes. 'I shouldn't have gone with your suggestion. It's better to have husbands and wives bickering at the Centre rather than having one of them tied to a stake in the middle of nowhere, waiting......'

'....... waiting for money. Look, Mary! You must calm down! My men have been up all night trying to establish the full situation.'

'So you've known for some time?'

'Yes, he was taken on Christmas Eve. I took the decision that, until we had more definite news, there was no point in worrying you unnecessarily. We now know that the couple have been taken by a gang led by Freddie Magumba.'

'Oh my God!' Mary said. Her face had turned pale as she held her head in her hands.

'He may be known as "Mad Dog" Magumba, but it's not as bad as it sounds.'

'With a name like that, he doesn't sound too promising.'

'But you don't know Freddie.' Wayne said. 'and I do. We were good friends when we were growing up in Africa. When we were both sent to England to be educated, I was sent to Myndhams where I met John Smith, amongst others. Freddie went to Harrow where he fell in with a bad crowd and ended up with an education not quite to the standard his father had expected. He returned home, determined to make a difference for his people and for himself. With my Daddy and then my Uncle in power, Freddie always remained a very outspoken member of the Opposition. Good for democracy, as long as he didn't get into power. When

Freddie found that politics wasn't giving him the material rewards he felt he deserved, he went into the property business.'

Mary listened intently, her jaw dropping further as the story progressed.

'With this sub-prime crisis affecting East African property values, Freddie's own credit crunch has resulted in what some might see as a seamless progression from property speculator to highwayman of the seas. So, with banks not lending him because they have no money, he has resorted to other means.'

'Well, *we* don't have any money. I suspect that Roger's pension won't go very far.' Mary said, as shock was being replaced by rational thought. 'He may have got a few stocks and shares hidden somewhere. It won't add up to millions, which is what I presume this Freddie wants.'

'It's not so much the money. That can be arranged through the credit card. The problem, Mary my dear, is time. We cannot be seen to give in so readily to Freddie's bullying tactics. Negotiations might take several weeks. The good news is that I have an assurance that both Roger and Diana are being well looked after. They will come to no harm.'

Mary sighed as she watched Wayne's fingers fiddle with the buttons of his gold blackberry. She contemplated whether she should send off e-mails to her children to tell them that everything was under the control of a very capable and very handsome African Chief. She was succumbing to clearer rational thinking.

'I suppose, Wayne, that....' Mary wiped her eyes and took in a couple of deep breathes. '..... as long as we have Mr Magumba's assurances that Roger is being well treated....' Mary's tone sounded more considered. '.....maybe you shouldn't feel that you have to rush things on my behalf. Roger's a fit man. You must remember that he's retired now. He's got all the time in the world.'

Wayne looked up from his Blackberry. There was one more message that he needed to send. He watched Mary Mortlock swivel on her chair back to face the computer screen and the display of website for bed linen.

After a short while, Mary turned back to Wayne. 'I don't know about Miss Vowlds, but I'm sure that she's a game girl. She can probably put up with a bit of hardship. They might find that they'll have a lot to talk about with Freddie. Roger likes a good argument, especially with Harrovians.'

Wayne tapped out his final message on his screen and pressed the "send" button. .

++++

John and Candida stayed up late. They watched the news channel for any further developments in the story. As they sat on a cane sofa on the veranda, drinking more than they should have, John did his best to reassure that Roger and Mary's situation was best left to experts. Candida snuggled up to John.

'No more news from your man on the spot, then?'

'Nothing since his last text. I keep checking.'

'I don't see Mary being very good at being a hostage. She wouldn't want to be sitting around doing nothing. She's probably done the kidnappers' washing, whilst trying to convince them how they've got this ransom business all terribly wrong. She can be very direct.' She added sleepily. 'I'm tired, but I can't go to sleep knowing that my friend is..... locked up or tied to a stake somewhere. I'm just not used to having my friends kidnapped.' John had been watching the black screen of his Blackberry as he listened to his wife's outpourings. He realised that she was extremely concerned for her friend. He felt equally nervous for his business partner. Suddenly, the phone buzzed into action and pinged its tell-tale announcement that a message had been delivered. John scrolled onto the text screen. Candida had closed her eyes.

"Have agreed that R & D should have extended holiday as requested. All under control. W"

'It's from Wayne.' John paused. 'Still no news. He will contact us when he hears more.' John deleted the message from the phone's memory.

'So that's it, is it?' Candida asked as she stood up and moved to go indoors. 'We go to sleep whilst our friends are being prepared for the pot. Hell, Johnnie, I feel so powerless. Normally, I can do something.'

'You'll be needed when Roger and Mary are released.'

'How long will that be?' Candida had considered how she was going to address herself to the task. Would she have time to learn her role of counsellor? Many of her friends had become counsellors. It seemed to Candida just another excuse for prying into others' misfortunes.

'It could be weeks. It might be months.'

'At least, Mary and Roger have got each other. What about the other poor woman? Who is she? I'm sure that I've seen her somewhere. She looked vaguely familiar.'

Both had moved to the small bedroom. Candida had changed into a grey sloppy t-shirt and was lying on the bed. John had taken off his shirt and shorts and was displaying his best Bahamian Bronze. He was glad to be rid of the last tell-tale signs of his fancy dress antics. 'The picture on the screen was very indistinct. Maybe she's another volunteer at the school. Let's change the subject. There's nothing more we can do from here, thousands of miles away.'

Candida's eyes were closed in drowsiness. John stretched out his arm and pulled her towards him as the distant sound of rushing waves filled the silence. John asked quietly.

'Tell me about these ten extra horse boxes for the stables? How much do you think they would cost?'

Candida opened one eye and looked up at him. A smile extended across her face. Her hand started to play with the hairs on his chest. 'Lots....' Her eyes glowed in the bedroom light. '.....if you've got it. Maybe....' Her hand had moved further down as her husband started to respond to her touch. 'there could be a bit of this as well, if you want it.'

'Nothing that's going to break the bank then?' John replied as he gave in to one of the more pleasurable benefits of retirement.

Candida decided that there would plenty of time to provide not only a more lucid answer, but also to prepare questions of her own.

END

Acknowledgements

Like all authors, we would not have got this far without help from others. So, roll the credits......to our respective wives, Diana and Sarah, for providing us with their constant support and encouragement throughout the time that it has taken us to complete the book.   To those tutors at the Open University Creative Writing course and others elsewhere, for instilling in us the techniques needed to make you want to continue reading what you had started. Lastly, to you, dear reader, for sticking the course, (unless you're browsing or snooping - in which case, come on, enough is enough! Order your own copy!)

Bruce Lawson